PLAYLIST

New Am...
River (feat. Ed Shee...
rockstar – Po...
I Like M...
OT – ...
More Than a Feeling – Boston
Californication – Red Hot Chili Peppers
Nexus – Niykee Heaton
Ride Or Die – Yelawolf
In This World - Bonus Track – Yelawolf
Have A Great Flight – Yelawolf
Heartbreak – Yelawolf
I Run - Feat. Yelawolf – Slim Thug
Like Father, Like Son – Struggle Jennings, Joshua Hedley
Like A Sewing Machine (feat. Yella Wolf & Struggle) – Alex King, Yella Wolf, Struggle
Ex-Factor – Ms. Lauryn Hill
Nowhere Fast (feat. Kehlani) - Extended Version – Eminem, Kehlani
Catfish Billy – SupaHotBeats
Buffalo Bill – Eminem
Arsonist's Lullabye – Hozier
Work Song – Hozier
Mad – Ne-Yo
Knockin' On Heaven's Door – Guns N' Roses
Two Weeks – FKA twigs
Candy & Dreams – Yelawolf
I Said Hi – Amy Shark

Demons – Jelly Roll, Lil Wyte

Nice For What – Drake

Smells Like Teen Spirit – Nirvana

Heart-Shaped Box – Nirvana

I Don't Wanna Know (feat. Enya And P. Diddy) – Mario Winans, Diddy, Enya

Had Some Drinks – Two Feet

Demons – Jelly Roll, Lil Wyte

Now You're Gone - Video Edit – Basshunter feat. DJ Mental Theos Bazzheadz

Quick Musical Doodles – Two Feet

Never Tear Us Apart – Bishop Briggs

Eyes Closed – Halsey

Taste (feat. Offset) – Tyga, Offset

Solo (feat. Demi Lovato) – Clean Bandit, Demi Lovato

Glycerine - Remastered – Bush

Fly Away – Lenny Kravitz

Hunger in My Stomach – Overtime

El Chapo – The Game, Skrillex

Savage (feat. Flux Pavilion & MAX) – Whethan, Flux Pavilion, MAX

Birthday Sex – Jeremih

pop a pill – gianni & kyle

Remember When – Bad Wolves

Lost Without You – Delta Goodrem

Privacy – Chris Brown

Digging My Own Grave – Five Finger Death Punch

Do You Mind – DJ Khaled, Nicki Minaj, Chris Brown, August Alsina, Jeremih, Future, Rick Ross

Get You Right – Pretty Ricky

Your Guardian Angel – The Red Jumpsuit Apparatus

Sunrise – Our Last Night

Medley: Let Me Talk to You / My Love – Justin Timberlake, T.I.

FLIP TRICK

AMO JONES

Flip Trick

a novel by
Amo Jones

Cover design: Jay Aheer, Simply Defined Art

Editor: Ellie McLove, Gray Ink

Proof reader: Gray Ink

Lonely Day – System Of A Down
Better Than Me – Hinder
Third Day Of A Seven Day Binge – Marilyn Manson
The Love You Need (feat. Rashad) – Mase, Rashad

DEDICATION

To the girls who had barbie dolls because their ninja turtles needed bitches.

Love is a theme park, so let's burn this bitch down...

PROLOGUE

AMETHYST
Seven-Years-Old

"Mommy won't be long. Okay, sweetie?" my mom said as she climbed out of the car. She was in one of her weird moods again. I had been picking up the shift in her attitude for some time now.

I sighed when she got out, resting my head on the cool window. Glancing at the cassette player, I considered turning the radio on, but when I reached forward to turn the keys over, I grasped air.

She had taken the keys with her. Lucky for me, it was a mid-summer day, so my window was cranked down and the sun was pelting down over my skin. I kicked my feet up and let them cross on the door. Beginning to get impatient with my mom, I started whistling to a song I had heard on the radio this week.

I wondered why my mom always came to Krispy Kreme, and why I always had to sit in the car. I had a feeling she was seeing someone, but I wasn't completely sure, and why would she hide him from me? It's not like she was married or even had a boyfriend. I didn't know why she didn't do this on a weekday while I was at school, either. It was like she was tormenting me just by doing it. She knew I had ADD, she knew this would drive me crazy having to sit in the car for so long. As if on cue, the familiar shiny black car pulled up beside ours. I tightened my ponytail, inching down the seat a bit more until my top rode up over my belly. I had on loose cargo pants, a tank top, and Circa skate shoes. I'd always preferred boy's clothes to girl's clothes. I don't know why they made our clothes so tight—even at such a young age. Tights, for example. Hideous.

When the door of the car beside me closed, I peeked my head over the top to see if I could catch a glimpse of whoever it was. The windows were darker than normal cars, so dark that I couldn't see in, so I inched farther up and saw a man in a dark suit entering the donut shop. I sunk back into my seat, huffing out an annoyed breath when I caught the window of the car beside me slowly wind down. My head snapped toward the movement and a young boy, probably a couple years older than me, looked over. He had a cap flipped backward on and dark olive-green eyes. He was cute, that much was obvious, but boys had cooties.

"Hey," he said, nodding his head.

I shuffled uncomfortably. "Hi."

I realized that my voice sounded deeper than I intended, so I cleared my throat and tried again. "Ah, you like donuts?" My cheeks heated. Why would I say that? Who even...I'm so awkward.

He chuckled, and that's when I saw two perfectly crafted indents dip into his cheeks. He had dimples. "My dad does. He comes here every Thursday."

"Mine too," I answered, annoyed once again at my mom. "I mean," I corrected. "My mom comes here every Thursday at five. She only ever walks out with my tiramisu donuts. I like donuts, so I guess it's worth it."

"Tiramisu is gross, and it has coffee in it. Not good for your height." I ignored the bright flashing logo of white, green, and red hanging against the old brick.

Glancing down at my legs, I'd always been taller than most girls my age, so I snapped, "My height is just fine, thank you."

He turned up the volume to his car stereo. The song I had

heard last week was playing. "Hey," I nudged my head. "Who sings this?"

He gave me a side glance. "Lenny Kravitz. It's called 'Fly Away'..."

"Cool." My head bobbed to the song, and he slowly inched up. I smiled at him, and he caught it, giving me a small one back. Fifteen minutes later, his dad walked back out. I waved goodbye before they departed. A couple minutes after that, my mom was walking out with a smile on her lips, carrying a box of donuts.

She scooted inside.

"You know, it's a good thing you're a very active kid."

I took the box from her, flipping it open and taking out a donut. I bit into it. "Why?" I asked around my mouthful.

"You are going to have to learn etiquette one day," she whispered.

"Maybe." I scooped out some cream with my finger. "But not today." I rubbed my finger down her cheek, smudging the cream onto her skin.

She gasped in shock, and then laughed, taking out a donut for herself. I loved seeing my mom like this. Happy, content. Her and my dad have a friendship, not a relationship, and it was all I'd ever known of them to have. Nothing romantic at all. They separated before I was even born, but it works for us and our dynamic. At the same time, I had never seen my mom with another man either.

The following Wednesday night, I was giddy and slightly excited that I got to see the boy again the next day. Mom came into my bedroom, just as my eyes were closing.

"I see you smiling a lot lately, Cherub." She sunk into the bed beside me. "Anything I should know about?"

I pulled the blanket up to cover my mouth and shook my head. There was no way I was going to tell her that my chest does a funny twist thing every time I thought of the boy with a pretty smile and strange eyes. I mean, she didn't even know that he and I had met. Aside from all of that too, my dad was FBI, and he and his partner, who I call Uncle Marcus, always liked to remind me that the day their "princess" got a boyfriend, was the day they'd plant evidence on him just to get him locked up.

They scared me.

"You sure?" Mom asked, pulling the blanket down from my mouth. "I could swear... is that..." Then she pulled a candy bar out from under the bed.

"A Goo-Goo Cluster!" I shot up onto my elbows and then reached for it.

She giggled. "Don't tell your dad that I give you candy before bed." Then she ruffled my hair and kissed my head. She walked to the doorway and switching the light off. Instantly my head was swimming with images of the cute boy with a bright smile but tormented eyes.

"You've never tasted a Goo-Goo Cluster before?" I asked, almost offended. "That's not good."

"How is that not good?" He snorted. "Should I be worried about your sugar addiction?"

I squinted my eyes at him, turning the radio up. We were both sitting in my car this time, and our parents were taking extra-long today. I didn't mind. I really liked spending time with him.

"Where do you go to school?" I asked, chewing on my candy. He bit into his and paused his chew.

"That's actually really good." Then he looked at me sideways. "I go to Charming Prep, you?" Of course, he goes to private.

"Malfroy Elementary." I picked at the frayed parts of my jeans. "Have you ever skated before?"

He shrugged. "I sometimes do, but I prefer more hands-on sports." He looked me up and down. "You obviously skate."

I nodded. "Yes. What's your favorite color?"

"Blue, yours?"

"Pink."

"Huh." His eyes slanted. "You don't look like a pink girl."

"I don't look like a lot of things, but I am some of those things."

He paused. "Interesting."

"I am not interesting."

"You are to me." His finger started tapping on the side of his leg, his attention drifting out the window. "Do you have any brothers or sisters?"

I sucked the chocolate off my finger, shaking my head. "Nope. You?"

"Two brothers."

"I always wanted a big family," I confessed, crumpling my wrapper up and tossing it into the middle console of the car.

"You really don't," he replied flatly.

"Hey, you're pretty good at that!" He pointed down to the picture I was drawing. I shrugged. "I like art. All kinds of art, but my favorite is creative writing." I smudged the lead into the paper. Both our eyes connected briefly, and my heart did that stupid thing again.

He cleared his throat and both of our heads snapped back to the front doors to see my mom and his dad talking near the entrance. They didn't see us again.

Not even when he slipped out of our car and back into his Lincoln.

Not even all of the weeks after that when we saw each other.

Every Thursday, my mom met this man. And every Thursday, the boy and I would sit together.

We never exchanged names, I don't think it ever crossed our minds to ask. I felt a connection with him, one I had never experienced before. I had seen movies that would talk about soul mates, but who finds their soul mate at seven? And what if someone doesn't have a soul? Do they still get to find someone?

Not saying the boy doesn't, but sometimes I wonder if a soul is even real. *ADD.*

April first was the last time I ever saw him, and my mother never went back to that Krispy Kreme again.

PART ONE

"Disobey.
Don't comply.
Rebellion is fucking romantic."

- Jonny Ox

AMETHYST

SOME PEOPLE SEEM TO MISUSE THE WORD "BROKEN HOMES." Like it's a dirty thing, and I honestly think it stemmed from the word "bastard." Oh, he's a bastard child. Now it's 'Oh, he comes from a broken home.' Fuck your stereotypical small box of a brain, Susan, not all split homes are broken. Some are filled with more love than one normal home. Who needs normal, anyway. Normal never makes history. I don't come from a large family, either. I'm an only child whose parents are also only children. My dad's parents died in a car accident and my mom's family? Well, I never really asked—and sort of didn't want to.

There was this one-time when I was a young kid, I must have been around two? The memories are murky, but for some reason, I remember snippets out of this particular day—hence the not asking about my mom's family. It was summer, and I remember my 'grandma' taking me away from my mom who was busy with another child. I don't remember the other kid much, and I can't remember if it was a girl or if he was a boy, but Mom later told me that the child was her friend's who was getting out of a bad relationship, it's why I only remember her from that day. So anyway, my 'grandma' decided to take me for a walk to the local park. I was sucking on my popsicle, and I can still taste the tangy juice from the icicle trickling down my throat, the sun warming my skin, and the loud slap of my sandals hitting the heel of my foot with every step. I remember squeezing her hand with mine while skipping all the way to the playground with her. She had pointed to the swing set and said she would be right over there, and further pointed toward an old rusted bench seat. I trusted her. She was my family, and furthermore, she was an adult and as a child, I was told I should respect adults, right? I just wasn't old enough to understand that this only implied to certain adults, not all.

So, I bounced my happy self toward the swings with my frilly white daisy dress hitting my knees with every skip. Fucking hated that dress. My mom probably soaked up all the time she had putting me in dresses. Little did she know…

I clutched onto the cool chain and took a seat on the rubber strip, smiling from ear to ear. I looked to where my gram was, to show her how high I could go on the swing, only the bench seat was empty. In that moment, the swoosh of the trees intensified and suddenly, I could hear crickets chirping off in the distance. A sob escaped me once I realized she was gone, nowhere to be seen. I jumped off the swing seat and hid underneath the little playground shelter where a slide was nailed against it. I curled into a ball and cried until my skin was as rough as sandpaper, and my hair clung to my damp face.

My mom came two hours later, I'm not sure what took her so long. I never really asked her about that day because anytime I'd raise the question, she'd clam up like a shell, so I left it. Dad was there later that night too. He came as soon as he felt something wasn't right. But by that time, my tears had long since dried. Since that day, it's just been me, my dad and my mom. We've never spoken of the grandma since that day. She's like Lord Voldemort in both homes.

The great thing about coming from a split home, is I get two. New York City, where my mom lives, and Spring Valley DC, where my dad lives. He's the lead detective in his division, and my mom owns her own business. I'm thankful that I at least have my mom within a car ride to the college, but I miss my dad and sometimes hate that I have to drive four hours to see him. My mom owns her own little coffee shop-slash-book-

store that is in the heart of Brooklyn. She lives in the apartment above it in a comfortable little loft. Money wise, my dad
is pretty well off, but my mom barely makes enough, let alone
to get me through college. I mean, she does okay and basically
survives off of the loyal customers who have been coming in
since she opened twenty-or-so years ago, but I was lucky
enough to snag a great scholarship. All I have to do now is
work for my living expenses. Dad always says that he could put
me on an allowance while I'm here, but it never felt right. He
and Mom have taken care of me all my life, I always vowed to
myself that once I hit college, I was going to be an adult and
not expect any more from them. They have done more than
enough. They've both made sacrifices for me throughout,
some, like my mom, her own family. Anyway, it just doesn't
seem fair to expect that from either of them now that I'm old
enough to take care of myself.

"Ame, hang these for me," my co-worker-general store
manager-slash-best-friend says, breaking through my past
daydream. She hands me a white silk minidress that is clinging
to a hanger. I take it, walking toward the white section of the
boutique. I've been working at Dust Boutique for three months
now, about two weeks after I started Columbia. It's only
weekend work and some Thursdays. Or when some highflyer
rich girl bounces in splashing money around, then, we're only
allowed to close once she's done shopping.

"Helloooo?" Leila waves her hand around like a maniac.

"What?" I ask because I didn't hear what she said.

"Amethyst Lilly Tatum. Did you just zone out on me
again?" Leila places her hands on her slim hips, cocking a
perfectly arched eyebrow.

"Sorry." I smile at her. "I was just thinking about that day
with my evil grandma."

Leila stops, her face falling slightly. This is no surprise. Leila
hasn't heard me speak about my family, and even though she

and I have only been friends for three months, our friendship has developed to be one of those unicorn friendships. The kind where you hate each-other in the beginning, barely tolerate each other, but then you decide you sort of love them and before you know it, a bond is formed, and you grow attached to one another. We also share a dorm room, so that's every single day for three months that we have spent together. We fight and bicker, but we love and shelter each other too.

"Okay," she sobers, walking back behind the counter. "Want to talk about it? Or want to drink about it?"

I laugh, shaking my head. "I don't really want to drink about it."

She sighs, rolling her eyes. "You never want to drink about it."

I shrug, going toward her just as the bell rings to alert that someone has walked through the door. "I know, right? It's a good thing too, considering who the hell would take care of your drunk ass every weekend."

She laughs. She knows I'm right. Not only is she a difficult drunk, but she also has this bad habit of disappearing. In my defense, I haven't done much living in comparison to other girls my age. I've had a very different childhood background than Leila. She only works here to basically, flip the bird at her wealthy parents. Yes, that's right, she's working to be rebellious. A luxury most of us cannot afford. Her father is a senator in the current elections and if anyone found out his youngest daughter was working at a fashion boutique, even if the honey diamond chandelier displayed the lavishness of her working space, it would still be a catastrophe.

Lucky for her.

Me, on the other hand, am very lucky to have this job. My mother and father both worked their butts off, saving enough money for me to be considered. Obviously, my grades and 4.0 GPA got me in, but without mother dearest and daddy daddio, I wouldn't be here, and for that alone, I owe them both the world. But I can't afford the world, so for now, me working will have to suffice. Dad and I are just as close as my mom and me. Their story is a strange one. They were best friends since they were three and then decided one drunk night after they both hit sixteen that they would be each other's first. They did the deed and then laughed afterward, vowing to never do, or speak of it again. Only a couple of months later, my mom found out she was pregnant when mother nature decided to dodge her monthly visit. It was touch and go for a while there between them. Mom said that my nana kicked them out or something, so my Nona and Pop took Mom in. They helped and supported her throughout her entire pregnancy, and then when she had me, they set up a nursery until Mom and Dad purchased their first home. They both passed away in a wreck not long after that.

It sounds weird, I guess, but I've never known my mom and dad to be romantic, they've just been best friends. I wouldn't have it any other way either, the dynamic between our family has always been smooth. No jealous fits on either end because there have never been romantic elements. They're still best friends to this day, which admittedly has caused some issues within their own love lives—more with my mom than my dad, who has been with the same woman since I was a little girl. Lara is witty, funny, and one of the top lawyers in DC. She and Dad are complete opposites, but they work and they make each other happy. My mom has never settled. She dated a douche when I was a bit younger, but something happened between the two of them and she never spoke about him again.

"So, we are drinking tonight?" Leila repeats, locking the till and dropping the key back under the desk.

I grab my bag, tossing it over my shoulder and shrug. "I don't really see the harm in it." Except I sort of do, because there have been two times I have ever gone out with Leila, and both times ended in her being arrested.

"Oh, come on, Ame!" she whines, flipping her hair. "I promise I won't get arrested this time, and besides, I've never seen you drink."

"Yeah," I agree, unzipping my handbag to get my wallet out. "That's because I don't drink."

"Boo, you need to. It might loosen you up a bit." I follow her toward the front door as she flicks the keys around in her hand. Maybe I should take Leila up on one girls' night since my life is epically tedious right now.

"I can't afford to loosen up, Leila, some of us have to stay glued together in a little puzzle in order to not only survive college but to actually pass." Once we hit outside, I turn and lock up for her, sick of her twirling the keys around aimlessly. It's just after six p.m. on a Friday night, and I already know she's not going to drop this. It would be much easier if I only needed to fend off Leila's over the top peskiness at work, but unfortunately, she's also my college roommate.

I turn to face her, whistling at a taxi that's driving past. "Fine. One drink."

Her face goes from pouty-child-begging-for-a-cookie to spoiled-bratty-child-who-just-got-told-her-parents-purchased-the-whole-freaking-cookie-store.

"Yay!" She claps her hands in glee, then her face falls. "Oh no, honey, are we really catching a cab?"

I clutch the handle of the bright yellow taxi, pulling it open. "Yes, now get in." She pretends to hesitate, but then thinks better of it and slides into the back seat beside me.

"You know," she murmurs, putting on her seat belt. "I totally know where we can party tonight."

The taxi drives forward after I tell him where to go. "Really? Well, I was kind of hoping you would say that, you know, since you did invite me out."

She waves her hands in front of herself. "Oh, I know, I just didn't think you'd finally say yes, but…" She taps her temple with her index finger. "Good thing I'm so resourceful." Yeah, sure, alright. The taxi continues to drive us back toward the campus, so I take this moment to shut my eyes briefly.

I know I have to visit my mom this weekend. I've been sort of putting it off for the past few weeks after finding out that she has finally met someone, and although I'm trying really hard to be happy for her, I'm ashamedly scared. I'm terrified, because although Dad has been with Lara for so many years, I know that he can take care of himself—emotionally, not physically. Every time I go home only proves this with the cooking he still likes me doing, and his shirts that still need ironing. Even though Lara always says to leave it and that a woman isn't supposed to take care of a man, and that this is the twenty-first century where women work, feed, and provide for their families and cue pro-woman power (fist punch), I just can't seem to allow it to happen. She takes care of Dad in all the best other ways though, the ways I'm sure he enjoys, but the ironing and baking his favorite cookies, is just something I like to do every time I'm home. Whether they're still his favorite cookies or not, he allows me to continue. Probably for my own ego and not so much his needing to be taken care of.

Anyway, my mom is a different story entirely. She's quirky, loving, independent, and a true romantic at heart. Which is why I'm hesitant to meet this new man in her life. He could hurt her, and I don't think I have the mental capacity to even think of that probability.

My phone vibrates in my pocket and I unlock it, sliding it open to see "mom" flash over the screen.

Crap.

I'm really not good at snubbing my mom, and I feel like shit every time I hit "ignore," so this time, I exhale loud enough to catch Leila's attention and put the phone to my ear.

"Hi, Mom."

There's a long silence, so I watch as the passing trees illuminate past from the streetlights. I know we're getting closer to campus because I see the 7-Eleven Leila and I basically live at.

"Honey, why haven't you answered my calls?"

"Sorry, Mom, I've been busy with work and studying." I look up to Leila to see one perfectly arched eyebrow perched to the high heavens. I divert my gaze quickly. I feel like shit for lying, I don't need her judgy little glare.

"Oh, well, I figured. If I didn't get your texts, I would have called a search party."

"I'm sorry, Mom. I promise I'll try to make myself more available."

"Listen, the reason I called was—"

I sucked in a breath. Here we go. The big "I want you to meet a man." Though she didn't know that my dad let it slip a couple weeks ago that she was seeing someone.

"—I met someone, honey!" Her voice almost popped out of my phone, that's how ecstatic she was. I instantly felt like a bratty shit for ignoring her. What if he doesn't hurt her and it's the real deal? Surely by her tone, he must be something special. My mom doesn't sway easily. She may be frilly, but she's also smart. Very street smart and savvy. A ninja, if you will.

"Really?" I try for surprised, but when I look back to Leila to find her giving me the raised eyebrow look, I know that I haven't sounded as smooth as I thought I did.

"Yes! Oh, Amethyst, he's amazing. I truly want you to meet him, honey. It's important to me."

I shuffle in my seat. "Oh, well, how long have you been seeing this dude?"

She giggles. "Well, a while now, actually. We've been taking it slow because he has children too, and it's very complicated."

"Oh great, siblings," I mutter. It wasn't actually supposed

to come out loud. I sigh, instantly regretting my choice of words. "Okay, Mom. Fine."

"You will come?"

"Yes." Good thing I'm hanging with Leila tonight. I fear I might need a distraction even if that distraction is her getting arrested.

"Ok well good!" she excitedly answers. "So this weekend?"

"Ah." The taxi pulls up to the campus and we both jump out, Leila paying for the ride. "How about next weekend? I'm a little busy this weekend."

"Oh, well, ok, but it's just that next weekend—"

"—Mom? I gotta go, I just got home. I'll see you next weekend?"

"Ok, honey."

I exhale, my heart twisting in my chest. "I love you, Mom."

She sighs. "I love you so much, honey."

Then the line goes silent and I take a few beats to collect myself. "I guess I'm meeting my mom's new thing next weekend."

Leila hooks her arm around mine as we both head toward the dorms. "Don't worry, Ame. Your mom is a badass."

I tilt my head back and laugh. "No, she is not. She's probably—"

"—Ame, your mom is not stupid. Let her be an adult. I mean, she's gotta get some some time. Can you imagine not having sex?" She pauses, and then regards me up and down. "Actually, don't answer that."

I roll my eyes and shove past her through the doors, passing the reception desk where Dahlia is holed up with her feet perched on the counter, chowing down, what I'm guessing is her fifth donut within the last hour. We could probably be friends.

I bang on the elevator key. "Actually, last time I had sex wasn't that long ago."

"Oh really," she teases, coming up beside me just as the doors slide open.

"Yes!" I hiss, borderline insulted. Stepping inside, I crossed my arms. "Like, six months."

She snorts. "Six months is truly horrifying, and so your last sexy time was with Shane?" Shane was my ex of four months. Leila always says that I shouldn't count him as my ex because we were dating for less than six months, and though I should agree with her because Shane was a dick, I just can't bring myself to admit I wasted four months on such a jerk. Four months is still four months.

"Of course!" We walk out of the elevator and toward our dorm room. "I don't do one-night stands, Leila, you know that, and it took him a month to even come near my fortress."

She bursts out laughing while opening our room door and tossing her jacket onto her bed. "Your fortress? Well, sorry to say, but I'm going to need your 'fortress' to be trampled in a lot more than once every six months, not to mention after one month of seeing a guy. Loosen up, Ame! Trust me. The best feeling ever."

CHAPTER 2

AMETHYST

EVERYTHING HURTS. MY BRAIN THUDS LIKE A HUNDRED thousand bass lines were thundering through it at the same time, and when I reach up to caress my head, my hair almost damn near scratches the palm of my hands—that's how rough each strand is.

"I'm dying." I try to pry open my eyes, but my eyelashes are stuck together like glue. My stomach rumbles in hunger but aches in pain, and my mouth is dryer than anything I'd ever experienced before. Worst feeling ever.

I prop myself up onto my elbow, but all the pain and discomfort I was experiencing slams into me like a massive semi-truck carrying an entire store of Ikea crap.

"Oh my God." I give up, flopping back onto the bed, only that causes my head to spin furiously and my throat starts to swell from food reaching up my throat. I quickly cover my mouth to stop the spew coming out, but out of instinct, I lean over my bed—

"Bucket!" Leila orders from somewhere across the room, but before I can open my eyes fully to focus on where the bucket is, vomit is coming out of my mouth, flying across the floor. Now my eyes are open. Wide, freaking, open. I sigh in relief when I see that in my blind state, I managed to hit the bucket and didn't get a speck of vomit anywhere else. That I could see.

I groan, my hand coming up to my forehead as I laid back onto the bed. "This is horrendous. I think I'm dying. No, actually, I'm already dead and I've woken in hell."

Leila chuckles from somewhere in the room, I'm guessing her bed.

"You're evil."

She giggles again, and screw her because she actually sounds normal. "Actually, you were up to quite the shenanigans last night. I'm a little impressed by your actions."

"My actions?" Though my eyes were wide open now, my view was solely on the ceiling of our dorm room. The hideous pale pink suddenly making my stomach queasy again for no apparent reason at all. That reason could be tequila. Or vodka. And whatever the hell else I decided to drink last night.

"You don't remember a thing, do you?" Leila chuckles before diving right into her story.

"Dude, I broke into his house to save you after you called me and said that you had a one-night stand with—just saying —the hottest guy on campus—and I, in my drunken state, took your ultra-drunk directions to his house. Well, actually, I gave my phone to the taxi driver, who oddly, knew exactly where you were because, and I quote, *'I've been there many times. I know where she is'*, and then I climbed up the garden ladder outside his window, where you were waiting in nothing but your bra and—"she pauses, her gaze dropping to my chest as she waves her fingers around— "well, that."

I look down at my shirt to see I'm wearing a black Raiders top that I don't recognize. My mouth drops open in shock.

She continues on. "You left with nothing else but that top, but not before he woke, shocked the living shit out of both of us, and your hands went flying, dignity went flying –along with your phone, and then we both fell out the window, landing on taxi dude who was waiting down below. As hottie was leaning out the window to laugh at us, we both bolted to the car, with taxi driver hot on our heels. He floored it out of there quick-smart. All of us were in fits of laughter."

"Oh my God," I gasp, just as memories start flashing

through my head like a bad movie. "I remember." Leila's phone vibrates on her dresser, she reaches for it aimlessly. I swing my legs off the bed, letting my long hair fall over my face while massaging my temples. "God, I –"

"—Oh!" Leila giggles smugly. "Oh, this is great."

"What?" I answer, still caressing my temples. I peek at her from behind the loose strands of pink hair. "Wait don't tell me, you hooked up with the taxi dude."

She doesn't answer me, but I feel a weighted thud land beside my thigh. "No. I mean, I did consider it, but that text," she points to the phone near my leg. "Is for you."

"What?" I ask confused, and then grab the phone, opening the text.

Ame: MMS loading…

"Oh…no…"

"Oh…yes…" Leila mocks in my tone, nodding her head up and down and tapping her fingertips together like the evil wench that she is.

I swallow nervously, and then click "Open"…

"Tequila shots are the way of life." Leila shoved a shot glass into my hand. "Come on, Ame."

She started dancing to some hip-hop song playing through the loud speakers, and for a brief second, I thought about going home. I was dressed in a tight black bodysuit that dipped down between my breasts and a mini skirt that cinched around my waist, but that's as far as I let Leila go. She tried to get me into heels, but before she could pull out her god-awful

Louboutins, I was already tying up my —what she calls—goth boots. They're not goth boots, or maybe they are, either way, I'm not bothered. They're comfortable and all I've really loved to wear since I was a kid. If it's not my black Doc Martens, it's something casual like Chuck Taylors. I would never, ever, be seen in any kind of heel. She shoved some thigh-high fishnet tights into my hand and demanded I put them on first, and then she would allow me to wear the boots, and I figured instead of hearing her go on and on about it all night (because she was very capable of doing so), I threw the stupid things on. I don't wear makeup, and that didn't change tonight either. I brushed on a smudge of blush—though I don't need it—and some pineapple flavored lip balm, that had more scent and taste than what it did display wise— let my pale pink hair down from the tight bun I usually always leave it in, took my reading glasses off, and we were on our way. But as I was standing there with a shot glass of clear liquid in one hand, and a slice of lime in the other, I was beginning to regret every decision—including becoming friends with Leila—that led me to this point. She must've sensed this like the little spidey-sensor that she was, because her arm wrapped around my waist as she pulled me into her.

"Oh come, on. Just think… this time next weekend, you'll be wishing you were ass deep in tequila shots while you're meeting your mom's new man and kids."

She was right. I was being a softie. I don't do kids, and they don't do me. I don't really like being told all my flaws in under thirty-seconds flat.

I raised the glass to my lips and tilted my head back, swallowing the sharp, disgusting drink, then quickly shoved the lime into my mouth like I had seen in so many movies.

"Wooo!" Leila raised her arms in the air. "That's my girl. Now, let's get another."

A few more shots in, I was dancing up against Leila, the

room sort of spinning. She dropped down in front of me to rub
her ass all over my front in a seductive manner, giving a clear
view of the crowd in front of me. My smile fell when I saw
what, or who, was staring back at me. Dark brown hair sticking
out of a cap that's flipped backward, intense eyes that summon
all of my senses at once. Soft, tan skin, and then he stands, his
still on mine. He has to be around six-foot. His lean body
carries nicely fit worn jeans and a black shirt. He swallows his
drink while his focus remains on me, then pats his friend's back
and then—"Oh no." I muttered, just as Leila came back to
standing, laughing and tossing her hair over her shoulder.
"What?" She pulled her bottom lip into her mouth, handing
me another drink.

My palms were sweaty, so I rubbed them down my skirt.
"He's—comi—"

"—Who?" Leila caught my eyes, following my line of
sight. It was as though he was walking toward us in slow
motion. I held my breath as he got closer and closer, and—
his eyes flicker over my shoulder, a sexy grin tickling the
corner of his mouth, displaying a tiny show of his straight
white teeth, and then he brushes past me, going straight to
the bar.

I let out the breath I was holding, my shoulders sagging in
relief.

Leila chuckled. "Oh, I see you've noticed Maddox Stone."

"Maddox what now?" I asked. I felt as though I was
floating and the walls seemed to warp. "I think I want more
to drink."

"Sure you do." She wiggled her eyebrows.

I rolled my eyes, trying not to look too obvious in how
disappointed I was that he walked past us. I'd never seen him
—ever, but then again, I don't go out much, and when I do go
out, I'm almost always trying to stop Leila from killing herself.

"That's not what I mean, I just mean," I paused, deciding

on distraction. It always worked with Leila. "I mean that I need to get more drunk. I think."

"Well." She hooked her arm in mine. "Who am I to stop you?" She pulled out a stool at the bar, ordering four shots and two Jager bombs.

"Um," I said, eying the shot glasses with my index finger raised. "I don't think this is what I me—"

"Scared?" a voice said from beside me and out of instinct, I looked directly at him. I faltered slightly, my mouth going dry.

Shit.

"Not scared, just… wary."

His gaze stayed on me and goddamnit, he was more beautiful up close. His cheeks, though his skin had a slight golden tint to it, had a smidge of blush, probably from the alcohol. His eyes were a dark avocado green, which were framed by eyelashes that were thick black. His jaw was prominent, his cheekbones slightly high, like a model's. His features were so sharp and breath-taking, I almost faltered. Both arms were covered in tattoo's, with another big one on his neck. He also had a gold ring in his nose. Something about him seemed menacing. He definitely gave me the bad boy vibe—*not* my type. I liked the quirky guys. The nerds who liked science over parties. I could never date a guy who skated like me, they always found it intimidating when I could out trick them, so I liked quirky guys, and I liked them for a reason, because guys like Maddox Stone, they broke girls like me. I realized I was being judgmental, as I didn't really know his story, but at the same time, I wanted to be aware. Even if I was at a bar full of drunk people—me being one of those people.

He scooped up my shot glass, his eyes pinning me in my spot, and then brought the rim to his lips, tipped his head back and shot it back. He sucked on the lime and then tossed it into the glass.

"Try it. It's fun."

"What? You trying to get me drunk?" I picked up the other glass, shot it back, and then grabbed Leila's other one and shot that back too. "All you had to do was ask."

His eyes narrowed and then moved over my shoulder, landing on Leila, I was guessing, then came back to me. "I'm Maddox."

"Right." I try my hardest to not look out of place. "I'm Amethyst, but people usually call me Ame."

"Ame?" He grinned. "It's cute. I like it." Then he glanced over to the table I saw him at before. "Come sit with us?"

I cast a quick look to Leila, who was glaring at me like what the fuck was I waiting for, so I shrug. "Yeah, sure." He picked up the rest of his drinks that he came for and we followed him back to the table. I spun around quickly when I knew I was out of earshot from him. "Tell me everything about him."

There was no surprise that Leila knew who he was. She had either slept with him (which I was really hoping she hadn't), or she had been with his friend.

"I fucked his friend, and, hey!" Her arm caught mine. "Homeboy can be a bit of a player. Never had a girl, but he plays the field, if you feel me."

I searched her eyes, bored. "I don't feel you, so spit it out."

"Wrap it up."

"Leila!" I whacked her with the back of my hand, but then realized if I was to have my first one-night stand, would he really be the worst candidate? No. The answer was no, he wouldn't. My face fell at this revelation.

Leila must catch it because she busted out laughing. "Girl, do it, but let's continue to drink first."

She brushed past me and headed to the table.

"Hey! Rosé!" a voice yelled from behind me.

I turned back toward the table, and that's when I realized eight sets of eyes were watching me. Did he just call me Rosé? As in the wine? I walked toward them, and because Leila, like the little wench she was, had taken a seat beside one of the other guys, that left me to take the only empty spot.

Right beside Maddox.

"Rosé?" I gritted my teeth slightly, scrunching up my face in distaste. The guy sitting opposite me, and who had called me that, resembled Aquaman.

He grinned, his dark green eyes curving in mischief. Soft brown hair hung down his thick shoulders, and his jaw was hidden behind a heavy beard. That wasn't where the resemblance to Aquaman stopped though, oh no, this guy had the arms and body to match. He was scary but cute. If that could even be possible. I had a little bit of hair envy over his long locks, too.

"Yeah, your hair!" He gestured around my body, his demeanor relaxed.

"Oh, right, the pink." I slowly sat down, suddenly feeling way out of my element. I picked up my drink and took a long sip.

"It's different." He hid his smile behind his glass. "Is all I'm saying."

"Mmmhmm, I know." I put my glass back down. "It's sort of why I dyed it."

Maddox, who I could see out of the corner of my eye was still staring at me, put his arm over the top of my chair. Aquaman caught his friend's body language, and then slowly sunk back into his seat, a playful grin on his face.

Maddox pointed from the guy beside Leila. "That's Wolf." I followed his finger and my focus fell on another set of green eyes, only, where Maddox' were a little more mischief mixed with torment, this guy's were a little more…reserved. He looked similar to Maddox, though. A little bit. He was a tad shorter and leaner than Maddox. Maybe a cousin. Good looking, obviously.

Maddox gestured to Aquaman. "That's Talon."

"Aquaman sounds better, just saying…" I murmured, downing the rest of my drink. When I put my glass back on the table, everyone at our table started laughing. "I said that out loud, didn't I?" Then I looked to Leila pleadingly. "Lei…"

She swiped tears from her cheeks. "Aw, honey, it's ok."

Sinking back in my chair, I swallowed my nerves. "I'm going to need another drink."

Many drinks later, we'd all fallen into breezy conversation. My muscles had relaxed, but I was well aware that I was at a non-respectfully drunk stage. Even Maddox, who had picked up the PDA, had one hand on my knee, which was causing heart palpitations. "Aquaman and Rosé, has a ring to it, doesn't it?" Aquaman—Talon, winked at me from across the table.

Maddox's grip tightened on my leg. It was fleeting, and I almost missed it.

"I think I'll let you call me Rosé, but only because I will call you Aquaman."

Talon's head tipped back, his laugh erupting out of him. The music and the chatter in the room was drowning out my anxiety—or maybe that was how much alcohol I had drunk.

I giggled, more to myself, and turned to face Maddox who was still seated beside me. Our gazes caught, and the intensity of his stare sucked out all of the voices. My heart was banging against my chest, my breathing shallow and desperate. His eyes dropped to my lips, his head tilting to watch me with interest. I swallowed when I saw the corner of his mouth tip up in a taunting smile. *Why did he feel familiar?* Something about him. Or the drinks were playing tricks on me—yes, that would be it.

"Amethyst?" His tongue wrapped around each syllable of my name, and suddenly, I wanted to know what that tongue felt like pressed against my flesh. What his rough voice sounded like groaning out my name.

Jesus Christ, I was drunk. And I was still staring at him.

"What?" I asked, ignoring the rising heat climbing inside

my body.

Suddenly his face was closer to mine, so close that I could feel his breath fall over my bottom lip. *I wanted him. Bad.* Fingers latched around the back of my neck, pulling me closer until our lips were lightly pressed together, not kissing, just there —existing.

"You and I are leaving," he growled over my lips, conjuring all of my senses and possessing them with five simple words. "Now," he finished.

Make that six words.

We were stumbling down a long hallway after climbing tedious stairs. Everything was constantly obscured, reality now tainted by my blurred vision, but my lips were always on his. His tongue dominated my mouth, and just as we reached his bedroom door, he picked me up by my ass. I wrapped my legs around his waist, pulling off his shirt as he kicked his bedroom door closed again and slammed me up against it. I didn't remember exactly what happened between leaving the bar to getting here, and I didn't really care. This man who I had just met, lit my insides up in every way possible, and I felt like I was going to combust from the inferno that was raging through me. Or maybe that was the alcohol—I mean, alcohol was flammable, right? Who cared, it felt great. He laughed, and his mouth connected with mine again. He expertly massaged my tongue with his while his hands went everywhere, then he placed me back on my feet and tore my clothes off, leaving me in nothing but my fishnet tights. He picked me back up then he threw me onto his bed, stepping backward, his step faltering slightly. He was obviously as drunk as I was. He lazily took in my naked body, as his tongue came out and licked his lip. Jesus, I think that was by far the hottest thing I had ever seen, then he removed his jeans and boxer briefs—nope, *that* was definitely the sexiest thing I'd ever seen. I gulped, either I was seeing double, or his dick size was frightening. I yanked my attention away from everything south and took in his hair. Ruffled, brown, and just the right length to yank on it. My eyes dropped back down his chest and my breath caught when I took in all of his tattoos. They filled a quarter of his chest and both of his arms. Couldn't make out what they were, but I saw large Old English style writing going over his chest. D E S T R—nope. I've got nothing.

He grinned, then latched onto my ankles and yanked me down the bed. I screamed out excitedly just as his hand slammed over my mouth. His body lightly fell over mine, each of his legs stretching mine open until he was resting right there. I could feel him pressing against me and I tilted my hips up to him, wanting friction.

"We doing this? Because if we are, this is the only time I'm giving you an out. After this, your ass is mine."

"Jesus," I exhaled, my eyes rolling to the back of my head. His smell was everywhere, rubbing off of his skin and onto mine. Leather, whiskey, clean soap, and mint.

He chuckled. "Not Jesus, princess." He sucked my bottom lip into his mouth and tugged, before unlatching it and whispering, "*Maddox.*"

"I'm no princess, but ye—"He pushed inside of me before I could finish my answer.

I moaned, everything fuzzy and coming in and out.

Sweat, tongue, dick, pleasure, pain....

Back to the now, Maddox has sent a photo of him with his cap on backward, no shirt on, his pierced tongue sticking out between his lips and his fingers spread on either side of his mouth.

"Cheeky fucker," Leila mutters, looking smug from beside me.

"Oh my God, Lei, I can never see him again! Like, ever!"

"Don't be dramatic! It's only Maddox. He will have already forgotten your name. I wouldn't sweat it, but you do need to collect that phone! Girl, iPhones are ridiculous, unless you finally want to move to Samsung." She heads into our bathroom and swings a towel over her shoulder. She sighs once she sees my panicking is not subsiding. "Honey, it's fine, honestly, I've had tons of one-night stands. The trick is to not think too much into it."

Another text comes through and I scream, throwing the phone across the room.

Leila rolls her eyes, picks it up and stands. "You might need this phone, Rosé, but I'm keeping these..." She pauses, then her lips curl as she tries to stop her laugh. She turns her phone around to face me, and it's a freaking photo of my red panties.

"Shit."

Leila laughs. "I'm hitting the shower, boo, you should text him back. If Wolf texts me, tell him I'll see him later."

"Wait!" I stand from the bed. "You're actually having a thing with Wolf?"

"After last night? Hell yes. His D game is on point."

"Oh, see, I'm not cut out for that."

"For what?" she asks, tilting her head.

"That!" I gesture to her. "The whole casual thing. Like, shit."

"Ame, it was a one-night stand. Maddox has them probably every weekend with girls who he deems worthy of him." she rolls her eyes again, and I sense something there. Maybe there's something she isn't telling me.

"You're right, but I'm not going to get my phone or my damn panties back. I'd rather never see him again."

AMETHYST

"Do you have everything?" Leila asks as we make our way down to the student parking. I pop the trunk of my little BMW hatchback. It was the one thing Dad said I couldn't fight him on buying. I always tried to stop him and my mom from spending unnecessary money on me, but the car was the thing he needed me to own. He yapped on about the five-star safety rating and how European cars are the safest cars to own. I knew that it was his cop coming out of him, and I knew Dad had seen some horrendous accidents in his time, so I allowed it. She's red, has leather seats and is a stick shift. I learned on a stick, and it has stuck with me since.

"I do, and I'm only going to the other side of town."

I put my bags into the little trunk and turn to face Leila. "I'm sure he will be nice. I like to think my mom is smart."

"Your mom is smart. Like, street smart," Leila agrees, tapping on the passenger window so I wind it down, just as I get into the driver's seat. "I'm sure his kids will be great. Hopefully they're not like, in diapers or anything."

That's what I fear. I'm hoping they're at least in their teens, but the way my mom spoke about them makes me think that they may be younger. Great.

I give Leila another quick goodbye kiss through the window and drive out of the parking lot. After a quick stop to buy a new but cheap phone, I'm singing along to Halsey's "Bad at Love" when a phone call comes through my Bluetooth on the radio. They transferred my number quick.

I push the green phone button on my steering wheel.

"Hey, Mom, I'm on my way."

"Hey, honey, I forgot to tell you, I've moved into his house, so you'll be staying here for the weekend."

"What?" I snap, shocked at how quickly things have moved. "Mom, I don't even know this person. And what about The Cherub? You can't just abandon that…" The Cherub is the name of her bookstore, she named it after me. I used to hate the nickname growing up, but now I don't really mind it. I'm finding it strange that she would just pack her life up and move after knowing this man for— "How long have you known him?"

She sighs. "Amethyst, you're too old to be asking these sorts of questions. I'll explain when you get here. I'll send the address to you now."

I exhale. Maybe I am overacting a bit. "Ok, Mom. I'll see you soon."

"See you soon, sweetie."

A couple minutes after she hangs up, her text comes through, and I illegally punch it into my GPS, using one hand still on the steering wheel. Armok? "Who the heck is this dude." Armok is, from what I've heard, a town filled with filthy rich people. Now I'm worried.

The drive there is fast, and it's not long before I'm pulling up to an old concrete high fence. The gate is closed, not surprisingly. I get out of my car, pushing my sunglasses to the top of my head and pushing my long hair back with them. I shield the sun with the palm of my hand, and then my phone starts ringing from my car. I launch for it, tapping answer.

"Mom?"

"I'm opening the gates, sweetie!"

"Thanks…" I struggle to keep the dry tone out of my reply, ending the call. I get back into my car and wait. A few beats later, the heavy metal gates separate and open to a long gravel driveway.

I put my car into first and drive forward, passing the trees
that are littered with burnt orange leaves hanging dramatically
from the branches. There are post lights lined between each
tree, with iron cladding clawing around the bulbs. This
driveway itself screams wealth. When my eyes land on the
mansion that overlooks the driveway I came down, I gasp in
shock. Old Victorian stone is molded—no— perfected
through-out the entire structure. Windows are scattered delicately around the front with black frames. I pull up the brake,
coming to a stop in front of the marble steps that lead to two
heavy rustic wood doors.

"Okay, Mom, what the actual effing shit is going on here."
I reach for the handle to my door, swinging it open.

"Oh, you didn't have to do that!" a deep voice declares,
coming closer to my car. I haven't looked up yet, too lost in my
own thoughts about how revealing everything has been since
driving a few miles from down the road. He must've taken the
handle on the other side of my car because the door stretches
open farther.

"Thanks," I murmur, a little confused. I eye the slacks, and
then slowly travel up the fine, obviously very well-built body.
"Am I in the right place?" I ask while still making my travels up
to his face.

When my eyes land on a thick dark neck, I gulp. Nice neck.
My focus finally came crashing to his and my mouth went dry.
Covered in beautiful dark skin, smooth like chocolate, was
probably one of the most handsome men I have ever laid eyes
on. He's young, I'm guessing around late twenties, and then he
smiles, and my legs shake. Straight white teeth lit up the dim
area, and two deep dimples sunk into those mocha cheeks. My
God. He was... mouth-watering. I need to snap myself out of
whatever stupidity I had just walked my butt into.

He smiles softly, or politely, probably more politely because
he had just witnessed my embarrassing reaction to his appear-

ance. He has to be at least half African American or something
exotic. Closing the door and gesturing to the steps, I notice his
accent. British. Someone is taking me for a ride, and it's not
him—unfortunately.

"Amethyst? I don't believe you are mistaken. Your mother
and Mr. Stone are waiting for you." It's official. I have a crush
on the guard.

"Ah, than—thank you?" I step out of his way, almost falling
on my butt. His eyes are like a dark brown orbits, only the
intensity makes me feel like I'm swimming in a pit of hot lava.
Okay, my obsession with him has reached new heights. This
was beginning to be a little more than embarrassing.

His lip kicks up a little as if he's amused by the fact that I
found him interesting, then he points to the trunk of my car.
"I'll get your belongings and put them in the guest room in the
west wing."

"West wing?" I quirk an eyebrow, unable to hide the shock
on my face. "This place has a west wing?"

He seems to think over my question. "It's a manor,
ma'am."

"Oh, right." I have no idea what he's yapping on about. A
manor? "Well, thank you, I guess."

Then I head to the front door. With each step, my throat is
closing more and more. I can't believe my mom managed to
find someone so rich. Maybe he's really old. But the kid thing is
throwing me off. Unless his ex-wife is a twenty-something-year
old gold digger who got knocked up on purpose, then yeah,
that could actually be it.

I look around the area again. The gardens splashed with
color and vibrancy that obviously showed they were taken care
of by an expert. Not my mom, obviously, because the only
thing my mom does with her hands is flip pages from a book
Which is never a bad thing. I was reading classic romance
novels at a very young age, what with Jane Austen and Char-

lotte Bronte on our shelves, just high enough for a child to
reach. But Dad read too, only his book covers had dragons on
them and half-naked people. Actually, come to think of it, I
probably saw my first tittie because of the cover of one of
Dad's weird, dragon erotic novels.

"Cherub!" The front door swings open and my mom steps
through with arms wide. She's wearing a—somehow—stylish
straw type hat on her head, a yellow sundress and white-
rimmed glasses that are way too large for her small heart-
shaped face. She also has a cocktail in one hand. This is a
different side of my mom that I haven't yet witnessed. She has
always been single, sporting knitwear and jeans, and she always
had a coffee mug grasped between the palms of her hands
while balancing a book on her thighs. Never a damn cocktail
and a fancy hat.

Ah… realization seeps in. I get it. She's finally lost her
mind. Knew it was coming but I was hoping it would be later
rather than sooner. You know, I sort of wanted a sane nana for
my kids. If I wanted kids… did I want kids?

Damn, my ADD was acting up today.

"Hi, Mom!" I embrace her, wrapping my arms around her
tiny neck. Mom is smaller than me. She's petite, where I'm a
little more on the curvy side. By a little more I mean my ass
would jiggle if you flicked it.

"Come in, honey! Come and meet Elliot!"

Oh. He has a name. I follow her into the large entryway.
It's decked out in mahogany wood and accented in pristine
white paint. There's also a glistening chandelier in the middle
that drapes delicately above your head. I remove my leather
jacket, hanging it on one of the hooks, all while keeping my
eyes on the sparkling crystals hanging above.

"Mom, you really outdid yourself here."

"Oh!" She brushes away my accusatory tone with a simple

flip of her hand. I continue to follow her toward the open plan living room which steps out to the pool in the backyard.

She plops down on a sunbed and pats the one beside her. "You got here early, tell me, how's college? Tell me everything!" She sips on her drink, just as a maid comes toward us balancing a silver plate on her hand, carrying a couple of fancy looking cocktails.

"You still prefer pina coladas?" She takes both of them and hands me the milky one.

"Yep!" I take it from her and smile politely at the maid. The backyard has a massive lap pool in the middle and a fountain toward the end. Trees lined the yard and a pool house hidden behind a few shrub bushes. Mom swats my arm, gaining my attention.

"That's where Elliot's sons stay when they're here because it's close to Scar, their home play-thing."

Right. The kids.

"What? On their own? A bit neglectful, isn't it?" I chuckle, sucking down the cool, creamy cocktail.

She inches her sunglasses down her nose. "Amethyst, whatever do you mean?" Her gaze shoot over my shoulder, and then a bright smile beams up her features. "Ah! Here they are!" She stands, stumbling a little, but hastily collects herself again.

I don't bother looking quickly, I just stand slowly while taking the cocktail from her. I place it on the little table that separated our sunbeds. "Yeah, I'm cutting you off."

I hear a chuckle from behind me and turn, rolling my eyes. Obviously, I'm going to have to try to brave the little shit devils since I will have to play nice with them, possibly forever, if I'm reading the vibes of love my mom is shooting out correctly.

"Hi—" Everything stops.

My breathing catches in my throat and I squeeze the glass in my hand. My heartbeat drops to a deep, slow and alarming bass and my palms itch with sweat. My knees start to quiver. Shit. Shit. Shit. Shit.

There, standing in front of me, were three—not boys—men. Not toddlers, grown fucking adults.

One, was Aquaman.

One, was Wolf.

And the other? Was fucking Maddox Stone.

AMETHYST

I SWALLOW, MY EYES FLYING BETWEEN THE THREE OF THEM. I look at Mom. "I'm sorry, wait, what?" My mumbled confusion probably doesn't go unnoticed by the trio, so I do what I always do when I'm nervous. I shut my mouth.

Maddox's eyes are like green marbled magnets. I'm drawn to his observation of me, and then before I can help it, my eyes collide with his. His hand comes out to mine, a cocky smirk spreading over his lips. "I'm Maddox. You're the daughter?"

I realize what he's doing. If my mom found out about us, it would drive her into a spiral of anxiety— on crack. Anxiety on crack is my mom's specialty.

"Hi." I put my hand out to him. "I'm Amethyst. And you are?" There's a double dig to this. I try to make it sound as if the night before wasn't worth remembering, but obviously, it fails because his laughter breaks through my insult.

Aquaman steps forward, dramatically shoulder barging Maddox. "I'm Talon, but this hot chick I met recently, calls me Aquaman, and well, I think it's catchy, don't ya think?" he asks me with a mischievous glint lighting up his murky green eyes. I narrow mine again. His grin deepens.

I'm a lost cause because I have no control over the smirk that comes to my mouth. "I think it fits rather well."

He winks at me, and then Wolf stepped forward, his hand out and his face seemingly frozen and emotionless. "Wolf."

I shake his hand even though it feels more like I'm shaking a stiff, cold corpse. I don't remember much of the night before, but I do remember how stand-offish Wolf was.

Running my fingertips through my hair, I swipe it all out of my face and then look back to my mom. "Well—"

"—Oh! I told the boys how you're such a tomboy, with skating all your life and all that…"

"—Mom—"

"—No, no, so they had said that there's a raspy thing down the road. Y'all should take her. Ame, honey, did you bring your skateboard?"

She didn't actually need to ask me that, because she knows damn well that I take my deck everywhere. "Yeah, Mom, it's in my car, but I have to be back later tonight. I have a really important paper that I need to be studying for…"

"What are you studying?" Wolf asks, taking a seat on one of the sunbeds. I feel awkward standing, fiddling with my fingers, and I know that Maddox is watching me with careful eyes, so I sit back down. Despite the fact that last night made my thighs clench, my bones scream, and my soul roar with anarchy, it also made me painfully somewhat aware of how lethal Maddox Stone is.

I bring my glasses back down to my face to shade my eyes. "Ah, bachelor of fine arts, actually."

"Actress?" he questions, an eyebrow quirked in interest. I'm not sure if that interest is genuine, but I go with it.

"Mmm, not by choice, really. I actually want to be more behind the scenes, so I'm majoring in dramatic literature and screenwriting, but I guess we all have to start somewhere, so yeah, actress."

My mom swipes her mouth with the cushion of her thumb before blurting out, "Amethyst has been doing small acting gigs since she was a child. We knew when she was just a little girl that she was going to do something in that line of work. We tried to get her into modeling as a child, but she threw a tantrum that could be heard in China."

"Mom…" I'm about to stop her from her information

overload, but she carries on, only changing the subject and going back to her previous subject.

"You are staying for at least one night, you can head back tomorrow."

I think about fighting her, and then I think about it again, and I watch as the sun begins to set in the sky, igniting orange hues over her tanned skin. How the wrinkles on the edges of her smile look a little deeper since the last time I saw her. Despite my earlier critique, I appreciate the carelessness in her body language. She is happy, at ease. Not that my mom was ever unhappy before, she was just…mom. But I notice it, and the least I can do is spend one night with her, you know since it will be a very, very long time until I come back here. If ever. Actually, I'm already thinking of excuses to get out of all the up and coming family events that I'm sure she has planned.

I sigh and then squeeze my mom's ankle. "Okay, Mom, fine, I'll stay. One night, but you owe me a damn donut."

She giggles, her head tipping back and her neck tightening from the movement. "Okay, honey, I'll call Elliot and get him to pick some up on his way home from his meeting." The boys are quiet, so I glance back at them. Talon and Maddox are both watching my mom and me, but Wolf has disappeared somewhere. I'm not surprised, from all that I have seen of him (which is only a few hours in all, but first impressions and all that), he seems the more emotionally detached brother. He seems reticent, distant and cold. Either that or he's just down-right sketchy. Either way, a side of me relates to his personality. I have always been an outcast, never fit in anywhere. I'm still trying to figure out why Leila even tolerates me, because we are worlds apart. I like me this way and I'll never change. I've never been interested in fitting in. I like diversity and anything that's contrastingly authentic. You can't put a personality inside a box and say; 'That's what she's like.' We're human, we're supposed to shed raw emotion and be violently different. More people need to embrace their differences. You don't want to look back at photos when you're eighty years old and think Damn, none of those opinions really mattered. I should have just been me.

"I'll go in search of another cocktail!" Mom stands up, but my hand goes to hers.

I shake my head. "No, it's okay. I have barely touched this one."

Mom's face falls into a soft smile. "Ame, you're in college now, you're going to have to get used to drinking. I want you to have fun."

I gulp while trying my hardest not to look at Aquaman and Maddox. "Thanks for the talk, Mom, but I'm good."

"Alright, suit yourself." She continues toward the house, mumbling a few words.

Maddox takes a seat opposite, just as Aquaman plonks beside me. "How's your head?" Maddox asks, his eyes gleaming complacently.

I pinch my lips between my teeth and fight the stupid girly blush that wants to run rampant over my face. "It was really bad this morning. I feel a little better now."

Maddox' grin only deepens, and then I feel a nudge against my arm. "You know, we ain't that bad," Aquaman says playfully.

I let out a slow, heavy exhalation of breath. "Really?"

Aquaman shoots a sneaky smirk to Maddox and then sobers when he comes back to me. "Of course not…"

Sarcasm.

What's that saying? It's the lowest form of wit or something.

Aquaman stands and stretches his thick arms above his head. "I'm gonna hit the Scar before Dad gets home. You wanna come?"

Maddox doesn't answer, and when I finally allow myself to

look at him, his gaze is fixed on me. Burning holes into me with imaginary lasers. Our eyes stay connected, and before I can force myself to break the contact, he answers, "Nah, I'm good. I'll double up tomorrow." His eyes stay on mine, absorbing me.

"Bro, you have a fight this weekend. You need to train." Aquaman's eyes follow his line of sight once he notices Maddox isn't going to look back at him.

Maddox's lip tips up, and then he finally stands. He glares at his brother. "I'm undefeated, pretty sure I got this."

Aquaman shakes his head but goes on his way, disappearing behind the pool house. Maddox takes Talon's seat beside me and reaches into his pocket. He hands me my iPhone. I exhale a huge sigh of relief. There are so many photos and memories on this phone.

I take it from him, ignoring the zap of electricity that passes through our touch. When did my life become a cliché? "Thanks. I wasn't sure whether I'd see any of these photos again."

He unzips his hoodie and throws it onto the end of the sunbed. I try really hard not to look at his rippled arms and the way they tense when he grips the chair—much like how they tensed when they were on either side of my head. One thrust, two—sheesh. That escalated quickly.

"I knew, also, you need to put a lock on that shit." He laughs, picking up a water bottle and taking a sip. I watch as his throat contracts from his swallowing, and then quickly divert my staring when I realize I was watching his throat like a creeper.

"Wait," I say once I have managed to calm my erratic thoughts. Throats. "You knew? That you would see me again?"

He pauses and then slowly twists the cap back onto his water bottle. "My dad and your mom have been seeing each other for months now. You're her pride and joy, there are damn photos of you in their room. Yeah, I knew who you were when I walked into that bar." his eyes drift to my hair quickly, and then he chuckles. "And if I wasn't sure, the hair would've given it away."

"You don't like my hair?" I'm offended. I usually give no shits about what people think of me, but I'm offended by this, and then I'm offended that I'm offended by this. Prick. My hair has been this shade of pink since I turned thirteen. It was me rebelling against my mom and society. But at that time, mainly my mom was still trying to get me into modeling. I didn't have the height, standing at five-two, but apparently I had the cheekbones (whatever the hell that meant). Only I was riding on four-wheelers and BMXs when (according to her), I should have been riding on her dreams to become a model.

"I didn't say that, Rosé." He grins, using my nickname from last night. His eyes search mine. "But I didn't intend to fuck you. Smashing back Jessica's little Cherub? Yeah, hell naw, that wasn't my intention at all."

I'm offended again. Can I hit him? I'm going to hit him. "Um, there are so many things I want to say in reply to that, and they all have the word cun—"

"Mad?" A tall, blonde haired girl, waltzes through the doors while pushing her oversized sunglasses over her silky white hair. "Hey, baby, sorry I'm late."

CHAPTER 5

AMETHYST

My eyes close. I shake my head, attempting to calm my breathing.

He has a girlfriend.

Of fucking course he does, because men.

"Hey, Stace, what are you doing here?" He also seems surprised to see her.

"I know, I know, it's me again, but I just wanted to make sure you're hitting your macro count and getting ready to cut for this weekend." She hands him a bottle of some murky colored drink as her eyes fly to me. They drag over my body, and at first, I could make out the scowl that threatened to surface, but then her focus lands on my shoes (my Docs), and she visibly relaxes, putting her hand out to me. "I'm Stacey, Maddox's girl. And you are?"

Apparently, the chick who fucked your man last night.

Leila warned me about this in a way. Well, no. Actually, she had said that he wasn't the boyfriend type, she failed to mention it was because he already had a girlfriend. I'll be having words with her. I'd never, ever, sleep with another girl's boyfriend, no matter how hot he was or how shitty she was, it just wasn't in my nature to do something like that. Until now. I'm beginning to think I'll be having a lot of firsts with my new stepbrother. Asswipe.

I take her hand in mine. "I'm Amethyst, my mom is—"

"—Dating Elliot!" She nods, clicking her fingers together in recognition.

"Yep."

I refuse to look at Maddox. I can't believe this asshole.

"Stacey is my ex-girlfriend, slash old friend…" Maddox declares casually, getting to his feet.

Stacey rolls her eyes while caressing his arm possessively. "For now," she adds, throwing me a wink. Okay, that's an Olympic sized drama pool all on its own, thus, I will not be diving into that. Me plus drama equals a gold medal no.

"I better take this inside. It was nice meeting you, Stacey."

I finally allow myself to look at Maddox. I hate the way the sun shines through his liquid ink hair. It makes me want to tear the dumb thing from the sky just so I never have to watch how it warms against him. His face profile is square, chiseled perfection. Just the right amount of tormented bad boy with a slight dash of Abercrombie. Again, totally not my type. I should stay in my lane. The very reason why I stayed away from guys like Maddox all my life, was this reason right here. They're the devil's work, and I don't sin.

Much.

Today.

Well, since last night.

Hail Mary full of grace…

"You too," Stacey whispers to my retreating back as I make my way back inside. I know she is lying. She hates me, I can sense it. I can practically feel the sharp daggers she is shooting into my back.

I find the kitchen fairly easy, because we passed it on the way through. I empty the rest of my drink down the sink, and I'm about to rinse my glass when I catch the fancy tap that has a spiral-like tube. I better not touch it, just in case I break something.

"Hey, Cherub, you met Stacey?" My mom comes in, her glasses off and her hat placed on top of the kitchen's oak counter. For the first time ever, the name Cherub sits weirdly with me. Maddox and his filthy mouth.

"I did."

"Poor Maddox. They've known each other for a very long time, so he doesn't have the heart to get rid of her."

"He has a heart?" I ask, shocked.

Mom sighs. "He does. He's just particular with who he allows to see it. Like someone else I know."

I ignore her jab. "Yeah, well, they dated…"

Mom giggles. "Oh, for two weeks. They were always friends in high school, and Elliot said she was always in love with him," she pauses, going to the fridge and taking out a jug of juice. She better not be making more cocktails. "Maddox felt he owed it to her to give it a shot. He figured out rather quickly that he only had friend feelings for her. If you ask me?" No one was asking you Mom, and please keep your voice down. She leans closer toward me, clutching her glass. "She's a bit crazy."

I can't help the laugh that escapes me. I guess that made it a little better. At least he wasn't as douchebag-y as I initially thought he was. I glance out the large window that hangs above the sink, overlooking the pool, and watch their exchange. Maddox shakes his head, his eyebrows crossed. Her face pulls in sadly and then her shoulders drop. His face sinks and sympathy falls over his features. He tugs on his hair slightly and then reaches for her. She takes his sympathy eagerly, stepping into his arms and resting her head on his chest.

Drama. Central.

MADDOX

Dinner is just flat out awkward. Amethyst hasn't so much as glanced at me the entire time, regardless of the fact that I've been seated directly opposite her.

I stretch my legs wide until my foot collides with hers. Her eyes shot to mine, almost instinctively, and then they narrow. I'm pissing her off—good.

"So, Stacey," my dad starts, poking at his steak. "How are you liking college? I know it's your second year, but I remember when you started like it was yesterday."

Stacey clears her throat, reaching for her drink. "It's been very good. I'm just glad I get to see Mad a lot."

Talon snorts, biting into his bread roll and tugging at it viciously. He continues to glare at Stace from across the table. I know he hates her, hell, my whole family except for my father dislikes her, but her story is shit. She got a shit hand, and I took it upon myself to help her. Her mom, though she is trying to get better, is still a shit mom—even on her good days.

Dad pauses, glares between me and Talon, then grunts in obvious disapproval. Dad is a hard ass. He was a professional MMA fighter all his life until he retired at forty-four. He always had money from my pops' business that he ran on the side, then when he retired from fighting, he took on the business full-time. My pops passed away not long after that. My brothers and I now carry on his legacy. Well, more me than the other two. Wolf prefers illegal dealings in the underground and Talon prefers football. My brothers and I, we don't let people get close to us. We've always only had each other and that's how we like it. It's why not many people know about us, only hear about us. Talon is the guy that has the most friends though, with his social butterfly personality, and Wolf has more enemies than friends, and I somehow fall in the middle. I've always been the medium between the two of them. You could say that I'm more balanced. My eyes fly to Amethyst.

Usually.

"So, Amethyst, your mom says you're doing something in drama?"

I watch as her fingers tuck her long pink hair behind her ear. On the exterior, everything about her is perfect. I follow the precise line of her cheekbone and how it angles perfectly down to her jaw. How her chin has a small indent in the middle, sort of like the dimples on my cheeks. How she's obviously not wearing any fucking makeup, yet her cheeks manage to wash over in a pink tint every now and then, and her dark lashes fan out on her pale white skin. Her eyes are unusual too, the lightest blue I have ever seen, close to a cyan color. She's drop-dead fucking beautiful, in the most disturbing way possible. Disturbing because she doesn't realize what she does to mankind. She doesn't fucking see how beautiful she is. She doesn't flash it around or use it as a reason to be a shallow bitch. I've watched her tonight, and even last night. She's effortlessly herself, a 'fuck what you think' personality in a small five-foot-two little body with pink hair.

I wish I could say that I felt like shit for not stopping what went on between us last night and that I had zero intention of ever doing that again, but that would make me a decent guy, and that's something I'm not. They say that if someone maintains eye contact with you for three seconds or more that they are either plotting your death, or they want to fuck you. The sex and anger she exuded, proves that both dance in her pretty little head. The pull is strong between us, even at such an early stage. Too fucking strong for me, and that made me a little bitch because I put grown men to sleep with my right hook. The only thing I have to figure out is whether I play with whatever the fuck it is we have going on here, or leave it alone.

Never been one to leave anything alone, much less a challenge.

"Maddox?" my dad calls from the head of the table, cutting through my thoughts. I'm still fucking staring at her. She's sitting there, her doe eyes fixed on mine with a direct line to my cock.

I shuffle in my seat. "What?"

"I said what time's your fight this weekend?"

"Oh, ah, seven." I finally look back at him, cracking my neck. I either need to fuck something or break something—or both simultaneously.

"Good," he answers, digging into his steak. "Brian Lynard will be there. You need to accept his offer."

Brian Lynard has been trying to sign me under his name for years now. I just don't want to accept.

"Yeah, but I don't know if I want to go the celebrity way—"

"Oh, honey, you should take advantage of what everyone has to offer," Jessica adds, flashing me a smile. I like her. I've known her long enough to warm up to her, the one who hasn't warmed up to her is Wolf.

My focus goes to Amethyst, and I grin, leaning back in my chair. Making her uncomfortable gets my dick hard, and not a lot gets my dick hard. "What do you say, Rosé? The celebrity MMA fighter and the actress. Has a ring to it, doesn't it?"

She gapes at me in shock, her jaw basically hitting the table. She quickly checks everyone, only no one paid any attention to my comment. Mainly because they know what I'm like. She's about to get schooled. Talon scoffs at my comment, grunting into his meal again. The only reason he would have heard is because he likes her enough to pay attention. I don't know what kind of like that is, but I know someone who would have something to say about it.

She clears her throat. She's cute as shit when she's blushing, but deadly when she's trying not to blush. She's a rebel without a cause, and her soul is fucking reckless, but I want it.

I want all of it and her.

She seems a little more innocent in the sex department than the ones I usually go for, but cute and exotic, nonetheless.

She takes a sip of her drink and then gazes back to me. "Not unless that ring is from the bell at your funeral."

I laugh, going back to eating my dinner.

Fucking wish I was face deep in her right now.

CHAPTER 6

AMETHYST

Clearing my throat, I reach for the glass and take a sip of my water. I've been trying my hardest to keep my gaze away from Maddox. My phone starts vibrating in my pocket, but I ignore it, figuring it would probably be frowned upon in this house to answer calls at the dinner table.

A foot collides with my shin and I flinch, my eyes shoot to a grinning Maddox. Such a freaking jerk.

"Ame, are you going to that audition this weekend that your dad was talking about?" my mom asks as she poked her fork into her lettuce.

"Mmmhmm," I nod, tossing the tomatoes around on my plate. "It's just a small role for a new Netflix show coming up, but it'd be a lot of fun to play."

"Oh yeah?" Maddox interjects into our light conversation. "What's it about?"

I lean back in my chair slightly. "A young detective who is starting out on the force, but she has superpowers. It has Marvel vibes, but I think it'd be a great starter. More than great, actually."

I look to Mom. "Did you get the donuts?"

Stacey clears her throat. "Seems a little far-fetched, though, right?" Then she laughs, probably hoping that everyone else would join her, only no one does and she's left looking like a dick. She stops abruptly and then clears her throat again. "So, what do you do for fun? What are you majoring in?"

It feels like an interrogation, but I answer anyway because I don't really care for her or her bitchy attitude. I'm well acquainted with mean girls, and there's one thing that they always forget; they have more to lose than us. Their pride, their image, all that plastic stuff that they care entirely too much about is a lot to lose against a girl who doesn't give a shit.

"I skate for fun, and like I said earlier, I'm majoring in dramatic literature and screenwriting."

She stops, her mouth slightly ajar, then my mom comes to the rescue again. "It's true, my girl is smart. I guess I'm lucky she spent more time at skate parks and less at parties during school."

I pat my mom's hand from under the table.

Aquaman interferes. "You're hot and smart?" Then he pauses, looking between Maddox and me. "Whoever has you has got to be one lucky guy."

"—Oh no," my mom once again chimes in. This time, I'm thinking I'm going to be a little more annoyed than I was before. "She has only had a couple of boyfriends, isn't that right, honey." She places her knife and fork back down onto the table and seems to think over what she's going to say. I try to widen my eyes at her, as in shut the fuck up, but she abruptly blows me off. "Oh, Shane was his name."

I cringe, sinking farther down into my chair. "Mom—"

Elliot interferes. "I'm sure she doesn't want to talk about that, love."

He's right, I don't. Elliot seems like a nice man, a bit hard around the edges but soft in the middle. At least I think he is, especially when he looks at my mom or his sons. I'm feeling drained, so I get my mom's attention as the maid walks in to take away our dirty plates.

"I'm feeling a little tired. I didn't get much sleep last night." My excuse comes out way, way the fuck out of left field to those three boys at the table and sounded more like I was taking a dig at Maddox when I wasn't.

"Were you skating last night? Must be tiring," Stacey asks

unknowingly, her slight scowl pinned on me. Gosh, was she that intimidated by me? I want to roll my eyes at how cliché she is being.

Wolf chuckles. "She was riding something…"

I feel my cheeks heat. I'm itching to get out of the room, it feels as though the oxygen is getting sucked out minute by minute. Pretty sure I'm about to die in here.

"Oh, you don't want your donuts?" My mom's eyes come to mine.

I shake my head, suddenly, my escape plan sounds more appealing than sinking my teeth into frosted fried dough. Or did it? Yes, yes it did. I start to contemplate an escape plan that will get me back to my dorm. "No, I'm okay."

"But they're tiramisu," she declares proudly before continuing. "Amethyst could never get enough of them when she was a child. I'd buy her them all the time, but only tiramisu. Weird flavor for a child."

I smile softly at my mom. Even though she drives me crazy, she has so much to give and loves strongly. "It's okay, Mom. I might just go to bed."

My eyes unconsciously go to Maddox, who's now searching the dining table as if he's in search of something, then he visibly stills. His fists clench as his eyes slowly come up to fix on me. He pins me with a glare. "What's that song… you know, the one…"

What?

"The song?" I entertain him. "What song?"

He starts humming, and I instantly answer, annoyed with his tricks. "'Fly Away' by Lenny Kravitz."

I go to kiss my mom on the head when I feel the atmosphere drop to deathly cold levels. Did someone open a window? Goosebumps break out over my flesh as I slowly look back at him. His face has gone pale, his eyes flat. Now he's looking right through me, instead of at me.

"Why'd you just ask me that?" Oh no.... My eyes dart between my mom and Elliot. "Wait! How long have you both known each other?"

Mom stares up at me in confusion. "I've known Elliot since high school, he was your father's best friend."

"This just got weird," I mutter, swiping away the bead of sweat that's breaking out on my forehead.

Maddox slowly stands, his eyes cutting to me, but instead of the light, sexy stare he usually gives me, it's now seeping in disdain. I flinch.

"She was who you were having an affair with?" Maddox growls at his dad, but his eyes were on my mom.

Elliot pauses, and then puts his knife and fork down onto the table. "As she said, son, a long time…"

I narrow my eyes on Maddox as two stories click together inside my head, like a problematic old rusted puzzle. "Oh my God, you were the boy from Krispy Kreme!"

Mom sucks in a mouthful of air from beside me, but I ignore her.

"Can someone please tell me what the hell is going on?" Aquaman announces, his eyes frantically going around the table.

Stacey agrees with a simple, "Mmhhmm."

No one says anything, and the room goes ghostly silent. Wolf slowly stands from his chair, the sound of the legs scraping against the hardwood floor piercing through the tension. "Dad has been having an affair with Jessica since long before Mom died." Then he simply turns and barges out the door.

"That's fucking why Wolf didn't like Jessica!" Maddox almost yells at his father. "Because he knew about your fucking affair."

"Watch your tone, son, you're in my house. You will not raise your voice at me or at Jessica."

Maddox turns to face me and then flicks his focus to my mom. "Fuck Jessica." his focus comes to me. "Fuck Amethyst." His eyes go to his father. I ignore the verbal punch to my gut because he's obviously angry. "And fuck you and your house." He goes to stalk out of the room, but stops at the threshold and turns his head slightly over his shoulder. A dark sadistic smirk shades his mouth. "Oh, and Jessica? I fucked your daughter last night, too." His eyes slightly come to mine, his lip curled. "Maybe you could teach her a thing or two about sucking dick since your abilities are good enough to break a home."

My head bows in shame, but my cheeks flare in rage. That was shitty, and now I'm mad. "I'm sorry, I can't do this right now." I stand abruptly and run toward the doors that lead to the entrance room, all while swiping the tears from my eyes. I'm not watching where I'm going because I collide into a hard chest.

"Wow." Hands grip around my arms, steadying me.

"I'm sorry." I rub my nose and sniff, then I look up to find the driver or whoever he was from earlier staring down at me.

"No need to apologize, Amethyst. Do you want me to show you to your room?"

"I don't." I shake my head. "I don't want to be here. If you could just help me put my stuff back into my car, that'd be good." He doesn't answer, so I brave a look back up at him. His eyebrows are furrowed in. "I don't think it's a good idea for you to be driving while upset."

"I—"

"—I'll go with her," I hear a voice say from behind me. I turn slightly, even though I recognize the voice. Aquaman.

I smile softly. "He'll take me."

The guard searches my face, and then they go over my shoulder for a beat, before he reluctantly nods. "Ok. I'll be back in a few minutes with your bags."

Once he has disappeared up the stairs, I turn around to face Talon completely. "You don't have to do that."

"Yes, I do," Aquaman assures, stepping forward while clutching a duffle bag. He continues through the front doors and disappears into the dark night. I follow him, going straight to my little car and beeping her unlocked. Aquaman, or Talon, which is what I should get used to calling him, slides into the passenger seat, tossing his bag over to the back. I get into the driver's seat and push the key into the ignition.

"Before you start asking me about Maddox and Wolf and their anger, and why I'm not angry like them, it's because I recognize that it's not your fault. My brothers have always been hot-headed. I, on the other hand," he grins, giving me a wink. "Have always been the voice of reason. It's why I have more friends than both of them put together and is why I feel it is my duty to take you home."

I glance out the window ahead, starting the car. "Well, actually, I wasn't going to ask about it. So maybe you can just fill me in on the parts that you want to fill me in on."

It takes ten minutes into our drive for Talon to say, "Our mom died in a car accident."

"Oh," I answer absently, then realize how insensitive that could've sounded so I quickly add, "I'm so sorry."

"Thanks," he grunts. Bet he's heard that a lot. "It was a long time ago, not that you ever get over losing a parent, but I have had to say that line a few times."

"Um, when did it happen?"

"April first. It always felt like some sick joke that we lost her on April fools. If only that were true."

After dropping Talon off to their house, the house I didn't think I'd ever see again, I drive back to campus. My phone has been going crazy in my back pocket the whole way, but I ignore it, knowing full well that it will be Mom. She broke up a home? A marriage. Now that woman is dead? History is a bitch, and somehow, I've managed to fall into that pool of drama I was so adamant that I didn't want to so much as dip my toe into. The information is swimming around in my head, threatening to drown me. The only person I want to talk with right now is Dad. I have a feeling he could shed some clarity on this foggy situation.

I barge into my room, throwing my bag to the other side before belly flopping down onto my mattress. I need to gather enough energy to get up and call Dad, but fatigue sinks into my bones and I fall into a deep sleep.

The loud crunching of granola wakes me the next morning. My eyes peel open to find Leila, shoveling her face with spoonfuls. "You know, you slept a whole ten hours. I'm impressed."

I chuckle, dropping my arms down onto my blanket. I squint against the bright morning sun that's blasting through the cracked blinds. "Well, I'd rather be sleeping. God, my simple family life just got all messed up."

Her chewing slows, her head tilting. "Do you want to talk about it or drink about it?"

I shuffle under my blanket more and glare at her. "No, Leila, drinking about it is how this whole thing pretty much started. I don't really want to talk about it right now. Maybe later."

She heads off to her first class and I go back to sleep. There's no way I can face the world without more naptime.

MADDOX

"Bro, you need to pull all that shit in. I'm serious," Talon says, blocking my hit.

I bounce around on my toes, stretching my neck. "Why, Talon? It's not like you were in the fucking car!" I reared my elbow back, jabbing him straight in the jaw.

One, two, three. The combinations are a little savage. He has no chance. He throws his hands up to block my hits, but trips backward, falling onto his ass. I rotate my shoulders and gesture for him to get back up.

He shakes his head. "Hell naw, man!" He yanks the gloves off his hands and tosses them across the octagon.

We're at Dad's, training in the shed that we transformed into a Mixed Martial Arts gym when we were in high school. It's rough around the edges, but it's ours. When I was just shy of thirteen, my dad kicked up my training schedule and threw me in with a professional gym, one that my coach runs. I trained there six days a week for four years solid before I started fighting underground. At first, Coach didn't know. But when he did eventually find out, he kicked me out, which is how "Scar" was built. Personally, I would have rather call it Mufasa, but whatevs. There are boxing bags hanging from the wired structure and a large octagon made up of rope and a whole lot of padded flooring. There are speed bags, three treadmills, a few benches and a shit load of weights. It didn't look flashy by any means with the dirt floor, but the equipment did its job. I'm back with Coach now. When I stopped the illegal bullshit—just before I got out of high school—Coach took me back. This is where we all train when we're home, and I still prefer this place to my flashy ass gym in the city.

"Get up, you're getting weak," I teased, grinning at Talon.

He flips me off. "Fuck you Mr. I'm Undefeated."

I slip through the rope and grab my water bottle off the bench. I take a sip, then swipe my mouth with the back of my hand. "I can't get over it. I'm fucking irked at her."

"Why!" Talon yells, getting to his feet. He saunters closer and rests his arms on the rope, his head hanging between his shoulders. "I get it, bro. You were there with Mom when it happened. You were her pride and joy—"

"—We all fucking were, Talon. Goddamnit," I breathe in and out, in an attempt to calm my rage.

You know those moms who were just perfect. The house is always clean, there is always fresh cookies or cake baking in the oven, and dinner is always served with a smile and peck on the cheek. That was my mom. I can't comprehend why my father would ever cheat on that, and honestly, it makes me mad as fucking hell that it was happening under my nose, and was still happening without me even realizing it. I get humans and all their mistakes, but Jessica obviously wasn't a mistake. It felt more like he thought my mom—was.

"Talk to me, brother," Talon murmurs, searching my face. "Don't go into that dark hole in your mind. Regardless, Amethyst isn't the issue here—our father is. We can't punish her for her mom's decisions either. She's as innocent in this as we all are—hell! She has it even worse."

I tilt my head. "How do you figure?"

"How do I figure what?" he asks, climbing out of the ring.

"That she's worse off." I toss the bottle onto the ground and take a seat on the bench. I'm going to need to hit some reps since this fool is lacking stamina.

"She's alone, bro. We've all got each other. Amethyst is an only child."

I hate when this fucker is right.

AMETHYST

Flipping my Tony Hawk cap backward, I let my long pink braid fall over my shoulder. Standing on my deck with one foot, I push off the concrete with my other and then balance on the board. I had Boston's "More Than a Feeling" playing through my earphones, and it felt good to be out here, away. Free. I smile gently as the sun licks its rays over my skin and the air zooms through my trucks, pushing me to intoxicating speeds. I'm in my zone. I head straight for the halfpipe, going up and then kickflipping back down again. The breeze flew through the loose strands that had fallen out from my braid and goosebumps prickle over the flesh on my thighs. I'm wearing ripped, slightly baggy, cut-offs, and a red bikini top underneath my white tank. I can skate in anything, but the looser the better.

God, I missed this. The adrenaline that I get from skating is close to the feeling I get during sex. It's addicting and euphoric, so nothing can wipe the smile off my face as I continue to skate around the park. This park, in particular, isn't new to me. Kingsville is where I always come to when I need an out. It has a basketball court beside it, with hoops so old the netted baskets have torn off. A few metal bins are scattered messily in places, and there's graffiti artistically splashed on almost every inch of the half-pipes and ramps. I've always been completely aware of how bad of an area this was. Every second person who walks past is pushing dollars and baggies into their back pockets, but they leave me alone. I think they just got used to me being here.

Eminem and Ed Sheeran's song "River" starts playing as I skip off my deck, tapping on the bottom until it flips up and lands in the palm of my hand. Tearing my earphones out, I stroll to where my things are, picking up my water bottle.

"Your mom said you'd be here."

I freeze, recognizing the voice, then turn to face him.

"Maddox, hey."

I'm not sure what version of Maddox I'm about to get, so I figure a simple 'hey' would make an average opening. He slowly starts walking toward me, his eyes moving down my body and then coming back up again. He takes a seat on the ramp, leaning back on one elbow. I can't help it. I'm obviously an idiot, but I can't help checking out all that is Maddox Stone. Seriously, had he never gotten a pimple as a teen? His skin is ridiculous. I have skin envy. My mouth starts to open, when I internally register what I was probably about to do—ask him about his skin—so I bite down on my tongue and quickly change the subject.

"Is there a reason why you're here?" I place my deck down beside him and take a seat on top. "No offense, but this doesn't really seem like your scene."

His tongue creeps out to wet his bottom lip, and I catch the shine of his tongue ring. Lord, help. I quickly look away, staring straight ahead.

"This yours?" He picks up my gold link chain. I always take it off when I skate, so I don't lose it. I bought it for myself just because I liked it. Treat yourself is my favorite saying.

"Yup." I smile at him. He unclasps it and puts it around his neck.

"Hey!" I shove him playfully in his arm.

"I'll look after it for a while."

I think about protesting this but don't.

He clears his throat, his face falling serious. "I was eight when she died."

My mouth opens, but then realize I have nothing to say. I don't want to fill the empty pause with pointless words, so I let him continue.

"My mom and dad, they weren't on good terms when she passed. It was that night——" He stops and glares up at me. His eyebrows come together as he searches my face, going from my lips to my eyes. "It doesn't seem fair, right? That I got out of the car without a scratch, but she didn't even get to walk out."

He's still penetrating me with his stare, so I figure he wants me to answer. Only I'm not very good at pep talks or condolences, so I hope I don't fuck this up epically. Usually people who are comfortable enough to open up to me about something so deep, already know I suck at these things and forgive me before I open my mouth.

I clear my throat, keeping my eyes locked on his. "I guess it would seem that way to you, but I bet she wouldn't have had it any other way, Maddox."

He pauses for a beat like he is trying to figure me out. "I guess," he answers, finally breaking our eye contact to gaze forward.

The sun is beginning to set over the old abandoned buildings in the distance, and a car alarm has started going off from somewhere close, but all that matters right in this moment, is Maddox.

"There was just so much left unsaid and unfinished. I've always felt like she was robbed that night, because" —he halts, clears his throat— "because she had just finished finding out about my dad's affair with your mom. She was so angry, I had never seen her that angry. I wasn't even scared that she was crying so hard, or that the speed on the speedometer was pushing over a hundred at eight p.m. at night. I was terrified because for the first time in my eight years, I was watching my mom fall to pieces and I couldn't fix it."

My heart clenches in my chest thinking back to the

Maddox I remember. The eight-year-old who let me sit in his fancy Lincoln, and even sat in our beat-up Toyota—just to listen to music with me. Tears threaten to surface at the corners of my eyes, but I swallow them quickly, afraid that I didn't earn those tears, or that he wouldn't accept them.

"Anyway," he continues, changing elbows. "It was a second later that she took a corner too fast and wrapped us around a tree."

"Maddox…" I whisper without realizing how much emotion my tone gave away.

"Amethyst, I'm not telling you this for sympathy," he swallows. I watch as his Adam's apple bobs. "I'm telling you because I'm sorry."

"Sorry? For what?" What could he possibly be sorry for.

"For how I acted last night. I snapped at you, and I shouldn't have. I'm sorry." He looks back at me.

I give him a soft smile. "It's okay. Friends?"

He searches my face, his eyes softening. They turn lazy as they drop to my mouth before coming back up again. "Yeah, babe, friends sounds good."

I get to my feet. "Ever skated before?"

He freezes. "No, and I'm good with that."

"Oh, come on…" I nudge him with my hip. Leaning up on my tippy toes, my lips skim his ear. "Live a little…"

"I'd watch your proximity if I were you, friend, and I live just fine."

I drop back to the soles of my feet, struggling against the tingly feeling that starts to twirl deep in my belly.

"Fine, how about this…" He takes the deck from me. "If I go down this ramp without falling on my ass, you'll come to my next fight in three weeks…"

"I don't like fighting…"

"…I don't like skating."

I narrow my eyes at him.

He narrows his back. "What will it be, Rosé?"

"Fine," I agree. "Because I can't wait to see you fall on your ass." The dip is deep, there is no way he wouldn't fall as a first-timer.

His lip slowly curls up into a grin. It is so cocky that it has me second guessing him, so I quickly take another look down the ramp. Yeah, no, there was no-freaking-way—he flips the deck down onto the rim of the ramp, resting on it expertly.

What?—

He licks his lip, winks and says, "I'll have the boys pick you up at seven, princess." Then leans forward and I watch as he smoothly, not only makes it to the bottom, but drives up the halfpipe, flips back, and then drifts back down again.

I look down to the pit of the ramp. "You cheated!" I yell, though I can't help the cheesy smile on my cheeks. They burn with pride.

He chuckles and flips me off. "Whatever you need to tell yourself, princess."

CHAPTER 8

AMETHYST

I RETURN TO CAMPUS A LOT HAPPIER THAN HOW I FELT WHEN I left. After Maddox took my ass to church on the halfpipe, we split up as he came back to school to catch his final class. I hit the school gym quickly in an attempt to burn off all the food I have consumed. I learned a bit from today, and training only helps my brain process all my thoughts.

For instance, one of the things I have come to terms with is that it might be too late. I think I already like him. Did I really ever stop from when we were kids? The crappy thing about meeting someone at a young age is that a crush can turn into an obsession the older you get. It either manifests or burns out. I don't think the latter is what has happened between Maddox and I. The fact that we slept together probably doesn't help either. It's shit. I hate being human. I obviously already like him enough to call him a friend. But it couldn't go further, even if I want it to. Our family's connection is obviously deeper than what I had initially assumed. Not that I'd need to worry about it going further. Just like Leila said, he's not that kind of guy. I really should have spent more time on the social side of college, then maybe I would know what I was up against as far as the Stone brothers were concerned. I have always kept my head down, and I'm embarrassed to admit that even if I had passed them previously on campus, I may not have looked at any of them a second time. I'm just not aware of my surroundings as much as I should be. I have missions in my head, and if you're not on my daily mission, you probably won't get noticed.

Maybe it's time to learn about these brothers. I fire up my laptop and see if I can search them on Facebook to get an idea or even an inkling as to what they're really like. I have a feeling that wherever they go, people know, they watch. The way Leila reacts to them says a lot, too, so maybe I really have been that oblivious to everyone. Not that it's hard to gain Leila's attention, but it is almost impossible to keep it. She'd forget your name as quickly as she learned it—but not these boys. I need to research a little.

I get onto Facebook. Notifications (0). I have two messages and three friend requests, though. I go to the messages first because sometimes my dad uses Facebook to send me funny memes and videos. He hasn't quite figured out that you can tag people in the comments section instead of sending it to them in a message, but baby steps. He is getting there, and I am proud of him.

I begin removing my shirt when I click on the bubble. Sure enough, one was from Dad. I open it and see it's a YouTube link. I roll my eyes and type out a reply.

Me: Dad, I'm not opening that.

My eyes snap to the side, catching a box of donuts with a note sitting on top. I tilt my head, reaching for the note.

Figured I can start sending you donuts now that we're FRIENDS?
   P.S. Check your Facebook.

I laugh, shaking my head while putting the note into the drawer of my computer desk. I reach blindly inside the box, gripping onto any donut and pulling it out. Tiramisu. The perfect man. He'd make someone a lucky girl one day.

I bite into it and moan, knowing full well I'm the only one in here. After surviving the carb and sugar attack the donut launched me into, I click the Friend Request tab.

Wiping my hands on my shorts, I swallow when I see "Maddox Stone has requested to add you as a friend on Facebook. Do you accept?" I think about pushing decline, but he did just send me donuts, so…

I accept his friend request and then go to the other two. The one below Maddox is Talon, and then below Talon is some weird name I don't recognize. I have no friends in common with him and they don't have a profile picture. Dodgy. Decline. I hit accept on Talon and then go back to the Messenger tab, remembering I had two messages, not just one.

Maddox: You get the donuts?

I start to type out a reply, but figure I owe him now. Pulling out my phone, I turn the camera on and flip it to selfie mode. Biting into the donut, I cross my eyes like I'm experiencing the best feeling ever, and then snap it. Licking the powdered sugar off my fingertips, I shake my head at the image. I look a mess. I have sweaty post-training hair, with a sweaty post-training bra on. My pink hair is a mass of hay piled onto the top of my head in a messy bun, and I have on zero makeup, which isn't too surprising. I don't wear it anyway, but my cheeks are still slightly flushed and my lips continue to hold their natural red tint. I open Facebook Messenger on my phone and hit send.

I see my dad has replied.

Daddio: Are you okay? Your mom said you might be upset about something. What has she done now?

That is sobering. I'm not entirely sure how I feel about my mom at the moment. I need more time to process her, and then maybe, when I'm not so weirded out about it, I'd ask her for her side. But I don't like cheating, and I despise cheaters. I get that life is sometimes difficult and things aren't black and white. I'm a strong advocate for the color grey, but that will never excuse adultery. I sort of expected more from my mom. I wanted more from her.

Me: I'm ok, Dad. I'm not ready to talk to her yet.

Daddio: Do you want to come home this weekend?

Me: I'm truly ok, Dad. I'll make a trip back when I can. I love you. I'll call you this week.

Daddio: Alright, baby girl. Watch that video. I love you too.

I roll my eyes before scrolling back up to find the link, clicking on it. My damn dad and his dry ass sense of humor. It's a video of a goat terrorizing a village. Only my dad would find this amusing. God, I love him.

My eyes catch the new message, but I shut my laptop and pick up my phone, going to the dresser to take out some clothes. As much as I loved that donut, I need real food, stat. And a shower. I open up Maddox's new message.

Maddox: You're cute as shit, Rosé.

I smile, typing back a reply.

Me: It took you that long to reply with 5 words? Do I need to help you in English?

Maddox: My English is fine. You can help me with human anatomy though. I might need some help there...

I roll my eyes again. There is no way that this man needs help there.

Me: I'm sure you don't need me for that.

There is a pause in the texting, so I quickly grab my clothes and towel, heading for the shower. We're lucky we have our own small bathroom in our dorm room. I don't know how I managed to get into this room, must have been sheer luck. It takes me about ten minutes to rip my sports bra off. I swear, my life always flashes before my eyes every time I need to get one off, and I am about to slip under the steaming water when my phone dings. Like a crack fiend, I reach for it and open up his latest message.

Maddox: You sure about that?

What kind of stupid reply is that? I put my phone down and slip back into the shower, relishing the pelting hot water rolling down my body with the smell of lavender and sage dancing in the steam. After quickly washing my hair, I turn off the faucet and get out, wrapping the towel around my body. My phone lighting up catches my eye, so I pick it up, opening it onto another message. Only this one is from Leila, the selfie we took during work one day flashing on my screen.

Lei: Did you get the donuts? He came over while you were at the gym.

Me: Yes. They were delicious.

Lei: You didn't save me any!?

I snort, heading back into our bedroom.

Me: I don't share, remember?

Lei: Good thing I stole one this morning then. Xo

I gasp and check the box, sure enough, there's two missing.

Me: Wench.

Lei: ((hugs))

I scroll through my photos and then open the selfie that he had sent me the morning after our night. Cheeky fucker. I assign it to his number before opening his message again to finally reply.

Me: Hungry?

A text comes through instead, and the image of him that I saved under his number does weird things to me. Maybe I should remove it.

Maddox: For...

I don't think I'm going to survive this friendship.

Me: Food!

Maddox: Sure. I'll come pick you up in ten.

That was going to be my line, but whatever. I freeze. He's coming in ten minutes? Shit. Diving into my wardrobe, I pull out a pair of loose ripped boyfriend jeans and my Metallica shirt that hangs off one shoulder. Dashing back into the bathroom, I fire up the hair dryer, but only get halfway, leaving my hair with some strands still wet. This won't end well, my hair always frizzes when left half damp. There is a knock on my door. Surely he wouldn't come up here, I mean, guys aren't allowed in the dorms here. And besides, with Dahlia at the front desk, there would be no way Maddox could sneak past her. Unless she was otherwise occupied with donuts. I really need to make her my friend. We obviously had something vital in common.

Raking my hair out of my face, I open the door to Maddox leaning against the frame, already smirking at me. He doesn't have his cap on this time, now he's in dark jeans, a white Henley hiding underneath a heavy leather jacket, and by the looks of the dampness of his hair, I'd say he just got out of the shower not long ago. The smell of soap laced leather and a dash of cologne consumes me in ways that I don't really want to be consumed right now. He smells like man with a lot of sin. Or like sin with a little bit of man. It's intoxicating and forbidden, and probably poisonous, but a real nice way to wake up dead. My mouth waters. Fuck.

"Hi." Suddenly, I was shy.

His eyes drop down my body, right down to my toes before coming up again. "Hey."

I hitch my thumb over my shoulder. "I just need to grab my shoes and wallet. Come in." I leave him in the dust to grab my things.

Him in my space feels…strangely normal, but it is doing funny things to my imagination, which I don't appreciate. Tying up my original Vans, I snag my little coin pouch from my bed. I have a small obsession with coins, and I hate anything big and extra. So I've always carried around a small leather coin pouch. It's big enough to hold my cards inside and some cash while being easy to push inside a pocket.

I catch him looking at all the photos that are scattered around the room.

"Want a donut?" I ask, unable to hide my smirk. His eyes meet mine. I take this chance to see what photo he was looking at. It's one of me and my dad after a football game. I would have been around eight, so pretty much around when I first met Maddox.

He shakes his head slowly. "I'm good. Let's go."

Walking out of our room and down the hall, we fall into an easy silence. Once we hit outside, he heads toward a black muscle car.

"Um…wait, is this your car?"

His eyes fly between me and the car. "Yeah, why?"

I grin like a small child left unattended in a candy store. "This is freaking amazing."

His shoulders visibly relax a little. "Thought you were about to tell me it's old, then I would have had to cancel our friendship."

I chuckle a little, reaching for the door handle. "Nah, no way. It's beautiful."

Driving there is long-ish, but without Maddox's driving, it could have been longer. He takes a turn down a long gravel road, lined with overgrown trees and ancient brick statues.

"Are you taking me here to kill me?" The sun is just setting, so there's a beautiful burnt orange hue setting fire to the sky.

He does his half smile thing, and it's mysterious, smart, sexy and…nope. "If I wanted to kill you, I wouldn't drive so far out to do it. Do you know how much gas that would use?" He quirks an eyebrow at me and I shake my head, smiling. "In all seriousness, I thought you'd like this place."

Before I can stop myself, I blurt out, "This where you take

all your dates? Or just Stacey…" Abort, abort. I shouldn't have gone down that road. I close my eyes and internally cuss myself out.

He sighs. "I don't date. Ever. I fuck and that's it." I open my mouth to give him points for his crass mouth when the sight of bright fairy lights catches the corner of my eye. I look straight ahead. Words get stuck in my throat because my God, this place is beautiful.

"Wow…" The setting is outstanding. It's a two-story cedar cottage, the aged wood stained in dark brown tarnish. The windows glow in the center of white trimmings. The front patio that overlooks the driveway has tables and chairs scattered around neatly. Bright fairy lights illuminate every inch of the cottage structure. More lights hang around the patio, up the steps that lead to the front entrance, and even curve around the window trimmings on the outside. Maddox pulls us to a stop, the deep rumble of his V8 vibrating under my butt. The gloss black Hemi Cuda is long lost in the back of my brain now. All I can see, all that takes up the entire vicinity of my head, is the beautiful setting in front of me. I must have been staring a long time because my door opens, and Maddox stands with his hand out, waiting for me to take it.

I smile appreciatively up at him, placing my hand in his. "Maddox," I whisper as he guides me across the gravel, handing the car keys to a valet boy waiting at a podium. I feel slightly under-dressed, and for the first time in my life, I care a little. I don't know why, but this place feels sacred.

"I know," is all he says. It isn't in a cocky way, it was in an appreciative way. He guides me up the stairs where an older man greets us. He wears a dark maroon suit and has aged, tired eyes. "Good evening, Mr. Stone. Will you be sitting at your usual?"

I freeze. I realize I'm being a little irrational, but it's my first instinct to jump to conclusions. So, he did bring other girls here? I'm not stupid enough to ask again, though.

Maddox shakes his head. "No, a booth."

The doorman, who is named Billy by the looks of his nametag, simply nods politely and then gestures for us to enter. "I'll escort you to booth four."

Maddox follows him with me not far behind. The inside is just as striking as the outside. There's no harsh lighting. The entire interior is filled with more draping fairy lights. Some hang professionally from the roof like droplets of water, while others simply line the tables, chairs, and walls. Two candles light the center of every table, one tall and one short. It is breathtakingly different. I have never witnessed anything like it. I can't be mad at him, even if he has brought girls here. It's not like we were dating, are dating, or are even going to date. I think at this point, we just generally enjoy each other's company.

I think.

For now.

Well, I don't mind him, but then again, I don't really know him. Shit.

Billy points to a small booth in the corner where a curtain hangs above the seating, giving more privacy should we want it. He then points to the menus on the table. Literally, on the table. As in a tablet on the table.

"As Mr. Stone is aware, we're trialing a new system. You place your order using the touchscreen on the table. Drinks, entrée and main dishes, all come out rather quickly after ordering, so we advise not to order all at once but rather separately, once finished. There's the drink menu beside the salads and the desserts underneath it. If you have any questions, push the red button on the tablet and I will come to you. Have a lovely evening." Then he bows his head before disappearing.

I sigh. "I want to live here." I run my finger over the tablet, seeing everything lined up easily. There are tabs defining which menus you want to order from. I start with drinks, just one, to calm my nerves. I hit "White Russian" because I'm craving something velvety, then continue to order the steak salad.

"You like it?" Maddox grins up at me proudly while tapping on the tablet.

"I more than like it," I admit, my eyes fluttering around the place. "It's like a hidden treasure. It's truly stunning. What's it called?" I didn't pay attention to the name because I was too busy admiring everything else. There are people in almost every booth, and more outside on the patio, as well us upstairs too, probably. I'm not sure what could be upstairs, maybe a draaanking bar. Leila would be up there in a heartbeat.

"Dutch!" he says, running his index finger over his lip.

I smile appreciatively, then realize I'm watching his finger. I need a distraction. "So, now that I know that you, Talon, and Wolf are brothers, who is the oldest brother?"

He clears his throat, leaning back in his chair. His eyes glimmer with mischief. "Who do you think?"

I pretend to ponder over my answer, but I already know who. "Talon." It isn't just his size, because he is a lot thicker than Maddox and even bigger than Wolf, but it's the way he holds himself. He just seems like the protector of the three.

"Interesting. And where do you think I place?" He cranks his neck, his eyes swaying manically. What was I doing? Was he enjoying this? Probably.

"Middle. I'd say Wolf was the youngest."

He tilts forward, his elbows resting on the table. Another waiter, a young girl this time, brings out our drinks and then bows her head at Maddox. "Sir."

Sir?

I quirk my brow at him questionably but tuck that in to ask him about later.

He didn't even acknowledge the waiter, his eyes remaining

solely on me. He chuckles, shaking his head. "Well, I guess you got it right. Sort of."

"Sort of?" I ask, tilting my head and sipping my drink.

"We're triplets, Ame."

"Oh, wow." Then it sinks in. Their poor mother had to give birth to three, probably above average-sized boys. Ouch.

We fall into easy conversation that ranges from sports to his fighting, to my dreams and aspirations.

"So you're still fighting?" I ask around a piece of steak.

He takes a sip of his drink. "Yeah, I do. It's a little more serious now, though. Sort of takes the fun out of it."

I nod. "Yeah, that's probably one of the reasons why I never thought to go pro in skating. I just always thought, I don't know…" I don't want to insult him.

"Say it," he urges, doing his head tilt thing again. If he didn't exude fear, I'd say that little move was cute.

I exhale. "That when you use your talent as your career, it's either going to soar, or it's going to kill it."

He chuckles, watching me carefully. "And what do you think it does for me?"

Licking my lower lip, I shrug. "I haven't watched you fight, so I can't answer that."

He grins wickedly. "We'll have to change that real soon."

I place my knife and fork onto my plate, just as the waiter comes back to clear our plates and replace our drinks. I truly only intended to have one, but it went down a little too smoothly.

Before I can ask him more questions, his foot collides with mine from under the table.

I freeze.

"So," I change the subject, picking up my drink. "What are you majoring in?"

"Business. Boring, but it's something my dad has me doing since you know, I'll be taking over one day."

I take a small sip of my drink. "What is it that he does? I don't think I caught it at dinner with all the drama flying around."

He rubs the side of his face, exasperated. "Tell me 'bout it. We own Stone Properties."

I gulp. I recognize the name, I just didn't put two and two together. "As in you literally own most of New York?"

He gives me a tight smile. "Yeah."

"Wow," I say, just as dessert gets placed on the table. Tiramisu. My eyes go to his as I stab my fork into the spongy cake he ordered for me. "Thought tiramisu was bad for my height?" I take a bite off the fork.

"Guess I think you're perfect."

Friendzone.

I clear my throat. "Why you and not the other two?" My palms sweat and my thighs clench. Everything he does is attractive to me—what the fuck is up with that.

He shrugs. "Yeah, I mean, my brothers have their own shit that they've always been working toward. Talon with his football and Wolf with law, and besides all that, I was the only one who always took an interest in the family business when Pops was around."

"Oh okay." It makes sense, I just get the feeling that it's not something he wants to do, rather something he feels he has to do.

"What are you doing this weekend?" he asks casually. My eyes follow the tattoos that trace down his arms.

I'm feeling thirsty, and it's not for water. I'm pathetic.

"Probably studying, and then hit the park at some point. Why?" I eye him skeptically.

"Talon is throwing a party at the house this weekend."

"Right." I put my glass down.

He searches my eyes, making my tummy feel queasy from the mere connection of it. "You should come."

Clearing my throat, I shuffle in my seat. "Well, I'll have you know, contrary to how we reconnected, I'm actually not a party girl."

He stands, tossing his napkin onto the table and grabbing out a few dollar bills. "I sort of got that feeling. Come on, I better get you home."

On the way back to campus, he stops at a parking spot on the skirts of the city near Brooklyn Bridge. I tilt my head back and fix my attention on the roof. "This sort of feels dejavu-ish, right?" I can't fight the smile on my face. "With us in a car."

"Yup." He pulls up the brake, reaching for his cap in the backseat and flipping it on backward.

I feel like everything about him is taunting me. From his eyes to his lips, to his skin. I'm not one of those girls who are crazy about guys with tattoos, but I admire the reasoning behind why people get them. But he, all that is him, is provoking me right now. How am I supposed to have him as a stepbrother if I am barely coping by having him as a friend. The attraction is undeniable, and it's being a stubborn bitch. Like Eve, I am tempted by the apple...with Maddox being the apple. The question is, is the bite worth the venom? I shouldn't ask myself that because, in my stupor, I will probably say it would be.

"What?" His voice is low and reaches something deep inside of me.

I lick my bottom lip and watch as his eyes catch the move-ment. Tilting my head, his eyes snap back to mine, and I don't know if it is the semi-lack of lighting or the shadows the street lights are casting over his features, but his eyes darken.

"Nothing." I quickly interrupt whatever he is about to say. "I just" —gazing out the front windshield, I watch as people stride across the walkway— "I guess I had fun tonight."

"You did?" His voice is still low, but it's almost distant. Still close enough to send goosebumps over my neck, nonetheless.

"I did. I still sort of feel guilty about my mom," I add, fidgeting with my fingers. I feel responsible in some way.

He visibly stills, but then shrugs. "I guess shitty things happen all the time."

"I guess," I answer softly, trying to tread carefully around the subject, but still wanting him to know that I care.

"Can we do this friend thing?" I ask, resting my head on the window.

"I don't know, guess we'll see..." He winks at me then starts the car. "This is my place of zen. I run down here almost every Sunday, and any other time that I might need to clear my head." He puts the car in reverse, pulling out.

"It's nice. If I ran, this would be the place I'd want to do it. You know, away from the road and traffic."

He takes us back to campus, only a lot slower than before. "Will you come this weekend to Talon's party?" He looks between me and the road.

"Ahhh." I shuffle uncomfortably in my seat. My muscles have long since relaxed from being around him, now it's moving into scary territory because being around him is starting to feel easy. "So, you want me to come to your fight and to the party?"

He shrugs, pulling into the school. It is late now, and all that illuminates the courtyard are the big street lights. "Yeah, why not? It's not like I'm making you come to my fight this weekend. You have a couple weeks to warm up to it."

I pause, my hand resting on the handle. I smile softly. "Ok, I'll come to both. Maybe. I mean, I'll try to come to the party."

He reaches forward, his eyes still on mine. His face comes so close that I can feel his breath falling over my lips. I freeze, internally battling with myself on what the fuck I'd do if he kissed me. He leans a bit closer, his lips only slightly brushing over mine. My eyes close, and just when I'm about to kiss him, he leans sideways and flips open the glove compartment, ruffling through papers. Motherfuck! My eyes pop back open as I collect myself quickly, even though my cheeks are on fire. Damnit. Was that a test of friendship? Did I imagine his lips slightly brushing mine? Oh God, I need help.

Pulling out a lanyard, he hands it to me along with a couple of rectangle pieces of paper. "Two tickets, and that," he points to the lanyard. "Is for you. It gives you back entrance to my room. During the fight, you'll both be sitting with Talon and Wolf."

I clear my throat. "You want me to come and see you before?"

His face softens, which turn my insides into molten lava. "Yeah, Rosé, yeah I do."

I have approximately three weeks to pull myself together whenever he's around—or I'm screwed.

Later that night after my shower, I'm lying in bed with the cover pulled right up to my mouth, smiling from ear to ear.

"Good night?" Leila asks from her bed. I can't see her because the room is pitch black, but I can hear her grin.

"Amazing, Lei."

"Just…" she sighs. "Be careful."

AMETHYST

"SHIT, SHIT, SHIT, SHIT, DOUBLE FUCKING SHIT." I RUN through the empty corridors, coffee in one hand, and my books in my other. Yes, okay, so I'm late because I got coffee, but in my defense, if I don't have it, I wouldn't be able to learn anything, because I'd be too busy killing everyone in plain sight. That's right. I am a profound java addict, and although I have recently cut down my intake to four shots per cup, I still need it like I need air. I shove through the doors to my English class and the room silences.

"Hello, Amethyst, how lovely for you to grace us with your presence."

"I know, I know, I'm so sorry, Mr. R. I promise, it wasn't intentional," I say, slowly stepping backward up the steps to one of the back tables.

"Let me guess." He quirks an eyebrow just as I plop down onto a chair. "Your coffee truck was late." Oh yes, and it was also no secret how much I loved Satan's juice.

I give him my best and cheesiest smile.

He pushes his glasses back up his nose, dismissing me. "As I was saying, the counterparts of a…"

I pull out my books quickly, skipping to a blank page to take my notes. I'm old school. I could never type fast enough for my notetaking, and I'm a scribbler by nature. I'd jot down incoherent notes from class that only I could understand, and I liked it that way. Can't do that on my Mac, no matter how fancy and pretty it is.

"Psst."

A voice catches my attention beside me and after clicking my pen, I look at him sideways. "Hi?"

"You know, that stuff is bad for you, right?" He uses his pen to point at my coffee cup.

I snatch it and cuddle it close to my chest. "My precious." I'm joking. Anyone who couldn't point out a LOTR (that's Lord of the Rings), reference, couldn't sit with us. By us, I mean me because I don't have a gang. Well, I have Leila, even though I did have to make her sit and watch the entire series with me. She now gets the references, so that's why we're best friends.

He chuckles, sitting back in his chair. "Smeagles, huh? Must be some good coffee." He winks at me and then focuses his attention back on the professor. Since he's no longer looking at me, I finally let my eyes take in Mr. Coffee Hater. Clean shaven, almost military cut hair, a collared shirt and tidy jeans on. No sign of tattoos, and no air of danger. He seems, normal. His features are nice with his long eyelashes fanning out over high cheekbones. He is more my type. Safe. And—shit.

"Getting a good look?" He cocks an eyebrow without looking at me.

"Sorry." I'm terrible at being a girl. This shit sucks.

"Don't be," he answers so low I almost miss it.

"Don't be…what?" I ask, jotting down some notes, but ending up drawing swirls.

"Sorry."

"Oh," I lick my lips. "I'm Amethyst." I guess a little chit-chat can't hurt.

"I know." He gapes right at me, his eyes connecting with mine. Two of the softest blue eyes look back at me with dark eyelashes only intensifying the color. "Mason."

Lunch comes around fast. I take in the food options as I wait in line in the cafeteria. Option one, we have carbs, fats, and more carbs; option two, more carbs, fats, and some added sugar. I'm not a gym nut or a nutritionist per se, but I do maintain a healthy diet (for the most part). Donuts don't count.

I hear a loud whistle. My head turns toward the table Leila and I both always sit at, only she's not there. I go back to the lunch menu, snagging some sushi rolls and an apple.

Another whistle echoes out.

"Rosé!"

Maddox is grinning from across the room. He waves me over, but I hesitate, then I see Leila and nod. She's looking cozy beside Wolf. Traitor. Maddox is wearing destroyed light blue ripped jeans, and a semi razed AC/DC shirt displaying all his muscles. He has a flat cap flipped on backward too.

I make my way to their table, ignoring how the entire cafeteria has taken a front row seat to watch Maddox and me.

Fighting the urge to roll my eyes, I slide my tray onto the table. "I see you have quite the audience."

Maddox winks. "Oh, you've just noticed that?"

"Mmm." I bite into my apple while taking a seat. "It's the year of the thirst, apparently." He leans back in his chair, a smug smile on his face. "Don't look at me like that, Maddox."

"Like what?" A toothpick flicked around inside his mouth.

"Like you know what."

"So anyway!" Leila interrupts, glaring at us both while taking a piece of lettuce and putting it into her mouth like a bird. The way she eats is a little uncomfortable. It's borderline painful. She has the unhealthiest obsession with food. Eat it or don't, don't half-ass food. It deserves our full ass.

Maddox is still smirking at me.

I kick him under the table, my foot hitting his shin. "Ouch!"

"Oops. Sorry." I bite into my sushi.

His eyes narrow. "You don't look sorry." They drop to my mouth and then come back to my eyes.

"Because I'm not." I suck the soy sauce off my finger.

"Hey! Mad, got a minute?" a girl says from beside us. I'm too busy eating my sushi to look up at her. As I said, food deserves your full ass.

His focus stays on me, dropping to my mouth briefly.

"Maddox?" the voice repeats nervously.

He continues to pin me with his stare. It's like a competition of who is going to break contact first. It won't be me.

"Sup?" Maddox finally glimpses up at her, dragging his attention away from me.

I exhale slowly and quietly so no one can hear it, then nudge my head at Aquaman. "Now why are you looking at me like that?"

Talon continues to smile, but I appreciate it. It takes my attention away from whatever Maddox is saying to whoever is beside us.

"You coming to the party this weekend?" Talon asks, biting into his sub.

"I was thinking about it."

Talon's lip kicks up. "Got any other hot friends?"

"Hey!" a girl's voice pipes in. "Settle down, tiger." She softly places her tray down, her eyes going around the table, then they settle on me. "Hi, I'm Liza, also known as Talon's girlfriend."

Talon has a girlfriend? Could have fooled me.

I shoot Talon a confused look, okay, I could be glaring.

He winks, pulling her onto his lap, where she sits comfortably. I wonder if she knows that her man has cheated on her. I'm almost certain he has. She rolls her eyes. Was I that transparent? I'm not happy. I'd worked hard to not be so obvious.

"We have an open relationship."

Leila chokes on her food.

I don't falter, mainly because I don't really care. It isn't unheard of, and she seems relaxed about it. She gives me hippie vibes with her long maxi dress, moon shaped earrings, and long blonde braid. She's classically pretty and very petite. Talon would break her for sure.

The next question comes out of my mouth as fast as it comes into my head. "Do you guys swing too?"

The girl who is talking with Maddox is now sitting on his lap.

Maddox coughs. "What?"

I ignore the girl, glaring straight at him. "I asked if they were swingers since they had an open relationship."

"Who the fuck would even ask that. Gross," blondie mutters, flipping her fake long hair over her shoulder.

"That's just cruel," I mutter to myself, biting into my roll of sushi.

"What is?" she snaps, one perfect eyebrow arched. Bet she pencils that shit in.

I shrug. "The fact that you stole some poor horse's tail and are now using it as hair."

Her jaw drops open.

Maddox chokes on a laugh.

Leila snorts, along with Liza and Talon.

"Who the fuck—"

"—Hey! Watch your fucking tone," Maddox snaps at her, moving his knee so she falls to the ground.

My head hurts from all the drama in a very short span of time. I want to go back to my bubble, to not existing. I like Leila because we have a natural bond, but as far as my people skills went, that is about as far as I am willing to go. I don't want to be the asshole, but I'm well aware that it almost always comes off as that.

I stand, picking up my small backpack and throwing it over my shoulder. "It's fine. I'm not feeling well, anyway."

"Mad!" Blondie brushes her hair out of her face, standing from the floor.

Maddox doesn't give her any attention because he's still watching me.

"I'll see you guys around."

Maddox is about to open his mouth, but I cut him off by turning on my heel and heading straight for the doors. I shove through them, continuing to hold my breath. I was supposed to go to the halls, but instead, I found myself going straight to the student parking lot. Pulling my keys out of my pocket, I push the button to unlock my car and throw my backpack into the passenger seat. I exhale softly, my fingers gripping around the steering wheel and rest my head against my hands, closing my eyes.

"Too many people."

Starting my car, I reverse out of the parking spot. I can't be here right now. I drive all the way to the other side of town and park my car in my usual spot. My heart relaxes, my airways expand at the mere sight of the halfpipes.

I push play on my playlist, shoving my earphones into my ears. Red Jumpsuit Apparatus "Guardian Angel" starts playing as I drop my deck onto the concrete, leaping onto it and kicking off the ground. What the fuck is it with Maddox, and why do I let him get to me so damn much. Yes, there's that connection from when we were little, but it's gotta be more than that. Surely. The song switches to "Lonely Day" by System of a Down—perfect. The deep strumming of the song relaxes me as I fix my focus on the stairs that take you down to more ramps. I do a three-sixty hardflip down, landing smoothly, then push myself toward the launch ramp. Driving up one of the launch ramps, I do an ollie onto the second one. A few seconds later, I head toward the halfpipe, but before I hit it, I squat all my weight down slightly, and kick up, landing the Dragon Flip perfectly.

Boom! I fucking love the Dragon Flip.

I keep going to the halfpipe, tail stall at the rim, then flip it one-eighty and head back down. My muscles clench and sweat drips down my skin as I lead myself to the full pipe. I kick off my board and make my way up the steps. Resting the tip of my deck on the rim, I position myself onto it slightly before leaning forward. My heart races as I head up the ramp, I crooked stall on it briefly before flying back down the ramp onto the other side. I drive up the ramp smoothly, and then put all my weight on the board before kicking up, landing on one hand upside down, grabbing my deck with my other hand. My heart pounds as I hold the move for a couple seconds, Two Feet "Go Fuck Yourself" pounding through my eardrums, then I let go, diving straight back down in a perfect landing, and up the other side of the ramp again. I stay until the night sets in and my clothes are drenched in sweat. Usually I have clarity after a major session like this one, but my thoughts are still a mess when it comes to Maddox.

I'm standing under the shower when I replay all of what has happened over the past few days. Maybe I can get some answers under the pelting hot water. One thing I know for sure is that my small circle has somehow expanded to a medium size square. I'm not sure how I like it. I'm not good with change.

I turn the shower off and wrap the towel around my body, wiping the condensation off the mirror. I have always thought that I'm plain looking, no real cute attributes to this face. I like it that way. There are no cute dimples in my cheeks. People have always complimented me on my eyes, but I don't see what's great about them. They're blue. I have blonde hair— until I dyed it pink. I like my pink hair. It's like a big fuck you to the universe for only giving us three options of hair color. My cheeks are baby soft and my eyes are almond shaped. I'm not sexy looking, I'm just. Me. Amethyst. Rebel.

I squirt moisturizer onto the palm of my hand and rub it into my face. Quickly throwing on some grey sweat shorts and a grey crop top, I towel dry my hair and toss it into the basket, pulling open the door into our room. The fresh air slashes my face, setting goosebumps erupting over my skin.

"Hey!" Leila sits up in her bed. "Are you ok?"

"Fine," I grumble, pulling over my cover.

"Was it Maddox and Tasha?"

"Ta—ta—what now?" I know who she is implying, but I don't really want to get into it with her right now.

"Ame." Leila sighs.

"No, it's not. I just needed to get out for a bit." My head hits the pillow, blanket slowly falling over my bare legs.

"Ok." Leila yawns, turning off her bedside light. "Ame?"

Here she goes. "What?"

"You shouldn't sleep with your hair damp."

"Mom, you need to put all your older books to one side and then so on. This is getting ridiculous."

"Honey, your OCD has been working on overtime lately. Are you sure you're ok?" she asks, handing me a Styrofoam cup of coffee. I place the old but not original edition of The Great Gatsby onto the small table she had in front of the worn old couch. I blow onto my coffee. "My OCD is just fine."

She gives me the look she always gives me when she knows I'm lying. "And how is school?"

"School is great, Mom." I take a small sip, burning my upper lip. "Any other questions?"

She shakes her head slowly. "I guess not."

I stay for the rest of the day and help her out. Mom's bookstore is urban and safe. I miss this place. It's almost as comforting as a halfpipe. The burgundy drapes that hang over the front window and the leather chairs that have aged wrinkles indented into the arms. It's all home to me.

I check the time on my watch. "It's almost six. We've been at this all day." I lean on the counter as Mom takes the money out of the till and bags it.

"We've had a good day. I've missed this," she says, rubbing my arm. "You know You're welcome at the house any time. It's your home now too."

I push off the counter and reach underneath the till to get my handbag. "Thanks, Mom, but I don't think so."

"Honey, I know that you aren't exactly happy with—"

I cut her off. "No, that's not it, Mom. I mean, you and Elliot have history, and I get that. It's just… I don't know. I'll need a minute."

Her eyes soften around the edges. "Okay, sweetie. I can give you a minute."

"Do you want to grab a bite before you head home?" I ask, taking my keys out of my handbag.

She beams. "Yes. I'm starved."

CHAPTER 10

AMETHYST

"I think I don't get it," I say, twisting my hair up into a knot on the top of my head.

"Get what?" Leila asks from the bathroom. She's getting ready to go out, and I'm staying in to finish this paper. Story of my life—usually.

I take the pen out of my mouth. "How you and Wolf are so easy with your arrangement. And did you see Talon and his girl? An open relationship? That's crazy. Y'all are all crazy. I swear, if I ever get into a relationship, I'll be carrying knives."

"What's crazy is that you're wearing sweatpants material as a crop top. That is… that should never be allowed."

"You can leave now!" I flutter my fingers toward the door. "You look great, Lei. Have fun." She does. She wears a little white dress and over-the-knee boots. Not something I'd wear—ever, but she always looks fantastic.

As soon as the door closes, I move my attention back to my paper. Writing has always come easy for me. It is the only thing—other than skating—that I am truly good at. I'm about to begin writing The Fundamentals on Action Verbs when there's a knock on the door.

Rolling my eyes, I head toward it. "Don't tell me, you forgo—" I pause when I see it's not Leila standing there, it's Maddox. "Hi?"

His eyes drop down my body, taking me in. "Nice clothes."

"Thanks." I cross my arms. "What's up?"

"You going to let me in?" he asks, his lip kicking up into a grin. We haven't seen or spoken to each other since that day in the cafeteria.

"Why?" I retort suspiciously.

"Do I need a reason? Damn. If I knew that you were going to need a reason, I would have made up some bullshit on the way here."

I go to close the door on him. "Goodnight, Maddox."

"Wait!" His hand interferes with my epic closure. "Because you owe me."

I widen the door, my eyebrows shooting to the high heavens. "Oh? Really? How so?"

"March twenty-seventh. You and me sat in your car, eating purple Hubba Bubba, and you said to me that you owe me."

"I don't recall."

I do. I remember that day exactly as it was.

His grin deepens. "You do so. I gave you your first ever Hubba Bubba and you said that you owe me for that."

"Please stop saying Hubba Bubba."

"I will if you let me in."

"Fine!" I open the door and wave my hand inside. "I would say excuse the mess, but I don't really care what you think."

He chuckles, walking farther into our room. I close the door and discreetly check him out while his back is turned to me. Jeans that had been washed a few too many times, white Adidas original sneakers, black shirt and a black jacket. Nice. I do dig his style, I'll give him that, but again, he's not my type. I dig his style because I would wear that.

"You're studying on a Friday night?" he asks, tilting his head to read the papers on my bed.

"Well, I did say that I don't really have a life."

He sinks down onto the edge of my bed and kicks his shoes off.

"What do you think you're doing?" I wave my finger down to his shoes.

"What?" He grins, so wide it almost (almost) makes me smile.

"Don't you have things to do?" I walk to my bed. He leans back on his elbow and shakes his head. "No?"

"I actually have to study," I answer, pulling my hair out of its loose knot to tie it back up again.

"Then study."

"Don't you have a girlfriend or something to annoy?"

"Nope. Study, and then, I've been given strict orders that you're to come out tonight."

"Ohhhh, I see, so it all makes sense now." I shake my head. Fucking Leila. She couldn't drag me out herself, so she got Maddox to do her dirty work. "She got you to do her dirty work? Man, that's rough." I laugh, picking up my pen and trying to read over my last paragraph. The essence of writing, I believe, comes fr—my cheeks heat. I look up from my paper, catching him staring. "Maddox! You're distracting."

His eyes go from mine to my lips and then back again. "Not sorry."

"You're a pain in my ass."

He grins and then pulls out his phone. There's no way I'm going to be able to get any writing done, so I toss my pen down onto my bed and get up. "Fine. You both win. I'll get ready."

I can hear him chuckling from behind me.

Twenty minutes later, I'm ready, and this was the best that they were going to get. Black shorts, white tank, and my Doc Martens on my feet. I straightened my hair and put on a bit of makeup to hide the new bags that have appeared, but other than that, I am ready.

"Don't look at me like that. I don't do pretty, slutty dresses. So sorry you have to be seen with me like this." I gesture down at my clothes.

Maddox stands and slowly prowls toward me. "I never said anything and honestly, Amethyst, you're fucking perfect." My stomach flips and my cheeks heat. Friendzone. Friendzone. F-R-I-E-N-D-Z-O-N-E.

He licks his bottom lip. "Come on, let's go."

We stop outside of a bar in Morningside Heights, but all the way over here I've been thinking about how it must've been for him to not only lose his mom but to be there when she died. It's something that I feel may always sit uneasily with me. I turn in my seat to face him. "Maddox, I know I sound like a broken record, but this whole thing? It just, I don't know. I still feel like I need to apologize for it."

Maddox' eyes search mine. "For what?"

"Your mom…" I inwardly wince at my choice of words. I wasn't joking when I said that I sucked at small talk and anything that could show any emotion. I feel awkward when faced with the issues, and then I get paranoid that they think I'm not being sincere because I try hard to look like I'm truly sorry, and I am, always. I can't imagine losing someone so close to you, but I struggle with expressing human emotions.

"It's not your fault, you don't need to be sorry." He gets out of his seat and shuts the door. I slide out and follow him as he makes his way to the bar entrance. Bright blue neon lights flash against the aged brick. It's more of a relaxed bar than a night-club, so there's no massive line or over-the-top bouncers, but there is one security guard standing near the door. Bald head, tight black top that has his muscles bulging out.

He tips his head at Maddox when he sees him. "Sup, man. Watch the fight this weekend?"

Maddox chuckles. "Yeah. Good fight, had my money on Grahams, though." Maddox pauses, his hand reaching for mine. I'm straightening my bra a little (because it feels as though my tit is about to flop out) when my other hand connects with his reflexively. Shit. Heat shoots up from the palms of my hand and up to my chest. Should I let go? Or would that be too obvious? Double shit. We walk into the bar, my hand still in his. He squeezes tightly while leading us to the back booth where Wolf, Talon, Liza, and Leila are sitting at a table, drinks already empty.

"Oh here are the lovers!" Leila announces, twinkling with joy.

"Fuck you," I mouth, sliding in behind Maddox.

As soon as his hand is gone, I miss it like a fool.

Friendzone.

Maddox rests his arm behind me, just as Leila gestures to the bar. "Let's get drinks."

I slide out again and head toward the bar. She hooks her arm in mine. "What's going on with you and Maddox? Spill."

"What?" I feign innocence. "Nothing."

"Yes… you guys have a thing. I don't know, it's weird." She shakes her head, pulling out a bar stool. "It's as though you've both known each other for years."

I snicker quietly. "You could say that."

"See!" She spins around to glare at me. "Spill!"

I shake my head. "Not right now." I let her order the drinks and pay for them. I don't have the energy to tell her that I wasn't in the mood to get drunk, so I figure one wouldn't hurt.

One turns into one too many real quick when you go out with Leila.

"Lei," I say, my hands resting on my forehead. "Honestly, I need to study. I have a pap—"

"Amethyst! Chill, girl. We're having a good night. Just relax." Talon pulls me under his arm. We didn't stay long at the bar before we all piled into a taxi and made our way to one of the many nightclubs in the city. Seriously, I really didn't want to go out tonight. Especially because the brothers were throwing a party tomorrow night. I will definitely not be attending. At all.

"Are you going to tell me what's going on between you and Maddox?" Leila asks again, inching forward while twirling her straw around in her mouth. I regret our friendship by this point.

I shake my head, leaning in towards her ear. "We knew each other when we were little. It's hard to explain, I'll tell you tomorrow."

She gapes at me, then tugs me back into her. "Are you serious?"

I look back at her and nod. "Yes."

She pulls me back, her hands clenching around my arms. "You guys are supposed to be together, Ame. I see it, we all see how you both are. Why are you fighting it?"

I cross my arms in front of myself, confused. "I don't know, Lei!" I throw my hands up for added effect. God, I hate when I'm drunk. Alcohol sucks. I'm never drinking again. Leaning back in my chair, Maddox slides in beside me, his arm going around my back.

I glare at him. "I hate drinking. This is your fault."

Sweat glistens off his top lip, his smooth tanned skin gleaming from the strobe lights. The Weeknd "Six Feet Under" booms through the speakers. His focus falls to my mouth and then come back to my eyes. "You're right, it is my fault. What you gonna do about it?"

I swallow.

He throws his head back and laughs, then his lips brush against the crook of my neck as he growls, "Mmm, that's what I thought." I feel like I'm going to physically combust, as his tongue comes out and slips across my flesh. The room shrinks, my legs shake, and my heart feels like it's going to pound out of my chest. I close my eyes and count to ten in a pathetic attempt to pull my shit together. God, I'm so disappointed in myself when it comes to Maddox. Why are you fighting it? I need to get Leila's voice out of my head, there's no room for her up there.

I shove him away playfully. "Stop it." He doesn't budge, his face staying against my throat. I can physically feel my breathing thicken. He kisses me below my ear.

Jesus take the wheel.

"Mmm?" His soft growl vibrates against my neck, and I shit you not, goes straight between my legs. Does not pass go.

His hand comes to my thigh. "Answer this one question honestly…"

I clear my throat, sipping on my drink. "Okay."

He leans back slightly just enough so he can study my features, but close enough that his lips almost touch mine. "You want this as much as I do?"

I search his face impassively and contemplate lying just to burst his ego, but my mouth didn't get the memo. "Yes."

"Why you fighting me, then?"

"I'm not," I pick up my glass again.

"You are."

"You haven't exactly thrown the first punch," I reply smoothly.

"First punch?" he taunts. "Amethyst, I fucked you until you couldn't fucking see straight, and you wanna say that I haven't exactly thrown the first punch? I'm undefeated, baby. Try me…"

My head snaps to him, only to find his cocky smirk on his smug face. "You're such an asshole."

He shrugs. "Never claimed I wasn't."

CHAPTER 11

AMETHYST

On Monday, I'm stumbling into class when my phone vibrates in my pocket. I pull it out discreetly, looking down at the screen while sliding into my seat.

Maddox: You didn't come on Saturday, why?

I typed a quick text back. I didn't go because I was hungover, yes, but after Friday night, I needed to recover. I'm not cut out for their lifestyle, and I have way too much to lose if I don't put my head down. After Maddox and I had our little push and pull in the city, I bitched out and snuck away from them. It wasn't until I was safely secured in the taxi and on my way back to campus that I sent him and Leila a text saying I had bailed and that I'd be busy all weekend with studying. I turned my phone off after that and I hadn't turned it back on until this morning. Not intentionally, purely because I'd been so lost in my assignments. There were a couple messages from Leila and only one from Maddox saying "Sweet." I wasn't sure whether he was mad at me or disappointed with me. Either way, I didn't really like it.

Me: Hungover. Sorry.

I push my phone back into my backpack, but not before it vibrates again in my palm. "Fuck," I cuss, quickly looking at the screen.

Leila: We need to talk…

Oh no. Here goes my old pal anxiety. I haven't seen Leila since Friday night, either, I'm guessing that after the club she went home with Wolf. Her staying away for one night isn't surprising, but two nights sort of is. I don't know what it could be that she would want to talk to me about, but whatever it is would need to wait.

Class went slower than I hoped it would, but that could have something to do with the fact that I am constantly glaring at my phone. Throwing my bag over my shoulder as soon as the bell rang, I slide it unlocked and open the text from Maddox.

Maddox: We need to talk.

My heart starts to pound in my chest. What the hell could they both need to talk with me about?

Me: I'll be there soon.

It is lunch, so I know that they would already be in the cafeteria. I want to know what they want to talk with me about, but—

"Hey!" Mason calls out, falling into step beside me.

I smile at him. "I've seen you twice in less than a week now. Are you stalking me?"

"What? Me?" He gestures to himself. "No, I'm totally gay."

I stop walking, my eyes bugging out. "Are you serious?"

His lips slowly crank into a smile. "I'm not, sorry…"

"Don't be sorry, I would be the one who would have to apologize. How shallow of me to think you were stalking me."

"I wouldn't say shallow." He opens the cafeteria door and gestures for me to walk in ahead of him. "I would say, intuitive."

"Intuitive?" I grin, looking at him like he has lost his mind. "Intuitive would mean my assumption had some sort of intelligent ground to build from. I was being shallow." I grab a couple of trays and hand him one.

"You aren't being shallow, Amethyst. You're being human, and anyway, when I first saw you, I thought you looked interesting. Shallow people don't look interesting, they look bland."

"You thought that of me?" I reach for a chicken sandwich and an orange. It surprises me that he thinks that of me. I've never been called interesting before.

"Sure." I could see him watching me out of the corner of my eye, so I allow myself to look at him. His soft blue eyes watching mine with deep sincerity. "When I first saw you, I thought you looked interesting but shadowed. Like Banksy's finest art sitting beside some cheap mundane knock-offs of the Mona Lisa."

I smile sadly, licking my lips. "That is really sweet of you."

He shrugs as if it's nothing and goes back to piling his plate with food. "It's the truth. In a world where everyone is wanting to be hot. Sexy. Seductive. The Mona Lisa's, if you will—even though they're obviously cheap and non-authentic—you're an art of Banksy, pulling the middle finger splashed over a brick wall while carrying a pot of dead flowers. You're everything

that the world tells you not to be—and that's why you're inter-
estingly beautiful."

I'm speechless. "Mason…"

"Mmm?" He bites down on a piece of carrot.

"That was probably the sweetest thing anyone has ever
said to me, and I don't even like sweet words… but
that was…"

"Interesting?" He quirks one perfect eyebrow.

I burst out laughing, turning to face the loud cafeteria.
"Yes, interesting. Where are you sitting?"

He nods over to the college football table. "With the boys."

My eyelashes flutter. "Of course you play football."

"Hey! What's that supposed to mean?" All his buddies are
watching us carefully. Most of them with smug expressions on
their face.

"Interesting…" I add, and then walk off toward my table,
leaving him behind.

"Hey!" he calls out. I smirk while slowly turning to face
him, walking backward. "I need that number!"

I pretend to ponder over his request. "Maybe. Only
because I like the word interesting."

His head jerks and a wide smile spreads over his mouth,
showing his straight teeth. I shake my head, turning back to
slide into my seat.

"Hi," I shrug off my bag and sit down. Noticing no one
greets me, I look up at all of them, throwing a celery stick into
my mouth. Talon is watching me carefully, along with Wolf.
Leila seems uncomfortable, blatantly glaring at me, and then I
finally sneak a peek at Maddox who's opposite.

His eyes are flat. Expressionless, blank and dead.

"What?" I snap at them all. "I had both of you" —I
gesture to Leila and Maddox— "Text me to tell me we needed
to talk—so talk."

Maddox' eyes cut straight to Leila.

Leila throws her hands up. "Hey! I wanted to talk with her about girl shit—not your shit!"

Maddox tilts his head at me. "Why'd you skip the party?"

I chew on my celery stick. "I told you, I was tired and I needed to study."

"And did you?" He inspects me closely.

"Did I what?" I ask, peeling my orange. I love oranges, but I hate peeling them because my fingers smell like citrus for hours, and they give me an acidy stomachache every time I eat them, but they're my favorite fruit so I tolerate it.

"Study."

My eyes go back to him. "Yes. Why are you snappy today? How was the party?" I ask around the table, sucking the juice off my thumb.

Maddox's foot hits my shin under the table and I scowl at him. "Ouch!"

"Don't do that."

"Do what?" I snap. I've almost had enough of his moody bullshit. Mason's table is looking rather appealing right now.

His eyes slant on my mouth.

"Oh, that," I murmur.

"It was...eventful," Talon grunts, taking a bite out of his burger.

"Amethyst won't want to hear about it. She hates drama," Leila chimes in, chopping up a tomato into small pieces.

"I don't hate it. I just don't care about it."

Leila rolls her eyes. "Everyone secretly loves watching it when it's not happening to them."

"That's so disturbing to me, Lei, like you have no idea." Leila starts yapping on about some random fight that happened between two girls at the party, but I tune her out and look back to Maddox. "You ok?"

His jaw clenches, and then he abruptly stands. "Yeah. See you guys later."

He leaves, and I glimpse at Talon. "Did I do something again?"

Talon watches Maddox closely, and then stares back at me. "Sweetheart, you've done nothing at all. Wanna take a walk?"

I unscrew my water bottle and then look to Leila, who gives me a reassuring smile. "Ok."

After following Talon down the empty corridor and out the front doors of campus, I fall into step beside him. "So, are you feeling like the extra cardio today, or do you really want to talk?" I start braiding my hair to fall down one shoulder. I'm wearing a small white crop top that shows my belly and ripped jeans with white Nike Air Force 1s.

He chuckles, pulling me under his arm. "You're the little sister we all wanted, that's for sure."

I relax against his warm chest. "I think you speak for yourself, not for Wolf, who hates me, or Maddox, who also hates me but also—"

"—Maddox doesn't hate you, Amethyst." Talon leads me under a flowering dogwood tree that expands under the bright sun, shading us. I plop beside him on the grass, crossing my legs.

"Care to elaborate?"

Talon sighs. "Maddox had a girlfriend once."

"Lovely," I answer. "I assumed he may have." I am being a smart ass, but it is worth it to see Talon smile.

"—Not Stacey," he quickly interrupts my thoughts. "Stace was nothing but a charity bang. This was in high school."

"Wait, why are you telling me this?" I'm going to ignore the charity bang thing.

"I'm getting there!" He shoots me a playful glare.

I relax.

"She disappeared on him after dating for over a year. He searched for her, and then eventually fell off the rails. As in drugs, money, and bitches."

"Talon, don't refer to us as 'bitches.'"

He snorts. "The ones he was messing with? Were. Anyway, he hasn't had another since Cassidy. I guess that's why he's probably acting up right now. Maddox likes control, and he exercises it in almost everything. Cass fucked him up when she left." Talon admires at me over his shoulder. "But he didn't even look at Cassidy the way he looks at you, Ame. Think that scares the shit out of him."

I ponder his words, yanking the grass out of the ground. "Well, it's mutual, so I don't know why he stormed off instead of talking to me about it."

Talon grins. "He's only just realized it. I saw it the first night I met you. Now." He stands, yanking me up with him. "Whatcha doing this weekend?"

"I'm going to see my dad, you?" We start walking back toward the cafeteria.

"Liza has a birthday thing she's throwing for one of her friends."

"About you two…"

Talon laughs, shaking his head. "Oh no, I'm not getting into that."

"That's not fair!" I call out as he jogs back into the school.

My toothbrush is sticking out of my mouth as I'm tugging out clothes from my closet when there's a knock on the door. "Coming!" I mumble around my toothbrush, dodging stray clothes that are strewn around the floor. I dive for the handle, pulling it open.

Maddox chuckles when he sees me. I let him in, jogging for the bathroom. Spit, rinse, and repeat.

"Hey!" I come back into the room.

"Hurricane?" Maddox asks, gesturing around the clothes that are on the floor.

I chuckle. "Nope. I'm going to my dad's for the weekend, and I left everything to the last minute to get ready."

Maddox watches me before slowly lowering himself onto my bed. "What are your plans for this long weekend?"

It's Independence Day on Monday. Thank God, because even though I have managed to get a lot of studying in, it's still not where I should be with Leila and her partying ways rubbing off on me.

Maddox shakes his head, watching me carefully. "Did you forget my fight in a couple of weeks…"

"Um, no?" I lie, blindly tossing a few more items into my backpack. It may have slipped my mind. "Where is it going to be anyway? Here?"

When he doesn't answer me, I turn to face him and then instantly regret it when I see the look he's giving me. He's intense, guarded and a little hard to handle. I'm still trying to figure out whatever we have going on. There's no denying we have a connection of some sort, but I'm not naive enough to think I'm special just because his brother has said that I am, and his actions are a litt—okay. Maybe I can explore the idea that maybe I am… but he's Maddox Stone, renowned playboy. I just, I have trust issues, I guess. I usually like to walk into the den when I know what kind of animal is lying on the other side. Not wait until it's too late and I'm locked in the cage with a hungry Lion instead of a harmless bunny.

I'm trying hard to stay focused, but when he's staring at me like he is now; it disarms all my senses. Even just for a few seconds. How long does it take for a lion to take its prey?

"Amethyst," he demands my attention, his alluring gaze still on me.

"Huh?" I tilt my head. Shit, was he still talking?

He smirks. "I said my fight is in Vegas at the Cox Pavilion. It's great exposure for me and my team. Hopefully snag a few sponsors while I'm there."

"Should I be excited or scared? Or both? And will Dana White be there?"

Maddox grabs my hand and tugs me into his chest. He takes a seat, pulling me down onto his lap. "I'm a little turned on that you know who Dana White is, but you don't need to be scared. I've been throwing right hooks since I was a kid. It's what I do. If I get enough attention there, then hopefully I'll be selected for my weight division in the MGM Grand fight. Big fucking deal, babe."

My legs hang sideways over his, his arm snaking around my back as he pulls me in closer. Shit. His lips press under my ear.

"Why would you be scared?" His voice is low and deadly, his warm breath dancing across my flesh.

My eyes close. "Why are you doing this?" I whisper. I'm about two seconds away from losing my mind and I'm not sure if I'd want it back. His hand glides up my thigh, his grin pressing against the surface of my neck. He sets off flames in places I thought I had extinguished.

"Come with me."

I turn to face him, the tip of his nose slightly brushing against mine. He's so close my eyes damn near cross. "Why?"

His hand comes up to the back of my neck and he pulls my face to his. "Because I want you. I want all of you. I want to fuck you until you can't walk or talk, or fucking see straight. I want to ruin you, break you, and make you bleed so I can make it up to you again. I want to fuck you so hard that I leave an imprint of my cock inside of you, so everyone after me knows that you're mine."

My thighs clench and wetness pools down there. Distraction. "I can't be owned, Maddox," I say, swallowing down all, and every feeling that is rushing through me. I want him. Goddamnit. Want him. I want him to do all of those things to me and more.

His lips skim over mine, then he kisses me. I open my

mouth slightly as his tongue gently dips inside mine. He pulls away, his breathing labored. "You're right, Amethyst, you can't be owned. Because a young boy already claimed you when you were seven years old."

I lick my bottom lip. "You're not my type."

"Ditto, baby." Then he flips me onto my back, stretching my legs wide with his and sinking into my crotch. Oh Lord. He grinds his hips into mine, a smirk on his mouth. I can feel the thick trunk of his cock grind against me and I need to fight all that is inside of me not to rub myself against him until I come. "How about this…"

"Are you about to proposition me?" I quirk an eyebrow.

He chuckles. "I am. Why? Wanna fight me?"

"I'd fight you," I say, challenging his stare.

His glare intensifies, his grin deepening. "Oh, you would?" he mocks being shocked. "I'm terrified."

"You should be." I nod my head.

"Fucking shaking in my boots," he adds, circling his hips into me.

My eyes narrow, and I bite down on my bottom lip to stifle a moan. "What's this proposition and can we do this with you not being on top of me? It's distracting."

He bites his bottom lip. Straight up, bit his lip. As in white, perfect teeth sinking into soft plump lips. I grab the back of his neck and yank his face down to mine, kissing him roughly. He stills for a beat, and then relaxes into me before dropping down, his elbows now caging my head in. Sucking on his bottom lip, I trail my tongue over him then go back to pretty much sucking his face off.

He chuckles. "You done?" he asks, leaning back slightly.

I nod. "Yep." There is no shame in my takeover game —clearly.

I can feel his arousal pressing against me again. I close my eyes. "You're going to have to get up for this to work."

"Agreed." He jackknifes off me, stands and readjusts himself. I sit up from my bed, letting my hair fall all over the place.

"Neither of us do relationships, so what about we do this… and other shit, without any labels."

I tilt my head. "You want a free pass to do what you want with other girls?"

"Amethyst," he says dryly, his eyebrows raised. "I don't fucking want anyone else and I can't see the future me wanting anyone else, but like you, I hate labels. Not because of the commitment, because I already know that I won't be going elsewhere and you and I both know how much I despise cheating… but because fucking society says that we need to have a label in order for us to work."

He makes sense, and for the first time since being reunited with him, I can see why I had blindly chosen him.

"Fuck society." I smirk.

He pulls me up from my hands and into his chest. My eyes close as I inhale his scent, allowing it to wrap around me like a safety blanket. "You're annoying."

He laughs, kissing me on my head. "You'll come next weekend?"

I nod, stepping out of his grip to continue packing up the rest of my belongings. "Yes! Now I need to get my stuff organized."

His lip curls. "Mmmm, not yet…." He picks me up from behind my legs and throws me back onto the bed. I scream out in laughter as he drops down onto the bed with me.

AMETHYST

"Mom, I'm driving." You would think she would be more maternal, but no, she's on a mission to see what's going on between Maddox and I.

"I know, but you have Bluetooth. Just, please. I know that you're probably still angry at me."

"I'm not angry." It's true. I worked most of my anger out with Maddox about three hours ago. Meaning, I may have used his dick for my personal use—angry sex is great like that. Which also means, I'm still a little over an hour away from Washington. Great. I am excited to be back in DC, though.

"Anger is healthy, Ame. I worry about you and how you keep your emotions inside. That is not healthy."

I roll my eyes.

"So you and he? Are you dating?"

"We're not dating, Mom. We're fucking, now are we done here?"

"Amethyst Lilly Tatum!"

"Mother," I answer. "Listen, I need to go. You're cu—cu—ting—" I hang up on her and turn my phone off. She can be exhausting on the best of days. I soon realize I need music. Fuck.

My dad's home is all cedar stone with heavy windows that have so many miles on them it displays through the wrinkles in the paint. He moved here when I was one, which meant that I had to stay with Mom pretty much full time. I wouldn't have minded as much if my dad lived closer so I could see him more. I love my mom, but I've always been close to my dad.

I climb out of the driver's seat and stretch my arms wide.

"Ame!" Lara, my dad's partner and world-famous defense lawyer opens the door. She's in a white flannel two-piece suit and slippers. "Hey, girl!"

"Hey!" I smile, going straight for her.

She's carefully watching my reaction. Her brown eyes to my blue. She has long ash blonde hair and what I call mouse features. She is good for my dad and has always been nice to me. Her and my dad have been together since I was five, I think, so she's always sort of been there. She pulls me into a hug and I relax.

"Your dad is out back playing with the BBQ. I'm a little scared."

I laugh. "Yes, I don't blame you. Make sure Rocco is away from the grill." She opens the door wider and I step inside, shutting it behind us. Rocco is my dad's German Shephard.

Following her deeper into the house, I pass through the sitting room and kitchen, right to the doors which open out onto the patio out the back.

Dad's flipping patties wearing the apron I bought him for Father's Day a few years back wrapped around his waist that reads "Don't Leave me Alone with the Grill" and a beer in hand. I lean against the door frame, fighting the smirk that's on my mouth. "Hey, Daddy."

Dad turns quickly, a smile radiating across his face. Dad is classically handsome. He has salt and pepper hair, a dusting of crinkles around his eyes and smile lines in his cheeks. He has an infectious smile and laugh that can flip even the angriest of people. He has tons of friends and is always the life of the party. But he's also a little scary when he wants to be—especially when it comes to me.

"Hey sweetheart, how was the trip?"

I shrug, walking forward until his arms wrap around me and I sink into his warmth. "It was rather long considering Mom kept calling me."

"What's your mother hassling you about now and why is she calling you while you're driving?" he asks, going back to the patties.

Dad and Mom have an odd friendship. They joke and call each other names and even pretend to despise each other. But everyone knows that they'd kill and die for one another. When I asked them why they broke up if they loved each other so much, my mom replied, "Sometimes, love isn't enough to keep a relationship or marriage working." I then shot back, "But you do, you both have friendship, too!" She said, "Yes, we have friendship and love, Amethyst, but we don't have the kind of love that sets your soul on fire, and that's the only kind of love that you should ever settle for." I must have been really young. Maybe four or five, because their not being together has never, ever bothered me. I think it helped me in a way. Two happy homes are better than one broken one, and I learned at a young age that you should always keep your soul and intentions real.

"Jonathan…" Lara warns, using my dad's full name. Everyone usually just calls him Jonah. She gives him a warning glare while placing the knives and forks onto the outdoor table.

I chuckle, inhaling the smell of freshly cut grass and fresh lavender from the garden down below. I love this place. It has always been home to me. I know I'm lucky. I have so many homes, but the thing I loved most growing up was two homes, two separate rules. They were always eating out of the palm of my hand when I was a teen—it was great.

Lara hands me a beer, and I take it, popping off the lid. Taking a swig, I shrug. "Well, I met my new stepbrothers."

Dad grunts.

"Dad, you never told me that you knew Elliot?"

Dad grunts again. I figured that's all I was going to get out of him for now.

"Anyway," I add. "It turns out that I may or may not have met his son the night before at a bar."

Dad stills, tilting his head to look at me from over his shoulder. I take a seat on one of the chairs.

Lara laughs, placing the large salad bowl onto the table and wiping her hands on a dishcloth.

"Girl… you did?" Her smile beams briefly, before obviously realizing old daddy dearest is listening, so she collects herself and straightens her shoulders.

God, I love her. No evil stepmom here, nope. Lara is a few years younger than Dad, and when they met, she was still in college, just shy of graduating law school. Most college people, me, for example, would run if a guy had a kid. But she didn't. She has always treated me like a friend. I respected her a lot more for it. I have two parents, everyone has two parents, I didn't need three. She let Mom and Dad parent me while she played the cool role. Sort of like a cool aunt but only better.

"What do you mean, at a bar?" Dad asks, his eyes narrowing on me.

"I mean as in we did something."

My dad and I have always had an open relationship. As in I've never hidden anything from him because I knew he'd never judge me or be disappointed. But he would kill anyone who'd hurt me. My dad is my safety blanket. He's something no one could take from me. Sure, I love my mom, and I'd never compare the two loves because they're completely different, but Mom has always been… Mom. She's light, funny, and can at times, be a little…away at the fairy's. But Dad? He was my constant. I knew no one could take him away from me, so I knew he could handle anything I did in life. I like to test this theory a lot.

"Amethyst." Dad shakes his head, turning the patties again.

I make my way to him, inching up on my tippy toes to kiss his cheek. It felt like rough leather against my lips. My poor pops is getting old that's for sure.

"Anyway." I resume my seating. "I remember Maddox from when we were kids…" I pause, looking back to my dad. I didn't want to rub it in or make him feel bad. Or get my mother in trouble.

His face relaxes. "Amethyst, I know about Elliot and your mother. I've known since we were kids."

"That's not like, weird for you?" I ask, watching as he starts piling the cooked meat onto a tray.

He shakes his head. "No. I stole her from him to begin with, it was only fair that they would be together again."

I massage my temples. "Lord have mercy. This whole family shit is a little messed up."

Dad takes a seat opposite me, taking off his apron and popping his beer. "You're telling me, but baby girl, it's fine. I know everything. Now, tell what happened with you and Maddox. The PG version, please. Too young for a heart attack."

I take a piece of meat and some salad, ignoring how Lara is hanging on the edge of her seat for all the details.

"I don't know. We pushed and pulled for a bit, but I can't deny that there's a bond with him. It's easy, and not complicated. He has a bad reputation on campus, you know, womanizer and because he beats people's faces in for a living, it only adds to his bullshit appeal." I suck in a deep breath. "But he's not any of those people when he's with me, which is what makes all the difference. You know me, Dad. He's not my type at all."

Dad quirks an eyebrow. "I know. But maybe this is what you needed. Those nerd boys you messed around with were little fucks."

"Dad!" I snort, taking another sip of my beer.

Lara sighs, brushing us both off and taking a long, hard sip of her wine. "Well, what's the problem aside from the not-your-type thing?"

I push the meat around with my fork. "Mom doesn't like it. I think she thinks it's like incest."

Dad scoffs, taking a bite out of his bun. "Don't listen to your mother, Ame."

"I guess." I pop some meat into my mouth. I shouldn't listen to her, and she shouldn't really be judging me.

"Tell him not to lose his fight this weekend. I got two-hundred large on him. Marcus is rooting for the opposition."

"Of course he is." I roll my eyes. My uncle Marcus is fiercely overprotective of me, so I can't wait until I see him. He's not really my uncle, he's my dad's friend and has been for as long as I can remember. Where my dad is the life of the party and has lots of friends, my uncle Marcus is broody, moody, and dangerously cold. But, he loves me.

"Wait!" My eyes narrow. "How did you know I was seeing him?"

Dad gives me the look. "I didn't know you were seeing him like that, but I know who they are, Ame."

"Right." I sigh, digging back into my food. Stupid question. Of course, if they didn't run backgrounds on everyone, they'd know who they were just from knowing Elliot in high school.

"I guess you have a lot to think about with the whole Maddox thing, but I'll always support you, darling."

"Thanks, Daddy."

"I will kill him if he hurts you, though."

"Of course."

The rest of the night goes easy like it always does at Dad's. I finished my meal, and then Lara brought out her famous pecan pie. I ate way too much (with added cream), it's near eleven at night and I feel like I need an extra push to get any shut-eye.

I make myself hot cocoa and tiptoe back upstairs and into my bedroom which is exactly the same as it was when I was growing up. Splatters of bright neon pink and blue paint is splashed on the wall, with a bright blue blanket covering my bed. It's like going through a time machine. I tell Dad to change the room every time I come home but he never does. If you ask me, I'd say he's a hoarder. A hoarder for feelings.

I'm slipping under the covers when I hear my phone ding on the bedside table. Picking it up, I flip it unlocked.

Maddox: when will you be home?

Me: Sunday, why?

He doesn't text back, so I open another one.

Me: You know, since I've met your dad, it's only fair for you to meet mine.

But as soon as it sends, I instantly regret it. He probably thinks I'm some stage five clinger. My phone chimes with a text.

Maddox: Yeah? I'll see you tomorrow then.

I grin, stupidly like a little teenager. God. I send him an "Ok" text and the address and put my phone on charge. What am I doing? I feel like I'm doing something wrong. But how can something be so wrong when the wires that the warning signs are held up by are of feelings that feel so right?

MADDOX

"Do you know what you're doing?" Dad asks, pushing his hands into the pockets of his slacks.

"No? But fuck it, I'm going to do it anyway."

Dad sighs, sitting down onto the sofa. He wanted to talk with me about the fight this weekend, only when I walked through the door, Amethyst's name was the first thing that came out of his mouth.

"Maddox. She's not disposable like your other girls. If this ends badly, it would impact not just you, but me and her mother too."

My jaw clenches. "Careful."

I want to fly into a fit of rage and tell him to go fuck himself because I didn't give a shit about their relationship, but I don't. Because as much as I fucking despise everything that he and Jessica built their relationship on, I respected my old man. Ain't that a bitch.

"Maddox—you also need to stay focused on this fight, on your career. You can't have distractions. I thought you agreed you would keep it as friends? What happened?"

"She happened, we happened, that's what," I say, leaning back into the sofa and stretching my legs out wide. "Listen, I don't care much what you or anyone has to say about her. I'm going to go with what feels right, and right now, she feels right. If that changes in the future, I'll let her know nicely, which is more than what I've given anyone else and you know this."

"Do you have feelings for her?" Dad asks, watching me

carefully. I take my attention away from him and look to the gas fireplace. The flames lick around each other in an inferno.

"Not like that, not yet, and I don't know what will happen in the future. But right now" —I look back to him— "this is what's happening."

I head back to my place and pack a bag.

AMETHYST

If I were a nail-biter, I'd be chewing the shit out of my goods right now. I'm pacing up and down the front porch of my dad's house when my eyes lock on the fountain in the middle of the driveway. It has a sculpture that sprays water in the general direction of wherever you are. I hate that sculpture. He needs to change it. I hear Maddox's car before I see it. Anyone could, with its loud V8 awakening hell itself.

I lick my lips, squashing the cliché butterflies that were about to take flight in my gut. I'd chop their wings soon enough—just not right now, because like a sucker, I was addicted to the adrenaline. Like a moth to a flame, only the flame is way too large to just flutter over my fragile wings. It was going to ignite them.

He climbs out of his car. He's wearing a hoodie and jeans with a leather jacket over it. He stretches his arms over his head while walking around his car and slowly coming to me. His shirt lifts, revealing his abs and that glorious V that dips under his jeans.

"Hey," I say shyly. Suddenly, I'm not as badass as I pretend to be.

"Come here, baby." He struts to me and pulls me into his chest. I inhale quietly, sucking in the smoothness of soap and leather to comfort the loneliest parts of my soul.

Stepping backward, I lean up on my tiptoes and kiss him on the lips. "How was your trip?"

"Pretty fast."

I grab his hand and ignore the stupid pangs that shoot straight to my chest. "Come meet Dad."

"I've met your dad, Ame."

"When!" I turn to face him, just as we close the front door.

"When he was a lot smaller than what he is now," my dad answers, coming toward us.

Maddox grins, putting his hand out to my dad.

My dad takes it. I'm trying to decide what he thinks of Maddox. "I take it I don't have to have the talk with you because your old man probably already did it, and also, you haven't met her uncle Marcus—"

"Truth," I mutter.

"—Who is out back now."

I smile guiltily at Maddox. "Sorry. He was persistent and wanted to meet you."

Maddox shrugs, pulling me under his arm and kissing the top of my head. "Chill, baby." He wasn't even a little scared? It's almost insulting.

We follow Dad out to the back patio where Marcus is at the grill, who isn't any better than Dad. His wife, Shanika, is sitting at the table with a glass of wine, laughing with Lara. They both pause when we walk through. Lara's eyes fall on Maddox.

Shanika smiles politely at the both of us.

Lara stands, her hand extended. "Maddox? So nice to meet you."

Maddox smirks, taking her hand in his. "You too."

Dad introduces him to Shanika and then we both look to Uncle Marcus nervously, who hasn't stepped away from the grill. I chew on my bottom lip.

"Unc? Come meet someone!" I call out as casually as I can.

He pauses and then unwraps the apron before turning to face us. Uncle Marcus is old school. He has dark chocolate skin, hazel eyes that remind me of hot cocoa, and a deep soul that he guards with a brick wall. But if you get over that brick wall, his love is infinite. I love him like a second dad.

"You're on your own, kid." Dad pats my shoulder. I give Uncle Marcus my cheesiest smile, hoping my charm can still work on him. Maybe I need the messy top knot and my deck clutched under my arm, because his face remains hard, impassive.

He looks to Maddox. "I'm not a fan right now, and I might never be a fan, but I'd be damned if I ever come in the way of my Cherub being happy, but just know that if you so much as cause a single tear to drop from her eye, you'll have me to deal with, got it?"

"Jesus." I shake my head. We used to blame it on the fact that they could never have kids as to was why he was so over-protective of me, and that probably played a massive part in it, but I also am a strong believer in soul connections. And he and I had a huge one.

Maddox, being the cheeky shit that he is, salutes him and winks. "You got it."

Maddox is a badass, but as I said, Uncle Marcus is old school.

Unc turns to me. "Hey, Cherub." He squeezes my cheeks and I melt into him. He's a pain in my ass, but I love him.

"You do realize I don't have fat cheeks anymore, right?" My voice comes muffled because I'm pressed into his shirt.

"I know." He kisses my head and backs away. His gaze drifts to Maddox briefly who is taking a seat beside Dad, popping open a beer, then they come back to me. "Be careful, ok?"

"Your vibe thing?" I ask through a whisper.

Uncle Marcus is famous for his "vibes." I would say they were bullshit, but he cracked a lot of cases based on those vibes. Enough to find evidence against people. So my odds are not looking very good right now.

He offers a small smile. "No, just saying."

Lie.

Uncle Marcus is a terrible liar.

He goes back to the grill and I take a seat beside Maddox, who is now talking with Dad about the fight.

I zone their conversation out as Shanika and I start talking about her newest little project—a new clothing boutique. Great. Because the world needed more of those.

"Your dad, he's different from your mom," Maddox says, pushing me forward on the swing. The wooden swing that hangs off an old tree branch is still here from when I was a little girl. I don't think my dad has the heart to chop it down. Like I said, emotional hoarder.

I chuckle, looking to the patio that is now lit up with small tea lights hanging around the rails. The sun has set, the night turning the air damp. "He is. I think that's why it always worked with them, you know?"

He stops the swing and comes around to face me, dropping to my level. His eyes search mine. "Probably."

I divert my attention away from him, unable to allow myself to get lost in what feels like an endless ocean.

His finger hooks around my chin as he brings my face back to his. My eyes almost cross from the closeness of his face.

"Amethyst…"

"Maddox," I answer breathlessly.

"Are we doing this?" he asks, tilting his head.

"We can try."

His shoulders relax, his lips brushing over mine softly. "We can try."

We arrive back to campus the next day, me climbing the stairs to my dorm with a stupid grin on my face. Later that night, Dad had Maddox sleep in the guest room on the other side of the house—as I expected—but the next day, before we followed each other back to New York, we stopped at the old abandoned hospital I used to skate at when I'd stay with Dad. The aged cracked walls were still sprayed with rebellious graffiti, and the inside held a darkness that left sticky dampness clinging to your skin, but I loved it. It was haunting, but it fed my cravings for adrenaline. The walls, even though they were old, held memories of me as a kid, learning to skate. St. Catherine's old hospital was where my skating obsession started, the sign smudged from age on the front entrance.

"Where are you taking me?" he had asked, taking off his aviator glasses and tossing them inside his car. He shut the driver's door and glanced up at the building again.

I grabbed my deck out of the backseat of my car and balanced it on the ground. Tying my hair into a top knot, I smiled. "I'd come here as a kid a lot. It was here that I taught myself how to skate."

I picked up my deck, gesturing to the tall building. Maddox followed, taking my hand in his. "How often would you come to your dad's?"

I shrugged. "Almost every weekend, but also whenever I needed to."

We climbed the split stairs that led to where a door once hung off. It wasn't there anymore, and I wasn't the least bit surprised. The last time I was here, it was barely hanging on by an old rusted screw.

"How often did you need to?"

I gave him a small smile, letting go of his grip. "Quite a bit."

We headed straight to the main lobby. That's where the halfpipes were built. It looked the exact same as I remembered it. There were beer cans littering the floor and a couple of logs laying around everywhere, but for the most part, it was the same. Maddox gestured for the deck.

I narrowed my eyes. "You sure?"

He chuckled, licked his lips and then tore his shirt off.

I gulped.

His abs all tensed with the motion and before I realized it, I was checking him out. His skin glistened, all his tattoos on display. The word DESTROYER was inked across his chest in old English writing, and there was one massive skull that covered his belly. I licked my lips again.

"Ame…" His tone threw up warning signs.

"Hmm?" I took my greedy gaze away from his perfectly sculpted body. I was never big on the ab thing. I always dated boys who were probably skinnier than me, but there was something about Maddox. Maybe it was the fact that I knew those muscles weren't there for the sole purpose of him to flaunt around. They were a product of him being a walking weapon.

"Watch your eyes."

I roll them instead. "Show me what you got." I pointed to the deck.

He winked at me, tucking his shirt into the back of his jeans and did exactly that. Showed me what he had, which wasn't half as bad as I expected.

Snapping out of my memory, I toss and turn in my bed, unable to find sleep. Leila spent the night with Wolf—I think. Which means that she will be seeing Maddox. And the stupid side of me is jealous of this. Unable to get any sleep, I reach for my phone and type out a text to Maddox.

Me: Destroyer?

Probably a shit text starter, but I figure it's the less obvious way of saying "Hey, I'm thinking about you." My phone dings.

Maddox: My ring name.

Me: ahhh, makes sense.

Now I sound desperate.

Maddox: Why are you awake?

I bite my lip.

Me: Because I can't stop thinking.

I squeeze my phone until sweat slips between it and my hand.

Maddox: of what?

I can picture what he probably looks like right now. Maddox is a glorious sight when he's sleepy. Either waking up, going to bed, or interrupted in the middle of his sleep, he's pure sex. Messy hair, tight, tanned body, lips you want to bite, eyes that lazily scream "I'll break you, but you'll like it."

I start to type out a text, but then stop typing. Another text pops up.

Maddox: Don't do that. Send me what you just wrote.

Damn Apple and their fancy little text bubbles. Maybe I should take Leila up on switching teams to Samsung.

I draw in a deep breath and type.

Me: u

He doesn't text back, so I toss my phone across the floor and force myself to sleep.

CHAPTER 14

AMETHYST

IT'S FRIDAY WHEN I'M WALKING OUT FROM MY FINAL literature class of the day. Which means it's closer to Sunday.

Someone jumps on my back and I don't need to turn to know who it is. It's not that I'm unapproachable, but it's just that...yeah, I'm slightly unapproachable.

"Lei, you're heavy. Stop."

She shoves me playfully. "Please, if anyone can carry me—it's you. So, are we excited for Sunday? Or should I say tomorrow, since that's when we are leaving!" Leila chirps, clapping her hands together and falling into a comfortable step beside me.

"Yes and no."

She nods, looking at me in a way only Leila could. "And why is that?"

I inhale the crisp breeze and shrug, looking up at the old buildings around campus as we almost get to the residence hall. "I don't know. I am because then it will be over, I guess."

"That's bullshit!" Leila snorts. "This is going to be epic!"

"Yeah." I shove through the entry doors. "That's because it's not Wolf."

She waves me off. "I guess, but no. That'd be so sexy to see him throw down. Also, you have nothing to be worried about. Does the word undefeated mean nothing to you, Miss I'm Studying Literature."

I roll my eyes. Nothing has been so Leila than that statement right there.

Later that night, we're both holed in. Leila and I lock

ourselves in our room to finish our paper before flying to Vegas. We know that we have to get it done tonight or it isn't getting done, and the guys respect our wishes. Leila isn't impressed with their chivalry, but I am relieved. Yes, I don't mind acting. I rather enjoy it. It is a place I can lather a new kind of skin over myself, and then shred it before going home. Not that my life is torturous or sad, but I do enjoy the escape that acting gives me. But even still, I'd like to be a screenwriter one day, more behind the scenes. That's where my creative juice really needs to be squeezed into.

"I'm beat," Leila exhales, belly flopping onto her bed.

I take off my reading glasses and massage my eyes. "Me too. What's the time?"

But Leila is already snoring.

I giggle, shaking my head. Glancing down at my phone, I see it's two a.m. and drop down onto the mattress not long after.

It wasn't bad enough that I had the fight to work myself up for, but my mom and Elliot have also called a family dinner for tonight.

"Why." I massage my temples. Leila is sitting in front of her mirror, pulling a straightener through her hair.

"It won't be that bad, Ame, just chill."

"Lei, no offense, but it will be that bad."

There's a knock on the door and I jump over my bed to reach for it. I'm in an old beat up Rolling Stone shirt with holes in weird places and thick fuzzy socks on my feet. My hair is in a high ponytail and my reading glasses are still perched on my nose. Because yup, you guessed it, I'm still studying. I only have a couple more words to get in and then I'd be done. Good words. I'm not one of those people who will rush the pictures I paint with my words. I like my drawings to be clean cut and crisp, not smudged and unfinished. Shame I can't say the same about me as a person. Good thing I take my art seriously.

I pull the door open and sigh. "Of course it's you."

Maddox saunters in and laughs, kicking the door closed with his heavy combat boot. "I wanna see you before we leave." His fingers hook into mine and he hauls me into his chest. My arms wrap around him.

"I can't argue with that." I inhale his scent. Leather, soap and a hint of motor oil. It only adds to him. To all that is Maddox Stone. "I don't think I'm ready to see this whole thing."

"I get it now," Leila says from behind us. I pull myself away from Maddox and turn to face her.

"Get what?"

She smiles gently, and it has to be the softest I've ever seen Leila. She gazes out the window absently. "The whole soul mates thing." Her attention comes back to us. "I believe in it now. Because of you two."

My eyes widen, and Maddox's grip tightens around me.

Leila must notice both our discomfort because her eyes roll and she snorts. "Oh, please. Don't try to tell me that you both don't feel what we all see."

Classic Lei. Always has to speak her mind. I'm not sure what she's implying, but if it rhymes with Pikachu, then she better abort mission.

"Anyway!" I turn back around to face Maddox, whose eyes are doing that weak, lazy thing at me. I gulp. Ignore those fucking butterflies. "Shall we ride with you?"

He gives me a half smile. "Or on me would be good."

"Oh, come on…" Leila exclaims.

CHAPTER 15

AMETHYST

"So, Leila, what are you majoring in?" my mom asks, spooning salad onto her plate.

"Computer science," Leila answers smoothly. She's always so poised, and confident. It's the kind of confidence you gain when you come from money.

"Ah, interesting!" Elliot nods then chews on his piece of steak. His eyes go to Wolf, who is sitting opposite Leila. Maddox is right beside me, with his arm thrown over my chair. He hasn't made an effort to hide that we are an item at all tonight—despite my mom's obvious discomfort. I'm thinking he's doing it on purpose now.

"She's—" I pause when I feel Maddox's lips softly press against my bare shoulder. I kick him from under the table, but his hand flies to my knee and he squeezes so hard I almost squirm. "Very smart. Leila is very smart," I say breathlessly. "Is it hot in here? It's hot in here." I try to tug my leg out of his hand, but he only intensifies his grip.

Shit.

"Amethyst, stop being weird. Is that your ODC or whatever again?"

"What? I don't have OCD," I reply, taking a sip of my wine.

I try to yank my leg out from his grip again and he unlatches, which sends me semi-flying into Leila.

She widens her eyes at me. I know what she's thinking. She probably thinks Maddox has his hand down my pants.

I clear my throat, then catch Talon's eye from the other end of the table. He's grinning like a big stupid panda.

"So." Mom cuts into her sirloin. "Are you two together now?" It's eerily calm the way she asks it. Almost like she's asking about the weather.

I look to Maddox. His tongue snakes out and swipes at his bottom lip, then he half smiles, showing his annoyingly white teeth. "Yeah. We are."

Mom clears her throat and then looks to Elliot, who then looks to me. I look to Leila, who clears her throat and sips her wine. She's like Kermit right now, sipping tea. Just as I open my mouth, Talon steps in.

"You can't be surprised." He looks between Mom and Elliot. "I mean," his eyes catch mine, and then Maddox. "The evidence is there, always has been."

Mom takes a sip of water and then nods. "Ok." Her attention comes to me. "I'll have a talk with you later, but ok. Does your father know?"

Elliot grunts. "I can't imagine him being too…"

I shake my head. "Actually, he's fine. Maddox came to stay with us last weekend. Even met Uncle Marcus."

Mom almost spits out her drink. She swipes her mouth delicately. "Forgive me, I'm just a little surprised you have no broken bones, or I don't know, are still alive. He shot Amethyst's high school boyfriend."

"He's not that bad, and that shooting was an accident. He thought Adam was a fugitive." It's true, there was an incident in town when Adam and I were together. Uncle Marcus accidentally shot him in the foot. Nowhere serious or anything. Total misunderstanding. Also a complete coincidence that Adam was cheating on me throughout our entire relationship.

Mum snorts.

My shoulders relax for the first time since I walked into this house.

Elliot's tense voice breaks the smooth vibe. "Maddox, can I speak with you?" He stands and then excuses himself from the table.

Maddox doesn't move, he remains relaxed, but he watches his dad's retreating back. He licks his lip and then looks to Talon and Wolf. Without locking eyes with me, he leans over and kisses me on the cheek, then stands and follows his dad out.

I feel like I'm holding my breath with all the awkward vibes flying around the room.

"Rosé," Talon hollers, a beer near his mouth. He drinks beer. Is he the only one who drinks beer? Such a caveman. Actually, Maddox drinks beer too. I look to Wolf's glass, and as does he. But Elliot, he drinks whiskey. Why is that? "Hey!" Talon leans forward, resting his elbows on the table. "Relax." Talon's eyes soften around the edges, and I find myself slowly breathing in and out, counting to ten.

I exhale and nod. "Thanks."

"Um, should you go check?" Leila whispers to me.

Should I? Part of me wants to. I don't want Maddox to have to deal with our shit on his own, but at the same time, I know that he can handle it and will want to handle it.

"No, they'll be fine," Mom assures, sipping her drink. There's a lot of drink sipping going on tonight.

"Mom, seriously, why did we have to come for this dinner anyway?" I ask, itchy with annoyance.

Mom gestures to Leila. "Well, Elliot wanted to meet Leila, and of course, I did too. And you never come and visit me anymore."

I lean back in my chair, my eyes on my mom but my focus on the archway that separates the kitchen to the main sitting room where Maddox and Elliot are. "Well, you're not living in The Cherub anymore, so what am I supposed to do? Drive here every night?" My eyes fly to the door when Maddox walks in, chewing on a toothpick. He looks down at me and winks before pulling his chair out and taking a seat.

I search his face, ignoring that Elliot has taken his spot again at the head of the table.

I see the slight unease in Maddox. There's an inkling of uncertainty that bared itself for a split second, but before I can over-analyze it, it's gone and Maddox with his stupid cocky grin is back.

"So, where were we?"

"Are we going to talk about what happened tonight?" I raise my eyebrows at Maddox.

He removes his shirt and tosses it into the basket in the corner of his room. Every muscle tenses with his movements. "No need. Dad is just worried that I'll hurt you."

"Ha!" The laugh comes out forced. "Well, he doesn't have to worry about that."

Maddox pauses, his head tilted. My mouth waters. "Why?"

"Why, what?" I ask, confused about his question. I climb under the covers and try to ignore the fact that Maddox's scent is all around me now—seeping through his sheets.

His eyes narrow. "Why doesn't he have to worry?"

I exhale. "Because, it's early, and…"

Maddox starts walking toward me. My eyes drop down his body, catching him unbuckling his belt.

Shit.

"Um," I say, watching as he pulls at his belt and flicks open the top button of his jeans.

"Hmmm?" Maddox murmurs, unzipping his zip. His jeans fall lower, showing the rim of his Calvin's. "Why? Why do you think I can't hurt you, Rosé?"

I gulp. "Because it's early, Maddox. I've never, you know… been hurt…"

His knees hit the bed and he crawls over me, ripping the bed cover off my body. His eyes dip down and slowly drag over my form. His head tilts.

He chuckles, then his hand flies to my throat and he clenches tightly. Just enough to allow slow intakes of breath. My throat swells every time I swallow.

He licks his lip, then grins. "Challenge accepted." Then he presses my hands above my head and widens my legs with his.

The dampness between my thighs only intensifies as he grinds his groin into me. Clothes start flying off. Wrapping my hair around one fist, he yanks my head back to face him. His eyes come to mine, and then he licks me from the bottom of my throat up, to my mouth where he sucks my bottom lip into his mouth and bites down on it.

My hips begin slowly riding into his hips, but he doesn't give it to me, slowly inching away every time he knows I'm trying to gain traction.

His other hand comes to my throat as he positions himself at my entrance. "You think I can't hurt you, baby?" he questions and then slams inside of me.

I scream out embarrassingly, but his mouth drops to mine, his tongue savagely dipping inside my mouth, the ball of his piercing clinking against my teeth. "Gonna need to watch the volume of those screams tonight, baby. Don't want Talon to think I'm killing you," he mutters into his kiss. He pulls out, and then pushes in again, the grip on my hair tightening until I feel each hair slowly tearing out. Fuck. "Because he will think I'm killing you."

He rides me harder, his groin rubbing against my clit with every thrust. His grip around my throat tightens every few seconds, allowing me to breathe every now and then. I start whispering dirty words into his ear, words I will probably regret later when I'm not riding on a sexual induced high. His jaw marbles. Sweat drips down off his nose and drops to my mouth. I lick it off, then lean up and run my tongue over every sweat drop I can see on his neck and jawline, biting and chewing on my path.

He pauses, and then chuckles, getting off me.

"What are you doing?" I ask frantically when I feel the absence of him. I instantly need to fight the urge to pull him back on top of me. His heaviness pressing my body into the mattress.

He cocks his head, as I take in his naked glory. Tattoos seeping into his golden flesh. Flesh that's stretched to the max from his muscles. Not too big, but way bigger than lean. You wouldn't think it though when he's wearing clothes.

"You said I couldn't hurt you…"

"Yes…" I agreed, even when I said that I knew it wasn't true. Or I was in denial. Wasn't sure which of the two is more true.

My thighs clench.

Maddox' focus falls to them. "How you feeling down there right now?" he asks with a nod of his head.

I snicker. "Sore," I admit, but my wit gets the better of me, and I smirk. "But I mean, I can take care of it myself…"

His eyes darken, his smirk now completely gone.

He comes back and grabs me around my thighs, squeezing so hard I feel like the fat from my legs is about to pop out. Yanking me down the bed, he hovers over me, eyes to eyes. Nose tip to nose tip.

His jaw clenches.

Then he growls.

I gulp.

His hips circle into me, his cock pressing against my slit…

"What am I going to do with you, Rosé…"

I challenge him. "You can do what you promised you would do…"

He does his head tilt thing and bites his lip. "And what's that?"

I look between his lips to his eyes. Lock, loaded… "Hurt me."

And fire.

He flips me onto my stomach, slaps my ass cheek so hard I swear China could feel the sting that erupts over me and dives into my pussy from behind. His hand comes to my throat.

"You want me to hurt you, baby?" he asks, thrusting into me.

"Yes…" I whisper, even though every time his dick pounds inside me it slams against my cervix. I erupt. An orgasm washes over me in brutal storm-like waves. I scream out a line of swear words, my body trembling under his assault.

Cum drips down my inner thighs with every pulse.

He slaps my ass again and I cry out in pain. His other hand comes to my hip and he presses against it, slamming me against his dick. I feel it building again. That familiar brutality of pleasure. That's what it is with Maddox. It's not all just pleasure, it's pleasure, pain and games. It's survival of the fittest. I'm not very fit.

Just as I hit my peak, he bites down on the back of my neck and we both come undone together.

I fall onto the bed and twist myself inside his now sticky sheets. The last thing I remember is him pulling me into his chest and me rambling about him not having sex pre-fight.

AMETHYST

"HOLY MOTHER OF GOD!" LEILA'S MUG SLIPS BETWEEN HER fingers and smashes against the glass tiled floor.

"Leila!" I scold her, kneeling down to pick up all the broken pieces. "You're going to wake the monsters."

"Ame!" she whisper-yells. "Have you seen yourself?"

"What?" I brush her off, picking up the shards and then standing to walk them to the bin.

"You look like he beat the shit out of you."

My hand freezes over the bin and then I run to the bathroom.

"Oh shit." There are purple grip marks around my neck. I cradle my pink hair up and turn to look at my back. "Shit," I whisper, seeing the bite marks on my left shoulder. Pulling at my pajama shorts, I look in between my thighs to see even more bruising there and one massive circle on my hip that is clearly visible because my tank top shows a slice of my my lower tummy.

"I mean we heard you both, but daammmmnnn," Leila whispers. "He done fucked you up."

"Shush!" I whisper-yell back at her.

She shrugs and hands me the mug. "They need to wake up anyway. Our flight is at twelve."

MADDOX

Ame is pacing up and down the floor as Coach wraps up my hands. "You okay, baby?" I ask, even though I know she's not. She's been uneasy the whole way here.

Her pacing stops, and she pins me with a scowl. Anyone would think she was the one who was jumping in the ring. Then she looks to Coach and takes the gauze from him. My knee jiggles from the adrenaline. Coach glares between her and I, then back to me. He's been with me for a long time. He found me at an underground fighting ring in high school. He was there to shut it down but ended up seeing my talent, he likes to call it. My head bobs in approval and he takes a step back, giving us some space. She kneels in front of me and continues with the wrapping.

"Am I ok?" she asks, but I think she's more asking herself because her eyes don't meet mine. "Well, no, I'm not really. Just please don't die. Or get hit, please don't let him hit you." Her hand rests on my knee. My legs are spread out with the chair flipped backward. My elbows rest on the edge of the back. She goes back to the task at hand. "Promise me, Maddox."

I lick my lips. Promise her that he won't hit me? Joseph "The Man" Banderas has a record much like mine, unde- feated. But I knew then and there with those fucking blue eyes peering up at me that I was going to promise this girl that exact thing.

"Alright, baby."

She leans up and kisses me. I lose it for a second, my thoughts fuzzing in and out.

"Mad, you're up," Coach gestures to the door where Wolf and Talon are waiting for me. I stand from the chair and stretch my arms out in circles. Cranking my neck, Amethyst's shoulders straighten, and her demeanour turns defiant. Her hands come to my cheeks. She leans up on her toes until her nose tip touches mine. "You've got this."

"Do I?" I play with her, a smirk on my lips. I knew I had this, but I also know Amethyst. She needs to feel needed. Not in a superficial way, or a temporary way. In a way that a thunderstorm needs the loud clapping of chaos to reach its peak.

"Yes," she says, pressing her lips to mine again. "You do. Or I'll kill you."

I smirk and kiss her roughly again.

"Alright, lovers." Talon bangs on the door like a Viking. "Lettttt'ss ggggoo!!" I bounce around on my toes, my brothers in front of me and the coach in front of them. Amethyst is behind me, and out of instinct, I reach for her until her hand tangles with mine. She squeezes and then we're walking out.

AMETHYST

KO'd. The words flash on the oversized TVs that are hanging above the caged octagon.

What?

"Holy fucking shit. People paid big money for this fight and Maddox just ended it in less than ten seconds."

I gulp.

I find Maddox, but he's already staring at me with a cocky grin on his face. He winks and blows me a kiss.

"Girl, you need to marry this guy like, stat," Leila yells into my ear excitedly. There's loud cheering erupting everywhere and signs that have Maddox's name displayed on them. Panties and bras are flying toward the ring too, girls screaming at Maddox. Seriously, how fucking desperate. One sign catches my eye.

Maddox, you can destroy me any day!

She talks a big game, but she should see my bruises. Bet she wouldn't be swinging that sign around then.

I fight the urge to push Leila away at the mention of marriage. I don't want to hear the M word. I've never been a part of a wedding, or even attended one, let alone think about being a bride. My palms sweat, so I rub them against my jeans.

Maddox jumps over the ring like a damn lion and comes down to the crowd, ignoring the cheering and grabs onto my hand, dragging me back to the den. The echoing of voices invades our personal space, but I feel it. Whether it's from the surge that Maddox is sending off or the vibe in the air from all the adrenaline, I feel a smidge of why he does this. The same reason I skate. Because the rush of doing something that sets your soul on fire is foreplay, and the end orgasm is only reached by succeeding. And he did. In less than ten seconds.

He leans into me as we walk down the quiet hallway, the loud voices long lost. "So, is my talent gonna die or soar?"

I chuckle, shaking my head and leaning into his sweaty body. "Definitely soar, but next time give me a longer fight."

Later that night, we all hit town. I complained the whole time that my feet were sore and that I wasn't feeling well so I went back to the hotel early. I thought Maddox would stay with his team and celebrate his victory, he didn't. He came back to the hotel, pulled me in close and rode my body until my legs were numb. I fell asleep that night with a tightening in my chest that I didn't want to explore.

CHAPTER 17

AMETHYST

IT'S TUESDAY NIGHT WHEN WE DECIDE TO CELEBRATE—SINCE I'm feeling better. I felt guilty for being such a party pooper after the fight, so tonight was all my idea. Leila spends most of the night wrapped around Wolf, and Talon has some random skank on his lap. I really want to ask what his and Liza's deal is. Truthfully. They have the most bizarre relationship. I believe they called it "open." Through the night, we drink a lot, dance even more—until our bodies were dripping in sweat, and then I met Maddox's agent. He came crashing through the doors, holding his phone. He had to be around late thirties. Dark and brooding. Pretty good-loo— "I got you a deal, kid! A fucking huge one. It's going to set you up for life." The excitement in his voice is evident.

I down all of my drink. Whiskey, neat. Because why fuck around with something as lame as wine tonight.

Maddox seems pleased as he pulls his agent in for one of those awkward man hugs. They whisper something into each other's ears, and then Maddox grabs my hand and pulls me under his arm. He had long since lost his shirt—seriously? How is he allowed in a club with no shirt on? It's tucked into the back of his jeans. He has clean white sneakers on his feet. Adidas originals—the high tops. Totally not my type. I feel like a broken record. I don't usually date guys who have the same dress sense as me. It's weird. Only when we're together, everything is natural. Being with him is like breathing. Short breaths where my heart constantly feels as though it's contracting in my chest, but breathing, nonetheless. He downs his drink and points to me.

The agent's eyes come to mine. "And who do we have here…" His hand comes out, and I look at it briefly before shaking it.

My dad always told me that you could tell a lot about a man by his handshake. For instance, if it's firm, it means he's uptight and probably there for business and is keeping something from you. If it's relaxed, he's comfortable, a little more trustworthy.

"Amethyst," I yell over the music, adding a smile too.

He smiles back, and it's warm. I relax. His handshake is somewhere between the two.

"I'm Trevor Michaelson. This delinquent's agent." His eyes fall to my mouth and then come back to my eyes. He is good-looking for an old dude, but no one could stand beside Maddox. It isn't just Maddox and his obvious good looks. It is how he carries himself. His shoulders are always back in confidence, his walk filled with so much swagger it has you second guessing where he was raised. It's his obvious neglect to any and everyone who isn't someone to him. It only adds to his appeal. My stomach clenches and my heart twists. Shit. Was I in love with him?

I excuse myself from them both and dip out for the bar. Once I reach it, a twenty-something old guy grins at me. He flips bottles around his fingers so expertly it makes my head tilt. The neon flashing laser lights lit up the club to a certain extent, but the bar was lined with fancy string lights, so I have a clear image of him.

"Whiskey neat, please!" I holler, then look to the dance floor. Shit. Do I love him? I swallow.

"You here with Destroyer?" he asks. He's pouring my drink, but attention his stays on me. He's skinny with weird floppy blond hair. He has a perfect straight nose and small perfect lips. His jaw is somewhat clean. He has slightly smudged kohl under his eye and I look to his wrist where leather bangles are strapped around. He's a punk guy. I guess you could say that he's attractive in his own way.

I take the glass he's sliding to me. "I am."

"With, with him?" he asks with a quirked eyebrow.

I lick my lips. "Yes." He's gay, that's it.

He grins. "What's ya name? I swear I'm not hitting on you. I don't have a death wish."

I laugh at that. "I'm Amethyst."

"Wow." His eyes widen in shock. "That's a fucking rad name."

My cheeks heat. "Thanks." I appreciate the brief distraction from the fact that I'm probably in love with Maddox.

He slips me another. "On the house." Then he winks at me and goes to serve another customer.

That's when I see what he's wearing. Fucking suspenders. I snort into my drink. It's refreshing to meet someone not so perfect when you've been around perfection for so long. Even my best friend is perfection. I decide right here that I'll be making this club my casual. I sink the other drink just as Leila drags me onto the dance floor. I laugh, moving my long pink hair out of my face. Leila starts grinding into me to the beat. Some mash-up of Drake's song "Nice for What." Leila and I always had a good time when we went out, and it was always mainly because we could dance.

A week after Vegas, I swear I could still feel my head pounding.

"Rosé, better wise up before dinner tonight!" Talon whips my ass with a dishcloth.

"Ouch!" I scold him, rubbing my sore ass cheek. I don't know if it is from his little slip or from Maddox's daily assault on my body. Everything hurts lately. My muscles ache and my skin throbs. I'm pretty athletic, (not that I work out or anything), but skating has always kept me pretty fit and toned.

Talon laughs, as though he's reading my mind.

"Shut up."

I'm still rubbing my ass cheek when Leila walks in. Her hair in a mess all over her head. We haven't spent that many nights at our dorm lately.

I busy myself with making coffee. It's a Saturday and I plan to tell Maddox everything tonight. For the first time ever, Amethyst Tatum is about to tell someone else that she loves them. I'm terrified.

"You look like shit," she says through a yawn. Talon slips out the front door for his run.

"Thanks. So do you."

Leila takes a seat. "Lies," she mutters, resting her forehead on her arms. "Seriously. Why can't we skip college and go straight to jobs? My brain hurts."

I hand her a mug of watered down coffee beans and sip my delicious brew. I have creamer because I love myself.

"Because we don't know what we're doing." I blow into my cup.

Maddox ambles in, rubbing his eyes. He smiles when he sees me, his teeth flashing white. His muscles flex as he picks up my mug and takes a sip of my coffee.

"Morning, baby." He kisses me on the head and busies himself with breakfast.

Usually I make it, but I'm done for this morning. And anyway, watching Maddox walk around in those deadly grey sweatpants is way too much fun. Dick print anyone? My mouth waters.

I'm such a sucker for him.

Just him. I love him, and it's going to ruin me. I more than love him, I'm bordering obsessed with him. Does he feel the same way?

My eyes go to Leila, who is pointedly glaring at me over her coffee cup. I raise my eyebrows in question. She raises her back as in "what're you thinking?"

I shrug. "Nothing important."

Her eyes narrow like she doesn't believe me.

I shrug again. I don't give a fuck.

My attention goes back to Maddox. How did I manage to get him? The bad boy on campus. The guy every girl was thirsty for, and I got him. I didn't believe in fate or anything like that. I couldn't help but feel that when we were together, it was more than what we could see that was working with us. It was like a higher power had created us and put us in each other's path. Why me, though? Maddox, the possessive over-protector. The guy who'd stand over anything that belonged to him with his teeth bared. I was his, and now I just needed to tell him.

CHAPTER 18

MADDOX

I LOVE HER. I'M NOT EVEN FUCKING ASHAMED TO ADMIT IT, I flat out fucking love this chick, and I know she feels what I feel. Amethyst is a lot of things, but her main attribute is the way she can read people. When she gave enough of a fuck to do it, that is. She's a renegade. A girl who was raised in a good home but chose to rebel against society. She is loyal, fierce, sassy and feisty, but she also knows when to be soft. I loved her fire, but I caressed her soft side because she only showed it to me. I've spent the last couple of months studying her. Watching how she moves around certain people, that's how I know that she only bares her gentle side to me. That side makes me feral. Her softness brings out every single bit of bad inside of me roaring to the surface. Caging her like an obsessed animal protecting its prey. Amethyst is mine. She's mine, and I'm 'bout to make it official tonight. I don't give a fuck about our ages, or the fact that we might be going down different paths. Her with her acting and me with my fighting, I want her, and I'd move cities together just to make that happen, but I also know her and know us. As fucked as it may sound, I trust the connection we have. This doesn't lie, this is real. What I feel for her is real.

The little Tiffany box burns in my pocket the closer we drive to our parents' house. Amethyst is slightly headbanging to a Nirvana song and Leila and Wolf are in the backseats, being weird as per usual. She cranks the window down and I watch out of the corner of my eye how her hair dances around with the wind, sending the smell of dried lavender to linger in the air. My cock stiffens.

I pull us into the large circular driveway and we all make our way inside. I'll admit, I'm still not one hundred percent ok with Jessica, but Amethyst makes me want to be ok with her, for her.

We're halfway through dinner when there's a knock on the door. Jessica excuses herself and disappears to answer it.

I wrap my arm around Amethyst and pull her face into me until my lips are brushing against her earlobe. "I want to ask you something after dinner."

I inch back enough to catch her eyes dart up to mine. Wide and vulnerable. Her lips pinch together. "Ok."

Why does she have to be so goddamn beautiful.

Mine.

Jessica clears her throat from the entry. "Maddox?"

My eyes go up to Jessica, and then straight to the girl standing beside her. Long ash blonde hair, deep blue eyes. Fucking girl next door doe eyes. A face that looks familiar, so fam—I fly out of my chair.

"Cassidy?"

Cassidy Williams. My high school ex-girlfriend who I haven't seen in years, and who just up and left me with no backward glance, is here. What the fuck is she doing here?

She looks somewhat the same, only older. Heart shape face, slightly chubby cheeks with a slim neckline. Slim enough to squeeze. She's always been petite and slender, and that hasn't changed. She still seems all of five foot one. Tight jeans and a loose knit cardigan.

"Hi, Dux," she whispers huskily. That fucking nickname.

"What are you doing here?"

"Ah." Her eyes shot to mine with urgency. They glass over. "Can we talk?"

Six years. It has been six years. I healed over losing her, only just, and now she strolls back into my life like I didn't spend a whole year buried in pussy, drugs, and bad decisions to get over her. Fuck.

I nod, then start walking toward her. Fuck. Amethyst is watching our exchange. I retreat backwards and bend down, kissing the top of her head. "I won't be long, baby." I stroll out of the dining room and gesture to the formal room.

CHAPTER 19

AMETHYST

My stomach flips around as I watch Maddox leave the room. Everyone is silent, no one has so much as made a sound.

Mom sits back in her chair, giving Elliot a strange look. "Anyway, so what were we talking about?"

Typical Mom. Trying to run away from the issues at hand. Her chit-chat dies out into the back of my brain and I pick up my glass of wine, taking a long swig.

"Why is she here?" Wolf asks, finally breaking through whatever my mom thought was more important.

Talon comes around the table and sits in Maddox's seat. I don't look at him. I can't. I'm panicking. I can slowly feel my nerves work themselves up. Why is she here? What could be so important that she waited how many years it had been to come and make an entrance into Maddox's life again.

Talon's finger hooks around my chin and he tips my head up to face him. My eyes search his.

"Hey, cut that shit out. She doesn't mean anything to him anymore." I smile softly. He drops his grip and gives me my wine. "I promise. It'll be some stupid bullshit."

"Yeah, only it's Cass. I doubt it," Wolf answers smoothly. His head whips around to Leila suddenly. "Ouch." She must have hit him under the table. His tone is dry, just like him as a person.

"No nicknames, please. Her name is Cass-idy," Leila exclaims.

Mom sighs.

Elliot clears his throat. "Ame, I want you to know that you

are a part of this family now. So whatever happens, it doesn't matter—ok?"

I gulp. Shit. What if he is still in love with her?

"Nice, Dad. Real nice. Just go freak her out." Talon shakes his head, leaning over the table to grab his plate and move Maddox's away so he can continue eating. I like this dining room. It sits just off of the kitchen, and the whole back wall is one big glass window so you can overlook the backyard. There's a glass chandelier that falls delicately over the table. Art is hanging on the walls—and fuck.

I hate this fucking room.

I hate this house, I want to leave. The room feels like it's shrinking and clinging to my skin.

As soon as Maddox walks back in, my head whips straight to the entrance. I'll know instantly if it's good or bad. I'll know by what his eyes do. I suck in my breath and allow myself to focus on him.

I blow out my breath when I see his eyebrows pulled in and his knuckles are bleeding. His pupils are dilated, and his chest is heaving in and out.

Oh no.

This isn't good.

"Amethyst," he says, his voice dripping in anger. Then his eyes finally come to me, and his features soften a little. He licks his lip. "We need to talk, baby."

"Okay." I shoot off the seat and make my way to him. He watches me for a few seconds. His eyes going from my mouth to my eyes, as if he's trying to memorize something.

"Stop it," I grind out, getting annoyed with how he's looking at me. I shove past him and make my way to the living room. No sign of Cassidy. Thank fuck. Maybe he killed her. I'm probably not that lucky.

My eyes fly to the hole in the wall and I flinch. Something has happened. Something bad.

He closes the open doors to block out any other noise, then I feel him take a seat beside me. My eyes remain on the pool out the back and the bright blue neon that lights up the water. I want a swim.

"Amethyst…" Maddox says, but he doesn't touch me.

Why isn't he touching me?

"I—I—fuck…" he breathes out, seemingly frustrated with himself.

"Just say it, Maddox." I fight the tears that threaten to surface, swallowing past the giant rock that feels as though it's lodged in my throat.

"I have a kid."

Everything stops. I whip my focus to him, my hair slapping against my face. "What!"

He exhales and stands from the couch. He starts pacing back and forth. His hands go from his hair to his face back to his hair.

"I didn't know. Cassidy, she—" He exhales, pauses and looks straight at me. "She ran away when she found out she was pregnant. Not to get away from me, but to get away from her parents who would have made her abort. Her kid—" He pauses and I feel like I've been smacked over the side of the head with a brick. He continues. "Our kid, she's a girl. Her name is Kennedy. She's a little over five, and she has kidney failure, Amethyst. She needs me." He pauses, and I can't fight the tears anymore. They're rolling down my cheeks. It's not that I'm upset that he has a child, not at all, and that wouldn't change my mind on wanting to be with him, but I have a feeling it is an issue for him.

"I—I'm sorry, Maddox…" Because I am, and I'm speechless. What more can I say.

He continues, taking a seat on the leather sofa opposite me. "Cassidy isn't a match because she's A-. Kennedy is the same as me, she's O-. Cass tried to get in contact with her parents again, but they apparently died in a car accident not long after she ran away."

I want to scream. My insides feel like they're cracking, and my brain is running off of white noise. "Wh—um. What are you going to do?" I tuck my hair behind my ear and wipe the tears off my cheeks.

He buries his face into his hands.

Reality hits me at full force, he's obviously conflicted with what he wants. He wants to be with her, even if it is for his child, he still wants it, and who can blame him. I come from a split home, so I know how much they really do work and the dynamic can be great, but that's only if both parents share the same understanding. I get the feeling that if I fight for him now, and force him to stay with me, he might later resent me for doing it and maybe missing more time with his child. No, he needs to choose on his own. I need to leave before I beg him to stay with me and that I'd raise their child like she was my own.

"Don't worry," I answer, going to stand on shaky legs. "You don't have to say anything." My voice breaks in the end, and I feel my legs shake under my weight.

Two steps to the door, and then I can run. Run where? I don't know. I can get Leila to take me home. Only she came with Maddox too.

Run.

"Amethyst," his voice interrupts my erratic thoughts. I freeze with one hand on the door handle. Had I already made my way across the room? "Please, I don't—God I don't know what to do."

I swallow and take two breaths to try to compose myself. I slam my eyes closed.

"She's my child, and I have already lost five years, I don't want to lose another five. Cassidy, she's been getting by but she's struggling to pay the bills, and I don't want to be like my father and abond— fuck!" Maddox must stand and come straight to me, because he grabs me around my arm and spins me around until my back slams against the door. He searches my eyes frantically. "Tell me what to do, Ame! Fuck, I can't…" He is physically shaking, so I wrap my arms around the back of his neck, pulling his forehead down onto mine.

"It's not our time, Maddox. Maybe in another life, maybe in another realm, but it is not our time right now." I step back, already missing his flesh under my palm. I want his scent in my space and his sweat dripping on my body as he rides my pain away, but I can't, and I won't ever again. My heart feels like it literally breaks inside my chest. It hurts, everything fucking hurts.

"No." He shakes his head, searching my body up and down. "Fuck!"

Because he knew. We both did. Deep down, we both knew what he has to do. We have to let each other go and hope that one day, when he has enough time to ponder and make a rational decision, we will find each other again.

"You know what you need to do, Maddox. As much as I—"

His knuckles come to my cheeks and my stomach clenches at his touch. The walls feel as though they're caving in on me. "Please don't." My eyes slam shut to stop him from seeing my emotion.

His lips come to mine and I almost throw my restraint out the window. I let them sit there for a few seconds as tears pour over my face and into the crack of my lips, into each of our mouths. I take a deep breath.

"I loved you."

He flies backward, his eyes flaring with a fresh round of anger, but it's too late. I quickly pull the door open and sprint out.

"Amethyst!" he roars from the living room, but I pounce back to the dining room. Everyone is already standing, probably because they heard the beast be unleashed in the other room.

"We going?" Leila asks.

I nod my head frantically, my face wet with tears and my hair a disarray all over my face. I have no doubt that my mascara is smudged all over.

"I'm sorry, Mom," I whisper without meeting her gaze. "But I really need to go. Now."

Elliot gestures out the door. "Take her, Talon."

Talon doesn't miss a beat, he and Leila are following me out the door, leaving Wolf behind.

"Amethyst!" Maddox yells, launching for me.

Elliot and Wolf grab him, holding him back and I pick up the pace as Leila's arm hooks around mine. Talon has his hand on the small of my back as we hit outside and start jogging to Talon's parked pickup. I must have been in a hurry, because it isn't until we're pulling out that I see Cassidy sitting on one of the steps, tears in her eyes.

She catches me in the window, and then just when I'm about to somewhat feel sorry for her, her lip curls up in a smug grin.

I spin around to look at her but it's too late, Talon is flooring it down the driveway, kicking gravel up in our retreat.

"Okay!" Leila screams out. "Now someone tell me what the fuck is going on!"

Talon looks at me every two seconds.

My mouth dries. I have nothing. Nothing. I came here with Maddox, with a future, and I leave without him. I feel empty and alone, and every single inch of me aches from his absence.

I keep my head forward, tears still pouring down my cheeks.

"He has a kid."

Leila sucks in a breath. Talon curses.

"Her name is Kennedy, and she has kidney disease." I

swipe at my tears angrily. "She has the same blood type as Maddox. And—and—"

"—and Maddox doesn't want to be like our father and bitch out on his kid by shitting on the mother," Talon declares, finishing my sentence.

Leila's hand comes to my arm. "It's going to be ok, Ame. We've got you."

One month passes.

Two months.

Three months.

.

Four months.

Five…

CHAPTER 20

AMETHYST
One Year Later...

"AND THAT! IS HOW IT'S DONE!" LEILA PULLS ME IN FOR A HUG. "Can you believe it?" I look out to the crowd of people who are here. Families, friends, all mixed together. Amongst everyone else's loved ones, I see Talon towering over the masses of people with Wolf standing beside him and my mom and Elliot waving at me from the stage.

Leila squeals and jumps off the stage, tossing her hat into the air. She spider jumps on Wolf and he catches her by her ass.

Seriously.

I shake my head and laugh. As sour of a bitch as I am, I'm happy for my best friend. She helped me through some of the roughest days of my life…

Six Months Earlier

I shot back my—I lost count how many. Everything just needs to turn numb. Fuck feelings. Maddox once owned every part of my heart, but when he left, he took that part with him, so now all that sits in his replacement is a sack of void. A void I tried to fill every night with alcohol and sex. The sex was good while it was happening. I never saw their face, or their body, instead, I relished in the feeling. The great wave of euphoria that would wash over me as I reached my orgasm. That was what filled Maddox's space. For like, the few seconds that it lasted for, and then the thumping of loneliness would seep in again. That was how it circled and how it started. Every night after studying, I'd either get drunk or get laid—or both.

"Ame!" Leila barged into the bar, taking the glass from me. "Do not give her any more drinks, Trin!" Trin. Siiigghhh. Trin was my bartender-slash-obvious new best friend.

Leila looks back at me, hooking her arm in mine. "I'm taking you home."

"No." I shook my head, trying to pull myself away from her. "I don't want to go home, I want to stay here and drink and look at pretty Trin!"

Trin winks at me. "Text me, princess."

I pointed at him. "I will!" I thought he was gay when I first met him—wrong. He was bi-sexual, and ever since we had come into the bar with—he who shall not be named—I have been coming back, and Trin had a lot to do with that.

"Come on," Leila gritted through her teeth. "Unless you want Wolf and Talon to drag you out of this club, I would obey my orders."

I ran ahead of her and barged through the doors.

"Ame!" Bryce hollered, reaching for me. Bryce was one of the bouncers here. He was beautiful. Dark skin that I just wanted to bite into and big broad shoulders.

"I could climb him for sure." I paused, my hand going to my mouth. "Shit, did I just?" I looked up at Bryce doe-eyed. He smirked, and Leila shoved me from behind toward Talon's parked pickup.

"Come on, my sluterous, we're taking you home."

She opened the passenger door and pushed me inside. It took three tries because this truck was hard enough to get into sober, let alone drunk. I looked at the raptor label on the fresh leather dash. "Rawr."

"Jesus, how much have you had to drink?" Talon slapped my hand away when I went to touch his face. Marilyn Manson's "Third Day of a Seven-Day Binge" starts playing and I lean forward, turning it way the fuck up. Love. This. Song. We all have stripper songs, well I have about ten and they're all Manson songs.

"Your beard has grown. Why has your beard grown?" I yelled loudly at Talon, tilting my head.

"Someone shut her up," Wolf muttered from the backseat.

"Sorry, seems the only person who could do that or control her is—"

"—Don't!" I snapped, turning in my seat to face Leila. It was a sobering moment—the only sobering moment I had. My eyes connected with hers. Her eyebrows pulled in together.

"I'm sorry," Leila whispered.

I swiped the tear off my cheek and turned back to face the road. "I can't believe you called me 'Sluterous.'"

The boys burst out laughing. "You did?" Talon looked at Leila in his rearview mirror.

Leila shrugged.

I flipped them all off.

This was the last night I spent getting shit-faced or having sex. I was upset that I didn't get one more hoorah in before coming to my senses, but I was glad that I had. Maddox left me. I meant nothing to him. The nights I sat crying on an empty street with a bottle of Johnny Walker clutched between my hands? Yep. For nothing. The night two creepy guys were trying to lure me into their car late at night while I was curled up drunk and yep, you guessed it—crying on the pavement, was for nothing. Thank fuck for older brothers. Only, not Maddox.

Present

"I know…" I whisper, squashing the bad memories that haunt me from the past year. I put the mess in hot mess during that time, but the one thing I gained through all the mess, is two brothers. I have noticed that the family doesn't speak of him while I'm around, which I'm grateful for. There's a raw wound with no cure that is stabbed into my heart where he's concerned. I'm just handling it a bit better now. A little…well, as long as no one says his name, I'll be fine. `

"My girl is moving to LA." Talon pulls me under his arm. I relax.

"Amethyst, are you sure this is the right thing to do?" my mom asks, pushing her hat lower to shade the beaming sun from her eyes.

I go to answer her, but catch Mason in the corner of my eye, and he gives me a little wave. If only. I bet things would have been different had I taken his path instead. I wave back, smiling, and he disappears with his family.

"Yes, Mom." I reach out and touch her hand reassuringly. "I promise I'll be fine."

"Well." Elliot puts his hand in his pocket. "If you ever need anything, you know where home is."

I give him a warm smile. "I do and thank you." For a year now, this has been my family. I feel a little guilty for it because it is his family more than it is mine, but I have continued to go for Sunday dinners every week, he hasn't. No one talks about what he is doing, but I know they must all talk with and to him, it's just never announced around me.

MADDOX

"Dux, I really don't like it…"

"Cass, you've always known that this was going to be my life. You walked away and then walked back in with my kid. You can't expect me to change all of what is me." My eyes go to Kennedy, who's sitting on the sofa with headphones on playing with her iPad. "Why is she playing on that bullshit?" I gesture to the iPad.

Cass glares. "Maddox, don't change the subject. She's on that because it's the way of the future."

I sigh. I'd fight her on the electronic thing later. Cassidy has always hated that I do MMA. Even at school, but even more so as an adult.

"You don't need to do this, Maddox! You're rich, a business owner—even at your age, and I rest my case. You do not need to."

"Cass, I don't expect you to understand this."

Her shoulders stiffen. "Would she understand this?"

I freeze, narrowing my eyes on her. "Cut the shit, Cassidy." My jaw flexes.

She moans. "Fine." Then she comes toward me, her palms resting on my cheeks. I search her blue eyes and soften slightly. "I'm sorry. You know how I get with her."

I did. I knew exactly how she got with Amethyst. Even so much as a mention about her and Cassidy turns into fucking Ursula from the Little Mermaid. I made that connection after watching it endlessly with Kennedy when she went through her mermaid phase.

Cassidy is insecure by nature because of her rough entry into the world. Everyone who was ever supposed to be there for her wasn't. I was her constant growing up, and I'm not going to lie by saying that she didn't mean anything to me, because she did. She does. But did the feelings I had for Cassidy match the same ones I had for Amethyst? Not even fucking close. After a year of not seeing Amethyst, I can still feel the burning need for her simmering beneath the surface. The feeling is like a sleeping volcano waiting to erupt. It's why we moved away from New York, way away, and settled in Las Vegas. With my fights at the MGM center and others, it seemed appropriate to move here. I've been going home once a month for the past year. To check on Dutch and see the family. Talon is definitely Kennedy's favorite uncle. Every time I go back, I go on a Saturday. Talon had said that Amethyst is there on Sundays and he didn't think she was stable enough to see me, and I got it. Completely got what she was feeling. It's just easier this way —to not see each other. I feared the day our eyes locked again, not for myself or for her, but for everyone around us that would feel the aftermath.

Cassidy kisses me and then scoops up her handbag that probably cost more than the average person's first car. "Can you make sure you send those out, then?"

I ignore what she is pointing to and look her up and down. "Where are you going?"

"Out with the girls." She punches some numbers into her phone and then shoots out the door. My eyes go to Rocky, our driver-slash-guard.

"Want me to follow her, boss?"

I clench my jaw a few times then shoot back my whiskey. "Nup. She can do what she wants."

Looking to the pile of envelopes on the counter, I reach for the bottle of whiskey and rip the cap off with my teeth.

"You alright, boss?" Rocky asks, watching me carefully. Rocky used to work for my dad, but I took him with me when I left.

"I don't know."

AMETHYST

My house is in West Hollywood down St. Ives Drive. Its architecture is second to none with the clean glass windows and the infinity pool that demands the view of Hollywood Hills.

"Of fucking course," I cuss, shaking my head and switching on the main lights. The emptiness sets off chills over my flesh. It's cold, and new, and way the hell not me at all. This is what I get for letting my mom, Elliot, and the boys choose my house.

"I don't want to bother you guys with it! It'll be fine. I'll grab a small cute cottage in town. Somewhere close to the studio so I can walk to work."

"Ah, no," Talon declared, heading for the fridge to take out the orange juice. Mom snatched it off him and poured it into a glass before he could wrap his caveman lips around the rim. "No sister of mine will be living like that."

Mom handed him the glass. "Amethyst, please let me do this for you," she insisted, coming toward me, taking my hands in hers. "Please." Her eyes searched mine pleadingly, and I knew I had to. Mom had always wanted to spoil me and give me everything in the world but never could. Now that she had Elliot, I guess she thought she could.

"It doesn't feel right, Mom."

Elliot resurfaced from somewhere down the hall, probably his office. "Amethyst, please, I insist."

I sighed. "Okay. Please nothing over the top, and I am paying the rent there every month, so nothing too extreme either. Also, it will need to be furnished for now."

They all looked at each other and then agreed. "Deal."

Clearly, they broke that deal, because this house is something I could never afford.

I drop a couple of my boxes—the only box's I had—to the floor. The loud bang breaking through the eerily silence.

"This is way too much." I shake my head, reaching for my phone. When I drove up the cramped road, I passed what looked to be mid-range houses, but this is not mid-range, this is extravagant.

I dial my mom's phone first, but no one answers, so I hang up and dial Talon.

He picks up. "…Hey!" there's shuffling in the background.

"Um, did I interrupt something?"

"What?" He clears his throat. "Oh, no, no way. What's up? You got there safely I see!"

"Hear," I correct, and then tilt my head, taking in the space. When you walk through the front door, you take a few steps down into a square looking lounge room. The entire wall ahead of me is glass and opens out onto the infinity pool in the back that has lights beaming through the water. LA twinkles in the night below. It's beautiful, but it's too much. I step forward.

"Breathe." Talon knows me. He knows that I'd be silently freaking out about the price of this place. "It's yours now, just accept it."

I shake my head. "I can't." I crank my head to look up above. The high ceiling carries on and just to the left is the twisted flight of stairs that lead up to a hallway that lines almost the entire upper-floor so you can look down from upstairs. "It's a lot to take in and I can't afford it, Talon!"

"Amethyst," he sighs. I hear a sharp intake of breath, not Talon, someone else.

"Who is there?" I ask, swallowing through the lump that has formed in my throat. Even though I ask, deep down I know who it is. My blood turns cold. "I've got to go—"

"Ame, Wait!—" I hang up the phone. Squeezing my eyes closed, I try to shake off the panic attack that's seeping into me. I haven't felt like this since that day…

Past

I wondered idly if I could diagnose myself with insomnia. Like, is that what people did? They just declared "Hey, I'm a shit sleeper, I must have a condition"? I wasn't sure, but the tossing and turning lately had eaten into the routine I usually had. I looked at the alarm clock that sat on my bedside table. Three a.m. Wasn't that witching hour?

I sighed, sitting up in my bed and turning on the light. Leila was at Wolf's for the one-hundredth time this week. I closed my eyes while sitting up. Why did I miss him? His touch, his kiss, his everything. Why. Why did he have to consume me at every turn? The universe was a bitch, because I could never have him. He wasn't mine anymore. Those words stung more than anything, even if it was from myself.

My phone started vibrating on my bedside table and I reached for it. It was weird, someone calling me at this hour, then I freaked out when I saw it was a number I didn't recognize. It could be someone the police calling... shit.

I swiped my phone to unlock and quickly pressed it to my ear. "Hello?" My voice was breathless, what from all the freaking out I had just done.

Silence.

I looked down to make sure the call was still connected. "Talon, if you think this is funny I'm going to kill you when I see you tomorrow. You know how I get on no sleep." I snuggle deeper into my covers and hit the light off. I don't know why I didn't just hang up. My eyebrows crossed. "Who is this?"

There was a sharp intake of breath on the other line. I froze, squeezing my phone.

"Maddox?" I whispered softly.

He didn't reply, but the call stayed connected. I woke the next morning at eight a.m. and opened up my call dialogue. Maybe I dreamed it. It wouldn't be the first time. Maddox visited me in my dreams every night in the form of a nightmare.

But there it was. That number. Was it the same number he

always had? I wouldn't know because I deleted it when he left. I opened the info of the call.

Call length: 4:42.87 seconds.

He had only just hung up.

I threw myself into studies after that phone call to busy myself or I'd think too much into it. I knew it was him, every single bit of me tingled with need. That's why I had to throw myself into work, because if I didn't, I'd get myself excited, when in actual fact, Maddox Stone will never be mine again.

Present

I push my phone into the back pocket of my jeans and take a tentative step deeper into the entryway. There's a large U shape lounge that is facing the glass wall in the sitting room and a small mini bar in the corner. The kitchen is to the left and is…I pop my head around the corner, yup, all crystal white.

I hate white. White represents purity, something I am not.

I like black. Black represents rebellion, something I am. Something I will carry with me until I'm grey and old.

I sigh and open the fridge door. Fully stocked with food. Great. My phone vibrates in my pocket again.

I open it and see a new text from Leila.

Lei: We gt ur car shipped there 2. It's in the garage. Don't be mad, I mean angry, Ame. This is your family, you're basically a Stone, and they take care of each other.

I reply out a text, punching each key way too hard.

Me: I hate you

My phone dings.

Lei: Will you still hate me if I tell you that me and the boys will be there in two sleeps?

I immediately lighten. Yes, this place is way too big for me. And too wealthy. But I can make it work, and anyway, I'll be mostly working a lot. I shoot back a text to Leila.

Me: I love you.

MADDOX

"Hey, baby." I pick Kennedy up from the floor and hug her into my chest. Her long legs dangle down my body. "You need to stop growing."

"Daddy, I'm fine," she laughs, going back to the floor. She picks up her iPad and starts playing her game. Fucking iPad.

"Uncle Talon is still your favorite, right?" Talon grins at her.

Kennedy giggles and nods. "Yes. But don't tell Uncle Wolf."

Talon seals his lips.

Liza hands me a glass of whiskey. "You okay? This dad thing looks good on you, but I must say…"

"What?" I answer, looking up at her and taking a drink. "I don't look happy? Bullshit because I am."

Talon gazes at Liza and gestures down to Kennedy. "Give us a minute?" Liza searches his eyes and then blinks at Kennedy.

She swallows nervously. "Um, what do I do with it?" She points to Kennedy.

Talon rolls his eyes.

She eventually takes Kennedy out of the room.

"Now." Talon sits beside me on the sofa and I inch down, my head resting on the back and my legs stretched wide.

My whiskey is resting on my knee and I have to fight every urge to get out of this room. We're all scarily linked together. We mostly know when one of us is feeling off-balance, so it doesn't surprise me that Talon is about to ask some questions. "You gonna spill what's going on with you and Cass? She's never here, dawg."

"Because she prefers going out with her girls than being a fucking mom."

"What?" Talon's brows tug together. "Kennedy is six, What do you mean?"

"I mean, since I've come back into the picture, Cass has been pretty much shoveling everything onto me. She thinks it's a punishment to me for missing all the years, but it's fucking not. Love my fucking kid, but now that Ken is older, she's starting to recognize that absence of her mom. It's not that she's a shit mom, because she's not. It's just she's too busy punishing me and not realizing that it's fucking up Kennedy. I'm 'bout ready to bounce up out of here."

"Why don't you? You know you don't need to do this. It's the twenty-first century, Maddox. It's okay to walk the fuck away…"

I shake my head. "It's not, though. You know that. I don't know. I'm going to have words with her later, give her an ultimatum. I just want what's best for Ken. I don't want her to end up messed up just because her mom and dad couldn't pull their shit together. She keeps fucking thinking I'm cheating on her too."

"You're not Dad, Maddox, you wouldn't cheat on Cassie."

"Wouldn't I?" My eyes connect with his, understanding softening his features. "A certain girl with pink hair might change your theory on that."

He chuckles. "We're going to her place after we leave here. Just to check in on her. Big city, new girl and all that."

I still. Every protective bone in my body damn near fractures. "If anything happens to her, Ta—"

Talon raises his eyebrows, cutting me off. "—As I said, she's a big girl, she can handle herself. You need to calm down."

When Talon and Dad first started looking at houses for her, I didn't like it. I fought them at every turn. I didn't want her there alone, fuck that. Especially as a fresh actress in the big city, I hated it. Still hate it, but Talon promised that she'd get the best of everything. When I saw the house, I laughed.

Instantly knew she'd hate it, which is why I gave the all clear, hoping she'd hate it enough to move her ass home.

I sigh and look ahead. "It's pointless, because either way, I lose, right?"

Talon gets up and pours himself a drink. "You don't have to lose, bro. Just do what's right."

"Right for who?" I ask. "Hmm? Because my morals say to be here with Cassie, but my soul and heart were claimed a long fucking time ago, and there's no child or relationship that can change that."

"Kennedy," Talon whispers, and instantly, I know what I need to do. I hate it. Every fucking inch of myself was repulsed by this, but I knew.

I pull my phone out and type a text out to Cass.

Me: This weekend, then it's done. Deal? No fucking invitations. No fucking bullshit.

I snatch the bottle of whiskey from Talon and take a long pull from the rim.

My phone dings.

Cass: Done.

"Fuck."

Talon looks at my phone and then at my face. "Wait, what did you just do?"

I swallow harshly and throw my phone onto the couch. "Can you and Wolf make it back here this weekend? Without Leila? And can you both keep a fucking secret?"

Talon's jaw clenches. "Yeah." He clears his throat. His knuckles turn white from gripping his glass. "Why, Maddox?"

I grit my teeth. "Because I'll need you to attend my fucking wedding."

CHAPTER 21

AMETHYST

JELLY ROLL'S "DEMONS" IS PLAYING THROUGH MY SURROUND sound system. It's wired to every room in the house, including outside. The crew is expected to be here any minute now, and I have just burnt the chicken.

Taking it out from the oven, I'm waving the dishcloth around in an attempt to get rid of the smoke when the doorbell rings.

"Oops."

I run to the front door, throwing the dishcloth over my shoulder. Swinging it open, my smile is about to break my face.

"Familia!" I put my arms out in front of myself.

Leila launches at me like I haven't seen her in years and I laugh, squeezing her tightly. "I missed you too!"

Our relationship is still odd, there's no denying that. We still fight more than we show affection, and I would still kill for her.

Talon snatches me out of Leila's grip, picking me up into a bear hug. I wrap my arms around his neck.

"Hey, T. I missed you!"

He puts me back down and Wolf takes me under his arm, walking me back into the kitchen. I give Liza a quick wave. Poor girl.

"Let me guess, we're eating take-out tonight?" Talon laughs, putting their bags on the floor.

"You are," I confirm, showing them into the kitchen. "At least I tried!"

Talon, Liza, and Leila go take in the view in the sitting room, but Wolf follows me into the kitchen.

"How you been, Rosé?"

I pull down some vodka and glasses, putting them on a tray. "How long do you have?" I wink at him. "I'll always be ok."

Nirvana's "Heart-Shaped Box" is now playing. We're all sitting around in the oversized sitting room, sucking down Chinese take-out and almost an entire bottle of vodka.

"This place is holy shit amazing," Liza admits, putting her empty box on the small coffee table.

"It is. At first, it was overwhelming, but I've decided I'm going to buy it off Elliot and Mom. I've sort of fallen in love with it. Obviously, it needs some Amethyst touches, like a skate rink by the pool, but it already feels like home."

I take a shot of my vodka. "Okay, so seriously, are you guys moving?" I ask Leila. She had said that they were moving away, but didn't say anything else.

"Yes!" She looks to Wolf, who then looks at me.

"I need to ask you something," Leila grins, shooting back her drink.

I wait.

"Will you be my maid of honor?"

My heart clenches in excitement. "Oh my God! Of course!" I fly onto her lap and squeeze her. "Holy shit, Lei!" I lean back and touch her cheeks. "Wait! Where's the ring?" I climb off her and tuck my legs under my butt. She pulls the ring out of her pocket and puts it back onto her finger.

"Tada!"

I gasp.

"It's beautifully over the top." I grin, looking at Wolf. "Therefore, it's perfect. Oh my gosh! It's going to be the wedding of the century!"

Then my heart snaps. My face falls and my blood turns to ice.

Leila clears her throat. "Yes, which is why I knew I had to be careful. Look, I totally understand if—"

"—No!" I shake my head, filling up my shot glass. "Fuck no. I'm totally over all of that shit. I can't wait! When's the date? Do we know?"

Hopefully it'll give me enough time to pull my shit together.

"Six months."

"Okay." I should play poker, I could win big with the face I'm pulling right now.

"Hey!" Wolf nudges his head at me. His hair has gotten longer, now hanging around his neck. "Don't even sweat it. Six months is a long time away."

"Totally," I wave them off, swallowing my drink. "A long, loonnngg time away." Someone should probably cut me off.

"There's something else," Talon interjects.

I don't miss the silent exchange between him and Wolf.

"What is it?" I start filling up all of their shot glasses.

"This weekend... Maddox is getting married."

The bottle slips between my fingers, splashing over Liza. It feels as though someone has punched me in the gut.

"Shit," I exclaim, picking up the bottle. "I'm so sorry, Liza."

"It's ok!" Liza runs into the kitchen and comes back with a dishcloth.

I'm going to cry.

No, you're not. You're going to boss up.

Nope, I'm going to cry.

I can do both because now I'm crying.

I sob, falling back onto my butt. I'll blame it on the vodka.

Talon wraps his arm around me. "I gotchu, baby girl. It's going to be ok."

I know now. Maddox and Amethyst were over for good. I had to close, not just that chapter of my life, but the whole damn book and start on a brand-new novel—hopefully with no typos this time.

AMETHYST
6 Months Later

MY EYES ACHE FROM THE TEARS THEY HAVE SPILLED, MY HEART is now tarnished by love. Love is supposed to be something that saves the world, but it couldn't even save me. I swipe the tears off my cheeks.

"I loved him," I mutter, so softly even though there's no one here to hear. I hate this place and these walls. "If these walls could talk, would they give away everyone's secrets?"

Probably not, I think to myself. I stand up on the single bed, looking out the window that demands the freshly mowed meadow. The sign *Hickleberry Psychiatric Ward* sways with the wind, but it's okay, because this will be the last time I see it. The last time I see anything.

Everyone thinks I'm crazy, and maybe I am, but that's because love. I may be crazy, but love drove me there. He's married.

I hook the rope loop around my head until it's resting around my neck, and squeeze my eyes closed.

"I love you."

Then I take the final step off the bed.

"Cut!" Tim, the director yells, pulling off his headphones. "You did well, kid!" I jump down from the step and unhook myself from the rope.

"Thanks, but that was..." I shiver, taking a Styrofoam cup of coffee from my assistant. I blow into the cup.

"Amethyst, I have you scheduled for an interview this weekend with E! Hollywood, if you give me some—"

I shake my head. "No, I can't. I have my best friend's wedding this weekend, so I'm heading home. I thought I told you about that?" I say, grabbing my handbag and oversized sunglasses.

The show has really, really kicked off over the last six months. Now I successfully have paparazzo's camping outside my house. Brilliant.

From being on a TV show.

I'm not Angelina Jolie huge, obviously, but famous enough to gain a lot of attention.

"No, you didn't," Alesha says, rubbing her temples. "It's okay, I'll clear your schedule this weekend."

"Thanks," I smile at her.

Arms wrap around my stomach, kisses pressing to the back of my neck. "Hey, baby, you ready to hit it?" Travis Deshell. My boyfriend-slash-co-worker.

"Yup!" I pop the P, pulling my glasses down over my eyes. We walk out of Studio 32 and head toward his red Ferrari. I sigh in annoyance.

It took me a while to warm up to Travis and his over-the-topness, but in all honesty, because of Leila, I am well acquainted with his breed now.

"Have you packed your bags?" Travis asks, looking at me over his arm.

I nod, drinking my coffee and being careful not to spill it on the upholstery.

"I like the black." I point to the new leather interior. Travis grins, flooring it onto the 101.

I touch my hair. "Oh, shit!" Pulling the very realistic looking wig off my head, I toss it onto the ground and take my freshly colored pink hair out of the ridiculous knot.

Travis groans. "Babe, I do love the pink, don't get me wrong, but I dig natural looking girls…you're twenty-three now. Don't you think it's time you go back to a natural color?"

I'm used to Travis's digs at my appearance. "Baby, you're so fucking exotic. Ditch the pink hair….if you were just a dress size smaller….babe, should you be eating that? Holy fuck, is that a zit?"

I never understood why he even started dating me if he was going to bitch about changing me. I, on the other hand, didn't really care. I'm not sure how I feel about Travis, but for now, he keeps my bed warm and the void penetrated—not filled.

I smile. "I'm good. Thanks."

"Alright, just saying, in the photos this weekend…"

I zone him out, my thoughts now dancing around in all the different scenarios this weekend could bring. The night I found out about Maddox getting married was bad. I drank two other bottles of vodka and ended up in the hospital getting my stomach pumped. I then had alcohol poisoning for the following weeks. Because I was still sick from that night, the weekend of Maddox's wedding I purchased an ounce of weed and smoked like Cheech and Chong's long-lost cousin. It wasn't pretty. I could've out-smoked Snoop Dogg. There was crying, Doritos stuck to my hair, and a lot of Lenny Kravitz and Marilyn Manson playing, but eventually, it knocked my ass out. I was thankful for that, at least. From that weekend onwards, I vowed that I wouldn't give Maddox another thought. He was a married man. Signed, sealed, and fucking delivered. Only, when the nights got cold and loud thunder clapped angrily in the sky, I couldn't help but curl into a ball in my bed and allow my thoughts to drift off to the bad boy I almost had.

It was hard, losing someone. I don't mean to death. Death was explainable. Mourning the loss of someone you loved who still lives, is unimaginable pain.

I'm over him now. I'm ready to see him.

We're boarding the plane when Talon texts me.

My favorite brother: Safe travels, Rosé.

I chuckle. He had changed his name on my phone a while ago, and put My moody brother under Wolf's name.

Me: Be there soon. Have the Vodka ready.

He texts back instantly.

My favorite brother: You better be joking…

I was. I think.

MADDOX

"Daddy! Nana wants your help with something!" Kennedy yells out from my dad's study. She's always called Jessica nana. It doesn't rub me the wrong way, but I wasn't sure how Amethyst would warm to it. I knew that she would love Kennedy. Amethyst would make a fucking great mom. It's just a little messed up. The thought of someone making Amethyst a mom makes me feel feral.

I walk into the study and see Jessica balancing on one of my dad's office chairs, reaching for one of the books on his shelf.

"What're you doing?"

She sighs in defeat and jumps off the chair. "I'm trying to get my family album from the top. It has a bunch of old photos in it, but mainly it has a photo of the day Leila and Amethyst met. They were both scolding each other, but you could see how much they were going to get along. It was their first day of college and they had just met in their dorm. I figured it was a great time to snap a shot."

My throat swells, but I swallow, knowing Kennedy is in the room.

"Nana, how come I've never met Amethyst? Isn't she my aunt?"

I choke on my spit and jump up on the chair. "I'll grab it down." There isn't a day that passes that I don't think of her—of course. I fucking watch every episode of that shitty fucking show she's on.

Four Months Earlier

The front door slamming had me launching out of my bed. I turned the light on and ran down the stairs.

"Oops, did I wake you?" Cassidy stumbled into the kitchen and tossed her house keys onto the counter.

I crossed my arms in front of myself.

Her eyes raked over my body. "Mmmm, all mine."

Hardly.

"What the fuck time is this, Cass?"

She squinted at the oversized clock that hung on the kitchen wall. "Um, it says four?"

I pushed off the wall and went to the fridge, taking out a chilled bottle of water. I shoved it into her chest. "Drink." Then I turned, ready to go back to bed when her words faltered my steps.

"Why are you so mean to me? You never used to be this mean in high school!"

I turned to face her. "I'm not a kid anymore, Cass."

Her shoulders straightened. I knew what was coming. She tucked her freshly cut jaw length hair behind her ear. "Because I'm not her?"

"Shut the fuck up and go to bed." I didn't like her talking about Amethyst.

"We don't even sleep in the same bed! We hardly have sex and when we do, you borderline hurt me! Speaking of connections, the only time we really have had one, Maddox, was after the transplant—then poof! It was like everything shifted and you went back to hating me again."

I chuckle, walking to her. "Yeah, because I did that for Ken, and I'd do it again and again if I needed to, but let's get one thing straight...I didn't want you, Cass. I didn't. I wanted my kid, but I married you because I thought it was the right thing to do, and yeah, I fucking hurt you during sex, wanna know why?" She gulped, looking up at me. I smirked, leaning into her ear and whispered, "Because I want to fucking kill you, Cass, but it's the only time I can hurt you without it being abuse." Then I straightened, pointing to her bedroom. "Leave it at that and go to fucking bed."

She shook her head. "I deserve more."

I snort. "That's pushing it, but sure thing, babe, whatever the fuck you need to tell yourself."

I walked to the sofa and drop down, squeezing my eyes shut.

"I love you, Maddox. I would do anything for you, for us and our marriage. Everyone knew it was us. We were meant to be together."

"Says fucking who, Cass?" I yelled, losing my cool and shooting off the sofa. "No one I know would say that! In fact, quite the fucking opposite. Take your ass to fucking bed. Now."

She finally left, sulking. It's not that she's a bad mom. It's that she can be neglectful at times, and she's lazy. But she loves Kennedy and spoils her. If anything, she's a good mom, but the drinking and going out with friends isn't good. I get that moms need to have a break, but she breaks every fucking night.

I flip on the TV and watch the reruns of Amethyst's show. Then click on "After Hours with the Cast." I had never seen that option before, it must've been new. I run my fingers through my hair and pushed play.

I shouldn't have.

Amethyst's pink hair glosses against the studio lights, her sharp jaw and nose still as perfect as ever. Her blue eyes look into the lens and it's as though she's in the room with me right this second. Every fucking beat. The air gets sucked out of me when I see her coworker kiss her on the neck.

"So how long have you and Travis Deshel been an item?"

I launched the remote across the room.

Fuck.

Present

"You'll meet her tonight!" Jessica says to Kennedy. I snatch the book and jump off the chair.

"Yeah, baby. You'll love her."

"Mom said that I won't."

I clench my jaw. Your mom doesn't know shit.

Jessica's gaze comes to mine, worry lines creasing her forehead.

I lean down to Kennedy and brush her hair away from her face. "Go and help Uncle Tal with the pool."

"Okay." She skips out.

I stand, looking at Jessica.

"She's bringing Travis—" Jessica starts saying, but I cut her off, shoving my hands into my pockets.

"I know," I answer smoothly, but everything inside of me is roaring to the surface.

"She doesn't know about you and Cassidy, or anything to do with you."

"I know," I repeat because I did know. Leila made sure to rub it in my face every chance she got that Amethyst was over me.

"How is Cassidy?" Jessica asks, leaning on Dad's office desk. I know she doesn't actually care, but she's making it out as if she does.

"Back to doing her own thing."

"She finally let you go? Even after the suicide attempt?"

I flinch.

"She had no choice."

"Are you bringing a date?" Jessica counters.

Jesus, it's like a damn interrogation. Cassidy and I split after that night. Cass was a lot of things, but she knew that we both weren't happy and agreed. That wasn't before she tried to OD on pills. She said it was an accident, and I wanted to believe her, because again, she was a great mom and loved Ken, but I knew she loved me too.

"Yes." Then I turn and leave the office. I didn't, and I didn't know that she was bringing fucking Travis or I would have. Now I have about four hours to find a date to this fucking wedding.

It took me thirty-seconds.

AMETHYST

Pulling into the familiar driveway, raw memories flash before my eyes, and every single one of them has one thing in common. Maddox.

God, I really hope he isn't here.

"You okay, baby?" Travis squeezes my knee. I look at him and smile, even though he's chewing that gum like his life depends on it.

"Yup."

I get out of the car, just as Rocky, the sexy driver for Elliot comes out the door.

"Well, hello there." I wiggle my eyebrows at him. It was just after mid-morning, so if he didn't catch my flirty tone, he would definitely see the smirk on my lips.

He laughs. "Hello Amethyst, so nice to finally see you again."

I grin, pulling him in for a hug. Hard muscles, everywhere. Almost as hard as—

Travis clears his throat.

I pull back. "Sorry, Travis, this is Rocky, my mom and Elliot's driver-guard. Rocky, this is my boyfriend, Travis."

Rocky gives a curt nod, then clears his throat. "Actually, I'm with Maddox now."

Travis glares.

"Anyway!" I clap my hands together, ignoring the mention of Maddox. "Where's the fam?"

Travis and I are walking through the front door when Leila runs toward me at full speed.

I catch her just in time, but we both tumble to the floor. "It's amusing that even after all this time, you both still can't behave yourself in public," Talon chuckles from somewhere.

I squeeze her. "Hey, lover. Wanna get up off me."

She climbs off and helps me to my feet. "You guys took so long!" she whines.

"Well, sorry to disappoint, but it's not like we could speed the plane up!" I brush my harem pants down and swipe my hair out of my face. I like to think that my dress style is essentially still the same, much to Travis's disgust. The harem pants, though, I've got nothing. They're comfortable, so they're a win.

"Stop wearing those Aladdin pants," Leila says, hooking her arm in mine. And there she is.

Mom comes around the corner with an apron around her waist. "Hi, honey!" She pulls me in for a hug.

"Hi, Mom!" I squeeze her back, realizing Travis is still in here and hadn't met anyone yet. I turn to face him.

"Fam, this is Travis, Travis, this is Fam. Everyone, be nice..." I smile at Travis.

"No promises..." That voice. It is like a mac truck plows into my chest. I suck in a breath and step aside for Mom to walk to Travis.

My eyes go to Maddox, and another truck slams into me. "Hi."

Maddox clenches his jaw.

He's mad.

A tight smile flashes over his face, but his eyes impassively stay on mine. "Hey, Rosé."

I lick my lips, needing a distraction from the silent room. He looks...well, how he always looks. Seems to have a few new tattoos on his arms and neck, but he's still delectable. Broad shoulders, a few day's scruff on his jaw, but not too much. Enough that you can still see his prominent cheekbones and deadly cut of his jawbone. Dressed in a casual

Henley and dark jeans, he's every bit of sexy that I remembered.

This doesn't help.

My eyes close. This is too much.

"I like your hair!" a little voice says, and my eyes pop open. I look down to the small girl and my heart starts pounding in my chest. I'd be lying if I said I wasn't nervous about meeting Kennedy, but, then she smiles up at me and I see Maddox in her.

Instantly, I relax. I kneel down to her level and pull it out of the high ponytail it was in. "Wanna touch it?"

Her lips tug in together and she bobs her head. "Yes please."

Her hands come to my hair, and everyone around me seems to go back to their chattering. Even if they didn't, I wouldn't know, because all I see is her. God, she's beautiful. Has long dark wavy hair, dark almond shaped eyes and squishy little cheeks. The cheeks must be from her mom, Maddox doesn't have those cheeks. But she has Maddox's square-shaped profile and thick dark eyelashes. My eyes drop to her lips. Pouty and pinched cherry. She's perfection.

"My name's Kennedy," she says sweetly, fiddling with my hair.

"I know," I answer. I can't help but smile. "You're beautiful."

She sighs. "So are you. Do you want to play with me?"

I chuckle.

"Ken, Amethyst just got here, I'm sure she's tired, baby," Maddox interrupts us.

My gaze darts over her shoulder and lands on Maddox. He looks like he's struggling with something internally, I'll leave that for now. "No," I shake my head. "I want to!" I pat her arm and stand, looking over my shoulder at Travis. "You'll be okay for a while. They don't bite." I gesture to my family.

Travis dips his head in greeting.

"I mean… don't I?" Maddox adds through a chuckle.

I glare at him, but he regards me with a grin. Winking at me, he ambles past and heads for Travis. "Chill, Rosé, you know how I like to play…"

Shit. I need to tell him that Travis doesn't know about him and I. People have always said how if you put Maddox and I in the same room together, the universe feels as though it stops. We had that undeniable pull toward each other. When we were together, it was our world, everyone else merely existed in it. I hope they were all wrong.

I touch my hair and notice Kennedy had done a crooked side plait. I take her hand. "Come on then."

I'm getting dragged away when I pass Elliot. I quickly wave to him and let the little minion do her worst.

"I like makeup," Kennedy says, brushing—I lost count how many layers of blush on my cheeks.

"I see that."

"But I also like fast cars."

I grin. "It's okay to be a little bit of both."

We're in her room, well the one she has when she stays here. It's pink and blue, just like my walls when I was a kid. The feelings I have for this little girl are already indescribable. I thought I'd be a nervous wreck meeting her for the first time, but I have nothing but love.

"My mom says that I shouldn't like boy stuff."

I hated her before, now I hate her more. "Well, you should always listen to your mom, but in this case, I would say not to. You should never change who you are inside for anyone. Not even your mom." And she's going to hate me too now. If she didn't already.

We spend the rest of the day together. Going from makeup,

to dress ups, to sneaking into my mom's chocolate stash she keeps under her bed. Kennedy found that super resourceful.

We're snuggled under the covers of my bed with the Grand Prix playing on the television when the door opens, revealing Maddox.

"Shhh," I push my finger to my lips. "She's asleep."

Maddox enters the room farther, his eyes going from her to me. He leans on the edge of the bed.

"She had a bath and got changed. She wanted to sleep with me tonight, but I said we could have a sleepover the last night I'm here."

Maddox shakes his head in amazement. "She doesn't like anyone."

I chuckle, slipping my arm out from under her. I wiggle the pins and needles loose. "Well, that's another thing we have in common."

"I see she had fun with you…" He gestures to my hair and face.

I snort. "Yeah, I forgot about that. I better have a shower." I want to get away for a second. Since being home, it's Maddox everywhere. I've gone from not seeing him in almost two years, to seeing him a whole lot more. It's hard being around him and not being able to *be* around him. I'm struggling already, and I shouldn't be because I'm with Travis. Travis, my boyfriend who I haven't even thought about for the entire day because I've been causing havoc with my tiny raven-haired princess.

I'm reaching the bedroom door when Maddox says, "Thanks, Rosé."

I throw up deuces on my way out, ignoring the stabbing pain in my heart.

CHAPTER 25

AMETHYST

"I'M A LITTLE AFRAID FOR THIS BACHELOR PARTY," TIFFANY says, pushing her tits up farther while checking herself out in the mirror. I hadn't met Tiffany before today. She's apparently Leila's new BFF and a bridesmaid, along with Liza and me. Not sure I like her.

"You should be," I tsk, tipping back my drink. We all separated this morning. The guys getting a hotel on one side of New York, and us on the other. Fitting.

Leila brushes us off. "Nonsense. It's going to be great."

Liza's eyes come to mine and widen. I chuckle. "Sure, sure."

Tiffany comes off as somewhat superficial. Not to be judgmental or anything, but when I met her this morning, I noticed the up and down look she gave me when Leila introduced us, and the fake smile she put on instantly after. Leila has a habit of making shitty friends. No doubt Tiffany is one of them. Straight long white hair and bright red lips, I didn't say she was unattractive, she's just. Fake.

Liza glides the wand of her lip gloss over her lips, looking at me in the mirror. I was ready before all of them, my hair took the longest because it's so long, but as far as foundation and contouring went, I didn't. Tinted moisturizer, eyeliner, mascara and smoky eyeshadow with bare lips was me tonight. I wave my hair out, but it still hangs to my tailbone. It is getting extremely long.

I pour some vodka in my glass and take a sip.

"You sure you should be doing vodka tonight?" Liza asks with a quirked eyebrow.

I chuckle. "Yes. Even more so."

"Aw, sweetie, can't you handle your alcohol?" Tiffany says, turning to face me with a hand on her hip.

I blink at Leila, counting to two in my head.

Leila laughs, waving me down. "Calm down, B." She winks at me and then scowls at Tiffany. "Amethyst can more than handle herself."

The limo pulls up outside our hotel and Rocky gets out, opening our door. "Hello, ladies."

Leila squeezes his cheeks before sliding in. I'm last.

I pat his cheek and tap his chest. "I promise to behave tonight."

He rolls his eyes and winks. He knows me well too.

The music is blaring with some old school 50 Cent and the girls are laughing. We pull into the first nightclub. Getting out, we make our way to the bouncers who instantly let us in. With a moaning line of thirsty women, and I don't mean for a drink, Leila flips them all off and we shuffle in behind her. Diva.

I'm a lot of drinks in when I draw Leila away from Tiffany and Liza. Liza glares at me as we leave her there to a chatty Tiffany in a private booth.

Leila and I start grinding against each other and dirty dancing to "Do You Mind" from Khalid and Nicki Minaj. I stand up onto the stage the DJ booth is on and grip onto one of the poles. My attention aimlessly drifts to one of the small TVs in the bar and I see Maddox on the screen during a fight.

I still. The advert that is playing is promoting his upcoming fight. Fuck.

The room starts spinning and all the faces in the crowd turn to a smudge of oil paint. I grind against the pole to the song.

I'm drunk.

For sure.

It feels good. God, why'd Leila have to get married.

I grip around the pole and twirl.

Why did my mom have to stay with Elliot.

My leg wraps around the pole.

Why did I have to still be in love with Maddox.

I roll my body off the pole.

Why—I'm tossed over a set of hard shoulders. Shoulders that are pressing into my belly.

My stomach hurls and I close my eyes, trying to ignore the juggling of movement.

"Put me down," I murmur, but my voice is drowned out by the music. Shit.

Finally, I'm swung down to my feet. Maddox is glaring at me. "You're getting me jealous, sit your ass down."

I gulp, taking a seat beside Leila in the booth.

"Um, why are you guys here?" Tiffany laughs. "You're not supposed to be here."

Leila and Liza both roll their eyes.

I snort. "They're Stone brothers." I cut my glare at Tiffany. "Like hell would Wolf allow his bride-to-be unleashed without him." I think I'm going to puke. My hand goes to my mouth.

Tiffany's eyebrow raises. "Hmmm, my kind of men…"

"Well, they're all taken!" I snap before I can stop myself. "Goddamnit. Fucking vodka."

There's chuckling around the table, but my eyes go to a now smug looking Maddox. "That right, Rosé?"

Yes, goddamnit. You're mine. That's what I want to say, but I don't. Thankfully.

I can almost feel Tiffany sneering at me.

"Had a bit too much vodka, huh, baby sis?" Talon grins at me from beside Liza. The flashing strobe lights are hitting the wooden booth chairs recklessly, it's making my head spin a little.

I nod like a child. I hate drunk Amethyst.

"Give her some water, Lei, we don't want another trip to the hospital…" Talon waves his hand toward me casually.

"I'm fine…"

Maddox's head snaps to Talon. "What?"

"You said those exact words about thirty minutes before you were ass deep in nurses." Talon glares at me.

"What the fuck happened?" Maddox leans forward, looking at Talon.

Silence, aside from Pretty Ricky's "Get You Right" banging softly through the sound system. A little weird for club music, they must be getting ready to close.

I stare at Maddox, who is already blatantly glaring at me, and now he looks pissed.

"For fuck's sake, Maddox!" I snap. "Why is it every time I look at you, you look like you're either going to rip my head or my clothes off!"

He tilts his head, his fist clenching on the table. "Because those are the two things I always want to do to you, Amethyst! Like fucking clockwork."

"Then fucking do it already!"

Oops. Wait, do what?

"Get up." He pulls me up by my hand.

"Ah, guys, as much as I had money on you both lasting shorter than this to finally start this whole push and pull thing again, need I remind both of you that Amethyst is taken?"

I rip my hand out of his. "And you're married!" Oops. Did I yell? Why'd the music change.

Maddox wraps his hand around my chin and squeezes, pulling my face close to his. "Was married."

"Ah." Too late, I'm being dragged out of the booth by the angry caveman as we duck and weave between the sea of sweaty corpses. Gross. Hitting the outside, Maddox has his hand in mine, our fingers intertwined together. He fist-punches a couple of the bouncers, tugging me under his arm. I don't pull away. I should. Vodka.

We start walking down the empty street when he finishes talking with the bouncer, heading toward God knows where. When the club is out of sight and it's just our breathing filling the space between us, he squeezes my hand.

"I can't do this with you again, Maddox." I can't breathe, everything is now moving in slow motion.

He stops and turns me to face him, his arm hooking around my waist and pulling me into his body. "Do what?"

I swallow. "This."

"Oh, you mean this?" He leans down until his lips touch mine.

"Maddox," I whisper hoarsely through a choked breath.

"That's my name, baby, but I preferred it when you were screaming it from my bed."

My thighs clench.

He chuckles and then licks my lower lip. He goes to step back, but before I can stop myself, I lean up on tippy toes, reaching behind his neck and pulling his lips to mine. He stills, probably in shock, and then growls into my mouth and picks me up from the back of my thighs. I wrap them around him. He leads us into a dark alley, his fist buried in my hair. Smashing me against the cold brick wall, I moan. He licks the space between my boobs and tears down one part of my strapless top, popping my nipple into his mouth. I grind against him. He pulls his jeans down slightly, his thumb pressing against my clit on his way up. He tugs my panties to the side, brings his fingers up to his mouth, his eyes staying on mine, and then sucks me off his finger.

He grins. "Mine."

I force my lips back to his and suck his bottom one into my mouth.

He pauses, his breathing so deep his chest rises and falls, pressing against mine with every second. He searches my eyes again. "There have been fucking countless times I've pictured this going down, all times with my dick in my hand." He growls again. "But, baby, I'm going to fucking ruin you right now. Remember when I said that I loved you?" He leans down to the side of my neck and bites my ear. "Hmm? Remember those times I told you I loved you, Amethyst? Answer me, baby."

I swallow. "Yes."

"Think of that for the next few minutes, because I'm about to fuck you like I hate you."

He pushes inside of me and my eyes roll to the back of my head. His hand comes to the front of my throat. He squeezes roughly, pounding into me. The grit from the brick wall is grazing against my back, but I feel nothing. Nothing but his invasion inside of me. It's not long until his lips come to mine, his tongue slipping into my mouth as both of us come undone.

He lowers me to the ground, both of us panting. I fix my top and hair, and then turn and walk away from him.

"Amethyst!" he calls out, chasing me down the street. I'm swiping angry tears away from my eyes when he finally reaches me. His hand comes to mine, but I pull away, glaring at him.

"Why!" I scream, hitting his chest. "Why the fuck me? You ruined me, Maddox! You left me! For her!"

"For Kennedy, Amethyst! Fuck!" He pulls at his hair. I kick

my shoes off. Stupid fucking heels. Whose idea was it to wear these stupid fucking things. I start running.

"You and I both know you won't run for long, baby," Maddox yells out.

Bastard.

I start huffing not even ten seconds in.

"Asshole." I slow to a very fast walk. He catches up again, his hand coming to mine.

"Wanna talk about it?" he asks, his thumb tracing circles around mine.

"No, I don't. I have a boyfriend—"

"—who is a fucking piece of shit."

I glare at him. "You don't know him!"

Maddox snorts. "Don't have to know people to figure out they're a fucking piece of shit, Amethyst. Some people don't hide their dirty fucking flaws, they air them out for the world to see—that's how shitty they are!"

"And you?" I ask, suddenly tired from the fucking and the fighting. "Where do you sit on the spectrum, Maddox."

"I sit right wherever the fuck you are."

He pulls out his phone and punches in some digits. "Stop here, I'll get Rocky to come."

I stop because I'm tired. And hungry. He leads me to a bench and I sit beside him, watching the branches on the trees that are lined down the street sway with the wind.

"I loved you."

"Love..." he corrects.

I pause.

He continues, "You're a lot of things, Amethyst, but you're not a liar, so do you want to prove me wrong and lie right now?"

His fingers interlace with mine. I draw in a breath. I smell of him, all over my clothes, on my skin. Inside me... he's everywhere physically now, not just in my head, not just some-where where I can hide him.

"Love." I yank away from him and rest my face in my hands, knees to elbows. "God, Maddox! I couldn't survive you a second time!" I turn to face him. He's looking forward, his jaw doing that tick-tock thing. It's like a count-down timer to how quickly he's going to lose his shit.

I have about three seconds.

"We'll speak about your little vodka and hospital trip later."

I roll my eyes.

"Don't fucking roll your eyes at me, Amethyst, or I'll fuck you so hard you'll question your need to live."

I sigh like a scolded teen. "You know what—" The limo pulls up and I stand. "Finally!"

I get into the back seat, my arms crossing. "Yours or mine?" Maddox asks, like he already knows.

"Yours, but food first."

AMETHYST

WHITE. THE WALLS ARE ALL WHITE. I HATE WHITE. WHY DO hotels use white? It's probably the worst color you could choose with how high maintenance it would be. How many fucking times would they need to do repaints? My head hurts. I moan, crawling out of bed but trying to not wake Maddox.

I go to the kitchen and busy myself with coffee, waiting for the guilt to hit me. I hate cheating, hate it, but why don't I feel guilty? I'd never in my life cheat on Maddox and I can say that with one hundred percent certainty. I'd rather tear off my arm than ever cheat on Maddox, so is the saying really true about leopards never changing their spots? I'm thinking it more has to do with who's worth changing them for.

I'm a slut.

Oh God.

I massage my temples. "Fuck me."

Maddox hooks his arm around my waist. "If you're offering and all that good shit, then..."

He kisses my head with a chuckle and goes to the fridge. I look up at him, glaring from under my eyelashes. "Why don't I feel like a bad human right now?"

He flips the lid off the milk and brings the rim to his mouth, his eyes staying on mine. He lowers it and I watch as his tongue comes out and licks the white from his upper lip.

Is it hot in here or what?

His hair is messy but still short. His eyes piercing, his muscles. Oh God, his muscles.

Abort.

Focus.

"Seriously, Maddox…"

He drops the milk carton to the counter, his triceps twitching with the movement. "Because you've always been mine, Amethyst. If anything, you've been cheating on me with him."

I freeze. "Fuck you. You got married!"

He flinches slightly, but before I can overanalyze his reply, it's gone and he has his cocky smirk back on his face. "Whatevz, baby. You know why I did it, my brothers know, hell, fucking Leila knows! It's you that still needs to figure it out."

I wince. "Kennedy is beautiful. Tell me about her."

He puts a couple bagels into the toaster and leans against the counter. I watch as his face lights up. "She's perfect. I can't believe I helped create her." He turns to take the bagels out and tosses them onto a couple plates.

I grin, blowing on my coffee. "And you and her mom?"

I had to fake that smile.

He shakes his head. "A mess. Nothing was ever there, but we gave it a good run, for Kennedy."

"And now?"

He stares at me. "Now, we remain good friends for Ken."

I nod, placing my mug on the counter. "I don't know what to do…"

He hands me my bagel. "Simple," he bites into his and smirks. "Choose me."

I lick my lips. "I do, Maddox," I exhale, raking my fingers through my hair. "No question, I'd always choose you."

"Then what's the issue?" he asks.

I pause and mentally try to grasp something. Anything. Mental list. I'll make a mental list.

Maddox: 100

Travis: 5

I groan. "I just…"

"Give me today. Give me today, and by the end of it, if you tell me no, I'll walk away from you forever and you'll never see me again."

I wince from the physical pain those words give me, my chest tightening. That should be my first clue that I'll never be able to walk away from him, but my hand comes to my chest and I exhale. "Fine."

We finish breakfast, and both get ready for the day. After our long shower, I flip my phone onto airplane mode after sending a quick text to Travis and another to Leila. I lied to Travis, but not to Leila. She's shit at keeping everyone's secrets, but she always keeps mine. Travis has been staying at the house, probably occupied by Mom, whereas the girls will still be at the hotel.

Pushing my phone into my back pocket, Maddox comes out of the bathroom after brushing his teeth. "You ready?"

I tug at the edge of my leather jacket. "Yes." Thank God Rocky went and rescued my bags from our hotel this morning, or I would have been screwed.

AMETHYST

WE START AT KRISPY KREME. HE ORDERS ME A TIRAMISU AND gets his cinnamon sugar one, then we get coffee and make our way toward the beach. After the beach, we head to the skate park and make stupid jokes about how much we'd changed since the last time we sat at that same halfpipe. The sun is going down and the air has a soft breeze to it. He pulls me under his arm and leads me back to the limo.

Kissing my head, he exhales. "Always loved you and always will."

I warm at those words. They're like drinking a hot caramel latte in the middle of a blizzard during a twenty-day sugar fast. He opens the door and I slide in. He gets in behind me and I wriggle back under his arm.

"I don't want this to end."

"It doesn't have to," he answers, kissing my head. "Just say the word, baby, and it's done."

"I—" I pause. Shit.

"I want to take you to one more place." His eyes catch Rocky's in the rearview mirror, then he nods gently.

"Ok," I say, mostly because I really don't want this day to end. I want to bottle it up and take it with me everywhere I go.

We drive into the country more, on the outskirts of the city. The car pulls off into a shoulder on a long stretch of road. "Where are we?"

Maddox's eyes drift out the window behind me. I turn to see where he's looking, and I know instantly where he has taken me.

The crash site.

He gets out of the car from my side and I take a couple deep breaths before following. Cars are zipping past at crazy speeds, my hair flying up from the force. I tuck some strands behind my ear.

"This is the first time I've come here."

I lean into him until his arm comes behind me. "Why'd you choose now?"

He kisses my forehead. "Because if I never see you again after today, I won't ever want to do this with anyone else, not even alone."

I swallow. We stand there for a few seconds, and I study the white cross that is implanted into the grass.

"She would have loved you."

"I think I would have loved her too," I reply, leaning my head against him.

We stay for around thirty minutes before getting back into the car. We were almost back at our parents' house when I turn to face Maddox.

I know what I need to do. There's no way I can walk away from him—ever. I never want to and I never could. There's no point wasting Travis's time when I want Maddox. How is that fair to anyone? Travis may be an ass, but that doesn't mean my principles have to lower.

I search his eyes and lick my lips. "I want you."

He glares at me. "I know. Now get rid of that fool."

My stomach turns in excitement. We're doing this, finally. Finally, Maddox and I are going to be together.

Maddox kisses me again. "Now, baby. I'm done with this shit."

I slip out of the car and head into the house. Everything moves in slow motion. Travis stands from the sofa in the sitting room when I enter.

Guilt tickles my belly, but not because I regret the day and night I spent with Maddox, but because I have a heart.

Travis smiles, but then his smile drops when his eyes go over my shoulder.

"I knew it," he whispers, but it was in disbelief. "I fucking knew it!" He roars and launches toward Maddox. Maddox dodges him, and Travis falls to the ground.

"I just stole back what was mine, don't make me beat your ass too."

Travis gets back up, but Elliot comes in, grabbing his shoulder. "You don't want to do that, kid."

"I'm…" I turn to face Travis, my throat swollen. The fireplace flickers in the distance and suddenly I'm cold. I wrap my arms around myself. "Sorry." I blink a few times. "I'm sorry, Travis. I should have ended things a long time ago. You deserved that."

He stands from the ground, and just when I think he's going to yell at me, he scoffs and leaves.

"I'm a terrible human," I whisper, swiping the tears from my cheeks.

Maddox comes to me and takes me into his arms. "No, you're not, baby."

My mom comes in singing, "Who wants margaritas?" Her smile falls when she sees the seriousness in the room and Maddox and I wrapped up in each other.

Leila clears her throat. "Actually, I could do with one…"

"Me too," Liza adds.

The wedding is in two days. We have been here for twenty-four hours and already, Maddox and I had flipped each other's world around. I'm just glad Kennedy is asleep.

CHAPTER 28

AMETHYST

We stayed in separate rooms for Kennedy, because we didn't want to confuse her with anything. Maddox and I both said we'd break her in, even though I'm sure she'd have no arguments about it, but I respected his decision as a father. Shit. Does that mean that I'm a stepmother?

I gulp.

The guys have left again, and the wedding is tomorrow. The atmosphere is electrified with love. I've thrown myself into the chaos to get my mind off Travis. There are sprouting flowers all over the house, all red and black. Even though the wedding isn't going to be here, Lei still wanted the theme to take over every inch of every single place where we were.

We are sipping cocktails in the bathroom, dressed in fluffy robes and rose plaited headbands and eating chocolate, talking about the wedding tomorrow and how much things have changed. I put my glass down.

"I need to pee."

I untie my gown and take a seat on the bowl. "You know," I laugh. "I wouldn't mind becoming an aunty. Kennedy has made me fall in love with kids. Though, she's a pretty special kid…"

Kids.

Babies.

Sex.

I look down at my panties and frown.

"Fuck. That, no. We've already decided we don't want kids."

She swipes black lipstick over her lips.

Her voice dies out.

My blood turns to slush. "Lei..."

"What?" she asks around her glass, turning to face me.

"The d—date…" I search the ground. "No. No way. Not possible." My eyes go to her.

"Ame, what the hell are you talking about?" She puts her hand on her hip. "What's wrong?"

Tears fall down my cheek and I scrunch my face up. "I'm late."

She straightens and then looks down to my panties. "Ok—oh! Fuck!" Her hand flies up to her mouth. "Wait!" She runs out of the room and I spend the next five minutes dying a few hundred times.

She comes back in and pulls out a small box from under her robe, like it's a drug transaction. "I had to get one the other day, but I got my period, so I didn't need it. I swear, we're in synch. I was five weeks late, but it turns out stress and all that shit play a major factor in how your bo—"

I snatch the box and tear it open.

"Give me your wine." I gesture to the wine. Reckless because of the potential of being pregnant, but I can't say that I'm feeling very maternal right now to care.

She hands it to me. I drink it in a beat and then order her to get the bottle. She comes back in a few seconds later with a bottle of Moët and shoves it into my chest. I wrap my lips around the rim and drink while praying for the first time in my life.

Oh God.

Oh God.

This can't be… I'm on the pill. I take that shit religiously. I'm not a stupid girl, I make sure I'm on my shit.

I piss on the white stick, and then pull my panties up and wrap myself back into my robe, washing my hands. Have I washed my hands? I don't know. Maybe I need to do it again just to be sure.

"Chill, Amethyst."

I viciously rub my hands on a hand towel and then flip the stick.

Pregnant

My knees shake and my lip quivers. "No…" I shake my head and throw the stick at Leila like it's infected. I clutch my stomach. "No!"

"Shit," Leila cusses, her hand going to her forehead. "Shit. It's okay, we will sort this. Okay?"

"Not okay, how is this possible? I'm on the pill!"

"I don't know, maybe it's wrong?"

I search the ground. "I'm so sorry, Lei. I'm being so selfish." I feel sick. Turning, I empty the contents in my stomach into the toilet and wipe away the residue. "I have to tell Maddox…"

"Tell Maddox—what?" Maddox is standing there, leaning against the doorframe. He looks so happy and at ease. Finally, we were going to do this. Now, I feel like I've been kicked off the cliff of sanity.

Leila gives me an apologetic smile and squeezes my hand. "I'll be here, in the room."

She carefully walks past Maddox and he steps in, closing the door behind himself. I open my mouth, but his eyes land on the box on the floor, then the empty bottles of wine, and then the stick on the counter with the instruction manual spread out. He steps in farther and picks up the stick.

He stills, his face turning to marble. Throwing the stick, he launches his fist into the mirror and it shatters into millions of sharp little shards. I scream, wincing. He flies out of the room.

"Maddox!" I yell, attempting to chase after him.

"What is going on?" Mom asks as I fly down the stairs behind him.

He's already out the door and in his car before I drop to a heap of mess on my knees.

CHAPTER 29

MADDOX

Rage.

Pure undiluted rage pulses through my veins like adrenaline I've never felt before. She's carrying his baby. That should be my fucking baby. I clutch at my hair and floor it toward the hotel I know Travis checked into. I know because I followed him to make sure he wouldn't be an issue. Now, he's a big fucking issue.

I pull up to the front of the hotel and don't even bother to park or get the valet. My face is known everywhere, they'll park it for me. I fly into the lobby and hit the button for his level. The elevator takes me up, the smooth piano doing nothing to calm my beast. The doors ding open and I run down the foyer, shoulder barging past a young family. Reaching his door, I kick it down and it smashes open, showing Travis on his phone already. His eyes come to mine.

"Too late, he's here." Was that her? Did she fucking warn him like she fucking gives a fuck?

I'll kill him.

"Explain, right fucking now."

He pushes his phone into his pocket, his hands shaking. He was scared. I laugh. Good.

"I love her."

I step closer. "Careful…"

He grins. "Now I've given her something of me, and you and I both know Amethyst…" He tilts his head. This motherfucker has a death wish. "She's a family girl with family morals."

I couldn't stop. My fist connects with his face and he falls to the ground. "You fucking—"

"Stop!" Amethyst screams from the doorway. "Please, stop!"

I hover over Travis, fist in the air.

"Get off him, Maddox…"

I don't fucking want to.

"Please, Maddox…" She uses her gentle voice. She knows her softness is the only thing that can calm my beast. I instantly climb off him, but not without kicking him in the process.

He laughs, blood covering his teeth and lips.

"Step away, Maddox," she whispers.

I go to the other side of the room, because she's right. I'd flat out kill this fool if he says anything dumb.

She looks back to Travis. "How?"

He pulls out a smoke and lights up, looking up to the ceiling. "How do you think? I mean, there were a lot—"

"—I'd be very fucking careful, princess…" I sneer at him. Fucking pretty boy.

He blows out a thick cloud of smoke.

"I was on the pill, Travis. I took it religiously."

He beams at her. "I love you, I want to marry you! I have the ring and everything. I was planning to ask you after the wedding…" He pauses, and I watch as her eyes close. "I've been switching your pills for a couple months now."

Her eyes fly open. "You what?"

"You fucking what?" My shoulders straighten, and I take steps toward him. Amethyst throws her hand out to stop me, but I slap it away, inspecting the piece of shit on the ground. "I'll fucking kill you," I growl.

"Maddox!" Amethyst pleads.

"Fuck off, Ame."

I launch toward him again, but four sets of hands are pulling me back now. Talon and Wolf.

"I'll kill you motherfucker!" I yell, wanting to tear his skin from his bones and send it to every fucking person who loved this stupid fuck.

"What will Ken do if you're in jail, dickface?" Talon says, shoving me against the wall.

I calm enough to look at Amethyst over Talon's shoulder.

She was looking at him. Appalled? With something else. Hatred? Commitment? Fuck.

"Ame…" I say, needing her attention.

Eyes on me, baby. "I'll take care of you and that baby. Raise it like it's my own."

Come on.

She doesn't look at me.

Her focus staying on Travis.

"Baby…" I whisper.

Her eyes close and tears flood her cheeks. I already know what she's going to say before she says it.

"Take him home, T. I need to stay here until I figure some shit out."

I launch my fist into the wall. Talon and Wolf both drag me out of the room, my shirt ripping off in the process.

"Let her go, brother, just let her go." Talon squeezes me in a hug.

"I can't…"

"Try," Wolf says. "Just fucking try, bro…"

I calm my heaving, staring at the now closed door. I clench my jaw then shove away from them, pulling my phone out of my back pocket as I make my way back to the elevator.

The doors open and I step inside, not bothering to see if Talon and Wolf are following.

Opening up a new text message, I swipe the sweat off my cheek with the back of my hand and text Tiffany.

Me: You're coming to the wedding with me tomorrow.

Everything inside of me has snapped. Yeah, I may be an irrational bastard, but god knows I'd bend hell for Amethyst. I don't feel hurt or broken-hearted, because what Amethyst and I shared wasn't as simple as love. It was fucking complicated, messy, and fucking deranged. My world starts and ends with her, but not anymore.

The Destroyer has just been destroyed.

PART TWO

"Sometimes following your heart,
means losing your mind"
- author unknown

~

"I hope my absence haunts you"

-achelei

CHAPTER 30

Six Months Later
AMETHYST

I ENDED THINGS AGAIN WITH TRAVIS ON THE WAY HOME FROM the wedding, but I didn't want to be with Maddox right then either. I knew that if I broke up with Travis in front of Maddox, he would beg me to stay with him. I needed space to figure out the solo mom thing and what I was going to do in regards of work. I wanted to be comfortable with the idea of becoming a mom before letting Maddox and I's shit consume me again. My panicking didn't last long because I lost the baby a week later. I didn't even make it to twelve weeks before waking up with blood-drenched underwear. Since then, I've spent the last three months finding myself again. I got my half-pipe built near the pool, exactly where I envisioned it. Sitting on the edge of the halfpipe looking over LA is quite possibly my most favorite place ever. When I've not been drowning myself in work, I spend my time skating. I've been working on a movie lately, it will be my first big move. I'm struggling to keep on top of the tv show and the "Reckless" movie, but it's been keeping me busy which I'm thankful for. The paparazzi seem to only be getting worse. Now I can't even go down the street without being recognized. I love LA, but I miss the simplicity of New York. I haven't been back since the wedding. The disaster of that day and time cripples me. The memories are way too much, and what Maddox continued to do that day snapped every bone in my body…

6 Months Earlier
  The wedding

"You look beautiful, Lei," I said, brushing down her white gown. Tiffany is late, and no one knows where she is, so it's been my duty to make sure Leila doesn't flip out and go into a panic. Fuck Tiffany.

"Thanks, Ame." She turned to face me, her hands grasping mine. "How are you feeling about all this baby stuff?"

I thought over her words and shook my head. "Let's not make this any more about me than it already has been." No one had seen Maddox since yesterday, and quite frankly, I was scared.

"No, seriously, Amethyst. You're my best friend, I care about you. I need to know how you're feeling. Distract me, at the very least."

Distraction, okay, I could do that for her. "Well," I sighed. "A little nervous, a little scared, and…" I looked at her and squeezed her hand softly. "Does it make me a bad person that I wish I never met Travis and that I regret it already?"

She patted her brown hair that's up in a bun and smiled. "No, babe. It makes you human and twenty-three years old with a whole life and career in front of her." She squeezed me back. "It's going to be okay. You have so much support. We're going to get through this, okay?"

I nodded in agreement, even though it wasn't going to be okay. Not even in the slightest. Then pulled her dress up to cover her boobs more. "You ready to be married?"

She whacked my hand away. "Yes, and leave the titties out."

I laughed, giving myself one final glance in the mirror. Leila had the bridesmaid dresses similarly styled to hers, only where she wore white, we wore red. Tight, strapless gowns with a cinched waist. They were classy and over the top, much like her. My hair was down in soft curls and my makeup was light.

Everything was classy, yet classic. I would've expected nothing less from Leila. The bedroom door swings open and Tiffany comes flying in with an angry looking Liza following behind her. Liza slams the door closed.

"Sorry," Tiffany said, fixing her hair. "Was a little busy…"

I looked between them both, but Liza didn't look back at me. She gave a silent look to Leila and then gestured to the door. "Shall we?"

Leila grabbed my hand. I stared back at her. "You okay?"

She searched my face, her eyebrows etched in worry, then she released and smiled. "Yes, I love you, Ame."

"I love you too."

I half expected Leila to walk down the aisle to Snoop Dogg, but instead, a soft melody played that I didn't recognize. It was beautiful and relaxing. I put one foot in front of the other and slowly made my way down the aisle, making an effort not to look at Maddox, who I knew was standing beside his brother. I felt fire shooting toward me from that side, but I drove through it. I could hold my shit together for Leila. This was her day. I'll raise that baby like it's my own. I closed my eyes as I reached the altar, then opened them onto the entrance to wait for Leila. I couldn't do that to him. It was not his issue, he already had his own child to care for. It wouldn't be fair on him, and it wouldn't be fair on Ken to have to share her daddy. Not that there's anything wrong with mixed stepfamilies, but for right now, I couldn't do it. Not to rule out the future, though. Tiffany was coming down, but she was distracted, seductively hooked on the groom's side. I followed her line of sight, and I shouldn't have.

Maddox.

His eyes lazily focused on Tiffany, a crooked grin on his face. His hair was messy, much like Tiffany's and his tie wasn't secured around his neck properly. He licked his lip and bit down, his eyes raking up and down Tiffany.

My heart snapped in my chest, my legs physically shaking unsteadily. I closed my eyes as scorching heat flushed through me. Just as my legs were about to give away, Liza was right there beside me, holding me up by my arm.

"It's okay, Amethyst. Just don't pay attention." I search her face, but she was already sneering at both Tiffany and Maddox. If looks could kill…

Leila started walking down the aisle. Her sole focus should have been on her soon-to-be-husband, but they were on me, her eyebrows pulled in again in worry. She could probably sense it. We always were strangely wired together. I needed to pull my shit together for her. Everyone warned me about this. Elliot being the loudest, but I didn't listen. It didn't matter how betrayed or hurt I was feeling right now, I couldn't shit on my best friend's wedding. I took a deep breath in and out, while counting to ten in my head, then straightened my shoulders.

Fuck. Maddox, and that whore Tiffany.

The reception was much worse. Maddox and Tiffany were all over each other throughout the night. It made me physically sick to watch. Could I blame him, though? It's not like I didn't come here with someone of my own. But in saying that, he did get married. My head hurt.

We didn't stay for long, leaving quite early on in the night. Travis took me back to Mom and Elliot's quickly so I could say goodbye to Kennedy. We were having hot cocoa in the kitchen with marshmallows when the doorbell rang. The babysitter, a middle-aged woman named Tessa, called out that she would get it.

"Hey, so!" I pinched her cheeks. "I've got to go back to LA."

Kennedy's face dropped. "Why? But I thought you and Daddy were going to be happily ever after?"

I froze, then quickly collected my wits. "Why would you think that?"

She shrugged, her shoulders sagging. "Because you look at each other in a Disney kind of way."

"Hey." I hopped down and kneeled in front of her, trying to ignore the fact that my heart was physically throbbing in my chest. "We're still family, sweetheart."

She smiled. "We are, aren't we?"

I nodded.

"Kennedy! Are you ready, darling?" Tessa said, holding Kennedy's bags.

"I'll walk her out." I took the bags off Tessa and gently caught Kennedy's hand in mine.

I was still looking at her when we reached the door and I saw Cassidy standing there. She looked slightly different from what I remembered. Her hair was now short, and there were a few bags under her eyes.

"Hi…" I said, mainly to test out her vibe.

She sighed like she was tired, then looked down at Kennedy. "Hi, honey, go and jump into the car. Jessie has your favorite ice cream."

Kennedy shot off and we both smiled after her, watching as she climbed into the Range Rover.

Cassidy looked back at me. "Listen, whatever is going on with you and Maddox, can you please not let it touch Kennedy. You're both so toxic together, I will kill both of you if it comes near my daughter—"

I interrupted her. "No, no. Nothing's happening." And you don't know anything about me and Maddox.

She glared at me like she didn't believe me.

"Seriously," I whispered, clearing my throat. "I have a

boyfriend and whatever was going to happen between Maddox and I—just, will never happen."

She searched my eyes. "You can say that, Amethyst, but everybody knows that's not true. You don't get a say in what happens between you and Maddox. I wish I was that girl for him, but I'm not, and no one ever will be, do you know why?"

I shook my head.

"Because there's only one you."

"Lucky me," I answered sarcastically, leaning on the door-frame. Were we bonding?

She chuckled. "That bad, huh?" Then she started walking back to the car. "We could probably have some drinks one day and a good gossip session."

I snorted. "Not likely, but thanks."

"Thank God, but at least I asked." She winked at me and then they shot off.

AMETHYST
Present

Cassidy and I have become somewhat friends. I know, right, weird. She added me on Facebook, and then started liking my photos and then the next thing I know, we're tagging each other in memes (and we all know what that means). But it also means that I get to see Kennedy through Cassidy, so I love it. I love the time I get to spend with Kennedy, which includes her and I working on my halfpipe. She's quite the artist, it has been our bonding time. Cassidy has only managed to bring her over twice, but both times they stayed the weekend and we spent all night and day splashing graffiti on the halfpipe. Ken does all sorts of cute drawings. A beaming sun, a pink frog, and curly hearts. So many hearts. But the one that really gets me is the stick family she drew. She says it's me, her and Maddox and we're all at the snow together. She even drew a little snowflake beside us, and a cat named Greg. Don't ask me why she named it Greg, she doesn't even know, she just said that she liked the name. Can't argue with that. Cassidy would always be sunbathing by the pool, sucking down cocktails while Kennedy and I were dressed in matching denim coveralls with paint splashed all over them.

The last time they were here, Ken did my hair in pigtail messy knots and we snapped a whole ton of selfies, uploading them to social media. I wasn't sure whether Maddox knew about Cassidy, mine, and Ken's friendship, and I didn't care to ask. I was just happy to still be a part of Kennedy's life and I'll forever owe Cass for that. Cass isn't too bad of a chick, though.

She's a princess, and a bitch, but she's a great mom and not too bad of a friend. I can always count on her to give it to me straight. When we first started hanging out, there was once that she came out and said she needed to clear something up before we could become friends. I was nervous because it's Cassie.

She then went on to tell me the gory details of her and Maddox's divorce. She said that she took too many pills one night and had a bit too much to drink and that everyone assumed she had tried to commit suicide. It was hard to listen to, but it was only a solid ten or so minutes, and then it was done after that and we never had to speak of him or that again. I respected why she wanted and needed to tell me, she wanted to make sure that I knew she wasn't some crazy ass ex-wife trying to get close to the real love of his life. I interrupted her when she said that.

Leila still isn't hot on her, but I can see her slowly coming around. Leila is a hard nut to crack, which is why I never understood her friendship with Tiffany—who is no longer a friend. After the wedding drama, Leila kicked her out of her life. I don't know about Maddox, though.

I answer my phone while unlocking the front door to my house. Today was a long day that started at three a.m. It's now nine p.m. and I'm beat.

"Hello?"

"Amethyst?"

"Hi, Daddy. Whatcha doing?" Hearing from my dad always puts a smile on my face.

"Good, baby girl. How you doing? Have you been taking it easy? We watch your show every week."

I toss my keys onto the counter and change ears. "Thanks, Dad. Everything is good, I'm tired, though."

"Has that boy been leaving you alone?"

I roll my eyes. I made a huge mistake telling my dad that Travis was hassling me when I first broke it off with him.

Travis went into a drug and alcohol spiral and the show killed him off. He was that bad. I had to use huge force to stop Dad and my uncle Marcus from physically hurting Maddox every time we went bust, but the shit with Travis and I? That was a whole new ball game. Dad and Uncle Marcus straight up had a plan and a plot of land for Travis' body. It took me a whole week to calm them both down.

"Yes, Dad. He's fine now."

"Good. It's your birthday soon, anything planned for it?"

"Um." I pull open the fridge door and take out a bottle of water. "Not yet. I was thinking of just doing something small. It's hard enough to get everyone on the same phone call let alone in the same town."

"Okay, baby, well stop being a stranger and come home soon."

"I will, Daddy."

Hanging up my phone, I jump into the shower, scrubbing off the day, then slip into my bed. I contemplate turning on Netflix but find myself enjoying the silence. No one yelling cut, no one screaming orders. No flashing cameras or screaming paparazzi. I turn to the side, tucking my hand under the side of my head. The whole wall is glass, looking out over the pool, my halfpipe, and the rest of LA twinkling like an animated backdrop. I know that I should go back and visit Dad. I haven't been since Maddox was with me. I sigh, flipping onto my back. I've fought the urge to ask anyone how Maddox has been. If he's remarried or had any new kids. Cass is always quiet when it comes to Maddox, and Ken doesn't talk about him either. Every time I chat with Leila, she doesn't even go near the Maddox subject.

I exhale, flipping to my back. Fucking insomnia. My phone starts ringing on the table top and I reach for it aimlessly, sliding it unlocked without looking.

"Yes?"

"Ame, you need to come home."

I sit up at the sound of Talon's voice. "What? Why?" I shove the covers off me and stand, my heart pounding in my chest.

"Something has happened, and we need you here. Don't turn on the TV."

"Who needs me?" I start ripping off my pajamas, putting my phone on speaker and tossing it onto the bed.

I fly into the closet and tear down clothes, throwing them into my suitcase.

"We all do. Get here, and don't talk to anyone. Don't turn the TV on, don't do anything."

He hangs up and I freeze, staring at the phone on my bed. "Fuck."

I throw all of my clothes into my bag and once I'm packed, I run out to my car, shoving a baseball cap over my messy long hair. I start to make my way to the airport, the flashing bright lights beaming over the highway. I punch the Bluetooth feature on the steering wheel.

"Call Alesha."

"Calling Alesha."

The phone rings a few times before Alesha's groggy voice comes through. "Hello?"

"Alesha, it's me, listen can you please book a flight to New York for tonight. The first flight I can get."

"I'm on it. Is everything ok?"

"I don't know, I hope so."

The flight was fast, even though I got no sleep on the way here. A hundred different scenarios went through my head—none good. I'm walking through the arrival lounge with big glasses and a baseball cap pulled over my messy hair when the TV catches my attention.

Travis's face.

My brows pinch together.

The video murky, aimed at Travis's bed.

Me spread out, naked with censored bits blurred out.

My walking slows, and someone slams into my back.

He taped us?

I draw in a deep breath, hot flashes coming in and out.

"Wha—what?" I whisper out, the room spinning. My head pounds, and then everything goes black.

I wake up to my head thudding and my eyelids heavy. Pushing up from the couch, I rub my temples together.

"What the fuck happened?" I clear my throat and wipe my eyes. When they come into focus, I'm staring at Leila, Talon, Liza, and Wolf.

I straighten. "Am I in trouble?"

Leila looks to Wolf, and then back at me. "You blacked out."

"Oh." My eyebrows cross, then the memories come back. "Oh…" I squeak, my head burying in my hands. "I can't believe he'd do that to me."

Talon, who has been silent, launches off the couch, his hand running through his hair. "This isn't good."

"Wait." I straighten my shoulders. "Is that why you called me here?"

Leila stares at me. "No, honey. We called you because Maddox has put Travis in the hospital."

"What!" I shoot up from the couch, my eyes darting between them all. "What do you mean?"

"I mean," Talon says, coming toward me and pulling me in for a hug. He's hard as rock so it's always a little awkward when he hugs me. "Maddox is in jail right now, but Dad has gone to bail him out."

"Why? Where? In LA? Why didn't you just tell me! I would have bailed him out! Why would you send me here!" I'm yelling. My chest is heaving up and down and I swear sweat is dripping down my face.

"I don't feel well," I add, my hand coming to my forehead.

Leila jumps up, catching my hand and pulling me into her, away from Talon. "He didn't want to see you, babe."

"What?" I ask, wiping the sweat from my head. "Seriously, I don't—" I lunge forward, running for the bathroom. I've only been here a few times, but every time I come here, Leila has done something new to the décor. They ended up buying in New York.

After emptying my stomach into the bowl, I flush the toilet and turn the tap on, splashing warm water over my face. Patting the towel over my cheeks, I put it back and open the bathroom door. Breathe in and out, Amethyst. Why wouldn't he want to see me? He just beat my ex-boyfriend's face in for me. What a head-fuck, like usual.

Leila's on the other side when I open the door, leaning against the wall. "Are you okay?"

"No." I shut the door behind me. "What's going on?"

Leila gapes down the long hallway, and then walks closer to me, tugging my arm and pulling me into one of the spare rooms in their condo. She shuts the door, her hands resting on her hips.

"Maddox has lost his shit." She starts walking back and forth.

"Why!" I yell, my hands going up in the air. "What the fuck is it to him?"

She pauses, turning to face me. It's the first time I've seen Leila sort of angry at me. "Amethyst, you fucking said his name."

"Wha—" I pause, my mouth shutting. Pure horror rushes through me. "No, no I didn't…I wouldn't…" Would I?

She smiles slightly, seemingly enjoying my discomfort. "Yes, you did."

I flop down onto the bed. "Fuck. Did I?"

Leila bursts out laughing, taking a seat beside me. "Have you not watched?"

"Why the fuck would I watch?" Now it's my turn to be angry. "Leila, I literally only just found out that there even was a fucking tape!"

"Wait." Her smile falls, her jaw turning stiff. "He filmed that without your knowledge?"

I bury my face in my hands. "Yes. I'm going to fucking sue."

My phone hasn't stopped vibrating in my back pocket since I left. I know I need to work, or call the director, Tim, to let him know I'll need a break, but I can't face the music right now. Right now, I need to fix whatever mess has just erupted.

I swallow, laying on my back. I'm tired. So tired my eyelids feel heavy, but I can't sleep. It's like my brain is trying, but my body is fighting it. "Why doesn't he want to see me?"

Leila sighs, lying beside me. "I don't know, Ame. We're all exhausted from your guys' back and forth. I mean, it's been years and you both still can't make up your minds."

I turn to face her, resting on my side. "It's hard."

She turns her face to look at me. "What's so hard, Ame? Fuck. It's simple, really. You've both been in love with each other since you were seven years old. What's so hard about that?"

"That is what is hard about that," I snort. "Jesus, Leila. I fell in love with him at age seven. That's not romantic. That's fucking sad, confusing and chaotic. I would have rather found him when I was older. Old enough to know my feelings. I fell in love with Maddox before I knew how to jump. Now I'm drowning."

Her hand comes to my cheek. "And what do you feel now?"

"Now?" I exclaimed, turning away from her. "Now I'm mad that he doesn't want to see me."

She sighs. "Elliot is bringing him back. But he's in trouble and I don't know what's going to happen with his next fight. Did you know he bought a private jet? Named it Flyaway."

"He what?"

I know that he's rich. He's on Forbes highest paid athletes list at number one. Number freaking one. Raking in a staggering three hundred million a year. He has just never been that person to me, or to our family. I stay away from the tabloids to stay away from my own drama, but it helps because I don't really see his updates either. He named the jet Flyaway, and I know why. Everything fucking hurts, I'm so sick of hurting. Maybe I should check Instagram. He doesn't follow me there, but we are still friends on Facebook. He hasn't logged into that account in years, though, probably around the time he got famous. He has ninety million followers on Facebook alone, his personal Facebook is that—personal. He only has a hundred thirty-four friends on that account, but again, he hasn't logged in.

"Yup. He bought a private jet to match his twenty-million-dollar superyacht."

"Jesus," I whisper, shaking my head. "And he named it after our song."

Leila leans forward, getting to her feet. "The Lenny Kravitz song?" Her face pales, and then she shakes her head as if she's drained. I feel a pang of guilt for that. "I don't know why he doesn't want to see you, but maybe it's a good time to ask him."

She leaves, shutting the door behind herself. I appreciate it, it gives me enough time to process my thoughts. I take my phone from my back pocket and send a quick email to my

assistant, asking her to put in time for work. Alesha emails back
instantly.

From: Alesha Hope
  To: Amethyst Tatum
  Subject: Re: Sex tapes ruin lives.
  I'm so sorry, Amethyst. Of course. Please call Lionel and
sue that son of a bitch. I've attached his number to this email.
Take as much time as you need.

Regards, Alesha Hope
  Personal Assistant to Amethyst Tatum

I chuckle, typing out a quick reply. Alesha is all of nineteen,
but she has spunk. I like her. I'm finishing off the email when
my smile falls. I click on my contacts and slowly scroll.
  Anne
  Bee
  Chantal
  Caro
  Don't answer this number
  Ellie
  Franci
  Gigi
  Harry
  Indy
  Justin
  Kim
  Lyla
  Maci
  Maddox

I hover over his name and then scroll down more.

Manda

Michelle

I scroll back up and before I know what I'm doing, I hit dial.

The phone rings. Keeps ringing. Just when I'm about to hang up, it clicks over.

Silence.

"Maddox?" It comes out as a whisper. I clear my throat when he doesn't answer. "I'm at Leila's if you want to see me."

More silence.

Then the line goes dead.

Well alright then. I throw my phone across the room and strip out of my clothes, leaving me in panties and my bra before slipping under the covers. I hit the lamp off.

So tired.

CHAPTER 32

AMETHYST

I FEEL THE MATTRESS SINK BESIDE ME AND MY EYES FLY OPEN. A dark shadow sits, head buried in his hands.

"Maddox?"

"Don't—" His voice breaks through. It's soft yet hard, completely contradicting itself. "Don't fucking say anything, Amethyst."

I smell the harsh scent of whiskey mixed with his cologne and cigarette. Or is it cigar smoke. "You smell like hookers and bad decisions."

"Yeah?" he asks, the shadow finally turning slightly to face me. The moonlight is subtle, but it's splitting through the blinds slightly from the window behind me. "That's not fucking hookers, that's a fucking jail cell, and bad decisions? Always."

I shuffle up the bed, pulling my knees into my chest. "You need a shower."

"I should hate you," he says, ignoring my suggestion about a shower.

"And you do," I reply softly, clearing my throat.

He snorts, getting to his feet and then gripping onto my ankles and dragging me across the bed. "That's where you're fucking wrong."

I swallow. "I'm never wrong."

"Yes, you are."

"No, I'm not. Not when it comes to you."

"Oh?" His head tilts, and his hand comes to my throat. His index finger traces my collarbone, leaving a trail of fear in its wake, then his hand wraps around my throat. "I could kill you."

I gulp. "I can't breathe."

"Good."

"Maddox, I know you don't want to hurt me."

"That's undecided, princess. I'm a different man now."

I whack his hand away, but it doesn't move. "Cut the shit, Maddox." His other hand disappears into his pocket, then he pulls out his phone, flashing the screen in my face. The light assaults my eyes, much like his hand is doing to my throat.

His lips come to my ear. "You wait until he's thrusting his cock inside your little cunt, and then you whisper out those fucking words to him, Amethyst, hmm? And not to me?"

"I—" He loosens his grip, but only after squeezing tight for a brief second. "I didn't mean to! I was—I was high and drunk. I don't even remember that day fully, I didn't even know that—" Wait. Hold the fuck up for a minute. Now is not the time to admit that he taped it without my knowledge. I'll tell Maddox another day.

"Say it…" Maddox whispers, stretching my leg wide. His rests between my thighs and presses against me. My eyes slam shut. I'm not saying shit. "What did you say, Amethyst?"

I shake my head.

His other leg comes between mine and he stretches my other wide. I can feel his cock pressing into my pussy. Oh God.

He must push play because my voice is the next thing I hear.

"*Yes,*" I moaned in the video.

Cringe.

"*You like that dick, baby? That's my pussy….*" Travis liked to talk a lot of shit. Cringe again.

"*Mine.*" He had said again. "*Say it, say it's mine.*"

Tears pinch the corner of my eyes as memories slowly drift back in from that day. The cocaine, the weed, the alcohol. The partying, the sex, the kissing, the threesome with another girl, more sex, more cocaine, and then the stumbling upstairs to that bedroom. Travis's bedroom. I trusted him. I shouldn't have. I was weak, weak from love. Weak from not having my lifeline, Maddox.

"Say it, Amethyst. Say that pussy is mine," Travis repeated. *"Who owns this pussy? Who owns you?"*

Silence stretches out. You hear nothing but the bed squeaking and the loud slapping of sweaty bodies, then my voice. So soft, so defeated, so fucked up, whispers out, *"Maddox Stone."*

Maddox grinds into me, tossing his phone onto the bed. I can still hear the muffled sounds though, the sounds of me trying to reach my orgasm. So forced, so fake. I thought of Maddox the entire time.

Maddox brings his hand to my thigh, pulling it up higher to rest on his hip. "Why the fuck didn't you tell me?" His tone sounds strained.

I'm trying not to meet his slow thrusts, but every time he grinds into me, everything down there is throbbing, aching to be touched. Meanwhile, my heart is thudding, pleading to be broken. Just do it, he's going to break it anyway because that's what he does. Maddox severs it every single fucking time, but he doesn't put it back together again afterward. He leaves the remnants of my heart on display for everyone to see, just so he can say, 'I did that. She's mine.' His way of owning me is by breaking me.

"I—I—" For fuck's sake, Amethyst.

His hand comes to my breast. "Why the fuck didn't you come to me if you wanted me that bad." He tears my bra down, his thumb skating over my swollen nipple. "Did you think of me every time he fucked you?"

His lips are now hovering over mine, his breath falling over my cheek. "Answer me, Rosé..." The tip of his nose glides over mine. "Did you think of me every time he did this?" he grinds himself against me, so hard. Hard.

"Fuck," I whisper, my eyes rolling to the back of my head. He pinches my nipple, the borderline of pain and pleasure starts to shake like it always does in bed with him.

"What about this?" He licks over my jawline and then traces his tongue down my throat. I bite down on my lip to stop my moaning.

Then his finger dips inside the rim of my lace panties, his bare knuckle sliding against my clit. His finger dips inside of me and I clench around him.

He pulls it out and brings it to my mouth. "Suck."

I do, opening my mouth and sucking myself off his finger. Liquid metal slides down my throat and my eyes pop open, counting the dates when I might be due for my period.

He chuckles. It wasn't a nice chuckle. It was dark and testing. "That's not you, Rosé," then slides his finger out of my mouth. "That's your revenge." Travis's blood? That should make me sick, but it doesn't. My body is on fire and everything south is screaming to be touched, fucked and ruined.

"Fuck me," I whisper, reaching for his mouth. I want to kiss him. I want him to kiss me. I need him like I need air.

He laughs again, leaning up on one elbow and making his way back to the foot of the bed. He stands, removing his shirt. I want to cry, that's how sexy he looks, even though I can't see him that well.

"As much as my dick is aching to see you lose your shit underneath me, no. You've been a brat and you need to be punished."

"So punish me!" I yell, a little too loudly. I hope Leila's walls are thick. I'll try my soft side, I know how much he loves that.

I crawl to him, reaching for his belt buckle and tug on it. He doesn't stop me. "Punish me the way I know you can,

Maddox." My finger dips under the waist of his jeans and I tug down. He remains statue still. I wish I could see his face right now. Bet that jaw is stone. "Make me hurt. Slice me open and break me, then lick my wounds better again."

He growls, and then pushes me back down onto the bed, tearing my bra and panties off. My hair sprawls out everywhere. He pulls the belt off his jeans, folding it over. A loud slapping sound breaks out, then silence. Shit.

"Turn over."

I gulp.

"Now, Amethyst or I'll double it."

I turn, putting my ass in the air. He presses down on my lower back until I snap into a perfect arch. Then he pelts the belt down on my ass cheek. "Who do you belong to?"

"Ouch!" I cry out, my face scrunched up in pain.

Slap. "Who, Amethyst?"

Slap.

"You!" I scream into the pillow.

Slap. "Say my name."

"Maddox Stone," I sob, relishing in the sting that's now traveling down to my opening. He dips his finger inside of me and swirls. "I'm still going to punish you, baby. Just in a different way." He snatches his phone and then the scene is replaying again. He puts it down under my face, so I'm looking straight at it. I clench the sheets.

"Who owns you, Amethyst. Mine."

I squeeze the sheets harder, wanting the video to stop.

Maddox's tongue slips inside me from behind, his thumb pressing on my clit. Pleasure, pain, and sadness consuming me.

"Why are you doing this?" I whimper, grinding myself onto his mouth but watching as my tears drop onto the screen of his phone. Pelts of tears smudge over parts of the video.

He doesn't answer.

My core clenches, my abs tensing. Sparks ignite behind my

eyes and I lose it, my legs shaking as pleasure ripples through me. My body jolts during my come down. The video is still playing. When Maddox fills me, it's playing. When he pulls out and thrusts inside of me, I hear Travis's voice. When I come undone again, I hear myself say *"Maddox Stone"* in the video. When Maddox thrashes into me relentlessly, the video replays. When he fucks me until I burst again, I hear *"Who owns this pussy."*

I scream out, "Maddox fucking Stone!" As he releases around me and I him, for the fourth time. We tumble down onto the sheets, both wet and panting. The video is playing again, but Maddox picks it up and throws it toward the window, it smashes through.

I flinch.

He pulls me into his arms, wrapping me up. We're both still trying to catch our breath when I yawn against his hard chest.

"Why didn't you tell me?" he asks breathlessly. I'm not sure if he's asking me or himself, but I answer.

"I couldn't. Why are you surprised, Maddox. You knew what it was like with you and I. Why are you surprised?"

"Oh, I'm not surprised," he says, rolling on top of me. His body is pressing mine into the mattress, his dick coming to my opening. I'm so tired, my body so drained, but with him there again, my body lights up like the Fourth of July.

His lips come to mine. "Do you love me?" he asks through a whisper, his lips skimming against mine.

"Yes," I answer truthfully. "I never stopped."

He groans, sinking inside of me. He slides into me softly and then pulls out. Finally, he kisses me, and it's the best kiss that I've ever had. His tongue slips inside my mouth and I moan softly, my fingers coming to the back of his head. I tug on his hair softly, grinding against his movements. We never break the kiss. Our lips staying locked the entire time. He fucks me slow and sensual. His tongue sliding in and out against my own in carnal movements. Sweat rubs between our bodies with each grind, his pelvic bone crushing against my clit. He circles my hips as our kisses turn sloppy. Our tongues and lips crashing together in a desperate attempt to get as much of each other as possible. I reach my peak and let go, my body now achingly sore as I jerk through my come down. He follows, his cock throbbing inside of me as he unleashes.

He collapses onto me, kissing my forehead and rolling off, pulling me into his chest again.

"Ditto, baby."

CHAPTER 33

MADDOX

I HADN'T THOUGHT TOO MUCH ABOUT MY ACTIONS IN THE PAST few days, but that's nothing new. I never did when it came to Amethyst, but even I'll admit that wasn't smart. Knowing I had a huge title fight coming up, I didn't need to risk my reputation by flying me and a few of my boys to LA to beat the shit out of a little fucking fuck that set out to hurt the only girl who has ever truly meant anything to me—aside from Ken. I saw the video when I was training, and I lost it. The boys were already there with me, warming up. We went straight to the airstrip and it was game time. Took roughly ten seconds to find out where Travis was. They say money can't buy you happiness, but that's a lie broke fucks tell other broke fucks. Money does and can buy you anything you need, but it's common intellect that it can't buy you. For instance, don't be a cunt. Money doesn't turn you into a piece of shit. If you're a piece of shit when you got money, then you're a piece of shit when you don't have it. What it did do was buy me his address.

I got there to Travis spewing hate toward Amethyst. He looked a fucking mess. Pale skin, purple rings under his eyes, ratty long hair, skinny little arms. I didn't want to hurt him, but then he said something dumb and I don't know, my fist sort of flew and connected with his jaw.

Snap.

I knew I broke it with one hit, but I couldn't stop. Flashes of him fucking Amethyst played in my brain. Flashes of him the last time I saw her when she was pregnant. Her telling me to leave. I took it all out on him with every hit, and before I knew it, I was wet with his blood and the cops were there. He's in a coma right now, which has put a delay on my fight. I thought people would be mad, but I guess rumors have started circulating and my public relations team have started to make a field day out of the whole thing.

The fans love it, it's like a fucking modern-day Romeo and Juliet story, only no one is dying because I won't fucking allow it. People are wondering what the connection between Amethyst Tatum and Maddox Stone is, and then making up their own stories. Photos have circulated online too of me and her when we were in college, then there are more articles about her mom and my dad. It's all a fucking mess, but I'm not going to tidy it up. My personal life is my fucking personal life, I owe no one any explanations—especially when it comes to Ame.

I slam my front door closed, heading straight to the fridge. I left Leila and Wolf's early this morning, needing to gather my thoughts. I don't want to go down this road with her again unless the road is endless. I won't do detours or fucking dead ends with her—not again. If this isn't it, I will never do it with her again, so I'm hesitant to jump into anything with her. Last time I went all in, she fucking folded on me when she should have spoken with me first.

I'm taking out all the shit I need for my protein shake when my phone starts ringing in my pocket. I throw the spinach and bananas onto the counter and then reach for it, sliding it unlocked. "Yo."

"Maddox, I need you to not get into any trouble right now, do you understand me?" Stacey screams into the phone, I pull it away and hit speaker.

"Yeah, I got it," I answer, putting my phone on the counter.

"I know you've got it, but has it sunk in? Like really seeped into that big brain of yours, because I know you're not stupid,

Maddox!" She sounds breathless, and she used my full name. She's pissed.

My eyes narrow. "What are you doing?"

She exhales loudly. "I'm—I'm…" The doorbell dings. "At your house."

I hang up on her. Of course she is.

I pull open the front door then turn back around, heading to the kitchen. She shuts the door behind herself. "Mad, I get it, I do, but you can't keep doing this to me. I'm tired. Okay? I'm tired, and I'm just—good Lord what the fuck are you making?" She gestures to my shake.

"My smoothie, and I know, Stace. Trust me. I just, I'm all fucked up right now."

"This bitch. She always gets you all fucked up!" She throws her hands in the air in frustration.

I chuckle, swallowing my shake and wiping the shit off the top of my lip. "Stace, you're a cool chick, and you do a fucking lot for me, but if you refer to her as 'bitch' again, I will clean my floors with your blood. Got it?"

She rolls her eyes, pulling out a bar stool. "Fine."

Yeah, Stacey is my ex, but she and I were over a long time ago. Well before Amethyst came back on the scene the first time. It just took Stace a little longer to catch on. There are no blurred lines now, though. She knows where her place is, and that's nowhere near my cock. She's also married with a kid now too. Ben, he's cute as fuck. Kennedy fluffs around him like a mother hen, and then always proceeds to ask me when she's getting a little brother. Stace's husband is a good guy. He's the complete opposite to her. Where she's loud and annoying, he's quiet and chill. I feel for the dude. She wears the pants in their marriage, but you see the love they have for one another.

"Okay, so I don't think we need to release a statement just yet. I will make one tomorrow, but until then, we can leave it. Your followers have bumped up another hundred thousand on

Instagram and you're currently trending on Twitter." She carries on, but I tune her out. I don't give a fuck about online presence, she knows this. She's all "it's the way of the future," and it's too exhausting to tell her to shut up, so I just let her fly off on her rants. With a nod and a casual "mmhmm," she almost always thinks I'm list—

"—Maddox! Were you listening?"

"Hmm? Yeah? Why?"

Her face goes flat.

My phone rings and I take it, thankful for the distraction. I don't look at who is calling.

"Sup?"

I wink at Stace.

She flips me off. "Fuck you."

I touch my heart in mock hurt. "You hurt me, baby, you do."

"Good."

"Hello?" I answer again, but the line goes dead. What the fuck. I look down at the caller ID and see Amethyst's number, so I call her back. She answers on the third ring.

"Hey!" She sounds over the top happy. Something's wrong.

"Why'd you fucking hang up on me?"

"Jeez, Maddox, when did you become so moody?"

"Around the time you left me for your baby daddy."

Silence. "Ouch."

"That hurt?"

"Yes."

"Good, because I'm just warming up."

"Think I'll call you back when you're in a better mood."

I push off the counter and take a swig of my shake. "Hang up on me and I'll use a stick next time, and trust me, there are other ways I can use one other than smacking you across the ass with it…"

"Yeah?" I can hear the humor in her tone and every

muscle inside of me loosens slightly. "Who said I was giving you a second time?"

I chuckle. "Who said I'd fuck you?"

"Oh Jesus Christ," Stacey massages her temples.

I lick my thumb and trace it down my stomach, winking at her.

Stace scrunches up her face and points to her ring, then mouths, "Married!"

I grab my junk and mouth, "Owned."

Stace blushes. I ain't lying, Amethyst owns my shit. Always has, but that won't stop me from walking away from her again if I think she's going to waste my time. I want her more than I've ever wanted or needed anything, but I'm also stubborn as fuck.

"Who's there?" Ame asks casually, obviously picking up on my being distracted.

"Huh? Oh, Stacey. You remember her right? You said she was a bitch."

Stace straightens in her chair, her face stiffening in offense. "Exxccuussee me, but—"

I laugh. "Shut up, Stace, I'm kidding. Go home to your husband and Ben, I've got this handled."

Amethyst is silent on the other end. She's probably sulking because she doesn't know about Stacey.

Stace picks up her shit and gives me one more glare before leaving. Once the door is shut, I sigh softly, gripping my phone.

"Baby…"

"Hmmm?" Amethyst says.

"Stop thinking."

"Maddox, I don't even know you anymore."

I laugh, gritting my teeth. That fucks me off. "Ame, you're the only person walking this earth that truly knows me, so shut the fuck up because you're beginning to piss me off."

Silence.

I exhale. "Come over."

She clears her throat. "I don't really want to."

"Come over."

"I should be getting ready to go back to L—"

"—Amethyst?"

"Yeah?" she replies softly.

"Come. Over."

She sighs. "Okay, send me your address."

CHAPTER 34

AMETHYST

"I DON'T THINK I SHOULD…" I ANNOUNCE LOUDLY, WALKING back and forth in the sitting room. I'm pacing, undecided with what to do. I glance at my packed bag, rake my long ass hair out of my face, and then look back to Leila and Wolf. Talon had to leave early with Liza, something about them arguing. I don't know much about Liza or her family, which is odd considering she has always been there. I wonder if Leila knows much about her. Focus.

Leila shuffles on the couch. "Listen, I think you should go…"

I pause. "Lei, look at my body! Last night was… was," I pause, searching for the right words. "Was so fucked up that I can't even form the right words. I'm sore, I can't walk because my vagina feels like it might fall out of me, my ass cheeks are on fire, I have bruises all over my arms and neck, but do you want to know what the worst part is?"

"No," Wolf answers instantly getting to his feet. "I fucking don't."

"What?" Leila says, tilting her head.

"It's what he did to my head. He distorted my mind just as much as he did my body, Lei!"

"For fuck's sake, we need some boundaries in this family," Wolf dashes out of the room, but we both ignore him.

"Amethyst." Leila stands and slowly steps toward me. Her hands come to my shoulders and I let my eyes drift to the floor to ceiling window that demands NYC. "I'm going to ask you this question, and you need to answer it."

"Okay." I look back to the fireplace and watch as the hot flames thrash together in an attempt to create heat.

"Do you want to be with Maddox?"

Instant. "Yes, but it's complicated."

She shakes her head. "It's really not. You're complicating it with your anxiety, nothing else. Go and see him. Give him a shot, give both of you a shot. For the love of God, it would make all of our lives simpler." She sags back onto the sofa and massages her temples. "Stacey is his head of PR and marketing. She's happily married to her lovely husband and they have a very cute son named Ben. Maddox hired her because, well, who she is as a person and she knew Maddox. He somewhat trusts her. Go and talk with him. You owe it to you both."

I leave the house, catching an Uber to the address Maddox sent me. I texted Mom briefly to see if she wanted to catch up while I was back, but she and Elliot went out of town after bailing Maddox out of jail. I told her I'd see her once I sort out this Maddox thing and this sex tape thing. People are about to be sued, that much I know. I get out of the car and slam the door closed. He lives on Long Island, which is even farther from Mom and Elliot, but close to Wolf and Leila. It's all modern-day glass with wooden railings. It screams executive beach home. I can smell the damp salt in the air and hear the crashing of waves, so I take it it's a beachfront home. I go to the door, but it's opening before I get there. Maddox grins, inspecting me closely. He looks bigger but leaner, then I remember his fight that's supposed to be on in a couple weeks.

"Hi," I say, tucking my pink hair behind my ear. I felt miniscule compared to his house, and him, but that really is nothing new.

"Hey, baby, come in." His hand comes to mine and he pulls me inside, shutting the door as soon as I'm inside. A spiral staircase is to the left, the railing woven with intricate swirls. The walls are bare—no artwork on them. There's furniture lazily sitting around with white sheets covering them. This house lacks the home touch. Even though every wall is glass, with the beach directly as the front yard, the air is warm.

"It's only one of my houses. I bought this for the trips home. I live in Vegas full time. Cass and Ken live there too." He disappears into the kitchen.

I want to say that I know, but I don't. I'll put that in the box with how Travis videotaped us having sex without my knowledge. The box will be labeled Things that will make Maddox explode. Handle with caution.

He comes back out holding a couple of drinks, then gestures toward another room. I follow him into the living area, my attention going to the roof. "It's…"

"Empty," he finishes for me, handing me a glass of red wine.

I smile. "Yeah." Then I take a seat on the large sofa. "So, any particular reason why you wanted to see me?"

"Yeah," Maddox says, sitting beside me. He's wearing loose grey sweats and nothing else. The band to his Calvin's strapped around his waist is taunting me. The tattoos—taunting me. The nose ring…I could go on. He must take that out during fights. "Gonna need you to sit on my dick again, Rosé…"

My eyes cut to his.

He bursts out laughing, wrapping his arm around me and pulling me into his chest. I sip my wine and count to ten.

"I'm kidding," he kisses the top of my head. "Sort of."

I shove him, kicking my sneakers off and curling my legs under my butt. "I'm sort of mad at you."

"Well, that's cute, babe, but I'm real fucking mad at you, so…" He gets to his feet, putting his glass on the small table and disappears into the kitchen. I quickly look around to take in anything else I can. But there's nothing. Most everything seems to still be in boxes.

"Are you going to be unpacking here any time soon?"

He comes back holding a box of donuts. I grin, my heart clenching in my chest.

He puts the box between us and sits back down. "How can you be mad at me now? I bought you donuts."

I hide my smile from behind my shoulder. "Tiramisu?"

He watches me, a dimple sinking into one cheek with his half grin. Goddamnit. "You know it." He licks his lip.

I take one out and bite into it. "Mmm," I suck the cream off my finger. "Are you about to tell me you're married again?"

He laughs, sipping his drink. "Nah, babe. No way."

"So, what, then? What's your story?"

"You mean what's my story since the last time we saw each other? Do you not watch TV or, I don't know, go on Instagram?"

"Oh, I do," I say, taking another bite and chewing slowly. "I just don't go on there for you."

"Ouuuccchhh." He smirks again. "Not much, Rosé. Ken takes up most of my time when I'm not training or running the businesses I have."

"Oh?" I say interested, leaning back on the sofa and putting the donut back in the box. I go to suck my thumb, but he snatches my hand before I can do it.

"Do that shit again and our talking is done." Then he wraps his lips around my thumb, his tongue flicking against the palm of it. He grins, his eyes connecting with mine. My lips part, my breathing shallows. He sucks off the cream and then bites my finger in his retreat. "Carry on." He takes another sip of his Whiskey like he didn't just blow my mind. Or my ovaries.

I'm still trying to gather my wits from the explosion inside my vagina when I clear my throat. "Ah." Fuck. Why does this fool always have a way of making me feel like a teen again. "Um, I didn't know that you had a business?"

"I've always had Dutch."

"Wait." I shake my head and put my wine glass onto the coffee table. "You own Dutch?" I remember the restaurant cabin he took me to. I didn't know that he owned it, though.

He nods. "Yeah, I do. It was my mom's and when she passed, Dad wanted to sell it. I begged him not to when I was little, and that I'd buy it off him when I was old enough. Wolf and Talon didn't want anything to do with it. The memories we have there are raw, and I hate going out there, but I kept it for her, unlike the rest of the bitches in my family."

"I loved that place," I whisper out. "I didn't think you were uncomfortable when we were out there, Maddox."

He shook his head. "Ame, things aren't the same when you're around. I can handle anything. I look down to the gold chain he's got around his neck. The chain he stole from me so many years ago. "And you still wear my chain?"

"Never took it off. It's always around my neck when I'm not fighting, whether it's under my shirt or not," he answers smoothly. "Want a tour of the house?"

I shake my head. "No. I sort of…"

He tugs me onto his lap so I'm straddling him, then buries his hand in my hair and yanks on it, forcing my head back. He licks my neck. "I'm hoping your next words are going to be want to fuck…"

I moan. "Yes, yeah." Only, I haven't told him that I'm leaving to go back to LA tomorrow.

CHAPTER 35

JESSICA

WHEN I FIRST FOUND OUT THAT I WAS PREGNANT, I WAS horrified. Not because Jonah and I were having a baby. That wasn't it, even though that was partly why I was terrified. We were friends. Best friends. Who got very drunk one night, decided to be each other's firsts, and in true my luck way, I got pregnant. At sixteen. Back then, that was scary, but that still wasn't it.

When Amethyst was born, she stole my heart, and Jonah's. We were so smothered with her love that we decided to take her away from my family and bring her to somewhere fresh, so we moved to Washington. Figured it was a safe enough area and far enough away from my family and most of their connections. Amethyst was two when my mother first tried to interfere when she found us. You see, I was raised in a motor-cycle club. My family wasn't just blood, and we sure as hell shed it. I didn't want Amethyst anywhere near that life. So, I took her away from everyone and we started fresh. I tried my hardest to make Amethyst choose a different college. I moved back to New York fairly early on and opened my bookstore when Amethyst was around four, only for the sole purpose of keeping a closer eye on my mother. But Amethyst was adamant that she wanted to go to Columbia, and her father and I aren't the kind of people to refuse something she wanted. She never asked for anything, never expected anything. She was never a bad child, so we felt we owed it to her to allow her to attend Columbia, even though we both knew the dangers of it. Elliot was Jonah's best friend through school. He and I had a long history growing up, so I knew he was here when I moved back. I knew he was married with the boys—but we still carried on our affair. I'd meet with him every Thursday at five at Krispy Kreme so he could give me an update on my mom and Satan's Angel's MC. Elliot ran this city, he knew who was coming in and who was going out. Nothing passed him.

Amethyst doesn't know about my family. The only memory she has is of when my mom took her to a playground and left her there. Well, that's the story we told her.

I needed to keep this secret.

Amethyst has gone this far without knowing. Because if she finds out about what happened that day, then she's going to find out the biggest thing I've kept from her and I risk losing her forever.

"Jessica." Liza comes into the kitchen, handing me her cell phone. "I don't know how long we have."

I clear my throat. "What do you mean?"

"I mean," Liza says, tucking her blonde hair behind her ear. Gosh, she was beautiful. "She is coming."

CHAPTER 36

AMETHYST

I STRETCH MY ARMS WIDE, TRYING NOT TO WAKE MADDOX. Reaching down to grab my phone, I check the time. Just past one a.m. I should leave, but I don't want to. I want this with him.

I look around the room, and even though it's empty with just the king-sized mattress we dropped in the middle of the floor with a few sheets, it felt full because I was with him. He is here. I bury my face in my hands. What the fuck am I going to do?

I stand from the mattress and make my way to the little patio that hangs off the room, quietly sliding the door closed behind myself. I suck in the fresh salt air, gripping the railing. My hair floats in the whisk of wind as the angry ocean waves crash against the heavy sand.

"You ok?" His voice pulls me out of my peace, and I smile. "Yeah."

I look out to the ocean, watching the waves pelting against the sand. It is therapeutic, and one of the many reasons why I loved the Hamptons, I love Long Island too though.

He cages me in from behind, an arm on either side of me. He leans down and kisses the side of my neck. "What are you thinking about?"

"I'm thinking that I have to face the music back in LA. I need to do something about this sex tape."

He stills, then his hands come to my hips and he spins me around to face him.

His index finger hooks under my chin, tilting my head up. "Tell me what you want to happen, and it's done, baby."

"No." I shake my head, swallowing past the fear that clogs my throat. "I don't want you involved in this, Maddox. You've got your own career."

"Fuck my career."

I yank my head out of his grip, but his fingers clench around my chin, pulling my face back to his. He leans down, his lips brushing over mine. "I'm fucking serious, Amethyst. If you need me, fuck anything and everyone else."

I focus on him, all of my attention just on him. People always said that I could handle him. That I was the only girl walking this earth that knew how to handle Maddox Stone, but that was a lie. I didn't know what the fuck I was doing. He terrified the shit out of me. His loyalty to me frightened me, because I knew without a shadow of a doubt that he would kill and be killed for me. How can girls want that? That's too much responsibility for me to handle. That means without me even wanting it, he could go and do something dumb and there's nothing I could do about it. So in essence, I had no control over him.

I lick my lips. "I don't want you to do that for me, Maddox. I can handle this my own. I have a team of people who can handle this all professionally."

He pauses, his jaw tensing. Now what have I done to piss him off. "I know I don't have to ask you this, but for my peace of mind, what exactly are you going to do about it?"

My eyes narrow. "Well, I'm not going to sell it to a porn company if that's what you think!" I snap, folding my arms in front of myself. "First, I'm going to sue him. Then I guess I'll go from there after I've spoken to my lawyer."

"Sue him? Baby, you can't. I mean, what he did was unethical, but you can't sue him for releasing it. You allowing him to video was you signing your right to do that. I guess you can send DMCA's to all the websites that are viewing them, but suing him?"

"That's the thing…" I say, gritting my teeth and unable to look him in the eye. "I didn't allow him to."

Silence. Then his hand comes to my chin again, forcing my eyes to his. "What?"

I sigh. "I didn't know he was taping me. I was on drugs, Maddox. Hard drugs. I was in a dark place. After we broke up, I was fucked up for a while. Longer than I care to admit. When I first met Travis, I dived straight into him. I snorted the drugs, inhaled the weed and sucked down all of the alcohol. I wasn't a good person. That night, we had done lines and bong hits and had been drinking since lunchtime that day. We had a stupid threesome." I wipe the tears from my eyes, slamming them closed. I don't want to look at him, I couldn't handle whatever way Maddox will be looking at me right now. "We went upstairs into his room and I couldn't even see straight. God." I open my eyes, staring straight at him. "I couldn't hear anything, I couldn't see, I couldn't feel. I thought I was going to die—that's how high I was. I don't remember that video."

Maddox bows his head, leaning back and gripping onto the railing of the porch. His shoulders are rising and falling, his breathing heavy.

"Maddox?"

He shakes his head, still not looking at me.

I've disappointed him. My heart snaps. "I'll show myself out."

I go to walk out, but he stands, his hands coming to the backs of my thighs and he lifts me off the ground. I wrap my legs around him, and it's then I see his face. His eyes are feral, frantic. Pure black and dilated.

"See this?" Maddox says, his nostrils flaring. Fuck, he's angry. "You do this to me, Amethyst. You make me fucking crazy!" He takes me back into the room, kicking the sliding door closed. He throws me onto the mattress and dives in behind me.

He pulls me into his arms. "I'll kill him."

"No, Maddox." I turn to face him, hiking my leg up on his hip. I press my palm to his face. "I mean it!"

He lets out a loud and long growl, then pushes me off him and slams his fist into the mattress. I don't flinch, no way do I flinch. I trust this man with my life. Even at his angriest, I know that he would rather cut off his left nut than make me feel unsafe.

Well, maybe not his nut, but like, his arm or something.

"Fuck, Amethyst. What you're asking of me is unreasonable."

I turn to face him. "No, it's not. And anyway, I'm going back to sort it all out tomorrow."

CHAPTER 37

AMETHYST

THE NEXT MORNING, I'M GATHERING ALL MY CLOTHES FROM Maddox's house when my phone starts ringing in my pocket. Maddox had to leave early this morning for something but said he'd be back to take me to the airport. I had to physically stop him from coming with me and said that he and Ken can come visit on the weekend. He agreed after I agreed that I'd take his jet.

I answer the call. "Yes?"

"Hi, so I've spoken with the lawyers, and they've said that on top of the Digital Millennium Copyright Act, and other laws that can help pull the videos down from websites, we can also sue him for damages in humiliation, embarrassment, emotional distress, and an invasion of privacy, but" —she takes a deep breath then exhales— "something really fucking strange happened."

"Okay?" I answer, dropping my bags near the front door.

"So, Travis woke from his coma last night and he said that he will be issuing you a formal apology and has already taken all of the videos offline. Now, you can still sue him for all of the other things, but—"

I pause. "What?"

"I know, right? He said that he got what he wanted. His intention has been met."

"What the hell does that even mean?"

She whistles, and then breathes into the phone. "I have no idea, but Amethyst, he's a weirdo and a creep. I would suggest you stay away from him."

"Got it," I say absently, hanging up on her.

None of this makes sense. I go into the kitchen and get to making a coffee. Why would he all of a sudden retract everything after causing a fucking shit show? What was his intention? To hurt me? To hurt Maddox? No, it has to be more than that, or maybe I am giving Travis too much credit. He's not that smart.

Maddox comes home and puts my bags into his Phantom.

"You own a mafia car…" I tease, getting into the passenger seat.

"I own many cars, baby."

"Of course you do."

I clip my seat belt on and wait until he's in the driver's seat. I turn to face him. "Hey so, Alesha, she's my PA, called me while you were gone. She said that Travis woke last night and is retracting everything. He's had it all removed from the net— even though we both know there will always be something somewhere—but he's issuing a formal apology too."

Maddox's head tilts as he drives us out onto the highway. "The fuck is he playing at?"

His jaw ticks.

I pause, hitting the radio. "Glycerine" by Bush starts playing and I turn it up. I love this song. His voice reminds me of Kurt Cobain. I won't tell Maddox that, he'll no doubt get offended. No one is Kurt Cobain but Kurt Cobain.

"I don't know," I answer, looking out the window at the passing concrete on the freeway. We pull into the airstrip and Maddox stops near his jet.

I shake my head. "Oh how far you have come…"

He stops, taking off his aviator glasses and putting them on the dash. "I'll be there this weekend."

"Okay," I answer. "And what are we doing?"

He licks his lip. "I don't know, but I know that you're mine and I'm not letting you go this time."

I smile. "Bringing Ken?"

"Yeah," he answers.

"Cool!" I say, opening my door. "Her and I need to finish my halfpipe." I get out and stretch my arms above my head, cranking my neck to look at the sun.

"What?" Maddox says, shutting his door.

I pause. "Shit." What a fucking idiot. "Sorry, I don't want to get anyone in trouble..."

He rounds the car. "Spit it out."

"Cass and I have sort of, well no not sort of, we have become close friends."

He watches me closely. "And?"

Maybe he won't be mad. "And her and Ken have come to visit me a couple times, staying for the weekend. Ken and I painted the halfpipe I got built at home. We took photos, a couple of them are on social media."

His lips pinch in, his cheeks turning red. "Really?"

"Are you mad?"

"Amethyst," he takes me in his arms, kissing my head. "Ken adores you and you her, why would I be mad about that?"

I sigh, relaxing. "I don't know, because you've been pretty moody lately."

"I'm sorry, baby," he whispers into my hair and then gestures to the waiting jet. "This Travis shit fucked me up, and us..." He says us, and it hits me in my chest.

I nod. "I know."

He grins, kissing my lips. "It's your birthday this weekend?"

"Is it?" I ask, my eyes going to the side. "Nope, I don't think so... you must have me mistaken. For someone else."

He shoves me playfully. "We'll be there."

"When you say we…"

"Yup." He reaches inside the car to grab his sunglasses. "I mean everyone."

CHAPTER 38

AMETHYST

I DRIVE HOME QUICKLY, DODGING THE PAPS ON MY WAY. I HIT call on Alesha as soon as I enter my house, she answers instantly.

"Yolo!"

"Stop," I chuckle, walking into the kitchen. "I think I need to get some extra security for a while, just until this sex tape charade stops."

"Yes, I think that's a good idea. I have a couple of people who come highly recommended. I'll give them a call and see if they're available. Do you have any preference? Would you rather male?"

"I don't have any preference, just a couple people to stick around for a bit."

"Done, anything else?"

"Yes, I'll be back in the studio tomorrow."

"Anything, anything else?"

I pause, shutting the fridge door. "Is there something you want to ask me, Alesha?"

She pauses. "Um…. Maybe."

"Spill…"

She clears her throat, but I already know what she wants to know so I jump in. "Yes, Maddox Stone and I have history, deep history, yes, we sort of have a thing between us, no we're not exclusive yet."

She screams. Full on girly screams. I push the phone away from my ear before the sharpness pierces my brain. "Okay, wow! Oh my gosh that's… that's…"

"Strange?"

"I was going to say hot, but yes and strange. So, you're not together right now?"

"As in a couple?" I ask, sipping my juice.

"Yes…"

"No." The uncertainty must be in my tone.

"…Are you sure?"

"No, I mean yes, I'm sure. I think."

"You suck at this."

I put the lid back on my OJ. "Okay, we already know this, moving on… get those bodyguards!"

I hang up the phone before she can interrogate me anymore. Were we? We didn't define anything before I left, now I'm confused. Fuck. I need a bath and some wine.

Grabbing the bottle of red I keep in my cupboard and a glass, I make my way upstairs into my bathroom, turning the tap on. I pour some bubble bath into the water and inhale deeply as the aroma of crystalized lavender dances in the air. I relax, reaching for the glass and pouring in the wine. As much as I loved seeing everyone, I really love being home and back in my space. I pull open the drawer and take out a lighter, sparking up all the candles. Removing my clothes, I catch my phone ringing and answer it.

"Hey, Mom."

"Hey, honey," she whispers softly. "Just making sure you got home ok. Sorry we weren't there to catch you."

"Of course I did," I chuckle, turning off the faucet and removing my panties. "Maddox wouldn't have it any other way, and no problem. I know you're both busy."

She exhales in relief. "Oh, that's lovely, honey. Did he go back to LA with you?"

"Hmm?" I ask, but it echoes because the goblet glass is in my face. "No? He's coming back with everyone this weekend for my birthday."

Silence.

I step into the hot bath, looking down at my phone to make sure it's still connected. "Mom?"

"Yes, honey, hey look. I might fly over tomorrow."

"Ok…" I sink into the hot water. I sigh, enjoying the stabs against my skin. "Are you okay?"

"Yes, yes. Do you have security or something there until I get there tomorrow?"

My eyes open. "Mom, you're being weirder than usual…" Realization sinks in. "Oh, this is about the sex tape isn't it?" I giggle. "Mom, it's okay. I've called my assistant and she's in the middle of getting some security. You don't need to come all the way here early. Come when everyone else does."

"Amethyst," she says, and just when I think she's going to say something, she exhales. "You're right, I'm probably overreacting. Can you have security tomorrow?"

"Yes, Mom. Okay, I'm going to go now. I love you."

"I love you, Amethyst. So much."

We hang up and I shake my head. I'm aware how lucky I am to have a mom who cares so much about me, but I'd be lying if I said that it wasn't overwhelming sometimes.

A notification for Instagram pops up and I open it.

maddoxthedestoyerstone started following you.

Hmm. A cheesy smile comes on my face. I click on his name, my heart pounding in my chest.

44 posts 66.4M followers 1 following

I click on the "Following" tab. My profile sits there: fliptrick. "Jesus fucking Christ."

I go back to my Instagram page, that has a comfortable 2.3M followers, but I'm following around a hundred-twenty people. I'm not a snob like Maddox. He's terrible. My Facebook is what I keep private. Well, I try to. I only accept people I know and family, but there are followers on there too.

A text comes through.

Maddox: Where are these photos of you and Ken?

I smile, typing out my reply.

Me: They're on my FB.

Maddox: Let me in.

I shake my head. **Me**: You're already on there! I've had the same Facebook.

Maddox: Oh, shit.

He disappears, so I open Facebook and sure enough, he's online. Messenger pops up **(1)**.

Maddox: Fuck, how'd I miss these?

Me: I don't know. You're not active on here.

A bunch of notifications pops up. Maddox Stone reacted to your photo. He liked them all, but "Loved" all of mine and Ken's selfies. There's one photo of us, both with hair in messy pigtail buns and of Ken painting a mustache on my upper lip. There's one of us pouting, pulling duckface, and then gangster faces. There's even one of Ken and I and Cass. Cass is posing, her tits sticking out while Ken rolls her eyes and I stick my tongue out between my teeth, my nose scrunched.

Maddox Stone commented on your photo: Jesus fucking Christ, Cass. Put them away.

A few beats later, I get another notification.

Cassidy Archer replied to a comment on your photo: Who let him in?

Maddox puts a rolling eye emoji.

I snort, shaking my head and place my phone back on the counter, sinking into the water. So good to be home.

CHAPTER 39

MADDOX

"The fight is going ahead, thank fuck. Travis isn't pressing charges and has taken full responsibility for the tape this morning by releasing a statement."

I squeeze my eyes shut, over the drama already. The fucker brought it on himself, but it still doesn't add the fuck up.

"Are you listening, Mad?" Stace says, pushing her glasses down her face. We've been here for all of thirty minutes and I'm already over her yapping.

"Yeah."

She takes her glasses off, just as Reva, one of my boys, takes a seat beside me. Stace chose this café, I didn't want to be out in public. Everything has kicked off even more since all this mess, plus throwing Amethyst into the midst of it too only adds to the hype.

Reva nudges his head at Stace. Stace smiles politely, but we know how uncomfortable he makes her, which only makes Reva intensify his bullshit. It's tiring. Reva is from France and has held the title for his weight division for going on four-years. He's built like a house, thick and heavy, and deadly.

"I don't bite, Stacey," he says in his accent.

I roll my eyes.

Stace swallows and then looks back to me. "Ah, so, when is Amethyst's birthday?"

I take a swig of my water, pushing my sunglasses up. "We're all flying out to her tomorrow."

Stace nods. "I need to come."

"Yeah, I don't think that's—"

"—Maddox, she's not the insecure type. She wasn't threatened by me when I first met her when she thought we were dating, she won't care about me now. And besides," Stace mutters, fluffing through her papers. "Have you seen her? She's like, perfection."

I grin. "She is."

Reva side eyes me. "She is."

My head snaps to him. "Yeah?"

Reva laughs, stabbing into his sausage. "Yes, she is."

But I can't be mad about that. Amethyst is perfection with a rebellious soul. She's unique, untamed and wild. Fuck. She raises my feral side.

"Maybe I should tell the fam to leave tonight. Can you do tonight?"

I rub my chest. I hate the feeling that stab there every time I think of her not being near me.

"Sit down," Stace orders, gesturing to my chair. "Your dick can wait one more night."

I crank my neck and sit back down.

"Now, so this Travis thing is a mess."

"Yeah." I pull my phone out, grinning at Ken and Amethyst's photo I saved as my wallpaper.

"So we need to answer the press on what you and Amethyst are…" Stace says.

"No, we don't." I shake my head. "Fuck that, I don't owe anyone shit."

"Maddox, you're a public figure. It's the least you could do, and it will give everyone a piece of the truth."

I clench my jaw. "I'll talk to Amethyst about it first."

"You are together now, right?" Stace asks.

"Yeah."

"So, she said that you guys are now a couple?"

I glare at her. "Stace, this is me and Amethyst. We don't need to define shit. You can't put a label on what we have, trust me, I've fucking tried."

After breakfast, I go back home and call Kennedy. I bought her a phone so I can call her whenever I want. Cass wasn't hot on it, but she allowed me to do it anyway. Considering she was Mrs. "this is the way of the future, leave her with her iPad," she really didn't have a leg to stand on.

"Hey, Daddy."

"Hey, princess, how was school?"

I make my way into the closet and pull out a whole bunch of clothes. "It was okay, but Linda was mean."

I pause. "Who's Linda? That a teacher?" I shove shit into my bag.

"No, she's a girl in my class. She was my friend, but she started being mean to me today."

My face scrunches. "Who even calls their kid Linda."

"I know, right?"

I clear my throat. Fucker. "Don't worry about her, baby. You have lots of friends."

"Yeah, I know, do you want to talk to Mama? She's in the gym with that guy."

"What guy?" I ask, taking a seat on the bed.

"She has a new boyfriend." Of course she does. "Melissa is cooking dinner again, but I like her cooking because Mom can't cook."

"This is true."

"What are you doing?"

"Ah, getting ready to fly to LA…"

"Oh?" That perks her interest. I wonder why. "Why?"

I smirk. "You got something to tell me, princess?"

She pauses, then sighs dramatically. "Fiiinneee, me and Mommy have been going to see Ame."

My smirk widens. "I know, baby, hey can you put your mom on?"

"Yup! Love you, Daddy!"

"Love you too, baby."

There are muffled sounds and music playing before Cass answers. "To what do I owe the pleasure."

I massage my temples. "It's Amethyst's birthday this weekend, we're all flying there tomorrow morning. I'll get you and the kid picked up."

She clears her throat. "Um, well actually, we're going there tonight."

"Of course you are," I shake my head. "Alright well, I'll see you tomorrow."

"Okay, and hey, Mad?"

"Yeah?"

"Don't fucking hurt her."

Then she hangs up. Why the fuck do people keep saying that. If there are any two people walking this earth who I will never hurt, it's Amethyst and Kennedy. I toss my phone onto my bed, just as the doorbell rings.

I jog down the stairs and swing it open to my dad and Jessica. "Everything ok?" I search the look on both of their faces.

"Yes," Jessica says. "But I need to talk to you about something."

I let her and Dad in and shut the door, gesturing to the kitchen. "After you."

CHAPTER 40

AMETHYST

Chris Brown's "Privacy" is blasting through my house and I'm dancing and singing around the kitchen. Alesha is here helping prepare the food.

"You know, we can hire people to cater all this?"

I shake my head. "No way! I'm old school. We can do it all ourselves."

"Amethyst?" One of the guys who are walking around my house to help set up comes in. "Yeah, the fire pit is all set up!"

"Perfect!" I suck down some more wine.

Alesha looks to the glass then back to me. "Should you be drinking during the day? Won't everyone be here soon?"

"Yes," I hiss, winking at her. "But they're my family and friends, Lesh, chill."

She has a Bluetooth thing in her ear still, answering calls. She leaves the room, pushing the button. "And drink something!" I yell at her. She's a brilliant PA, I can't fault her on that, but seriously, live a little.

I run upstairs and quickly get ready, throwing on some skinny jeans and a white strapless crop top that has the words "Punk Chick" splashed across it. It shows all of my stomach and is a bold move considering my diet lately consists of chocolate and potato chips, but dresses still aren't my thing. Besides, I want to wear my belly chain. I comb my hair and leave it in its natural state. Wavy and thick down my back. I'm excited to see everyone, but mainly to see Maddox and Ken. I feel bad because I haven't spoken to Leila much over the past week, but we have the kind of friendship that doesn't need constant interaction. Unicorn friendship.

Later that night once everyone is here, Maddox pulls me down beside him, lacing his hands with mine. He kisses me on my head. "You ok?"

"Yep, a little buzzed."

"Buzzed?" He laughs. "Baby, you're a little more than that."

I chuckle, sipping my water. Having Ken around makes me not want to be a mess. If she wasn't here, I'd be having shots.

Maddox's eyes drift to the halfpipe behind us. "Can't wait to see all this art tomorrow."

I follow his sight. "Yeah, it's something else. Maybe you can help us finish the rest."

"Sure thing, baby." His focus goes to my mom, then to Elliot, before coming back to me with a tight smile on his mouth.

"Where are Talon and Liza?" I ask, finally noticing that they're not here.

"Talon will be here a little later."

"Okay, and Liza?"

"Liza couldn't make it."

Cass and Kennedy left around ten p.m. I told them they didn't need to check into a hotel, but Cass didn't really want to stay with Maddox here. I guess the set up would be a little weird with her and I and him under the same roof.

I didn't push Maddox any further with where Liza was. I figure her and Talon must have had a big fight. It was nearing midnight and I was more than drunk.

We're all sitting around the fire pit, music in the background. "Birthday Sex" starts playing and my eyes dart around. They land on a smug and grinning Leila, sipping her drink and watching me.

I scowl at her. "Bitch."

My phone vibrates in my pocket and I stand, reaching to grab it out.

Unknown: Hey, Ame, it's Liza. I'm outside. Can you come and talk? Don't tell Maddox.

Confused, I stand from the log that's around the fire and send her a quick text back.

Me: B out in 5

Maddox grabs my hand as I stand. "Where you going?"

I gesture inside. "To get more ice."

He halts, his hand squeezing mine briefly and then he shakes his head and let's go. "Ok. Don't be long." He's being extra over-protective, more than usual.

"Awwww," Leila teases. "Y'all so cute."

"Shut up, Lei," he snaps, and I take this moment to quickly dip through the glass doors and jog through the sitting room, heading straight for my front door. Pulling it open, I jog out to the road, which isn't far from my front entrance.

A black limo is parked on the side of the road. I tilt my head, examining it. The car is on and the headlights are dim. Goosebumps break out over my skin from the sweep of wind that rushes through and I reach for my phone just as another text comes through.

Unknown: I'm in the limo.

My eyes go from my phone to the limo. I didn't know much about Liza outside of her and Talon. Didn't know anything about her as a person when she wasn't with Talon, or her family, mainly because I never thought to ask. So really, maybe she is rich, but I just didn't know. I head toward it, figuring I've been a pretty shit friend and stepsister-in-law for not asking more about her. She must be upset and that's why she hasn't come inside. I wonder what the hell Talon has done now.

I pull open the limo door and lean inside. "What's he done no—" I pause when I see Liza isn't in here. Just when I'm about to run, the sole of a shoe slams into the side of my head and everything goes black.

MADDOX

"Maddox?" Jessica comes over to me, just as I'm getting up to see what the hell is taking Amethyst so long. "Where's Ame?"

I look at the house. "She went to get more ice."

There's a long pause that passes between us, and then I sprint into the house. "Amethyst?" I call out, going into the kitchen. Everything is unmoved. Wolf and Leila come walking in through the glass doors, Leila giggling.

"What's going on?" she asks. When she sees the seriousness of mine and Jessica's face, her smile disappears.

I run up the stairs, taking two steps at a time.

"I'm sure she's fine, son!" Dad calls to me from below, but I've blocked everyone out.

"Ame?" I yell, slamming open every bedroom door. I run downstairs, almost tripping on a few steps and fly out the front door. "She's not here."

My heart pounds in my chest as my blood boils. Helpless. I feel fucking helpless and out of control. The street is dead quiet, no sign of life. Just black shadows from the trees and crickets chirping in the distance. My fists clench, jaw tense. Something catches my eye across the road, so I slowly make my way to it.

My heart fucking stops when I see it's Amethyst's phone. Picking it up, I clench it and storm back to the house.

"Maddox?" Jessica whimpers, clutching the necklace around her neck.

"They took her."

"What?" Leila shrieks, confused. I storm past her and head into the kitchen, just as my phone rings in my pocket.

I answer, unable to speak. I can't even fucking see straight let alone speak. *She was just here.*

"I still can't find Liza! I can't find her anywhere, it's like she's just disappeared."

"They took Amethyst," I whisper out, my vision fixed on the wall. "They fucking took her!"

"Who fucking took her?" Leila says, panicking and looking around the room.

Everyone who is anyone is in the kitchen now. The rest of the guests have started filing out and leaving. I look to Wolf.

"Get these fucking people out of this house."

I breathe in and out. I'll get her back, and I'll fucking spill blood in the process. Dad is already on his phone and Jessica is crying near the dining table. Leila was with her, rubbing her back and Wolf had disappeared to tell everyone to leave. Alesha comes in and catches my eye.

"I'll help get everyone out." Her eyes glass over. "Do you want me to alert authorities? Or is this going to be handled privately?"

I look to Elliot, who pauses his talking and covers the end of his phone. "Privately. Just try your best to make sure this doesn't spill into the media and the people who were here tonight shut their mouths."

She seems to swallow, and then slowly nods her head, but she looks terrified. I like her. I see why Amethyst had her. She wore her loyalty on her sleeve, a lot like Ame.

"I'll be there as soon as I can," Talon growls and then the line goes dead.

I put my phone on the kitchen counter and inhale and then exhale.

"Maddox?" Leila whispers, and my eyes finally go to hers. "What's going on?"

I look at Jessica. "Jessica has a past that no one knew about. Not even Amethyst."

Leila swallows. "Always knew you were hood, Mama J, but what's going on?"

I inhale and count to ten. "Jessica's mom runs Satan's Angel's MC. Turns out, Jessica had *two* daughters. One, her mom raised within the MC because Jessica had said she could. When Amethyst was little, her grandmother tried to take her, so Jessica made a deal with her mother that if she gave her one of her daughters, she'd leave the other one alone. She wouldn't interfere or try to come after them again."

"—Wait! What do you mean one of her daughters? She only has Amethyst!" Leila says, shaking her head like I had lost my damn mind.

I snort. "Yeah, well, it turns out that's not entirely true, is it *Mama J*." My lip curls. I fucking hate her in this very moment.

"Son..." Elliot warns.

My eyes cut to him. "Shut up, Dad! Just shut the fuck up." I exhale, squeezing the counter. "Liza is Jessica's other daughter. Her and Amethyst are ten months apart, making them Irish twins. Liza's dad is someone in the MC. Listen," I exhale, annoyed with this whole fucking thing and wanting my girl back. "Talon only just found out about Liza, and just because this has just come to light, we can't assume that Liza is sitting on their side. We don't know why or what the fuck they want."

Leila screams in frustration, then turns and launches her fist into the wall. I watch as she unfolds in front of me and I want to fucking hold her. In this moment, I know she feels what I'm feeling. I push from the counter and go to her, pulling her into my chest and glaring at Jessica.

Leila starts crying, her arms going around my torso. "I'll kill Liza if she has anything to do with this, Maddox."

Right now, we're just a girl's best friend and her boyfriend who are fucking falling apart.

"I know." I kiss her head. "But we need to fucking get her back first."

Leila steps backward, rubbing the tears from her cheeks.

"Ok." Her shoulders square and I know it's game on. "What's the plan? How long have you known?"

I shake my head, going back to the counter to get my phone. "Since fucking yesterday. I was going to tell Amethyst tomorrow. I didn't want to ruin her birthday."

"That story is true," Jessica clears her throat. "When Amethyst was two, Liza went with Paulette. Amethyst doesn't remember her much, and when she asked about the girl who she only remembers faintly from the day her grandmother tried to take her, I said that she was a friend's child and that's why she hadn't seen her again. It broke my heart to do it, but Amethyst never belonged in that life, Liza did from birth. Her father is the president now."

I narrow my eyes. "Did Liza know about Amethyst?"

Jessica swipes the tears from her eyes. "Yes and no, she didn't want to hurt Amethyst. She wanted to know her, but I pleaded with her not to tell her that she was her sister. Amethyst will never forgive me if she found out what I did."

I hit dial on my phone, Jessica's eyes fly to mine. "What are you doing?"

"Jonah, it's Maddox. We have a problem."

CHAPTER 41

AMETHYST

THE SWEET TANG OF FRESHLY PICKED ROSES AND CHERRY blossoms waft around me in a hypnotic-like aroma and I quickly reach for the blindfold that's secured around my head. Ripping it off, I shoot off the bed and allow my eyes to adjust.

Victorian ancient. Stone walls and white trimmed windows that overlook the backyard. Well, what I'm guessing would be the backyard judging by the tips of the trees I can see poking up in the window. I'm confused. I look around the room, stretching out my wrists that feel as though they've been tied together for months and get to my feet, quietly walking around the room. A small fireplace is built into the wall at the opposite end of the four-post bed and the walls are trimmed in dark maroon paint. There's an articulate painting hanging over the fireplace that looks to be two hands in one. A baby hand sketched onto an image of a real adult hand. There's dark smudged grey over the edges, but it's framed and, to be honest, a little eerie. The room is nice in appearance, but the empty pit in my stomach doesn't sit right with me.

A door opens and my head snaps there automatically, my heart pounding in my chest. A woman stands at the threshold, leaning against a frame. She has short grey hair that hangs perfectly around her jaw and familiar bright blue eyes. Guessing by the visibly aged lines indented into her skin, I'd say she's around late 50s to early 60s. Petite frame and not much shorter than me. She's wearing a leather biker vest over a long sleeved white V-neck and tight jeans with black leather boots.

Who the fuck is this woman and why does my head hurt.

"Amethyst Tatum," she announces, her voice husky. She smokes, for sure.

"Yes?" I look around the room in skepticism. "Excuse me, but why did you steal me?"

She laughs while walking into the bedroom more. I counter her steps by walking backward. She catches it and laughs again. There's a big man with an equally big beard who is standing behind her, wearing the same vest. I squint my eyes on the patch in the front, since his is much larger than the small one she bears, and I see the snake emblem with "Satan's Angels MC." Never heard of them, ever, then again, I don't have anything to do with motorcycle clubs. They kind of freak me out, if I'm being honest. The woman sits on the chair that is directly in front of the window, the sun bright behind her, her grey strands now casting shadows over her face. I can barely make out her expression. My head aches and just as I open my mouth, a sharp throbbing pounds at my temple again.

"Seriously, why did you hit me and where is Liza?"

Oh God. Liza.

I square my shoulders. "If you've hurt her, trust me, your biker friend there" —I gesture to the back of me— "has nothing on her man, or mine, for that matter."

The woman doesn't say anything, she merely watches me with interest. Then she tilts her head and clasps her hands on her lap. "You really don't know who I am, do you?"

I catch her eyes narrow when she moves her head. "No, I really don't, but if it's money you want, I can give it to you. If you let me go now." This has to have something to do with Maddox. Maybe he pissed someone off in a fight or something, who knows.

She snorts. "Amethyst, I am your grandmother."

My mouth drops open. "What?"

I fall onto the bed behind me, wincing again from the pain in my head. I press my palm to it, bringing it back down to see blood on my hand. "Oh."

Her eyes lift to my head and then come back to mine. "I can get someone to fix that if you want."

My lip curls. "Thanks, but I think I'd rather just take my chances." My stubbornness may just be the death of me. Maddox was right. I swallow, gulping past the pain his name alone rises inside of me. I don't want to think of him right now.

She laughs, leaning forward and resting her elbows on her knees. "You know, you're so much like your mother."

"You would know?" I ask, feeling dizzy. Sweat trickles down my face.

"Well, I guess I wouldn't really." She leans backward. "Not anymore."

"I'm your grandmother, Amethyst, and your mother hasn't been entirely honest with you through the years."

"That, I believe," I murmur, then close my eyes and try to calm the pounding of my head.

Thud.

Thud.

"Did you hear me, Amethyst?" she says. She? A voice?

Who is she? Oh, wait. "What?" My eyebrows pull together.

"Liza is your sister. She was raised in the MC, with me and her old man. She's ruined, I no longer have use for her, unfortunately."

"Who?" I ask, confused. "Why does my head hurt?"

I look around aimlessly. Smudged maroon walls, white trimmings. Four-post bed.

My eyes go to the strange woman on the seat. Her head tilts, confusion warping her ugly features. "Amethyst, I just told you three times. I'm your grandmother."

"My grandmother is dead. Where am I?" I ask, getting to

my feet. Everything starts spinning so I sit back down. "I don't think that's a good idea."

Silence.

"Listen," I say, resting my head on the side of my palm. "I need to get back to school. I have to study, and I have this new dorm chick who I don't really like because she's frilly and annoyingly rich and pretentious. I need to leave." I stand, but everything in my head tips upside down and I crash to the floor with blackness taking me over.

CHAPTER 42

LIZA

I MAY HAVE NOT BEEN SOMETHING THAT MY MOM WANTED AS A young girl. I probably wasn't pretty enough or wasn't Amethyst enough, but obviously, I wasn't enough. Because my father wasn't Jonathan Kelly, that means I didn't quite make the cut. Attending Columbia was always what I wanted to do, I didn't mean to run into Amethyst. I didn't mean to even start being friends with her. I knew she was attending because Gran had told me. I had every intention of staying well away from her. I hated her. I hated her so much it burned through my skin and almost killed me. As I got older, that hatred grew with me. Why wasn't I enough for my mom? I hated her more than I hated Amethyst. Amethyst I had envied, but our mom, I had despised.

Talon and I happened, and we happened fast. I met him my first day of Columbia and we hit it off instantly. He was everything that the men I was surrounded with weren't, but he wasn't a pussy. He could hold his own, and I'd later find out just how dark his bedroom fantasies were. He was big, tanned, muscled, and had a foul mouth on him. He was everything I wanted without my even knowing it. We started dating, but I told him from the get-go that I wasn't looking for a man. We were in college, there was no way I was going to end up like half the old ladies at the compound who are locked down with a bunch of kids they initially didn't want, just for the love of dick. He countered my offer with an open relationship, so I upped his offer by asking if swinging was on the table—it was. Swinging was our Sunday fun day activity, because Sunday is the Lord's day, so on Sundays, we sin. We started playing around a lot, but inside, my feelings for him grew, and his for me. We could never let each other go.

But the night Maddox and Amethyst ran into one another, I almost walked away for good. I disappeared that night and went back to the compound to gather my wits. I told my gram that Amethyst might start having a thing with Maddox, Talon's brother. Gram told me to just go with it. She wouldn't know who I was—ever. Gram told me that my mom didn't want me, but that doesn't mean that I had to hold that hate toward Amethyst, so I went back to Talon and officially met Amethyst. At first, I thought she was weird, uptight and a little snobbish. She wasn't popular, or anything like that, well, not in an obvious way. She never noticed it, but everywhere she went men would look at her. Women would be snide to her. She wasn't popular, no, but everyone knew who she was. No one spoke to her though, no one approached her, and I knew why, it's because Amethyst was elusive. She didn't have a face that welcomed you. She had a face that made you second guess your existence because she was *that* fucking perfect. Down to her swollen lips, everything about her was carved to perfection. I was average, so not only did she steal my mom, my life, and the looks, but she obviously had the kind of confidence about her that you can only get from a mom who loves you and a dad who adores and protects you.

My dad protected me in a different way.

It was two weeks, and a lot of conversations later that I felt that fire that burned inside of me slowly start to simmer. She wasn't really a snob, or up herself, she just didn't care about what was going on around her to pay it any attention.

Three months later I noticed she was kind, loving and attentive. She adored Maddox and he adored her. She was happy, and annoyingly so, I found that made me happy. I found myself becoming somewhat infatuated with her. How she walked, how she tilted her head back and laughed when Maddox would say something dumb. The way she wiggled her eyebrows in a nerdy way, but it came off as seductive. How not only did every man want her, but every girl hated her, while still respecting her. I was obsessed with her. I wanted her to like me. I wanted her to be my sister. I wanted anything and everything she would give me.

When she and Maddox broke up after Cass came back was the first time I felt fiercely overprotective over something. I never cared enough to give it before, not even with Talon. It's why our relationship worked so well, but when Maddox left her, I wanted to kill him and bathe in his blood. I wanted to keep in touch with her, but I didn't think she ever really warmed up to me, or just didn't care. I bet she didn't even know my favorite color, but I knew hers, and her birthdate, what she had for lunch the day before and exactly how long it takes for her to eat an apple. I became ferociously obsessed, following her every move on social media. When Wolf and Leila's wedding came around, I couldn't wait to get some time with her, hopefully tell her about us, about how we were sisters, but then she dived back into Maddox and then the drama with Travis. When I caught Maddox and Tiffany sucking each other's face, I had to fight every single instinct inside of me that wanted to knock her the fuck out. I wanted one of the brothers to slit a Chelsea grin across her smug face while I watched. I hated Tiffany but absolutely despised her after that. Thankfully, she wasn't around much after that because Lei woke up.

I cough, vision coming in and out. "Wake up!"

I wake, shaking my head. "I don't know who you are or what you want, but my family will come for you!" I scream, ignoring the blood that's seeping down the front of my throat from my mouth.

When Amethyst left after that, I felt empty and moped around a lot. I would soon realize that I was actually in love with Talon, and I lost myself in him. She wasn't around much when she and Maddox were fighting or separated, or both, so there were only a few times I really got to see her until she and Maddox happened *again*.

This morning, I was taken. I knew it was coming eventually, I lived a life that wasn't sheltered like Amethyst's life. The roof that kept me warm at night had holes as big as tires. I was somewhat warm, and sometimes sheltered, but there was always that drizzle of rain or that cold whisk of winter's air that would shiver over me. I wasn't untouched or protected like she was.

The men who took me, I notice are from our rivalry MC club. They've been at war with my grams and the SAMC for as long as I can remember. Last night Talon and I got into a fight. A big one, about Amethyst. Maddox had told Talon about her and I spilled everything. I told him everything about how I became obsessed with her, wanting to be just like her. We fought, then we fucked, then we fought again. Then he tied me to the bed and made me sit and watch while he fucked another girl. I kneeled, gagged, mascara running down my face, ropes tied around my wrist while he fucked this girl senseless all while watching me. I cried because I loved him, and we hadn't swung or been with other people in almost a year. This felt like cheating, and it was. He broke my heart when he fucked her savagely, but he shattered my soul when he made love to her.

After she left, he told me that he and she had been seeing each other for a while now and that I had neglected him by becoming obsessed with my long-lost sister, so in short, she essentially took my one true love too.

She took everything from me, yet I still would give anything just to have her notice me. To like me. For us to even just be friends, but that would never happen. Not ever. Now I don't even have Talon.

"I don't know what you want." I tug at the ropes around

my wrists. Somewhat similar to the ones Talon had me in last night.

Talon.

Did I love him more than I loved Amethyst? No.

Yes.

No.

It doesn't matter, because now I don't have either of them. Why was I still thinking of Amethyst in this very moment?

I'm dirty and unwanted. No one has ever claimed me. My mom, someone who is supposed to be wired to love me by nature herself couldn't even love me, that's how unlovable I was. That's how dirty I was.

The man laughs. I notice who he is. Gunner Lomoas, the president of Joker's Love MC. He's dusty and old, lines penetrating his olive skin. "Aw, sweetcheeks, we don't want anything."

"Listen, my family is going to come for you…"

"Your family?" He laughs, then stands and shoves a smoke into his mouth. His boots kick up the dusty floorboards, and it's then that I finally look around. I'm in a basement. "Your family are who put you here, sugar."

I'm confused, and my face no doubt displays that.

He continues. "Your grandma, the evil fucking witch that she is, ordered us to take you." He blows out a thick cloud of grey smoke and takes a seat on the aged chair in front of me. "To kill you."

I swallow. "That's not true."

He chuckles. "Baby girl, it's true. She wanted us to kill you, or, make you disappear."

I shake my head, unable to comprehend what he's saying as truth. There's no way she would, she's my grams. She was the only person I knew wouldn't disown me like a piece of shit. "No, she wouldn't."

"Listen." He butts out his smoke. "She did. I have a feeling you don't know your grams very well."

My head bows, tears stream down my face, smudging the dirt from my face. I have no one and nothing to live for. "I trusted her."

He leans back in his chair. "Doll, how are you only just waking up to see that Satan's Angels MC are grub. They're despicable and the shit on the sole of my shoe. The reason why we've been rivaling with them for so long is because they're uncontrollable."

I swallow, letting the tears from my eyes fall down my cheeks. The will to live is lost. I have nothing. No one and nothing. I mean nothing. Not even to people who I thought I meant something to. I'm damaged, broken and the darkness shades my vision so thick that I can no longer see the light at the end of the tunnel.

"Just please make it fast," I whisper, choking on a sob. I sniff my nose and look up to him. This man who I was raised to fear and to kill if I ever got the chance, blinks back at me.

"I won't make it fast, Liza."

My stomach feels hollow as those words break out of his mouth. "I understand." And I did. They're outlaws, they don't do anyone any favors.

"Because I'm not going to kill you, kid."

"What?" My head snaps up, my eyes connecting with his. "What do you mean?" Sweat drips down my temple, my eyebrows tugging in.

He sighs, tossing his cigarette onto the dusty floor and stepping on it with his old military boot. The door opens to the side and someone stands there, but I don't look because I'm too busy watching this man. This feral man who I had heard had done ghastly things to people, is suddenly not going to kill me. Is he going to rape me? Is that it? It's no surprise though. As a woman, we are always conscious of rape. We walk down the street at night and do you know what we're wondering? That's right. We're wondering if some sick son of a bitch is going to rape us.

"Liz?" That voice.

I turn to the door, my lips trembling. Maybe I'm imagining everything now.

He steps in closer and that's when I see him. Is he real? Or am I drugged too? "Talon?"

He leans down, pulling me into his arms. "It's me, baby." He kisses my head and I'm so shocked that I choke on my words. What's happening? He pulls me to my feet then picks me up, cradling me like a baby. He glares at Gunner. "We good?"

Gunner nudges his head. "We're good. Make sure you put in a good word to Maddox for me."

Talon sneers. "Sure."

Then he carries me out of the room. I close my eyes and tuck my head into his warm neck. I don't want to see where I am, I half don't think it's real. Maybe I'm dreaming, and God is playing a sick joke on me. Talon doesn't care about me. I feel the sunlight hit my skin and the scent of fresh cut grass and dried leaves hit me all at once. I squeeze my eyes closed from the bright onslaught of the sun. A car door pops open and Talon gently places me into the back.

"Liza?" It's Maddox.

My eyes open when the car starts off. Blue and pink hues throb in and out from the assault on my eyes. "What, Maddox?" I barely croak out, still overwhelmed with everything that's going on. My gram sent me there to get murdered, but why? I thought she…she raised me. My dad is a sack of shit—everyone knows that. He barely had anything to do with me growing up, so my gram raised me. I thought she loved me. So many memories I have with her, did she fake them all? Did she fake the soft caress her eyes would give me or the strength her arms gave?

I wipe away the tears. Again. I don— "Amethyst has been taken by Paulette, Liza."

I freeze, looking toward Maddox. "What!" My heart pounds in my chest.

"Yes, do you know where they could be?"

I nod, ignoring the fact that maybe Talon doesn't want me, that he probably just wanted me to tell them where Amethyst was. My heart sinks but panic sets in. "I know where they are."

MADDOX

"Stop here," Liza says, gesturing to the side of the road.

"This the compound?" I ask, confused by the location. We're in fucking suburbia. Middle-class family homes. There are playgrounds outside some houses.

Liza shakes her head, "No." She looks up at the house, her eyes broken. Liza has always seemed happy, lively, a lot to give and nothing to ask kinda girl. Something happened to her back there, and we will get to the bottom of it, but all I can think about right now is Amethyst. "It's my dad's house. They," she clears her throat. "They use this house as a halfway house. Somewhere where they don't need to bring heat to the compound if anything goes sour. No evidence there and such." Her hand goes to her chest and her breathing breaks out harshly as her attention comes to me. "God, Maddox, we need to go in there. Now."

I nod my head, then look to Wolf who is beside me, and my dad who is in the passenger seat. "Let's go."

She stops me, just as were all spilling out. "Maddox, they'll be armed."

"Yeah?" Wolf says, and she gets out of the car, shutting the door behind herself. "So are we."

Wolf goes to hand me an AR, and I glare at him, and then look to the gun, before looking back at him again. He takes the gun back. "Good point." Gives it to Liza. "Ever shot one of these before?"

I'm about to take it off her when she grabs it skillfully and cocks it.

"I take that as a yes…" Wolf mumbles, grinning at her.

Talon comes up behind her and swipes her hair off her shoulder. "We'll talk tonight, ok?"

She gives him a hard smile. "Ok."

Just as we're about to start walking up to the house, police cars pull up behind us with SWAT stamped across some of the vans. Leila jumps out of the car and runs toward us, wiping the tears from her face. "I'm so sorry, but I can't let you piss your life away! I called the cops in. I love Amethyst, but you all need to learn when you shouldn't be taking things into your own hands!"

Wolf shakes his head, lowering his arm as the officers start screaming at them all to drop their weapons.

I growl at Leila. Her head bows. "I'm so sorry, Mad, but I can't. I love Amethyst and she will be safe, she's too smart not to be, but the police can handle it now."

I growl again.

Talon steps toward her, his lip curled in a sneer. "You promised, Leila…"

They all drop to the ground, Wolf included.

"I know." She fiddles with her thumbs. "But my baby sort of will need her dad and her uncles not in prison."

Wolf's trademark somber scowl slowly lights up. He beams up at her from the ground, just as I drop to my knees. She's pregnant. Good for them.

"Holy shit," Wolf mutters, just as the police and SWAT pass us, guns raised and head for the house. Camera crews are all pulling up with the paparazzi. Wolf continues. "I can't be a dad."

"Both of you shut the fuck up," I snap, having had enough of their shit.

"Alright, up!" one of the officers says, coming straight to

me. I stand and then barge toward the house. I need to get my fucking girl.

"Maddox!" he yells from behind me, but I don't listen. The news crews and everything are set up now, talking into their cameras.

I ignore him and push forward, just as an ambulance rushes past me.

My walking speeds up to a run and I sprint toward the house. Why does this goddamn driveway have to be so long. I get to the door just as they're wheeling her out on a gurney.

Fuck.

My breathing stops, my legs shake. For the first time in my life, I feel physically afraid. Ever.

Her pink hair is now a dusty brown from the mess and the…she's bleeding. There's blood all over her face and her head.

She's not awake. Why is she not awake? I shove the medic out of my way, but an officer grabs my arms. "What's wrong with her?" I roar, launching to her bed.

I don't even fight the tears that I'm about to shed, because fuck, this is Amethyst. My fucking Amethyst.

"Sir, you need to get out of the way so we can get her to the hospital. Move the fuck out of my way."

I don't move, I'm so stunned by what I'm seeing that I'm lodged in the spot, my feet sunken into the cement.

The officer yanks me back and the ambulance takes off with sirens blaring and lights flashing. I scrub the tears off my face. My jaw clenches and I look to the house, rage erupts inside of me. Rage like I've never felt before.

"No." There are other officers there now, and my brothers, holding me back.

The officer looks into my eyes, and it's when I notice he's in a suit. Detective.

"I'm Detective Osborn, a very good friend of her dad. You

need to let us do our job now." He pulls me in and I physically have to force myself to calm down.

It doesn't work.

I try again.

It still doesn't work. I need to break something. I need to shed blood, I need to kill whoever did that to her.

He leans into my ear. "She's one of our own, Maddox. Whoever did this will never see the light of day again, and then when he's inside?" He pauses and chuckles. "We can have him be taken care of any which way you would like, for as long as you like, however you would like…"

A smidge of serenity settles over me. He steps back and stares right at me. A silent promise. "Her old man is on his way, as we speak, with an army of his people. Do you trust me?" he asks. I take in his gentle brown eyes, olive skin. Somethin' about him just makes me trust him.

He's sincere, I can feel it, so I nod.

"Good." He squeezes my shoulder. "Now go to the hospital and let us do our job here. You need to do yours and be there for when she wakes up."

One week passes.

Two weeks…

MADDOX

She's woken twice, both times she had no memory as to who I was, and even started swearing at Leila asking what the fuck she was doing here. We all stayed at the hospital on mattresses for the entire two weeks. Leila hasn't moved. Same as me. Wolf and Talon have been doing our food runs and general shit we need, as well as driving us home to shower, but then we come straight back. Liza hasn't left either. The hospital had moved Amethyst to a private room and asked us if we wanted beds moved in, but I declined. It would make everything feel way too permanent if they did that.

They had to do surgery on her brain. Christopher Lyon hit her across the head. It wasn't so much the impact of it, although that was bad, it was the timing and placing. I've been hit on the head so many fucking times I can't count, why didn't this ever happen to me? I'd take her place in a fucking heartbeat.

"Who are you?" Fuck. The absence in her eyes will haunt me for the rest of my life.

I run my palm over my hair just as the doors open and her dad steps in. He has aged a few years since this all went down, we all have.

"I would say go home and get rest, but we both know what good that would be."

I give him a polite smile, which is more than I've given anyone else.

The times I've spoken to Ken I've had to act normal. Cass and I decided not to tell her what's going on right now. There's no point in getting her upset. It's been hard to pretend like everything is okay and lying to my daughter every time she asks where her best friend is. I hate it.

I fly to my feet and start pacing the room. I go through

cycles of anger, sadness, and heartbreak. The TV is on in the background, talking about the arrests of Prospect Satan's Angels MC member Christopher Lyons and her grandma. Grandma got let out—fucking bitch Is going to have me to deal with when Amethyst is out of this hospital and back on her feet, but Christopher is getting tried for attempted murder. Little fuck.

I look to the bed where Amethyst lays peacefully. There are lines hooked up to her, around her nose. I asked the doctor how long she had been out for, if she had been out cold since being taken, but he said he didn't know. They wouldn't know the seriousness of her injury until she wakes completely.

If she doesn't remember me, I'll spend the rest of my life demonstrating to her exactly why she fell in love with me. I'll relive our most intimate moments and do it again and again and again until even just an inkling sparks inside of her head.

"She looks so peaceful," Jonah murmurs, brushing her hair off her head.

I nod, but I'm unable to say anything. My mouth is dry, my hands like sandpaper from rubbing them down my jeans. "I never knew about Liza." He pins me with his stare. "If I did, I would have raised her like she was my own."

I shake my head, resting my elbows on my knees. "I don't know you very well, but I believe you."

"Where is she?" Jonah asks, standing tall.

I gesture to the door. "Gone to get coffee. She hasn't spoken much since we saved her from Gunner."

"Gunner Lomoas?"

I bow my head "The very same."

"Interesting…" he says, putting his hands into his pockets. "He runs on the cleaner side of the law, so I'm not surprised he gave her back."

I didn't have the energy to tell him he gave her back yes, because he is clean, and yes, he had a daughter once that would have been around the same age as Liza, but also he did it because he wanted my respect. Men and respect go hand-in-hand. I didn't have the energy, nor did I really give a fuck enough to tell him. Another time. That time being when Amethyst wakes the fuck up. I'm going to beat her ass for this.

"She's going to remember who you are, son," Jonah says, gripping my shoulder. I cup my hands around my mouth and look at her. "What you and her shared, isn't something most people get to experience. Maddox, you both share something so rare that no amount of anything can erase it."

I don't reply. I just swallow past the boulder set in my throat.

The fear of not knowing if she's going to remember is damn near crippling. What if she doesn't want me? What if she doesn't allow me to show her? What would I do then?

I'd lock her in my basement and make her, that's what.

CHAPTER 44

AMETHYST

Brown curls wrap around this girl's face, her blue eyes twinkling with mischief. I hold the spray can in my hand and smile at her. "What are we doing?"

She laughs, deep dimples indenting into her cheeks. "You're so funny, Ame! We're spraying your halfpipe, remember? I'm doing you and Dad and you're doing the pink and blue splatters."

I look back at the splatters. "Why are they neon pink and blue?"

The little girl scrunches up her face, her little piggy buns bouncing. "Because you like fast cars, but also like dressing pretty."

"Huh," I murmur, staring off in the distance. "So I'm half tomboy and half girly girl?"

She nods. "Yup, just like me, remember?"

I don't remember.

"Um," I whisper. "What's your name again?"

She rolls her eyes. "Have you been drinking vodka again?"

I freeze. "No?"

"I'm Kennedy Stone, my—"

Memories invade my brain at one-hundred miles an hour.

Maddox and me laughing, him leaving me, us finding each other. Our first kiss, stumbling onto his bed during our one-night stand, falling out his window and laughing with Leila as we ran back to the taxi, him showing me Dutch, showing me the crash site. *"I love you."*

I shoot off the bed, sucking in desperate breaths.

"Amethyst?" Maddox flies off the seat he's sitting on. I look to him, then to Liza who is beside him, clutching a coffee cup with worry lines etched into her face. She obviously hadn't slept, then I stare to the ground to see the masses of mattresses scattered everywhere with blankets and pillows. Had they stayed the entire time?

"Baby?" Maddox tests, walking to my bed slowly.

I rub my eyes and then clutch onto the steel pole that sits on the other side of my bed. "Where's Ken?"

They both let out a loud exhales of breath. "Holy fuck." Maddox leaps at me, pulling me into his arms. I wince but then sink into him. "I love you."

"I love you too," I murmur, looking up at him. "But seriously, where's Ken?"

CHAPTER 45

Two Weeks Later
AMETHYST

I DON'T KNOW WHAT HAPPENED WHILE I WAS OUT OF IT, because I don't remember not remembering, but I remember the dream I had with Ken in it. When I told Maddox about the dream, he was speechless for days. It wasn't him who made me remember, it wasn't the love I had for him even though that love is infinite, it was the love I had for his child. My child, too. I've claimed her and no one can really do anything about it.

There's a knock on my bedroom door, just as I'm tossing clothes into my bag. "Hey, sugar!" Leila comes in, her hair in a high ponytail and her face free of makeup. She's gone back to brown since she's pregnant. I don't know, something about ammonia not being good for the baby. She's flipped and done a complete one-eighty and I cannot be happier for her. It also has me thinking about maybe having my own child one day. Half me and half Maddox. I don't know whether to be terrified by that or excited. But then again, Ken turned out perfect and her mom has a few screws loose, as much as I love Cass.

"Hey! Are you all packed?"

"Yup!" She sits down on my bed and gazes out the window. "Have you spoken with Liza?"

I gulp. Finding out she was my sister wasn't something easy to swallow, and I've not forgiven my mom for it, or even come close to forgiving her. I don't know when I will, but it won't be anytime soon.

"I'll talk with her when I'm ready."

"Wanna talk about this thing with your crazy fucking grandma?" Leila asks carefully.

I shrug. "Not really, but…" I inhale and take a seat beside her, brushing my hair back. "I don't fucking understand why she needed either of us. I mean, why? Why not just have left Liza and me with mom."

"Because power," Liza murmurs from the doorway.

I shuffle a little. "What does that mean? And you can come in…" I wave her into the room.

Liza falters, but eventually she comes in and takes a seat on the floor in front of us. Leila tucks her feet under her butt to get comfortable, I'm not sure I'll ever be comfortable listening to this story.

"Jessica was her only daughter, and the way the Satan's Angels work by presidency is by lineage. She tried to get pregnant after and before Jessica, but it never happened. If she didn't have someone to take over, then she would lose her presidency once she hit fifty. The reason why she didn't get the gavel taken from her ten years ago is because of me. Because they knew she was grooming me to take her place."

"What made her crazy enough to steal me then? No offense, but if she had you, then why would she start this drama?"

"Travis," Liza whispers, her eyes coming to me.

I freeze. "What?" I still haven't spoken to that little fuck-nut since the sex tape scandal. "What about Travis?"

She shakes her head in disbelief. "He was paid to get with you, make you trust him. He was already your co-worker, it worked. I was going to tell you! I was going to tell you everything. God, Ame!" She exhales, her voice shaky. "I've wanted to tell you everything for so long now, but I couldn't. I was too afraid."

"Afraid of her?" I ask, tilting my head, still trying to wrap my head around the Travis thing.

Liza shakes her head. "No, afraid I'd lose you. Lose you because I didn't tell you straight away, lose you, period."

"You wouldn't have and won't, Liza, but can you tell me more about Travis?"

She nods and continues. "He caused the debacle for a couple reasons, I'm gathering. One was to hurt you and Maddox, which is obvious, but the other is the not-so-obvious. He did it to draw attention to Gram." She clears her throat and straightens her shoulders. "Before I go on, I have to say right now that I can't have kids."

I feel for her, I do. "I'm sorry."

She shakes her head. "It's fine, I healed eventually, and it's a story I don't really want to go into, but my upbringing and the Satan's Angels MC is a nasty one."

I swallow. "When and if you ever want to talk about it, Liza, I'm here."

She pauses and I watch as her eyes glass over and her bottom lip trembles. "Thank you, Ame." Jesus, has no one ever shown her love?

I wave my hand. "Keep going."

She clears her throat. "When my grams found out that I couldn't have children to carry on the legacy, she was appalled. I was basically damaged goods, but she never outwardly said that. She always made me feel loved and wanted. When I told her about my infertility, She seemed sad, but I thought she was just sad for me, as the person who damaged me got 86'd around the time it happened.

I was wrong. So very wrong. She immediately concocted a plan to get you with someone, anyone. She watched your show and saw the connection you and Travis obviously already had and enforced it more, got in his head a lot. They jumped him, then threatened his life, then made a deal with him. He started taking your pills and replacing them to hurry the process. Then when he almost lost you to Maddox at the wedding, she threatened him again. It was shit luck that you got pregnant, but when he told Gram, she was ecstatic. Gram noticed the shift in me, how I was defending you a lot, coming to your defense when they'd talk about you. I tried to do things to stop it, but they started cutting me out of the discussions, so I didn't know anything. To be honest, now that I look back, I see it, where and how she started pushing away from me. She was losing me, but in her mind, I was already lost the second I got raped."

I pause, shooting off the bed and taking a seat with her on the floor. She snuffs her nose and shakes her head. "I'm so sorry, I didn't mean to say that."

"It's ok!" I wipe her tears from her cheeks.

Leila comes down to the other side of her. "Liza, we're family. We care about you as much as we do our own blood. Ok?"

I roll my eyes. "She is my blood, Lei."

Leila glares at me. "Wasn't talking to you."

I chuckle.

Liza giggles. She's used to mine and Leila's strange friendship.

Liza continues. "So, when you lost the baby and dumped Travis, I guess it all went downhill. She figured to get you another way." She looks at me. "I don't know what she had planned for you, Ame, but that house, my dad's house is only used for brutal things that they don't want to take back to the clubhouse. I don't know, but if you ask me, I'd say she had plans to keep you there. Travis's sex tape thing was a cheap way to break you and Maddox up, to separate you long enough to take you, I'm guessing. They just didn't know that nothing can really come between you two."

The information settles in my head like a carnival of psycho clowns. *Up and down and round and round…*

I exhale. "Well, at least it all makes sense now."

Liza nods. "If Maddox finds out about Travis…"

I shake my head and Leila bursts out. "No!"

We all look at each other and agree. "Maddox can never know."

We're all seated in Maddox's jet, waiting for take-off when he comes to sit beside me. Everyone is here except my mom and Elliot.

Talon and Liza, Wolf and Leila, Cass, Kennedy and Cass's new boyfriend. My family, basically.

Maddox's hand finds mine and he intertwines our fingers together. "You okay?"

I smile, snuggling into him. "Yes."

It isn't all a lie, I was okay, I just wasn't sure what to do about my mom.

CHAPTER 46

AMETHYST

Aspen was filled with a lot of laughs, a lot of alcohol, and in mine and Maddox's case, a lot of sex. My mom calls my phone for the hundredth time, so I slide it unlocked to answer. "What, Mom?"

"Hey honey, you answered. Listen, your father and I are on our way to your house, are you home?"

"What?" I sit up on the sofa, look to Kennedy and then make my way into the kitchen. Maddox isn't here tonight, he had to go to Vegas and Cass is on vacation in Australia with Aaron. We do have around five bodyguards all at the property though. Maddox still isn't set on Gram, and I don't think he ever will be. I'm not sure what he is planning to do, but I really hope he doesn't do anything stupid. The last thing we need is a beef with a motorcycle club.

"Fine, but what do you want to talk about, Mom? I know everything."

She sighs. "I know sweetheart, but it's something important and I really need you to understand."

"Okay." I give up. How long can I really be mad at her. I'll hear her out, but I really hope she has something new to give me.

I'm not even back in the sitting room when my front door opens and bodyguard number one who was outside the door pops his head in. "A couple old folks here, one is saying she's your mother?"

I can hear Mom yapping in the background.

I gesture toward him "Send them in." Then I look to Ken,

who has fallen asleep on the sofa halfway through The Greatest Snowman.

"Ame," my dad says, and I spin around to greet him.

"Hey, Daddy." I pull him in for a hug and then hug my mom. She's still my mom, even if I'm not exactly pleased with how she has handled Liza. I'm willing to hear her out.

"Meet me in the dining room, I'll just grab a blanket for Ken."

They both disappear into the dining room as I run upstairs to get a blanket out of the spare room that she sleeps in when she's here. It's Holly Hubbard, and I love it. I love that this kid for someone so young and born in this generation, has a rustic soul. She doesn't get sucked into the cool bullshit in the now, and she always loves to learn about the 90s. I can't wait to pull out the Hansen, Backstreet Boys and NSYNC posters. Maddox will just love it.

I tuck her into the sofa and kiss her head, then turn the TV off. I switch the lamp on that's in the corner of the sitting room, allowing a warm light to penetrate the dark.

I enter the kitchen, Mom and Dad are both seated at the dining table, like a pair of teenagers about to get the talk.

I sigh, opening up my alcohol cabinet and pull down a bottle of whiskey. "This is all I got." Then I grab some glasses and set it all the middle of the table, pushing the flower and glass centerpiece out of my way.

I take a seat. "So." I pour our drinks and then slide them across to each of them. "Let's chat."

Mom exhales, takes a swig and sets it back on the table. "Liza's father and I, we slept together a few times. We were actually together for some time." Another drink. "I had a feeling I was pregnant when I woke up the following morning feeling sick. You were only two months old, and I had only just moved back to New York, getting ready to set up the bookstore. I was confused with the world and struggling with you. I didn't have much help, and I didn't want to share with your dad about how much I was struggling at the time. That pride we share is a curse." Another drink, and a quick clearing of her throat. "I found out I was pregnant with Liza the same day Mom found me back in New York. I told my mom that I couldn't do it. I told her I didn't want my children in this life like I had been, that's why Jonah and I had left. She didn't like that. She needed at least one of you to take over when she passed. Sick fucking rituals they have."

I freeze because I've never heard my mom cuss.

She continues. "She came for you on your second birthday. She had you. You were at the playground and she had left a note on the kitchen table to give her Liza or she was taking you instead. Naturally, she wanted Liza more because of who her father was—"

I interrupt her. "I remember Liza sort of, from when I was a little girl. But not vividly, more like a couple still polaroid images embedded in my brain. I remember her more that day, but because I only remember her once or twice, I believed you when you told me she was a friend's baby you used to watch sometimes." Mom nods, her cheeks flashing in red. "Are you embarrassed by your lie, mother?"

Her eyes dart to mine, her fingers squeezing around her glass. "Of course I am, Amethyst."

I bow my head, semi-satisfied. "Very good, continue."

She does. "I don't regret my decision, Amethyst. There was no way in hell you were going into that life."

"Why didn't you fight?" I ask, tilting my head at her.

My dad shuffles in his seat. "You had Dad, who already admitted if he had known about Liza that he would have raised her as his own."

"Well," she takes another sip of her drink and I regret pouring her it now, because she's using it as a way to halt. "I thought I was doing the right thing at the time. I was young, I felt I didn't have many options, and I was afraid, so very afraid of her, Amethyst—with good reason."

"I'll drink to that." I lift my glass and sink the entire contents, and then reach for the bottle to do refills. Dad hasn't touched his, so I leave it.

"I want to make it up to Liza. So does your father, if that's ok with you?"

"Of course it is," I snap at her. "I can't believe you would even ask me that!"

"There's something else," Mom adds, clearing her throat. "Grams is dead."

MADDOX

I crank my neck and clutch the steering wheel of my Ferrari. I'm in the middle of getting all my shit sent to LA. Don't fucking like it there, but I'll need some of my things there when I'm visiting my girl.

I got to New York this afternoon, but I had a meet tonight and I knew I wouldn't be able to get away from Amethyst without her asking questions, so I lied to her and said I wouldn't be back in LA until tomorrow.

There's a knock on my window, and I pull my hoodie up over my head, winding it down.

"Come on."

I swing my door up and beep the alarm. We're down a dark alleyway in Brooklyn, not shady at all. My license plate is DESTRYR, and I'm pretty sure everyone knows who owns that.

A young patch member opens a heavy metal door and I walk in, straightening my shoulders. "He's out back."

I continue to walk down the empty white hallway, the light leading the way flickering on and off. I can hear loud laughter and cheering and smell the familiar scent of blood mixed with sweat. I push through the doors at the end, opening up into a restaurant kitchen. It's beat up and hasn't been used for over a decade because this is one of the locations they always use for underground fights. I know this because I used to fight here when I was in high school.

"Long time no see," Justice says, pulling his smoke out of his mouth. He stands and puts his hand out. I take it, and then sit down on one of the seats opposite him.

"Is it done?" I ask, my eyebrows up and my jaw tight. I clench my fist.

Justice chuckles. "Yes, it's done."

"And now you're the president?"

He shrugs. "It was always supposed to be like this, Maddox. I was always supposed to have the gavel, and that bitch was running this down to the ground."

I lean forward, pinning him with a glare. "And you'll stay the fuck away from Amethyst and Liza?"

His cocky smirk falls, and he takes a bit of tobacco from his mouth before looking back to me. "Yes, but if my daughter ever wants anything to do with me, I won't reject her."

"Fair enough," I say, leaning back in my seat. "Was it painful?"

"Very," he answers. "Wanna know the details?"

I want to say yes because I'd love to fucking dance with the images of her dying in my head, but I shake my head instead. "No. Amethyst knows if I'm lying to her, I can't risk having any information."

He nods, and I go to stand, satisfied with the outcome and ready to see my fucking girls.

"There's one more thing," he mutters, and I pause, tilting my head.

"What?"

Another set of doors open with a few more MC members walking through, holding up a tied and gaged Travis.

My eyes dart to Justice. "What the fuck is this?"

"Mmm," he chuckles, lighting another smoke. "Figured your little beauty didn't fill you in on this Muppet, so this is my treat to you."

I stare back at a frantic looking Travis. "You look like shit," I mutter to him, then look back to Justice. "What'd she hide from me this time?"

He snickers. "Let's just say, Travis had a lot to do with a lot…"

He continues, and I sit back down as he fills me in on every single gritty detail about Travis and the part he played in pretty much every-fucking-thing. My bones turn to fucking rage and my blood spins to lava.

I shoot off my chair, seething. "You motherfucker."

Justice gets to his feet, his hand coming to my arm. "Maddox, you can't wear any kind of heat. You want him gone, he's gone, but you won't have a part to play in it."

I stand there, fists clenched and thoughts running through my head. Then I chuckle and spit on the ground, my focus locked on him. "Naaw, it's all good. Let the fucker go."

Justice falters, looking over his shoulder to him then coming back to me. "You sure?"

"Positive," I affirm. "I don't want his shitty blood on my hands." Then my eyes fly to his. "If you so much as come within a radius of anyone I fucking know, you're done. Just like your acting career."

Travis nods his head, and the men escort him out the back.

Justice whistles. "That boy just got touched by an angel."

"Yeah, and that angel has pink hair."

I walk out of the bar and go back to my car with pent-up rage. I felt somewhat satisfied by Travis. He knows I have his balls in my hand. I zip through the city and drive straight to the airstrip. I want my fucking girl in my arms and I want her there now.

CHAPTER 47

AMETHYST

OVER THE PAST FEW YEARS, MY LIFE AND WORLD HAS RAPIDLY expanded. I went from being somewhat of a loner with an annoying roommate, to that roommate becoming my sister-in-law and my best friend. Then my boyfriend becoming my step-brother and then to actually having a real sister, and I turned into somewhat of a mother. Through the trials and tribulations that came with my journey, it was all worth it. I look at each of them and know that I'd go through the rollercoaster again and again just to have my life exactly where it is now.

My mom and dad left not long after our chat, around five hours ago. I promised them both that I'd come and visit as soon as I can, but with work eating up my schedule now because I've spent so much of it away, and dealing with my personal dramas, now my load is big. I've been watching reruns of Friends, trying to fall asleep beside Kennedy when the front door opens, and I lean over the couch, watching as Maddox tosses his keys onto the entry table. He pauses when he spots me and Ken on the couch curled up together. He treads farther into the house and then pulls the blanket back to slide in beside me. He kisses me on my temple.

"Everything ok with your parents?"

I nod. He makes me feel at ease, cures the itch that tingles in my veins. "Yes, it'll take time, but I think everything is going to be ok."

The next morning we're sitting out by the pool having breakfast when Cass comes out, pushing her sunglasses over her head. "What'd I miss?"

Oh you know, just the usual drama.

Maddox is still checking out the halfpipe when I walk to Cass, giving her a hug. "Not much, how was Australia?"

She sighs, taking a seat on one of the pool chairs. "It was amazing, Ame! So warm and the people, they're like a different breed. So friendly."

"Hey," I shove her. "I'm friendly!"

She clears her throat.

Bitch. I shake my head and chuckle.

"Mama!" Kennedy runs toward her at full force and Maddox follows closely behind.

"Hey sweetie!" she says, tugging her in.

They all walk into the house and Maddox grabs my hand, pulling me into his chest. "I want to ask you something…"

"Oh, oh…" I joke, the grin on my face smug.

He rolls his eyes and pulls me down onto the lounge when Cass has disappeared with Kennedy, probably to get her things ready. "Want me to move out here full time? I mean I have my fights that I'll have to fly back for, and then there's Dutch in New York and I want to open a few other little businesses here and there, but for the most part, I can be here. With you."

I can't fight the smile that spreads across my face. "Yes."

"Yes?" he repeats, as if in disbelief.

I beam excitedly. "Yes."

Two weeks later, Maddox and I are settled into our place. We're cuddling in bed, watching something on TV when his arm wraps around my waist and he brings his lips to my neck.

"How many kids do you want?" I ask, out of nowhere.

"Ahh…." He laughs. "I don't know? I guess I haven't really

thought about it. With you, I wouldn't have a preferred number, but I'm hoping for a lot. Why?"

I nod, my lips curling in. "Well, because." I reach for my bedside drawer and take out the white stick. "Don't get excited because as you know, I had a miscarriage an—"

He pushes up on one elbow. His face is impassive, and then a shit-eating grin spreads out. "Holy fuck."

"Yes."

I gulp. I haven't told anyone yet, not even Leila, but I know she's going to be excited that we're pregnant together. I haven't even thought of work, but we're over halfway through filming so I guess I have a bit of time, and anyway, FX and all that fancy stuff.

He rolls on top of me, pinning me with his pelvis.

I laugh, whacking him. "Maddox!"

I don't know why things happen the way they do, but I believe that the result is always the same. I believe in fate. If you veer off course, fate will help you back on. It wouldn't matter what direction you took, eventually, your life would lead you to the destination you needed to be at. Maybe that's like with Maddox and I. Maybe things could have been easier with him and me, but maybe I don't want it to be easier. Because every scar that I've received on the way to getting here has helped mold me into the person I am today. His person.

This isn't just about love and fate and all the sloppy stuff, though. This was just a boy who met a girl at a donut shop. I fell in love with Maddox as a child, I had loved him without even knowing it and because of that, the love we shared was primal and raw. It's an untouched kind of love.

Now, I get him for the rest of my life.

Two Months Later
AMETHYST

Leila and Liza are on either side of me, and the stench of damp bodies and testosterone fills the air. I'm amped, electrified by seeing Maddox in the ring. He's a work of art when he fights. I've watched him a few times now, a couple times on YouTube from his old fights, and one other time live. Every time I watch, the passion he has for it grows on me. This time is no different than the others. He's a lion, teasing his prey. It's like once he's in the octagon, he's a different person. He's no longer Maddox Stone, he's now "The Destroyer."

We're into the second round, after witnessing Maddox play with his opponent. He gracefully side-stepped every move, a grin on his face, then he'd lay a few light jabs on the other fighter. Then just when the other fighter would think: this is it, this is his time to start swinging on Maddox, it's too late, because Maddox is already laying perfect combos into him. One after the other, like a perfectly orchestrated performance. What makes him deadly as Maddox Stone, but a Destroyer in the ring, is the fact that he's always two steps ahead of people. Maddox bounces back on his feet, then lands one swift jab right in the center of the guy's face. The crowd's roars cut to silence as we all watch him in fascination as he drops to the ground, his body limp and lifeless.

The crowd bursts out in cheers and I exhale, dropping down to my seat.

He's built for this. His talent hasn't soared, it's damn near burnt up the whole damn world.

A week later we're all in New York, back at Kingsville Park.

"Baby…" Maddox warns. "Why do you need to still be

flipping ollies? Why can't you be like the other normal soccer moms who do yoga and shit?"

I scrunch my face and flip him off. "Like hell!"

Leila's laughing, with Talon and Wolf beside her. Liza grins, looking up at me from her sketchbook. "Seriously, girl. You are pregnant. You shouldn't be doing that..." Liza says, gesturing to my stomach.

Maddox glares at me.

"Just once..."

Kennedy giggles. "Do it, Ame!"

"I can totally land this..." I tell myself.

"Hey!" Maddox yells out from one of the wooden tables. "If you land this," he pauses and winks at our friends while jogging over to me.

"If I land this, what, Maddox?" I roll my eyes. I can totally land this.

"If you land this with a kickflip ollie, you have to marry me."

I inhale deeply, and everyone silences. Except Leila who squeals.

"Ah..." I lick my lips.

"Oh my goooossshh!" Kennedy starts jumping around.

Goddamnit, Maddox, throwing me off balance again. I falter my step. "You know I can land this, Maddox..."

He grins, pulling out a small white box and drops to his knee. "I know you can, baby. I guess the question is... do you want to?"

EPILOGUE

AMETHYST
Two Years Later

I MARRIED HIM. BECAUSE OF COURSE I DID. I WASN'T MUCH into planning the wedding, so I gave it all over to Leila to plan, with one exception: don't be extreme. We fought a lot. Cried even more. Fought some more and then hugged a whole bunch. In the end, we both agreed to have it at Dutch. At first, the guys bickered about it. It seems, my big scary brothers are actually big softies. They eventually agreed, of course, and the ceremony was beautiful. The wedding was at sunset with only fairy lights and lanterns illuminating the venue. It felt as though their mom, Lauren, was with us. It got a little emotional for Maddox and the guys, and even Elliot, but it felt like closure too. Now they visit Dutch all the time, and it's our go-to every time we are in New York. It was all a part of their healing process, which only makes the fact that Maddox and I married there so much more special. The reception was at our skate park. We had to get the all-clear from the council, but it worked. We had a Bedouin tent set up and more fairy lights lining the pipes and ramps.

Bradley was four months old when we finally tied the knot. There was no way in hell I was being a pregnant bride, and anyway, I wanted to drink. It was a beautiful night of laughter and good people. At the end of the night, we had so much left-over food that we opened up the tent to all the homeless on the street and the young kids. It ended up turning into a small party with a whole bunch of kids and people joining in with us.

It was perfect. Leila started swearing again but, in my eyes, it was perfect.

I'm pregnant with our second child, well, third counting Kennedy. Another boy and I'm slightly terrified. Not that Bradley is a hard kid, he's quite relaxed and makes this mom thing so easy. I'm not sure where he inherited his chill nature, probably from his uncle Wolf. We also have a Tonkinese cat named Greg, thanks to Kennedy, and Leila and Wolf have had two kids now, both girls. I'm starting to think they're going to have the girls and we're having the boys. Not sure who should be more afraid, but if they turn out like Leila, then Wolf definitely should be more afraid.

My mom and I have worked through our differences and her and Liza have a healthy relationship now. I guess it took time for Liza to trust her, but they got there. Now they have lunch dates without me and I think my mom has a favorite.

My dad has since moved to LA to be closer to me and Bradley. He and Lara packed up and he relocated here. He's at our place almost every weekend.

Liza and Talon are the cool auntie and uncle. You know, the ones who don't have kids and always have a clean house and come and pick the kids up, get them hyped up on sugar and then leave again. They spend most of their time traveling because they started their own travel blog. At first, we all sort of gave them a hard time about how they're just using it as an excuse to travel, but now they actually make money from it. I don't know why no one has thought of it before.

Maddox and I still want to expand business one day, but as of right now, we just have Dutch. We're both so busy with our career's and kids that we don't have the time. He's still undefeated. I know, of course he is. I'm hoping that one day someone will kick his ass, and I tell him this. But he counters it by saying there's only one person walking this earth who could probably do that—me.

What'd I reply with? Well, fighting isn't really my thing and he isn't really my type.

"A good book has no ending."
R.D. Cumming

cover coming soon

Wanna know what
I'm doing when I'm
not spittin' rhymes?
Bet you don't...

SNEAK PEAK

9.17.18

'MANIK

AMO JONES

'MANIK blurb:

I'm Beatrice Kennedy, but everyone calls me Beat. I live a low-key life, fresh out of college and drifting from town to town until I find my home. I love music, and how it stirs even the deepest and untouched parts of your soul. Depending on what you choose to listen to, would depend on what it touches. It's the drug we all damper in, only different strains. My strain is jazz. The smooth instrumental strums that take over me. The sound of cigar smoke, bourbon and an old dusty fedora hat. My strain wasn't rap, and it sure wasn't laced with some A-class shit like murky blue eyes cast down from the Lord and the Devil's handcrafted smile. I knew who he was—the whole world did. One fateful night set off a chain of events, events that no one was coming back from. You can't save people who don't want to be saved. You can't pull them up from the ocean when they've latched themselves to an anchor. Love was my anchor, destruction was the water that was drowning me, and the rope that was so tightly clamped around my ankles was woven with the lyrics of Aeron Romanov-Reed, also known as, 'Manik. He steals hearts from all around the world, but one night, he stole something that wasn't his to steal.

Me.

CHAPTER 3
Thug Love – Bone Thugs
BEAT

I search the room and take in a couple of things.

One, I'm in a basement. Not entirely old, or even beat up, just—a basement. There are dusty wooden stairs that I can see leading up to a door and a small window behind me. The thing I find odd, is the bed. The sheets aren't exactly used or old either, it's almost as though the bed is made. Like he was waiting for someone. *Was he?* Maybe he locks girls down here for fun. My head is pounding, my mouth dry and fluffy, and I need to pee like no one's business, but the slight fear of dying has these muted at the back of my brain.

I hear the door open, so I crawl backwards until I'm pressing against the wooden headboard.

Manik comes down the stairs, his chest bare and his grey sweat pants hanging off his lean hips. I gulp. At first glance, you would say that he's beautiful, but the second his eyes land on you, conjures any sense of the word beautiful.

He pins me with a glare, his eyes flat. "What the fuck am I going to do with you."

"Um," I clear my throat. "How about let me go?" I have to try.

His jaw clenches, and then he tilts his head as his eyes drop down my body. "How about, no."

"Okay, well can I go pee?"

His eyes narrow, his hands pressing into his pockets. "Do you know who I am?"

I gulp. "Yes. Aeron Romanov-Reed. I know *of* you, if that was the actual question…"

He ambles in closer, lighting a cigarette. He inhales deeply, his eyes squinting from the smoke and then blows out the cloud, clenching the cigarette between his thumb and index finger. "I can't let you go, *Voron*. You've seen too much."

"Can't, or won't?"

His eyes darken. "Still trying to decide."

"I won't tell anyone!" I suddenly blurt out. "I swear. Listen, I don't—it doesn't." I shake my head and he sits beside me on the bed, the mattress sinking under his weight. I exhale. "Are you going to kill me?"

The door opens again, letting in a slight crack of light. My eyes shoot towards it, but I can see Manik watching me on the corner of my eye.

I slowly look back at him. *His eyes.* I flinch.

"Manik?" A big guy—one of the guys who were there last night—says.

Manik slowly peels his eyes away from me, looking over his shoulder. "What?"

"Ah, your old man is coming over to make sure you've dealt with the issue."

"Me being the issue?" I whisper out, more to myself than to them.

I cradle my knees into my chest, only, I start to feel hot and flustered. I'm going to fucking die. Something happens when you surf close to the rip of death. It's as though you start to second guess every wave you rode to get there. I'll never get to surf again.

Who would miss me? I don't think anyone would. I don't have family. Christmas' were always spent alone, my birthdays, even more isolated. Truly, what is the point.

Defeated, I stand to my feet, ignoring whatever they're talking about and remove my leather jacket.

The chatting halts immediately, and I turn to face Manik. "Just, please make it fast. I know you don't owe me anything, but I'm hoping that there's some mixture of human essence under that hard exterior, and you'll just do me a solid."

I open my eyes when I don't get a reply, and Manik's are on my right arm. He's eating up every inch of skin I have. I look down at my arm, then back at him. "I like tattoo's."

He licks his lip and then looks back to the guy on the stairs. "Leave."

Oh god. Oh god here we go.

The guy glances at Manik, and then at me. He gives me a small smile and then turns and leaves. Manik stands and I clench my fists so tight my nails sink into my palms, forming little crescent moons. I can feel his presence. His heat is thrashing into me without us physically touching. I keep my eyes closed and watch behind my lids as little color dots dance around in various shapes.

My chest rises and falls.

Inhale, exhale.

A gun clocks.

I freeze. The silence is deafening, with nothing but the pounding of my heart and loud desperate inhales of breaths.

A cold metal ring presses against my forehead and I squeeze my eyes shut, my shoulders turning stiff. Sweat drips down my forehead and down the bridge of my nose, balancing on the tip.

He fires. *Bang.*

I flinch, expecting something. Anything, as I wait for death. I slowly peel my eyes open again and they land on Manik, dropping his other hand which held another gun, to the side of him.

My lip trembles, my knees shake. I drop to the ground in a heap and sob. "What?"

Curling into a ball, I rock softly, the tears soaking the front of my shirt.

"I changed my mind," is all he says, making his way back to the stairs.

I can't form words. My mouth is stiff and dry, fear and terror seizing my bones. When he finally reaches the top of the stairs, I swipe my face and ask, "When did you change your mind?"

He grins at me over his shoulder. "About one second before I pulled the trigger."

Horror. Pure undiluted horror. He nudges his head over his shoulder. "Bathroom is on the other side of the room." Then he leaves, the door slamming behind him.

As soon as he's gone, I dive toward where he gestured, finding the grungy pale pink door and kicking it open. Rushing, I dive head-first toward the bowl just as saliva mixed with whatever I last ate comes spewing out of my mouth. I dry reach a few times, until my throat burns with zest from my stomach lining, then sag against the wall, swiping my mouth of the residue. I know why I'm here, but I don't know why he's keeping me here. Maybe that's how he got his name, from being neurotic not with just his words, but with who he actually is. We all know his music is lyrically insane, and if that's even a slight glimpse of what's inside his head, then his thought process is not something I should feel comfortable dabbling in. God, I'm so fucked. I stand and rinse my hands in the little porcelain sink, taking a few sips of the water, then dry them with a cotton white towel, that is soft to touch. Why would a man who has everything want something like me locked in a damn basement.

I just want to leave. I feel sick. I've never had the feeling of homesickness, not even the slightest charge of feeling home-sick. Probably because I never really had a home. Aside from my parents house in Bondi, Sydney, I've never really felt like I had a home. Not the kind that most ache for when feeling homesick, but right now, I want my lonely life back. Better to be lonely than dead.

I head out of the bathroom and go back to the bed, crawling into a ball and slamming my eyes shut, thinking of slightly better days.

One, two, three. My feet move to the rhythm of the music, my body rolling like a perfectly orchestrated choir. Music is my life, and dance is my soul, one can't survive without the other.

"Yo! Beat! Hit this jam!"

Mi Gente by Beyonce started playing.

"Ohhh, I see what you did there…" I teased him with a wink. My head bobbed slightly, then when the beat dropped, my body broke down the syllables. I flicked my hands around, moving my hips with it. I was freestyling, which is where I loved to be most. I loved choreography, but freestyling was something else entirely. Less politics and restrictions. It was just where you got to let loose and showcase what you've got off the bat. Bey's verse came in and I flipped my hair, popping my ass out and shaking slightly. I had the ass to do it— and lucky for me, I've always had the small waist. Dancing has always given me a very fit body, so every muscle I had was defined and ripped. I wasn't a small girl, I was a fit girl. I ate as hard as I danced. The beat dropped again and I let it flow, dropping to the ground on my back and snaking my shoulders up in a wave motion before flipping onto my stomach and pressing the tips of my toes into the ground and shaking my ass as I came back to standing. The song finished and everyone cheered loudly.

"Damn, Beat!" Gerald slapped my ass. "That shit was tight. I'm putting that up on YouTube stat!"

I laughed, shaking my head while taking a drink of water. The next song played.

My skin prickles in shock and I shiver, my eyes popping open. The room is dark, with the only outlining coming from the small window above the bed. It didn't give much.

So cold, so dark.

"Jesus, he wasn't kidding," a girls voice whispers.

I quickly shoot up, crawling backwards to the head board and pulling the covers up with me. The girl walks closer to the bed, a slight crack of the light coming over her face.

Dark hair, that's all I can see right now, a slim body and long dark hair—much like my own. "Who are you?"

She tilts her head, the same way I've seen Manik tilt his. "I'm Katiya, Aeron's little sister." She takes a seat on the mattress.

I gulp. "What do you want?"

"Hmmm?" She asks, then her head turns to me and I get a full look because she's directly in front of the window. Large lips, pale skin, dark hair, and almond shaped eyes—can't tell the colour right now. Her face shape is different to her brothers though. Where his is clean cut, square and prominent, hers is round. Beautiful, almost baby-like. She smiles. "Oh, I'm not going to hurt you. Ae just told me that he had a girl locked in his basement. I thought he was joking, but he wasn't."

I swallow. "Ok." My voice is croaky. That earlier sip of water didn't do near enough to curb the age in my voice.

She leans over the bed and I hold my breath. She must hear the deep intake because she chuckles slightly, shaking her head and then sits up again, handing me a bottle of water. The cool dew slips over my fingers, taunting me. My mouth waters just by the thought of wrapping my lips around the rim, so I quickly twist the cap off and toss it across the ground, taking a drink. The first sip is like nothing I've ever experienced. The cool liquid soothes the dry cracks that had formed in my throat —best. Feeling. Ever. I drink the whole lot, and then slowly swipe my mouth.

She clears her throat. "You seem surprised to see me? Like you didn't know he had a sister," she says it with a slight scoff in her undertone. As if every person would know who she was. Maybe they did, I don't know.

"Because I was surprised. I don't know who you are, and you're right," I put the bottle onto the ground and slowly lean back against the headboard. I can feel the water rushing through my blood stream, hydrating my bones. I shiver, shaking my head. "I didn't know that he had a sister."

There's a long pause. "Really?" she was skeptical of my words, and that's okay, because I was skeptical of hers.

"Really."

"Huh." She shrugs, then points to the bottle. "Want another?"

I shake my head.

She stands slowly, and then starts retreating back to the stairs that lead up to the door. She turns slightly just before she gets there. "My brother has killed people for much less than what you've witnessed. He's relentless, and completely savage. Do not think under any circumstance that just because you're beautiful that he will let you live, because he won't."

I freeze, even though her words don't come as a surprise. "Why are you telling me this?"

"Because. If you're going to attempt to escape," she forces out the words *attempt to escape* rather obviously, like she's maybe hinting to me to do it. She continues. "I would do it fast, but know this, *Voron*, that if you speak of what has happened here, or what you witnessed earlier to anyone, ever, I will know, and let me tell you something. If you think my brother is evil, and my father is the devil, then wait until you've met Lilith— because that's *me*." Then she jogs up the stairs before I can ask any more questions, the door closing behind her.

Should I try? What if he catches me and kills me? But what if I stay here and he kills me anyway? What if what she said is a trap…

Rather live on my feet than die on my knees, right?

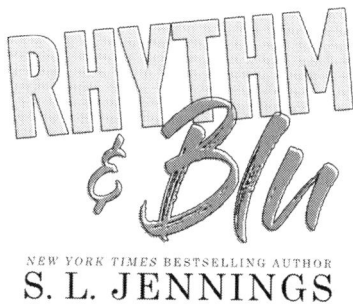

NEW YORK TIMES BESTSELLING AUTHOR
S. L. JENNINGS

Continue reading for a sneak peak into Rhythm & Blu by New
York Times & USA Today Bestselling Author S.L. Jennings

Before two minutes ago, there were three definitive times in my life when I felt more conflicted than I do right now.

The first was when Hazel Figaro, my best friend since grade school, butchered her hair to look like T-Boz from TLC. Somehow, the hairdresser selectively heard, "Make me look like Mr. T." I spent the remainder of the school year and most of the summer reassuring her that it wasn't that bad as it grew out.

Oh, hell fucking yes, it was that bad. Hazel looked as if she had been caught in a waterfall instead of chasing one.

The second time was the day I had to break down and tell my parents I wanted to put the kibosh on my plans for med school and pursue music. My very traditional Korean father and West Indian mother, both highly respected MDs in their chosen specialties, were not trying to hear that shit.

"Music is not a career," they said. "It's a hobby."

"But it's what I love...what I'm passionate about," I countered, feeling even smaller than my already pint-sized five-foot-one stature.

"Passion doesn't pay the bills, Roxanne. And neither will we if you don't finish your education."

And while I'll only admit it to myself, on days when I'm feeling particularly self-deprecating, they were right. Because music wasn't paying my bills. And since they had made good on their promise and stopped funding my apartment, car, and expenses, I had to swallow my pride and get a real job. While it was shallowly related to my passion, still, it didn't nourish my spirit and sing to my soul.

And the third time? Well, that's come back to slap me in the face hard enough to make me taste a decade worth of regret.

As I sit here staring at my laptop, rereading the email my editor just sent, I have to remind myself that rent is due on the 1st. And even though I traded in my ride for public transportation and a good pair of kicks, I can't damn well survive off of rice and beans for much longer. These hips can't take it.

He wanted me to do *what?*

I turn down the music pumping through my MacBook's speakers and I pick up my cell to scroll to his number. Surely Bari's email was riddled with typos and I don't want anything else to be lost in translation.

"This is Frost."

I have to bite down on my snort.

Frost is not Bari's last name. It's Feinstein. But…ok. These days, everyone has a moniker.

"Bari, it's Rox. Can you clarify your email for me?"

"What clarification do you need? I'm certain the assignment details were clear." I hear the squeak of his worn leather desk chair in the background, and can almost envision him reclining back in it, imagining that he's the king of the fucking world and not a prematurely balding dude caught in the hamster wheel of a mid-life crisis. Don't get me wrong; Bari is a decent boss. He tries to throw me a bone here and there. But he doesn't hear much outside of his own voice and his own self-indulgent bullshit.

"You know I don't do these types of pieces. Wouldn't this be a better fit for one of the Lifestyle writers? Or even Celeb Gossip?"

"Aren't you our resident music expert?"

"Well…yes, but—"

"And is he not a musician?"

"He is, Bari, but he's not the type of musician I usually cover."

He snorts in that condescending prick-ish way that's always

followed by something snide. "What? Grammy award winning artists are beneath you now?"

"Of course not, but—"

"Look, Rox. You asked for a shot. I'm giving you one. An incredible one at that. This is a huge deal for The Seattle Tea, so take it or leave it. But I promise you—a chance like this won't arise again. Most writers would be willing to suck their own dick at this opportunity so you should be grateful I'm even trusting you with a piece of this magnitude."

I heave out a frustrated breath. I'm not going to win this one. I could fight this until I'm as bald as Bari, but when it comes down to it, he's earned that raggedy ass desk chair in his corner office at The Seattle Tea. I'm still scrounging for stories, covering local bands and basement-dwelling artists that I'd hope the public would deem noteworthy. But truth is, the Seattle urban music scene hasn't been hot since Macklemore. And that's saying something.

However, beggars can't be choosers and my broke ass has been begging for a shot at a featured piece for the past year.

But why does it have to be *him?*

Of all people. Of all musicians. Why do I have to cover him? He's not even considered a local artist. Not since he ran off and sold out. But now after a stunt six months ago on one of those trashy reality shows on VH1 that damn near killed him and his career, the prodigal son wants to come home?

Please.

"So what am I supposed to do? Interview him?"

Bari chuckles. He's fucking with me. He knows how I feel about this assignment and the subject in question.

"Not quite. I want you to fully immerse yourself in his world. He's moved here to reinvent himself—to reclaim his sound. I want the scoop on his creative process, his goals for this next album, what he does to get inspired. Find out who he's listening to, what he's watching on Netflix, who he's banging. Shit, I want to know what his favorite breakfast cereal is and if he likes it with whole or skim milk."

I bite my tongue. Because I know he loves Captain Crunch but always picks out the green Crunchberries because he claims there is no such thing as a green berry. And he's strictly a 2% kinda dude.

As for who he's banging? I'm not touching that. No way. No how.

Out of habit, I bring my fingers to my chest, imagining the phantom coolness of metal against my skin. I'd worked too damn hard and for too damn long to bury that ghost. I wasn't about to resurrect him. But this was the real world and I had a real job that paid me just enough to pay my very real bills. I had to be an adult about this, haunted memories be damned.

"Anything else?" I ask, cosigning my own demise.

"That should be it for now. First meeting is tomorrow. I'll text you the address."

"Fine," I huff before hitting End. I don't even bother with the social nuances of a goodbye. That's reserved for people who aren't currently planning how to fake their own death just to get out of an assignment.

Car accident? Nah. Too public. And one would actually need a car for that.

Gruesome home invasion-turned-murder? Hazel would kill me if I got blood on the furniture.

Mysterious disappearance? My parents would have my ass on every milk carton in the country if I don't call at least three times a week.

Dammit. Even my fake death can't get its shit together.

I'm still staring at the screen when Hazel comes bustling in, arms overflowing with fabric samples in an array of colors and prints. She chucks her purse and keys onto our tiny kitchen island and tosses the swatches on our already cluttered dining table.

"How do we feel about his and hers matching dresses for spring?" she asks by way of greeting.

I shrug half-heartedly. "If Jaden Smith can wear a dress, I don't think it's too far off. Although I think matching couple 'fits in general are tacky enough, but what do I know?"

"Agreed." She flops down onto the couch and kicks off her Hunter boots, still speckled with rain, before snatching off her beanie. Loose, dark curls tumble down around her shoulders. "Apparently, being boo'd up excuses fashion faux pas. I don't care how good the D is, if I catch my man rummaging through my closet for something to wear, his ass will be ghost. He's not about to be stretching out my hard-earned couture with his hairy man-thighs!"

She cackles to herself for a good twenty seconds before realizing that I haven't budged, still too hypnotized by the words—or better yet, the name—staring back at me from the computer.

"Girl, what's wrong? You look like you've just seen a ghost."

"I have," I deadpan, meaning it. I sigh. "I got a job today."

"Aw, shit! That's great, Rox! We should go out and celebrate. I just got a dress so tight that it requires Crisco to get into." She busts into a shoulder shimmy reminiscent of the Bankhead Bounce circa 1995. Which takes me right back to my current dilemma.

"Yeah. Great."

"Then why do you look like you're mentally preparing for anal with a cactus?"

Unable to vocalize my disdain and overall frustration, I merely nod at the screen, prompting Hazel to climb to her feet and sashay her way over to my Ikea work desk. It only takes a quick glance to catch his name amongst the jumble of useless assignment details, as if it's outlined in bold, blaring neon yellow instead of flat, black Helvetica, size 12 font.

Riot Blu.

Top 40 fuckboi. Paparazzi player. Trashy reality TV trainwreck.

And heart-crushing life ruiner.

Ruiner of *my* life, to be more specific.

"Holy shit, Rox." Hazel takes a step back and brings her fingers to touch her lips to conceal a gasp.

"I know."

"Did Frost know about how he—"

"No. He only knows I don't care for his music, which is true."

"But he doesn't know that you—"

I shake my head. "He doesn't know anything."

"Fuuuuuck."

We both take a beat to reread the name that feels like a shank to my gut with every syllable.

"Well, we can still go out…" my roommate comments quietly.

"Do you not get what this means, Haze? Riot-fucking-Blu. I'm freaking out!" I snap with more venom than I intend.

"I know. I know. But you see…this dress. I was really hoping to get penetrated tonight. And we don't have to celebrate. It can be a last-night-before-the-end-of-the-world type of occasion, with booze and carbs abundant. My treat?" She bats her fake lashes and smiles in that way that looks like she's trying to feign innocence and hold in a fart at the same time.

She's going to get her way. That's how it's always been. Everyone gives into Haze one way or another.

Plus carbs and booze sound pretty damn good now that she's paying.

I roll my eyes. "Fine. Whatever. But I swear to G-o-d, Haze: No Scrubs. You are not sticking me with the broke, ugly friend to entertain while you get those cobwebs knocked outta your coochie."

"Cobwebs?" she scoffs. "Girl, bye. My shit is made of unicorn glitter and rainbow sprinkles."

I make a face and gag. "Sounds like a yeast infection to me."

The mood temporarily lightened, I heave out a breath and push away from my laptop. I can stew about Riot Blu later, after I'm properly sauced and am happily slipping into a carb-induced coma.

We shower. Dress. Pre-game.

And hours later, we're breezing into our favorite nighttime haunt in the heart of Pioneer Square. The upside of rolling with Haze? Always knowing where the party is. The downside? The party is most likely her.

As a fashion blogger and former self-proclaimed hoe (her words, not mine), Haze knows everyone who is anyone in Seattle. And if she doesn't know them, she isn't shy about forced friendship. Which is precisely how she foiled me into becoming her best friend of almost two decades.

I was the quiet girl with braces and Coca-Cola bottle glasses that would much rather spend her lunch period with a Walkman and a cassette mixtape. And Haze, all tanned legs and brazen attitude even back then, was the new kid, meaning she was a magnet for attention, the very thing I was hoping to avoid. Apparently, headphones were no deterrent for the California native, because she insisted on talking.

And talking.

And talking.

Until I finally got tired of pretending to read her pouty, pink-glossed lips and pulled off my headphones.

She never stopped talking, and I admittedly found myself listening. And soon enough, I was conversing with the super cool new girl at school whose parents let her wear eyeliner and baby tees that exposed the tease of her navel.

Not much changed from then. I got a little bolder, she got a lot louder, but the dynamic pretty much stayed the same. I was the Kelly to her Beyonce. The JoJo to her K-Ci.

Until Riot. Then...everything went to shit.

We sidle up to the bar, bypassing the pub tables and high-back chairs that are quickly filling up with patrons. It's Ladies Night, meaning two-for-one specials and plenty of men banking on cheap well liquor.

"So what are we drinking?"

I don't even know why she asks. Since before we were even old enough to drink, our spirit of choice has always been vodka. Tito's, to be exact. I only have to give her a pointed glance before she turns towards the bartender to flag him down.

"Hey, you!" she coos, batting her falsies and painting on a saccharin-laced, flirtatious grin. "I didn't know you were working tonight. I haven't seen you in a minute."

"What's up, Haze? Where you been hiding?" Manbun, beard, flannel. Typical PNW kinda guy. The bartender is easy on the eyes, with his emerald-hued irises and fit build, but he is so not Haze's type.

"Oh, you know. On my grind, always. It's so funny though...I was just thinking about you."

I bite down on a laugh and roll my eyes stealthily. Haze wasn't thinking about this dude. She can't even remember his name. *Hey, you* is code for, *Shit, who are you again?* And I feel bad. I always feel bad for the unsuspecting men that fall for Haze's charms. Her presence is magnetic and alluringly dangerous. It's like looking into the endless obscurity of an eclipse, knowing it'll scorch your eyes. And time after time, guy after guy, she renders them all blind.

She finesses us a couple double tall vodka sodas with lime before we claim a sofa and table set-up nestled on the other side of the lounge. It's dark enough that we have a veil of privacy yet gives us a view of the whole space. We're not ready to be seen yet—at least I'm not. But by our second round, the place is packed and the DJ on the ones and twos has the whole crowd vibing to the latest club bangers. Although I usually abhor anything on heavy rotation on the radio, I don't even recoil when Haze grabs my hand and tugs me towards the dancefloor.

There's something to be said about that moment when the rhythm slips inside you and sinks its hooks into your soul. Hands in the air, eyes closed, hips swaying and dipping to the groove, I am merely a marionette to the music. A slave to the rifts and melodies that flow through my veins like the liquor sloshing in my cup. This feeling…it's like a drug to me. I am weightless, boundless. A speck of glitter floating amidst a humid, smoke-veiled universe where each star is a dazzling note that ignites my soul with brilliant beams of rainbow light.

I'm so wrapped up in the moment that I don't even notice when our little party of two becomes a party of four. However, Haze is already welcoming the intruders—erm—newcomers back to our table. She turns to introduce me to her new friends just as I finish off what's left in my glass and attempt to flag down a cocktail waitress for a refill.

"Rox, this is Dane and Kaz. Guys, this is my girl, my ace, my bottom bitch, Rox Lee."

I flash a nervous grin and extend a palm, anxious to get the awkward intros over with and return to the carefree oblivion of booming basslines. But Haze gives me that look…that look that tells me that her dress has lived up to its promise of getting dickmatized tonight, so being anything but hyperaware is out of the question. I should have known the moment I spotted them. Dane is right up her alley. Tall, dark, and tatted up, with enough labels on his body to give Haze a fashion boner. He has skin the color of sunbaked sand and his eyes appear to be clear blue, almost gray under the strobe lights. He reminds me of Jeremy Meeks, the *Fine Felon* whose mug shot went viral after he was arrested. He's pretty, that's for damn sure. A little too pretty for my taste but judging by the way he's sizing up my roommate, he's already spoken for.

"What are you drinking?" the other guy, Kaz, asks. He's as tall as his friend, a little less muscular, and is much more conservative in denim and a black Henley with the sleeves rolled up to showcase tan, chiseled forearms. He's got a baby face, clean-shaven, and his golden brown hair is messily styled, but probably cost few bills to achieve its perfect waywardness. I'll never understand the notion of paying good money to look like you didn't do a damn thing roll out of bed and rake a hand through your hair, but I have to admit, it looks good on him.

While Kaz is admittedly neither broke nor ugly, I should have specified that I wasn't down with playing babysitter to *any* friend, scrub or otherwise. I have no doubt in my mind that Haze knew that these guys would be here tonight. She looks way too cozy with Dane while tucked under his arm, close enough to his lips that she could probably taste what he had for lunch.

I hold up my empty glass and shake it, the sharp tinkling of the melting ice cubes cutting into the mellow groove the DJ throws on next. "Nothing now. But…vodka."

"We'll have to do something about that."

Kaz signals the female server, who hurriedly comes over donning a wide grin paired with what I can only describe as a starry-eyed gaze. Her interest is obvious, but Kaz is all business when he orders a bottle of top-shelf vodka and all the appropriate mixers. The cocktail waitress nods and smiles in response, then in a much too obvious way that verges on desperate, straightens her back to make her perky tits even more noticeable in her low cut, midriff-baring tee. However, Kaz politely thanks her and turns his attention back to me. Nice of him, but not necessary.

"So, Rox Lee, what brings you out tonight?"

"My funeral." He lifts a brow, perplexed as expected, so I tack on, "I got the job of a lifetime, which is ironic, considering it'll kill me."

"Sooo…I'm guessing you're a lion tamer? Snake charmer?"

I shake my head and sigh. "Writer."

"Huh. Didn't know words could be hazardous to your health."

"Yeah, definitely. Ever get a papercut? Tragic."

"Oh, the horror. And I bet carpal tunnel is a bitch."

He laughs, and I notice that he has a gorgeous smile, complete with dazzling white, straight teeth and sensual, full lips. Ok, definitely not the broke, ugly friend.

The waitress brings over our bottle of booze and fresh glasses, and before I can go in for a refill, Kaz begins to fill two glasses. He hands me one and holds his own towards me for a toast.

"To a beautiful funeral for a beautiful woman."

I nearly choke on a laugh.

"What?" Kaz asks, an alluring smirk gracing his lips.

I shake my head. "Dude, that was…lame as hell."

"Too much?"

"Hell yes." I pretend to flag down the waitress and call out, "Excuse me, can we get some wine with all this damn cheese?"

Kaz laughs again, and I find myself just as tickled and feeling less awkward about being obligated to entertain a complete stranger so Haze can get her mack on. And after a few more drinks, I find that I'm really enjoying Kaz's company and am not at all thinking about the fate that looms just beyond the dawn.

That is, until the DJ cuts the music to make a special announcement. Consider it my eulogy.

"Aw, shit!" he hollers into the mic. "We gotta special guest in the building! Ya boy has returned home! Riot Bluuuuuu!"

On that cue, the DJ puts on Riot's biggest club hit from his last album, *Shades of Blu*, but it's completely drowned out by the raucous cheers and screams from fans storming the dancefloor.

I can't do this. I can't. I knew I would have to face him, but I thought I had one more night before it all came crashing down...one more night to prepare myself to confront the person I had vowed to never speak to again. He's already stolen so much from me already, yet I can't escape him. He's on my television, on the radio, in every fucking magazine that I flip open. I can't even have one last night before Riot Blu intrudes on my life, only to leave it in ruins once more?

This is bullshit.

"Huh? What was that?"

I don't even realize I've said that last thought aloud, so I shake my head. "Nothing. I gotta go."

Kaz looks confused and turns towards the stage, and I imagine he spies the person that's currently invoking my over-whelming urge to crawl out of my skin. I'm not certain because I refuse to even look in that direction.

"Rox!" I don't even notice that Haze has mustered the strength to tear herself away from her new boo. She grasps my shoulders and all but pulls me into her bosom. "I swear, I didn't know. You ok?"

I nod, but follow with, "I need to get out of here."

I try to step away, but end up stumbling on my own heels, right into Kaz's chest. My head is foggy, and I'm not sure if it's from the vodka or the fact that I've just been battered with a past I've worked over a decade to keep buried.

"I'll get her home," he pipes up. Haze and I both shoot him an unforgiving glare, prompting him to raise his palms as a sign of innocence. "That's all, I promise. The Square is about to be crazy once everyone finds out who's here. Neither one of y'all should be rolling alone."

Haze looks at me. "I can come with you now if you want. Just say the word." I know she means it, but I also know she doesn't want to leave. I can't ruin her night, especially since it took an act of God and a jar of Vaseline to squeeze her into that dress. And just because my love life is pretty much bankrupt that doesn't mean I should deprive her of a little momentary bliss.

I kiss her on the cheek and muster a smile. "Have fun, girl. I'm good." I peer over to Kaz who pretends to not eavesdrop. "I'll be fine."

I follow up by simply touching the bridge of my nose, which Haze mimics. It's been our unspoken signal since high school house parties, telling the other to stay alert, and if need be, use the pepper spray tucked in each of our purses.

Honestly, I can't get out of there fast enough, and I can tell Kaz is surprised by the way I power walk through the crowd to the exit. The crisp night air tastes of sea salt and impending rain, and I suck in as much as my lungs can take, hoping to sober myself.

"Damn, girl. Not a Riot Blu fan?"

I shake my head without looking up and pull out my phone to call a Lyft. "You could say that." I start walking towards a well-lit area towards the street.

"I'm surprised," Kaz remarks, following closely beside me, yet making an effort not to come off as intrusive. "Most women love him. "

"Don't believe the hype. This woman definitely doesn't."

Head down and preoccupied with summoning my ride, I lose my footing on the ridiculous heels Haze insisted I wear to complete my ensemble of tight ripped jeans, lacey black bra top, and coordinating lightweight blazer, which sends my cell flying from my fingertips. Kaz plucks it out of the air before it collides with the pavement while also catching my forearm before I do the same. Clearly, he's some kinda circus freak with octopus arms and can handle his liquor much better than me.

"Thanks," I mutter. He hands me my phone then pulls out his.

"What's your address?"

"For what?" I snap.

Noting my tone, he peers down at me, his expression pinched. "For your ride. They need to know where we're going."

"*We're?*"

"I told your roommate that I'd get you home, and I meant it. I'm not leaving your side until I know you're safe."

Too tipsy to argue, and admittedly a little touched by the chivalry, I tell him. In the few minutes it takes for our ride to arrive, I learn that Kaz is an only child, originally from Colorado, and a Pisces. Over the short car ride, I tell him that I have an older brother who serves as a doctor in the military, grew up in Redmond, and am a Virgo. By the time we pull up to my apartment building, I decide that he's cool. At least cool enough for me to invite him up for coffee.

I throw on a chill R&B playlist and go to prepare our hot brew while Kaz checks out the cluttered shelves of books and music.

"Holy shit. You still have CDs?" he calls out, his tone touched with mirth. "Do they even manufacture CD players anymore?"

I grab our mugs and make my way over to where he's inspecting my coveted collection. "Hell if I know. I've had the same stereo since '98."

"You're kidding." His eyes are wide as he takes the offered drink.

I shake my head. "No bullshit. Sure, I'm a big fan of modern technology and all; I'm not a dinosaur. But there's nothing like opening that CD jacket, reading the lyrics and discography, and remembering the excitement of hearing the new Jodeci or SWV or 112 for the very first time. Then playing it on repeat until every lyric feels like it was dedicated especially to you. And just like that, you're thirteen again, transported to your very first dance, and the way your date's hands felt on your body as you rocked and swayed to a slow jam. You relive those butterflies, those sweaty palms and the exhilaration of falling in love. Music is memories. And these are my photo album."

I don't even realize I've let my eyes fluttered closed until I open them and find Kaz staring down at me, the look on his face so thoughtful yet intense.

"That's…" he begins, his tone raw. "That's fucking beautiful."

I don't know if it's the vodka, or the quick trip down memory lane, or knowing that after tonight, my entire life will forever be altered, but I respond, "I think you're fucking beautiful too."

And as his hand snakes around my waist to pull me closer into his body and his mouth covers mine so his tongue can lick silent questions and taste my responses, I know that it's a combination of all three.

track two.

There's a fucking car alarm blaring inside my skull, yet it sounds oddly similar to my ringtone. The ringtone that belongs to the phone I can't find. The phone I can't find because every time I attempt to move or even peel open my eyelids, a stampede of baby rhinos Cupid Shuffle from temple to temple.

Fuck. Me.

What did I do?

I don't need to do a body check to know that my pants are missing, which probably means my bra and panties are too. Great. A hangover and a messy hookup with some guy I just met. And where the hell is my phone?

I dare to open an eye and bite through the ache that rips through my head. Surprisingly, the space beside me on the bed is empty. Hallelujah for small miracles. Drunken one-nighters are bad enough. The awkward morning after thing is damn near unbearable.

I manage to move my limbs enough to feel around for my phone, which stops ringing, only to resume seconds later as if the caller really, really needs to get in touch with me. *Shit!* Bari told me he'd hit me up with the Riot Blu interview details today. But more than that, Haze could be stranded somewhere and need me. I shoot out of bed with a renewed fire under my ass, squinting against the throbbing in my sockets, and rummage through the blankets and last night's strewn clothing.

"Hello?" I croak into the receiver the second I snatch it from its hiding place under my bra.

"Rox, are you fucking kidding me right now?"

"Shit, I'm sorry, Bari. I couldn't find my phone. I've been searching for it since early this morning," I lie.

"Never mind that. Your first meeting got moved up to this morning."

"This morning?" I'm instantly sober.

"Yeah. His camp had a scheduling conflict and needs to get started right away. Jot down this address."

I grab a pen and the closest scrap of paper I can find,

which funnily enough, is a receipt for condoms. Definitely not mine. "I'm listening."

Bari prattles off the address, but before I can even record a single letter or digit, the pen tumbles from my grip. "Wait. Where am I meeting him?"

"His home."

"His home? He's not staying at a hotel?" I was expecting a quick interview in the restaurant at Loews or the Four Seasons. Some place nice and public, yet tucked away from paparazzi.

"Nope. He bought a spot weeks ago, and just moved in. How did you not know this?"

Because I'd rather gnaw off my arm than occupy my thoughts with where Riot Blu lays his head.

"Must've slipped my mind."

"Well, get your game face on, Lee. They're expecting you in half an hour."

I glance over at the numbers illuminated on my digital clock display and curse.

"Don't be late," Bari commands. "Remember: this story could make or break your entire career."

We hang up and I jolt into action, sprinting to my closet and damn near tripping over my discarded clothes and shoes. I'm in such a hurry that I almost miss the little scrap of folded paper sitting on my dresser, marked with unfamiliar handwriting.

Rox,

Last night was great, and I wish I could have stayed. Early morning grind. I want to see you again, sooner than later. Call me.

Kaz

His number is scrawled under his name, but I don't have time to save it in my phone, let alone call him. My focus is completely singular right now: I'm about to see Riot for the first time in over ten years.

I once believed that nothing could fracture what we had. He wasn't just the boy next door, he was my first kiss, my first love, my first *everything*. There was nothing on this earth that I wouldn't have done for him, including defy my parents to be with him. And I did…more than he could ever know.

Still, he left me.

No goodbye. No note. Not even a phone call.

It was so easy for him too, as if those precious firsts I had surrendered to him had meant absolutely nothing. And being a young fool in love, I even tried to rationalize his disappearing act. He had left me behind to become a star. So I did what I thought was best for the boy who had left his mark on my soul and his music in my heart. I kept our secret so he could shine.

That was easier to do when my only access to him was in the form of MTV appearances and radio interviews. But when the loneliness became too much to bear, I soon realized that my Riot was gone. Maybe he was never really mine at all.

I don't know how I pull it off, but I manage to shower, dress, slap on some concealer and mascara, and run a brush through my hair in eighteen minutes flat. Normally, I'd call a ride, but by the time it arrived, I'd lose a good five minutes. Then we'd be battling traffic and detours from endless construction. I can hear Bari's bitchin' now.

I set out on foot, weaving through the morning crowd as quickly as my short legs will take me. Halfway to 2nd street, I try to recall if I put on deodorant, since the balmy Seattle summer coupled with my nerves are making for a very swampy situation. This is so not what I need right now, and definitely not how I wanted to present myself on such a huge assignment. Bad enough I'm hungover and my hair probably looks like I was caught in a wind tunnel with all this humidity. And while I'll only admit it to myself, I'd planned to look damn good the first time I came face to face with Riot Blu. Let him see how I've grown up and all that I've accomplished without him. Then let him be the one to sweat as he watched me walk away.

But you know what they say when you make plans. God has a sick sense of humor, it seems.

The tower on 2nd that houses some of the most luxurious (i.e. expensive) condos in the city looms before me, and I dash to the door with only seconds to spare. The doorman peers at me skeptically.

"I'm a writer for the Seattle Tea, with an appointment to see Mr. Blu," I blurt, trying desperately to contain my panting and not sweat all over his shiny, black dress shoes. "He should be expecting me." I even whip out my press ID to show him I'm legit, despite my disheveled appearance.

The door attendant offers a polite smile before turning to pick up a phone stationed on a small podium. He confirms my claim in a hushed tone then turns to me and says, "You're all set."

I follow him to the elevator where he punches in a secret code to grant me access to the penthouse. Before the elevator doors close, I extend my palm.

"Thank you…?"

"Harold," he answers, smiling, which makes the ends of his thick mustache curl up at the sides. He takes my outstretched hand for a shake. His grip is oddly gentle for such a formidable man. "Harold Faulkner."

"Nice to meet you, Harold," I manage to get out before the doors slide closed.

And then there's nothing but twenty-four floors standing between me and my absolute worst fear.

By the time the doors open to the foyer, I'm dizzy and I think I may faint. But I take a few deep breaths and force myself to keep it together. I can fall apart later, and definitely plan to, followed by eating enough salted caramel ice cream to slip into sugar shock. But for now, I'm all about my business, and not even Riot Blu will throw me off my game. I refuse to let him take one more thing from me.

However, any hope I had of maintaining my cool is quickly dashed away when I see a familiar form approach to greet me as I step off the elevator.

Oh-my-fucking...

"Kaz?"

ACKNOWLEDGMENTS

"I have so many people to thank, but I don't want to drag this on.

My children who inspire me daily.

My partner who puts up with my crazy, and my mummy who always has my back.

My brothers who are my everything, and my sisters who, even though we don't always see eye-to-eye, I will always be here for.

My best friend Lyla. I love you. 20 years of friendship and that's all I've got right now.

My best friend Amiria. Thank you for tolerating me.

My best friend Isis - I love you! Bitchface for life.

My readers who continue to support me and have my back!

My betas! Oh lord, these girls… I cannot thank enough. Caro, Franci & Sarah! Thank you so damn much for everything that you do. You rip my books apart so I can piece them back together, but do it in a respectful way. RESPECT! I love you!

Bloggers for taking the time out of their busy schedules to read, review and share me.

My agent, Flavia! Thank you for exceeding all my expectations and loving my books like they're your own.

Ellie! For editing my words. Girl, draaaannks on me in Vegas. I just said dranks. Bet you hate me now, if you didn't already. Tough, I have screenshots of you telling me you love me. Screenshots don't lie. Seriously, I don't know where I'd be without you. You spent so much time on my babies and treat them like your own. Thank you!

My PA Caro! She needs a pay raise. Like a massive one.

The authors who inspire, support, and encourage one another – my tribe!

Chantal! You're stuck with me.

Anne! You legit had no chance of running from me. Those heels won't help. But they preettyyy though! #IvyAndHarley

To Jaci – for keeping me sane most of the time, for our book dates and wine. And coffee. And red velvet cake. And general shit talking. Thank you!

My Wolf Pack – (howls).

Jay Aheer – I love you. Thank you for my beautiful covers. For learning my vision and nailing them every single time. Also, sorry for being a diva.

And lastly, to all the readers who may be about to read me for the first time ever: thank you for giving a girl a shot."

ALSO BY AMO JONES

The Elite Kings Series:
The Silver Swan
The Broken Puppet
Tacet a Mortuis
Malum (coming soon)

The Devils' Own Series:
One Hundred & Thirty-Six Scars
Hellraiser
Razing Grace: Part 1
Razing Grace: Part 2
The Devils Match
Lucky Hundred (coming Feb '19)

Crowned Duology:
Crowned by Hate
Crowned by Fate

Westbeach series:
Losing Traction
F*CKER

Standalones:

Flip Trick

'MANIK

'DYAVOL (Paranormal – coming soon)

More coming soon…

Website – amojonesbooks.com

Facebook – http://bit.ly/2GzzSq5

Wolf Pack (reader group) – http://bit.ly/2DNXohr

Bookbub – http://bit.ly/2DSH7rB

Printed in Great Britain
by Amazon

67828384R00232